To

Rosie with all my love

and in affection for the people of Exeter, Plymouth and Devon

ALSO BY J E HALL

Flashbacks (2016)

IStanbul (2017)

"Once more unto the breach... Cry God for Harry, England, and Saint George!"

Shakespeare's Henry V, Act III, 1598

"If you want to tackle extremism, you need to put hope back into their lives."

Stephen Lennon
(aka Tommy Robinson)

*"Oh, cry not that all creeds are in vain!
Some scent of truth, they have,
else they would not beguile."*

Rumi

Not all grey days in east London are dull. A kind of springtime was in the air. At last, after being dormant to the world for so long, The Circle was going to assemble and emerge from the shadows – not exactly as green shoots, but certainly with explosions heralding new life in mind.

After years of patient waiting, today a rare political opportunity had presented itself for an advancement of the cause in England. That early May morning, following the unexpected demise in a road traffic accident of a sitting MP not a month prior, the small matter of a parliamentary by-election had been triggered by the issue of a formal writ. The death had started the usual slow bureaucratic processes to expedite the election of a successor, in the corridors and then on the floor of the House in Westminster; these events, unknown to the powers that be, also spurred into life clandestine forces lying beneath the surface. No longer waiting in the dark, things were moving at last, they'd caught a glimpse of a grey new dawn beckoning them out.

The Marquess of Hastings, a tall thin man with aristocratic looks and a well-defined nose, had just agreed to The Circle's use of his house for the weekend gathering. They would convene by 10pm on Friday 19th May in his chateau, discreetly located in the woods of his country estate in the Forest of Hesdin in the Pas-De-Calais. Nearby was the site of the Battle of Agincourt. The Marquess disliked his own name's association with military defeat, albeit back in 1066, so to own a piece of France near Agincourt, where in 1415 a few English archers had roundly defeated the French, lifted his spirits. Back then Henry V had called his worthy troops 'we happy few, we band of brothers,' exactly how he saw The Circle. It was a body to be reckoned with, if not the right-wing power base entirely of his own creation, a group where his sympathy lay and which benefitted through his active, though distant, patronage.

It was now the job of The Circle Master's personal assistant to send out the invitations to all the pan-European contacts, ostensibly to attend the imminent 'boar-shooting weekend'. It had all the parallels of preparing for a coming battle and like the night before Agincourt itself, the assembling leadership must be sure to remain well hidden, protected by a veil of self-discipline and silence to avoid discovery.

Sending out e-mails demanded the utmost secrecy for there were listening ears and prying eyes everywhere. From his small flat in north-east London, the Master's PA, Carl Reynolds, knew he was secure from unwelcome attention. As he sat at his desk behind permanently closed metal shuttered windows, he read over to himself once again the message he'd just received from the Master, a three word encrypted text, 'Gather the eagles'.

Putting down his mobile, he powered up his laptop, giving an eerie blue glow to the poorly lit sparse front room. The invitations he'd prepared had been primed to go for days; the innocent looking encrypted e-mails with their hidden attachments sitting there on his desktop where he had left them ready just for this moment. In less than a minute they'd all gone with a single buzz, leaving as if they were electrically charged flies. Now all he had to do was wait for the acknowledgments to start coming back.

For some, getting to France was more difficult than for others, but The Circle infallibly drew everyone in. Absenteeism was not tolerated. Those instructed to be there would always find ways of crossing Europe's porous borders. North American brothers had to be particularly careful to avoid detection. Some accurately regarded their activities as an engagement in extreme politics and this consequently required in response, resourcefulness and an innate ability to operate using warlike strategies and subterfuge skills. They had all had to become adept at being social chameleons, masking their economic and political presence in a myriad of ways. They lived in the hidden places and preferred the dark; the darker the better, and black was the perfect colour of choice.

Making himself a black coffee, the thought crossed his mind that he belonged to an army. The warriors he pictured before him were like insects, winged cicadas, who, after years living hidden in the soil would shortly emerge, creating a deafening noise, the loudest of any insects to rule the world. Unlike the brief life of the cicadas, he had no intention that his army would rule for any less than a thousand years. There would be blood and toil, then victory.

Carl downloaded all the data on the laptop to his mobile and then ran a cleansing electronic wipe to take all traces of contacts, e-mails and correspondence from the laptop's hard drive, before shutting down and putting it away in a drawer. A gaping white waste bag stood leaning against the front door ready to take all his waste; blue forensic gloves included.

He then began packing what he himself would need for a trip to France. As PA his job was to front, point up, organise everything – accommodation, food, meeting room, and for those coming, the kind of entertainments they insisted upon. The Marquess of Hastings would have seen to his armoury. All would need their egos groomed.

Carl had allowed himself one personal luxury in this flat, a silver framed photograph of his old regiment. He'd done his final years of service in Iraq and Afghanistan and then got booted out at 40 with an army pension. That was several years ago. Like a cicada himself it was time he emerged, after several years of his shadow existence, to rise up at last – as he saw it. It was well past payback time for a society that had neither valued him or his fallen colleagues, a system that had spewed him out and left him to die alone. The Master recognised him as a man of two talents; one as an administrator with an exacting eye for detail, the other as a practiced operative in the field, able to use his well-honed military skills with competence. Carl couldn't live his life without both parts featuring in it.

Carl reflected on The Marquess, supporter and sympathiser, but not formally a member of The Circle. He was a man who understood what was required, and he left cars and drivers and catering and security staff at their disposal. With no Marquess himself present to tell them what they should do, Carl would need to arrive first at the country estate – Chateau de Montfort. The place, he'd been told, was named after Simon de Montfort who'd created the first Baron Hastings in 1263. The name de Montfort carried suitable resonances of political rebellion and reform that appealed as much to the current Marquess as to Carl himself. He smiled.

Using his mobile, it was the moment to check over the weekend's arrangements one more time, as well as to firm up the final details of the programme. This took him a full two hours, a few notes being typed on his phone to serve as an aide-memoire. He glanced outside through the blind. The grey day had slid into night and it was as dark outside in the London street as it was inside the flat.

4

Group mailing sent with replies already coming back, Carl knew no-one would refuse their invite. He had one more task to complete before leaving. The names of the candidates standing for Plymouth Moor View by-election had just been sent to him. An action was required.

He turned his attention to this other matter on his 'to do' list – to begin developing the Plymouth opportunity. Earlier, the Master had sent him a longer second e-mail, relating to the previous week's announcement of a by-election in the Plymouth Moor View constituency. This required Carl to busy himself on a more complicated task. In this, the anonymity of The Circle had to be protected at all costs. He knew he had to be certain that the particular message he was preparing to send, despite being delivered by a more primitive means of communication, would not lead to police enquiries pointing any further than the chosen postman. He reached into his inside pocket for his second 'anonymous' mobile (SIM card only) and made the necessary call.

'Greg Ward?'

'Yes. Who's this?' the hesitant voice of a young man replied.

'Let's just say, a friend. I've got a proposition for you – worth five hundred pounds. Are you interested?'

'You're on! I'm your man. What do you have in mind?'

'A sealed blue envelope will be delivered into your hand later today. Inside will be five hundred pounds in twenties and a letter in Arabic. The money is yours; the letter is what you are being paid to deliver.'

'That's fine by me. Where and when do you want it posted?' asked Greg, an air of uncertainty creeping into his voice, clearly not sure what to make of this caller with his London sounding accent.

'Now listen carefully,' said Carl hoping he had not given too much away by slipping into giving a military sounding order. Must be more careful.

Carl then gave a Plymouth address and detailed instructions as to when and precisely how the letter was to be delivered. For maximum impact the delivery was to be made at midnight – tomorrow, Saturday night.

By the end of the call Greg knew why he was being paid five hundred and that any failure on his part carried a much higher price. Times were hard and a trip down from Exeter to Plymouth to give a message didn't seem too much to ask of him. He couldn't see any difficulty with the job. After he'd given his mysterious caller his final affirmation that the delivery would be made as instructed, his caller abruptly hung up.

Admin done, Carl slipped out of the front door, his hoodie pulled up over his head, his two black suitcases trundling along behind him. Two streets away, after glancing round, he used his electronic key to open a lock-up garage door. He climbed into the driver's seat of the polished black Range Rover Sport SVR with its darkened windows and drove off in the direction of the Eurotunnel, France and Chateau de Montfort. He liked driving. He liked action. He felt alive.

As he drove, making his way slowly through the East End traffic, Carl reflected on the shifting political landscape in the UK; how UKIP at its height had spread its own right-wing reach to form a Europe of Freedom and Democracy Group. However, The Circle, whom he served, was not to be confused with their relatively gentle politics. Besides, UKIP was on its way out, soon to be regarded as a short blip in the evolving story of right-wing history.

He considered how, following endless internal wrangles, UKIP's power had waned as its leadership got distracted and minor figures fought it out with each other within the party with the inevitable disastrous political result – irrelevance. UKIP, he thought, had got sidetracked and had got themselves drawn into middle ground politics. Such foolishness to lose sight of the goal behind the vision, such weak leadership, he told himself, but looking on the bright side, hadn't they left the way open for The Circle to make its move and fill the political void?

In joining The Circle Carl believed he had truly found himself. As an only child he'd loved playing war games, first with models, then online. Going into the British Army had fulfilled a dream, but too often he'd been passed over for promotion – they'd told him he was a loner, not a leader. And all the painful memories of rejection and questions as to his mental suitability, they still hurt. It grieved him to think society didn't value him. Resentment ate into his soul.

But The Circle was the real deal, a secret and one hundred percent professional organisation living in the shadows of society. It allowed neither internal political distractions over policy, nor in-fighting over leadership. It prided itself on being self-disciplined, biding its time before revealing itself. That time had been judged to be now. Carl had been watching and waiting and seen it coming.

Extreme right-wing politics were now on an upward trajectory across Europe and the world, and those with him in the shadows were ready. People everywhere were discontented and were looking for inspirational leadership, a saviour even. After years of despondency followed by endless preparation, Carl's energy levels and optimism were surging. An extremely busy period lay ahead, but newly energised, he was up for it. He glanced at his watch. He'd make the Eurotunnel before midnight. France in the small hours.

For a moment, as he sped through the night, he wondered if he was a vengeful man, set on getting his own back on society, but quickly dismissed the thought – no, he was a loyal warrior serving a noble cause.

2

Some evenings seem overly long. From the very moment you send someone out to do something for you that really matters, time hangs still in the air. Stu Beamish had been gone two hours and still Harry McNamara had heard nothing back from him. Harry waited impatiently, drumming his fingers on the back of his mobile in frustration. Ever since he was a kid, Harry had only ever wanted to be a leader. This mattered.

Having taken his first steps on the road to political power, Harry was bothered that everything had, since the early excitement, so quickly slowed. Upon notice being given of the parliamentary by-election, he'd swiftly put his own name forward as prospective candidate for Plymouth Moor View. He'd toyed briefly with the idea of talking to UKIP and muscling in on their outfit, but hardly gave them a second thought when he considered the downward spiral they were taking. Standing proudly as a candidate for his new political party, the British First Democratic Party, he thought, as a free man, he'd be much better placed to give an unambiguous call to the electorate. In response, there'd been a flurry of initial press interest earlier in the week when he'd announced his decision to stand, but now, Friday evening, 19th May, nothing seemed to be happening.

The trouble was, his name had yet to be noticed. He'd been sidelined and he didn't like it. When he spotted a chance he took it. Though he'd quickly found ten of his mates to nominate him and his Dad had readily given him the £500 deposit required, in the six days of the campaign so far, nothing, absolutely nothing had happened and it was beginning to get to him. So far it had all been about the Conservative and UKIP candidates, supposedly fighting the seat out between them. Labour were also fielding someone, but no-one rated them with a chance. His hope was that tonight might have seen calls coming in, his phone ringing non-stop, and that he'd get some encouragement for he was changing all the tiredness of the usual politics.

Harry still had a few minutes before he had to leave the house and he tried to relax. Still clutching his mobile, he lay back on his bed looking up at a poster of Sir Oswald Mosley Blu Tacked on his bedroom ceiling. Mosley was seemingly looking back down at him, calling him to bring it on.

The poster was old and had once belonged to his grandfather. It had been found in the roof space of his grandfather's bungalow after he'd died. He'd only lived a few minutes away, but only now, four years after his death, had his intestate affairs been finally settled, and Harry's father able to sell the place.

There'd been this metal trunk hidden there in the loft all that time. No one knew of it until then. Inside it he'd discovered one neatly folded black shirt, some old letters, personal papers and copies of well-thumbed magazines from the 1930s, together with a few black and white photos and the carefully rolled Mosley poster, with its black ribbon to stop it unfurling. It was a strange find. Harry marvelled at how old the things were. His grandfather had been ninety nine when he'd died and these things, he quickly reckoned, were from the time when he was a young man.

When they came to clear his grandfather's bungalow, Harry's Dad was all for throwing the trunk out with the decrepit furniture and rusty contents of the garden shed. After all the years of waiting, his Dad, the sole beneficiary named in the will, wanted a quick sale, cash in the bank and all the rubbish gone.

Harry had liked his grandfather Michael McNamara and wanted to find something of his as a keepsake; one or two items to remember him by. So, he'd rescued the trunk with its memories, salvaging it from the tired and dirty furnishings tipped from the house outside on the street, and into a bright yellow skip his Dad had hastily organised for the purpose.

The battered grey metal trunk somehow spoke to Harry. He couldn't for the moment think why, but he knew, given time, its significance would become clear to him. For now it was a personal memento for him to keep, something tangible, a bridge between him and his dead grandfather. The trunk, if nothing else, would help keep his grandfather's memory alive.

The metal box now in his bedroom, stood across the end of his bed. He fastened the poster above him on the ceiling, the other contents undisturbed for the present. Harry gazed at his white designer trainers resting on it. At least the box was practical, he thought. Being a tall guy, it saved his footwear from messing the bed clothes as he lay down – his mind returned from its wanderings to his best friend – 'yes, I'm bloody well waiting to hear from you Stu,' he muttered under his breath.

'Come on Stu, call me,' Harry said out loud this time, feeling restless and fidgety. He calculated that it took a good deal less than an hour to get from Plymouth to Exeter's El Baraka Mosque. He reasoned that in the early evening any traffic delays wouldn't have been a problem for Stu on his motorbike.

Harry considered the possibilities. Maybe the Imam wasn't there when Stu had arrived. Yet Harry knew the Imam always turned up half an hour before he was due to lead the Maghreb, the sunset prayers. Stu knew exactly where he had to be and when, he knew what the Imam looked like, they'd been through it so many times. All he had to do was find the right man before prayers started and deliver Harry's message. What could be easier? What the hell had gone wrong?

Harry thought they'd covered every detail. Stu had even borrowed a dark blue suit from a friend and after much complaint had worn a shirt and tie, again borrowed; he'd shaved his head and although his black trainers looked slightly at odds with the generally smart presentation, Stu had made an effort to look slick and sharp. Harry had reminded him to show respect, and not to forget to remove his trainers when he entered the mosque. He hoped Stu had taken off his black motorbike helmet with Plymouth Chapter emblazoned on it and left it and his leathers with the bike outside. Well, there was only so much you could do to organise Stu, he told himself.

Harry wondered whether to risk a call, picked up his mobile, began calling, only to throw it down again on the bed, annoyed at his own impatience. He could rely on Stu, always had. Stu's instinct and judgement were invariably spot on. He recalled when they were in Istanbul only the previous summer for the pre-season international football friendly. It was Stu he'd first turned to when they were in a spot of bother. It was Stu who'd assessed exactly what the situation was and then Stu who'd been at his side as they piled into those Muslim terrorists.

That Istanbul trip was also Stu's stag do, and he'd got him safely back to Penny, his missus, hadn't he? Since then he'd hardly left Harry's side, helping him no end in the cause. Harry couldn't help but smile to himself, for on more than one occasion Stu's Penny had asked her new husband who he was really married to, Harry or her? Tonight though was a big occasion, it was time to get the political campaign properly under way.

When time stood still there was only one thing to do. He called downstairs.

'Mum, bring me a couple of beers up from the fridge,' he told her. She had to come up and downstairs twice. He'd had to remind her he drank his beer from a straight glass, and a fresh one had to be found. Two bottles of beer later and Harry's mobile finally came to life, patriotically ringing out 'the National Anthem'. It was Stu.

'About bloody time too,' said a relieved Harry. The relief was to be short-lived.

'Listen to me Harry. I'm sitting in a police car. They've let me make one call,' said an agitated Stu.

'What happened?' asked Harry, fearing a disaster. Had his political aspirations already prematurely bitten the dust?

'The Imam, he fell down and died when I gave him your letter,' said Stu.

'You what! Died! How?' asked Harry anxiously.

'I was late getting there, accident on the M5 motorway, caravan turned over, all lanes closed. Loads of Friday night traffic. I couldn't see him before he'd started his chanting, so I went inside the mosque. Having taken my trainers off like you said, I walked up to the front where the Imam guy was standing, tapped him on the shoulder and gave him your letter. That's when he died, fell forward on to the carpet.'

'No. No,' said Harry, his campaign also dying before his very eyes.

'A Muslim doctor guy tried to revive him, but he couldn't, even though he kept working on him until the ambulance arrived and took over. I didn't touch him Harry, you believe me don't you, you've got to help me,' he pleaded. 'Everyone thought I'd killed him. At first I thought they'd do me in, there were so many of them. I couldn't get away. They pinned me down on the carpet, sat on me and called the police.'

Something deep inside Harry stirred. He had to rise above this.

'Don't you worry,' he told Stu. 'You help the police like a good and upright citizen, but tell them before you do so, you want a solicitor present. They'll help sort it. You'll be home before you know it. I'll tell your missus you'll likely as not be back a little later than planned,' instructed Harry, beginning to see that the unexpected situation might offer him some promise. The phrase 'clouds and silver linings' crossed his mind, then there were voices in the background.

'I've got to end the call, Harry. I'll call again later when I can. The police want me. Thanks mate,' he said with some relief and with that Stu had gone.

Harry lay back on his bed. So the old bearded Imam had died as Stu took him the letter. He smiled, one less Muslim in Britain was his first thought – not something he could voice. Before he tried to get another Imam to hold a public debate with him, first he had to work out what to do next now there was a dead Imam. He began thinking through what he'd planned so far. He'd been fortunate in being born with a mind adept at organising and leading things. He could always marshall and order his thoughts clearly, and notwithstanding the beer he'd consumed, he focused and went over in his head events so far.

All Stu had done was take Imam Abdullah an invite. As the oldest and longest serving Imam in Devon and therefore the most senior and most respected, an invitation to a pre-election public discussion with Harry on 'the place of Islam in British society' was an inspired strategic starter gamble. He knew this was not something his political opponents would dare do. It was a risk, a punt at nothing, but one he'd decided worth taking. Now it looked as if this long-shot initiative, so early in the campaign, might just pay off big time.

Harry had anticipated a 'no thank you' response, to which he would have responded with a media campaign criticising the Muslim lack of openness and unwillingness to engage with British society. Harry had long been fed up and frustrated by the reticence of the Imam to speak out on any of the issues that had been in the news in recent weeks, issues that he believed the British people felt strongly about but weren't confident enough to challenge the Muslim leadership on. Harry said his political trump card was his own unique position amongst all the candidates in being prepared to 'speak with and speak out' – not a bad slogan, he mused. Now though, the debate was clearly not going to happen. A well laid plan had just fallen apart, or had it?

But wait, hadn't Stu just provided him with a public relations opportunity he hadn't anticipated: a dead Imam, scared by the prospect of an open debate. Perhaps he'd been so scared he'd had a heart attack, at the moment he was actually leading Friday prayers. There was bound to be more media coverage now and he could maybe put himself at the centre of it.

Harry thought hard. He had to appear both respectful of the deceased, people liked to see that; but also, at the same time, able to turn the Imam's death into a political debate about the necessary qualities required of a new leader in the current political climate. The good news was that now there was no Imam to respond to his views. He'd steal the show. The floor was his for the taking.

Might the mosque offer someone else? That could be tricky. A number of reasons quickly came to mind as to why the Muslim community would think the deceased Imam shouldn't be replaced by anyone else – he thought they'd all have a similar reluctance to engage. Harry began to see he could put the Muslim community on the back foot and get precious votes from true patriots by making his point. With ideas coming thick and fast, he reached across for his i-pad and began putting together an outline article he wanted his friend Cherry Thomas, a reporter with the Devon Evening News, to run with the next day, in Saturday's paper.

An hour later he read through his piece, changed one or two things, then picked up his mobile and called Cherry. Journalists who want good stories don't mind what time calls reach them and Cherry knew having first access when it

16

came to Harry's election campaign message was news worth having whatever time of night it came.

As it happened she was up late trying to make a boring piece about summer evening fishing in the lower River Dart Estuary sound remotely interesting for the morning's first edition. Seeing a call come in from a far right party candidate like Harry McNamara standing for election was all the lift she needed. He had her immediate and full attention.

'Hi Harry. You got something for me?' she asked.

'Have you heard about tonight's death at the mosque?' he replied. He heard the silence at the other end. Cherry clearly hadn't got the news yet. He took her reticence as the chance to press on.

'Well, the Imam died as he was leading prayers. Of course I'm very much saddened at this unexpected and tragic turn of events, and will be sending my condolences to the mosque. He was a good, well-intentioned man, even if a bit misguided, but it would appear that there is more to this story than people are admitting.' Harry paused to let Cherry listen out for what was coming next.

'You also might not have heard he had just been invited to come down to Plymouth and share a public platform with me to discuss the place of Islam in British society. He must have known he was going to struggle. We know that for a fact. People are already saying in social media the thought of an open debate was too much for the poor man and the strain in trying to advocate an indefensible viewpoint was what killed him. No doubt, in due time, the coroner will say what actually killed him but it was the strain of being anti-British that really killed him.'

17

'Oh,' was all Cherry felt able to say before adding, 'is there anything more?'

'Yes, you should know that, in connection with the Imam's death, the Exeter Police are currently holding a British First Democratic Party member, Stuart Beamish. In fact Stu was politely delivering the debate invitation letter to Imam Abdullah when he was assaulted by those in the mosque and forced to the ground. He was very careful to show respect and had taken off his shoes as required. I know Stu would want to help the police in any way he can, but you know, it seems to me there are dark forces at work in our police. There are policemen who want to interfere in this by-election. There are policemen who are inappropriately shy, police who should know better, who put political correctness before asking why mosques support terrorists.'

'Is that so?' asked Cherry.

'You tell me why they are detaining Stu Beamish if it isn't to try and discredit us? I'm sure a good natured young citizen like Stu will not want to press any charges, either against the Muslims who assaulted him or the police who are wrongfully detaining him. But you know Cherry, people should know just what's going on. Why don't you give the police a call, check out what I'm saying with the Chief Constable. Tell you what, I've put a few thoughts together on what's happening. Shall I send them across? Not for me to tell you your job, but a bit of a scoop for you this, Cherry,' said Harry trying to sound helpful, hoping he wasn't over-egging the storyline too much.

'It certainly is,' she replied. 'Send your material straight over and I'll get on to it at once. And thanks Harry. Oh, for the record, how do you think the other candidates will react?'

'The usual. I can't tell Conservative and UKIP apart, can you? So let's just call them the Tory/UKIP voice – their policies on immigration won't work, they are totally ineffective – just more of the same wishful thinking whilst numbers go up and up and through the roof. Well, they won't want to talk with or about Muslims, you'll see. It's their Achilles heel. Why? – well because they keep inviting more and more into the country and there's no end in sight. They've even made Plymouth a dispersal centre for overseas newcomers,' he added.

'For decades the Tories have been hand in glove with the others, welcoming Johnny foreigner whether they hate us or not. Don't get me wrong, legitimate victims of cruel regimes ought to be cared for, but they know they're really having a laugh at the people of Plymouth for being mugs and I'm the guy going to tell it how it is, you'll see. People who won't integrate into our way of life and threaten our safety and well-being have no right to belong here, do they?' he asked her. She didn't respond.

'They think the issue can be avoided and the election can be won by promising more jobs for the dockyard and better conditions for ex-servicemen. They'll make empty promises about social care and the garden of Eden that awaits us. That's a load of rubbish. What people really care about is who they live next door to, whether they are safe in their beds and whether they can trust their neighbours. What they care about most is whether the services they've paid for all their lives are there to serve them when they need them or whether they are being given away to queue jumping immigrants.' Harry was by now on his soapbox and in full flow.

'People want to feel safe not frightened by terrorists, have education for their children and health care when they're elderly. People want to speak English with their neighbours. That's why I'm taking the high ground on this campaign. The British First Democratic Party speaks for the British people, you'll see. Watch this space Cherry, you'll be the first to get news on our building campaign,' concluded Harry, thinking he'd said enough for now.

The call over, Harry knew that Cherry would already be ringing her editor. She was an ambitious young reporter, keen to make her mark and still naive enough to treat everything she heard in terms of the story's ability to grab reader attention alone, whether it came from the established parties or newcomers in the political field like Harry McNamara. He could see tomorrow's headlines now, 'Britain First Democratic Party – Victim Of Police Dirty Tricks', or alternatively and better still, 'BFDP – The Only Ones Calling Muslims to Account.'

In the morning he'd call South West TV news, line up an interview for midday and spin the story further. Hopefully by then, after Cherry's call to the Chief Constable, Stu would be free and standing at his side. Political support would start to swing in his direction from this, he just knew it. Earlier he'd been lying there waiting for something to happen, a man on the political margins, but now a corner had been turned. His dead grandfather would be proud of him.

Not so his father, he mused, a man who avoided politics and was to Harry's mind, too focussed on scrap metal collection and selling it on to China. His Dad could prove tricky to handle during the campaign. He made a mental note. Mind you, thought Harry, his Dad had given him some good ideas how his new political party could revive small businesses in the South West. That had been most useful. In times of austerity the economy might not be the spear thrust in his campaign, but he needed to have good ideas up his sleeve based on good solid local business experience, not the waffle of people remote from the grassroots.

His Dad was adamant he had no time for politics himself, he'd told Harry; he and his grandfather had often argued over politics, but that was all a very long time ago. But give his Dad his due, he'd coughed up the £500 deposit and he'd told Harry he could take as much time away from the family business as he needed for the duration of the campaign. In the meantime, he'd just continue to do what he knew best – make money from McNamara Metals. Harry got on best with his Dad when there was space between them.

Harry knew his grandfather Michael McNamara would have understood his passion to see Britain rise again. Strange though no one wanted to talk about his grandfather and his politics these days. Harry had long-sensed that in his grandfather he'd found a kindred spirit and when he had a spare moment he determined to know more about him and his views. He'd wished he'd asked him more about his life whilst he'd been alive, but his death had come out of the blue, caught them all out and now all that remained unsaid had died with him. Years on, Harry felt the loss and was almost upset, before checking himself and calling his Mum to get him another beer.

Like himself, he sensed his grandfather had stood up for what he believed in. Harry wouldn't rest until he'd learned more. Perhaps he'd start by finding out more about this Sir Oswald Mosley fellow, the man literally watching over him, looking down from the ceiling above, the man he knew for certain had an important place in his grandfather's life.

All he knew, as of now, was that Mosley had been a lively politician in the years before World War II, an elected MP, a man of the people prepared to speak out and for that he had been criticised. The man had stood on the political right-wing, was prepared to criticise and face immigrant communities like the Jews in the East End of London. Who hadn't heard of the Battle of Cable Street? But why did his grandfather keep these various items, why had he kept them all these years hidden in his trunk? Maybe there was someone still around who would recall those days.

He wondered whether his grandfather had aligned himself with Mosley's political campaign, certainly the possession of this trunk of memorabilia suggested a clandestine sympathy at the very least. He felt instinctively that his grandfather was, like himself, a political animal. They both had a knack for plain speaking and argument. Somehow, maybe, what he did then might help guide Harry now, and who knows, political aptitude might be in the family genes. OK they'd skipped a generation in his Dad's case, but he and his grandfather, well they both stood for British values in the face of misguided left-wing thinking.

Knowing his grandfather understood political struggle made Harry think he had an ancestral ally, had been left a spiritual legacy, support for what he was trying to achieve. It lifted his spirits. That and the fact today his own campaign had finally taken off, in no small measure due to the untimely death of an Imam.

At that very moment, as if to celebrate, his Mum gently pushed open the door holding out another bottle of beer in her hand. To Harry the days and weeks ahead suddenly seemed full of promise.

3

Next day, the news of the death of Imam Abdullah as he was leading Friday evening prayers at Exeter's El Baraka mosque created more than a stir. Someone present had taken a photograph of the Imam, lying there prostrate, dead on the blue carpet. Another had made a video. These had been promptly posted on social media and then gone viral. Tragic as it was, the death was a definite news sensation.

Fortunately for Stu Beamish and indirectly for Harry McNamara, Stu did not appear in the bizarre social media clips though he was just a couple of metres away. It was the awkward angle the Imam had fallen, his hands clasped in front, his head twisted fiercely to one side and both his bare feet sticking up in the air that provided an arresting image – giving the impression he had dived into a swimming pool only to meet a solid surface instead of water. It was the curious spectacle of the image, as much as the rumours surrounding the manner of his death that made everyone want to follow the story. In this case death had no dignity. Harry's eyes saw all this as political gold dust.

The news and photo had the effect of galvanising attention and then polarising the wider community in several different ways. This was reflected in the varied news media as well as the social media accounts that were circulating, the first postings being added cumulatively by the hour.

By lunchtime on Saturday, media myths and rumours were unsettling a significant section of the populace in Exeter, in Plymouth and across much of surrounding Devon.

Some were speculating that Imam Abdullah had been put to death by forces as yet unknown and opinions were starkly divided as to whether this was a good or bad thing. A can of worms had been opened. Others expressed the view that there were dark forces at work in the mosque itself, an internal power struggle going on between traditional conservative voices and the modernists, and the death of a conservative Imam would lead to more discord, to violent in-fighting and a desperate battle within the Muslim community created by the vacuum his death had left. Conspiracy theories as to which Muslim faction was leading an alleged mosque takeover bid were rife. Other worried voices asked whether an opportunity for extremist elements within Islam had been provided?

At the same time, in the heat of all the bitter and polarised comment, the kind the makers and sellers of news feed on, all moderate voices were being silenced; simply drowned out. A worthy statement promptly issued by the local Exeter inter-faith focus group, stating how much the Imam had done for his community over the past twenty years since his arrival from India was entirely lost, gaining just an inch of print on an inside page, as was an interview given by the Dean of Exeter in front of the West Door of his cathedral. The Dean achieved a mere two sentences.

In sum, amongst all the media noise, what the populace really wanted to hear was a fresh voice, a young voice – indeed Harry McNamara's message; and, much to Harry's immense delight, he was sought out for interview no less than eight times before lunch and his image subsequently splashed across the front pages. A posse of press men and cameras assembled outside the front door of his home in Plymouth, leaving the neighbours' curtains twitching.

As he stepped out on to the pavement to address them, Harry realised this precious air time, the very oxygen for life and success in politics, was all his for the taking in this gifted moment. What had, until then, been a lack-lustre political by-election in everyone's eyes, had now suddenly come very much alive. Interest in his Twitter posts began to rocket.

The message he gave everyone who asked him was a consistent one – that the Imam was neither faithful to his community, nor a true member of British society. He'd been afraid to debate with Harry because he knew he would lose. 'Not once,' asserted Harry, 'had the Imam condemned shariah law; not once had he supported sexual choice or gender equality; never had he approved of freedom of religion. And when did we ever hear him condemn terrorists from his own community? – No, he was an old fashioned conservative, one hundred percent backed by his mosque committee,' he told them.

Harry insisted for good measure that, 'Imam Abdullah and his kind had renounced their right to live in British society.' When news that some young men were reacting to Harry's assistant allegedly invading their prayers at the mosque, they had begun calling for Muslims to rise up and defend their community. Harry seized on this and immediately attacked the very idea, using the move as indicative of a wider dangerous militancy at work within the local Muslim community.

'Where is the rule of British law when people start arming themselves and running vigilante gangs? Do we know if they are armed? Is anyone now safe? Is this a new riot, an Islamist uprising in our midst and will our under-resourced police be able to protect us?' he asked, sowing seeds of doubt and fear to anyone listening. Harry felt his confidence in his message building the longer he spoke. He knew he was hitting home.

25

Reminding his audience of the Imam's many failings, Harry said the Imam had deliberately avoided any engagement with local politicians and had once described the ruling Conservative/UKIP council of Plymouth as his sworn enemies. It didn't matter to Harry that what he was saying wasn't literally true, he felt that the Imam's sentiment and intent was nonetheless being accurately reflected in his succinct analysis. More than once he was glad to remember the Imam wasn't around to contradict him. A little licence by politicians was fair enough, he told himself, it had always been this way.

Having spelt this out in his interviews some people had started tweeting and blogging – questioning whether Harry himself was a fascist. His answer each time was, 'no, not a fascist, but someone who believes in the historic British people and their democracy, cultural values and the traditional peaceful way of life we so value in the South West.' Harry had, in recent days, come to realise he had done with those selling out the ordinary people of Devon. 'Even UKIP were more interested in political power than telling it how it was', he said. 'How else was the Devon voter to understand why they were cosy-ing up to the Conservatives?'

By now some of his neighbours had come outside to see what the fuss was about and Harry found himself addressing a small crowd. He turned his interviewer's questions round, saying, 'it's those who give sympathy and support to extremists who are the fascists and they had to be stopped. It was the people of the mosque who tried to use a respectable public face of Islam to hide what they truly believed, and this sham needed to be exposed. If Harry was called an extremist, a fascist, for saying how things were, it just showed up how many voices raised were those of the politically naive if not blind! Couldn't they see the reality of the present time, wasn't it now patently obvious Muslims and extremists were placing extra demands on our public services, taking over our streets and infiltrating their way of life into the very heart of our society?'

'Come on,' he urged drawing in his crowd, 'open your eyes so you can see the threat before you, that you are standing on the very edge of an abyss into which you are about to fall.' He was finding being young and a fresh face on the political scene a definite plus. He was novel, interesting and newsworthy. Everyone wanted his photo, more neighbours and passers by stepping into the frame, happily posing for a selfie with Harry. Being outspoken, direct and quite unafraid gave Harry instant appeal and he instinctively knew it. Without any feeling of remorse, he silently thanked God for the death of the Imam, and meant it.

It had been only the previous week when the Chief Whip in the House of Commons had moved the necessary writ for the local by-election in Plymouth Moor View. Consequently polling day was set for five weeks hence, and with the unexpected events of the first 24 hours of the campaign, the heat was now being turned up high between the declared candidates. Of the four candidates indicating they were standing, from the main as well as minority political parties, Harry was, as of today, the only one generating media interest. The polite denouncements of Harry's position the other parties were trying to make were just not being heard.

Then, as if on cue, he was delighted to be joined once again by Stu Beamish. Released by the police without charge, delivered by police car to Harry's door, as Harry had assured him he would be, the two linked arms and beamed winning smiles at each other in front of the press. Harry was then able to steal more media time and attention telling what he called a 'public interest story' – how political correctness was not only clouding the judgment of the main parties, but the police service too.

'Even taking a letter to a mosque gets one in trouble now! Were local mosques no-go areas, like some Muslim areas of this country's towns and cities? Did people know it was the Muslims in Afghanistan who supplied the gangs locally with drugs? Did they know Muslim gangs use violence? Did people know the street collections by Muslims in London had supported the extremist Ali Muhammed's murderous campaigns that had so threatened stability at home and abroad?' he asked, pausing as each loaded sentence crashed upon the ears of the listening media.

Looking across to a crestfallen police officer, who had also just arrived in a second police vehicle to help manage the media scrum outside Harry's door, he added, 'The Chief Constable needs to make an apology to Stu here, she needs to explain herself. Why isn't she defending the loyal people of this country?'

A corner had been turned and as Harry and Stu turned to go back inside his home, he wiped beads of sweat from his brow, and knew he was successfully seizing the moment. He was a leader in the making.

By the end of the day Harry had lined up evening appearances in live shows on three mainstream TV channels – ideal peak Saturday evening viewing. A taxi was sent to take him to the first studio. Later, as he moved from one media session to the next, each in turn had that magic ingredient – public engagement.

Attention grabbing, visual, visceral even, full of acrimonious argument and name calling, Harry in his suit and tie rode out the storm like a god and came across as the most self-assured; the one with the single message, the common touch, with a message people wanted to hear. Harry could imagine his opponents were going to have to go back to their drawing boards and ask how they had so miscalculated the public mood, but then who, apart from himself, they'd be asking their advisors, could have foreseen an Imam's fortuitous death?

Around midnight, Harry was driven back to his Plymouth home by taxi at the BBC's expense. He was elated but exhausted. He couldn't have wished for a better day, and for a second time thanked God for the death of Imam Abdullah. Harry's phone hadn't stopped buzzing since lunchtime; there were pledges of support, questions from potential voters, and offers of help. It was all too much to handle for now, welcome though they were. He knew he needed to give more time to party organisation, he would have to step up his campaign a gear to a new level to keep up with his now developing campaign.

A final call was made to Phil Potts and Cathy Nicholls, his party secretary and political advisor respectively, telling them to come round to his place at eight thirty in the morning for an early Sunday breakfast meeting to plan their next moves. Then he decided, as his street came into view, to switch his mobile to silent. He needed time to himself.

Harry knew he brought one other great strength to his political campaign, the fact that he was a local lad and his family had for three generations lived and worked in Plymouth. Unlike the recently deceased MP, victim of a mysterious late night car accident, who had had to buy into

29

the constituency, or the new Conservative woman candidate who was a City of London business-woman, or indeed the UKIP candidate who had just moved from Exeter to Plymouth; Harry was an authentically local candidate, though with the name McNamara he could not entirely escape his family's southern Irish ancestry. Thankfully, the family's thriving scrap yard business was well known in Plymouth. Almost everyone had heard of McNamara Metals, and those who hadn't soon would.

Their family home was modest, somewhere local people could identify with. It was in Ham Drive, within spitting distance of Home Park, the Plymouth Rovers Football Ground where Harry had spent so much of his time. He was a well-known and popular character in the supporters' group – the Green Army. Ham Drive was the house and home the family had lived in for three generations since his grandfather had bought it in the 1930s. Fortunately, it had survived the bombing that had destroyed much of the city and its housing stock in the war. Gazing at his home Harry was convinced it too was an election trump card, one he would play when the time was right.

His modernised 1930s home was somewhat more spacious than the Victorian terraced houses in nearby streets, but still modest rather than large. There was a parking space out the front for a small truck from the scrap yard to park when needed, and a boxy garden mainly covered by lawn, out to the back. A nearby lock-up garage hosted Harry's car, his red Audi with wide wheels, a treasured possession – his Dad had bought for him three years earlier. He'd decided to keep it hidden from view since he began campaigning, not sure how sight of this particular motor would go down with his potential supporters.

Unable to settle for the night after the busy day, he grabbed himself a beer from the well-stocked fridge in the kitchen and went up to his room. His parents had long since gone up to their room. He carefully hung up his jacket and lay back on his bed wondering whether to put on his wall-mounted TV and watch his earlier efforts replayed on I-player. He had second thoughts, he needed a break from all that, so shoes off, feet swung up to rest on the trunk, he swigged deeply on his bottle of locally brewed Doombar beer. He felt good; today couldn't have gone better he thought as he toasted himself.

Ever since the previous summer he'd been convinced all Muslims had to be repatriated, expelled, whatever. Going to Istanbul had finally convinced him of it. Their threat to his way of life had stared him in the face and had almost succeeded in killing him and his mates. Now he knew what lengths these extremists were prepared to go to and he didn't want to see it happen here at home in Plymouth. It was personal. He saw Muslims as evil, threatening and supported by a book of lies. Considering himself to have nothing in common with them, a natural hatred just seemed to grow inside him. He didn't need to feed it, just keep it under control.

Harry considered his life as a football supporter had prepared him well for his new political career. His local loyalty to the Green Army, the Plymouth Rovers' Supporters Club, was second only to his commitment to the Barmy Army, of the England national football team. People in the game knew him – he had a reputation. As a supporter he'd learned how to lead a group of fans, he knew how the ordinary person thought, and carried all the authenticity and authority of a man of the street and of the people.

Out of town, at away game grounds, others had looked to him to protect them and he had. Big, strong, six foot two – he had a presence. More often than not, that alone was enough. At one time he'd joined the English Defence League when they started recruiting football supporters, had travelled to their demonstrations and rallies up and down the land, but then watched as the EDL fell apart leaving him nowhere to voice his politics; that was until now.

Over the years, there had been a few occasions whilst supporting Plymouth Rovers, when he'd missed the signs of where things were going. He recalled the time when Luton Town's supporters, the MIGs, and Rovers' supporters joined forces to fight the Bury Park Youth Posse Muslim gang, but he hadn't gone. He'd missed out. He hadn't understood then what the fight was about. He did now.

Today Harry saw with crystal clear clarity that Luton was a place that had gone all wrong. One time he felt he didn't have anything to say, any influence on the predicament of his community, he was in the shadows or even running away. But there had come a turning point. Since returning from Istanbul he had been a man on a mission to make sure what had happened in Luton and in so many other places would never happen on his watch in the South West. To his mind, his new political campaign held all the aces. Muslims had yet to get a proper foothold, numbers were still small, and the other parties were running scared of telling the truth and listening to local fears. Harry was a new broom politician, he knew how to use people's rising fears to his own advantage.

Then the trunk under his feet once again caught his eye and his earlier thoughts of his grandfather returned. He leant forward and opened the lid, pulled out a handful of what looked like political news sheets and began to flick through them. Were they worth keeping? Probably not. The papers were curled at the edges and browning with age. The top sheet had the banner, 'The Western Fascist – The West is Best' and was priced at two pence. Harry thought the name 'fascist' a liability in present day politics, but had no qualms in thinking The West to be best. All the news sheets were from 1933-34; Harry estimating his grandfather to be much the same age then as Harry was now.

The next thing that caught his eye was the subtitle. He couldn't believe it; it said 'Britain First.' The name was almost identical to that of his own Independent political party – the Britain First Democratic Party. Suddenly he believed his grandfather had been a man of political conviction with views like himself, someone who loved his country, even a man ahead of his time – Harry's curiosity was stirred, he wanted to know more. Not for the first time, he thought how he wished he'd talked to his grandfather more when he was alive. The warmth he always had for his grandfather was rekindled as he held his personal things. He felt charged up by the feeling of his close presence.

He started skim reading the newsletters and looking at the photographs. It was all about politics in the Plymouth area and the South West. In what he saw, he could recognise some of the same struggles to organise events, find resources and get popular support that he himself now faced. Someone, presumably his grandfather, had marked with a black pen against the dates for Saturday public gatherings in Plymouth's Market Place.

One fascist meeting held in 1934 had several thousand people in attendance. There were even notes about Sunday Church parades for the fascists. He read how, on Sunday 11

February 1934, six units of ten Blackshirts in each, paraded in Lockyer Street and marched to the church of St John the Evangelist on Exeter Street, where they were given a friendly welcome. They told the priest they stood for 'God, King and Country' at which he promptly admitted them to his church.

Harry dropped the sheet on to his bed. A nice tie up between Britain First Democratic Party and the church wouldn't do his campaign any harm at all. He made a mental note to self to follow the idea up later. There was some Archdeacon of Plymouth guy wanting to promote a joint political hustings, calling on all responsible citizens to vote – he might call him, sound him out – tell him that he was for 'God, Queen and Country,' and see where it led. His family had always had a link with their own parish Church too – also worth exploiting.

And there on another sheet of musty, browning newspaper there were pictures of huge crowds of right wingers in Plymouth proudly celebrating the fact their party membership had exceeded one thousand. It had happened once, thought Harry, why not again, the time seemed right. There were other bundles of papers, but he'd had enough, he was tired and slammed the lid on the past. The reassuring voices of the ghosts of the past had spoken, he'd seen enough to be convinced his time had come. The thought gave him unshakeable self confidence.

4

Lobbing a brick through an upstairs window needs careful preparation. Greg Ward had to obtain the necessary brick and some extras to be held in reserve; and then, to get the right size. A full house brick wouldn't do – too heavy and clumsy. It took half a day to find what he needed. Some local builder, cutting costs by fly tipping, had provided cost-free suitably anonymous half-bricks, just waiting to be picked up. No-one had seen him collect the ones he wanted early that Saturday morning, just as no-one had seen the builder drop them. He chose three that were evenly shaped and felt good in his hand and he'd decide later which he preferred out of the three.

Next, to choose the right gloves. A pair of cycling gloves proved ideal, exposed finger ends for good sensation, and stippled and padded gel-filled palms for a secure grip. The Velcro fastening strap allowed for a perfect fit. The caller's instructions to him had been precise, one brick through a specified window, marked on a photo, a screen shot image, taken he thought from a Google Street View; the brick to be thrown with a message in an envelope tied firmly to it with string and delivered at midnight, and all for a very good price – which satisfactorily settled the matter.

One final instruction had been given. He was to shake the recipient up – and hopefully by delivering it late at night, maybe shower him with glass in his room. Yes, someone really wanted to deliver a message and make a point, but then the customer's motives were none of his concern. Greg just had to have the right tools for the job and deliver exactly as he had been told. It meant an evening out, being driven from Exeter to Plymouth, then brought back. He couldn't see a problem.

Saturday evening and he was ready. He held the black balaclava he kept by for this kind of occasion loosely in his right hand, the heavy duty supermarket plastic bag with the bricks inside in his left. Just another lanky young man, anonymous in his dark jeans, a black top completing his attire. He was ready and felt conspicuous as he impatiently waited to be picked up.

The car arrived within five minutes of the agreed time, Matt's familiar face behind the wheel. Matt Briggs was reliable as well as being a careful driver. Matt swung into the pick-up point, the Victoria pub car park. Once the white Vauxhall saloon had stopped, Greg picked up his bag and strolled over to get in, greeting Matt with a put-on confident smile.

'You set then?' he said calmly.

'Let's go, get it done,' Matt replied, putting the car into gear.

Never relaxed, always attentive to detail to the point of obsession, Greg knew from past experience that it was the simple request that was most likely to go wrong. Last time he came out of prison, he stole a hire car some customer had dropped back to the car rental leaving the keys in the ignition. It was a gift! He'd helped himself, run a taxi business for weeks using it. Got a guy to drive it for him when he himself didn't feel like it. Excellent little earner, until his friend, the idiot, took a fare to the rental office. Then it was game over, arrest, and another unwelcome spell in prison. Now free, he let others drive him, less risky; using willing people like Matt, mates who were only too glad of a few extra quid in their pocket.

36

'Who's the lucky guy getting the message you're delivering?' Matt asked.

'Now there's a funny thing. I wasn't told. Be glad when this one's over and we're away from here,' he replied. 'Besides, best for you, you don't know, know what I mean?'

Greg knew for his part that the price he was being paid, even after he'd paid off Matt, meant that he was never going to grass on this one. Matt didn't ask more and focussed his attention on his driving.

It's hard to explain why you have a bag of house bricks and a balaclava if you get stopped, Greg thought, as he rolled over the top of the bag to hide its contents from his mate.

The drive to Plymouth took almost an hour, longer by the time they'd located the address in Ham Drive. The house in view looked ordinary, in a row of similar post-war boxes. Perhaps it was smarter than its neighbours, but nothing about it shouted out. It all looked too easy – had to be someone wanting to settle a score, Greg thought to himself. Maybe a drugs or money debt – it made him more nervous than usual as he thought once again of the money he was being paid. It made him alert. Put him on edge.

He was aware the pay for this job was way and above too much. Regulars would know putting a window in could be done for a fraction of the payment being made to him for this one. What's more, this mysterious paying customer was keeping himself more than usually well-hidden in the shadows – dark and unknown. Strange too, the whole transaction had been handled by a third party – a meeting in the pub, a verbal briefing and an envelope of cash. £500 for such a job – it was mega. Usually he'd have a feel for who or what he was about. What made Greg increasingly nervous as they approached their target was the realisation that the price of failure would be equally high. He shuffled in his seat.

'Let's get it done. That's the place. The one with the upstairs light on. Take us past it real slow, then park up over there,' he said pointing away from the house. 'There, the other side of that white van. I'll be back in two secs. Bloody well don't leave without me,' he ordered with a forced smile. Matt nodded to show he'd understood. He sensed the tension in his mate.

Before stepping out of the car, Greg reached down into his bag, pulled out his chosen brick and tied the letter from his pocket securely, double checking his knots to see the whole package would hold together.

'What's it say?' asked Matt looking on, his own curiosity building.

'Not the slightest idea, and since you ask, it was made clear to me not to read it,' he said.

Matt again went quiet. Greg, brick and letter in hand, left the safe interior of the car for the open street. It was so quiet in this street, the slightest noise, especially that of a car door, threatened to make curtains twitch. So he left the door slightly open as he made off.

This left Matt feeling exposed, the car's interior light remaining on, illuminating him for all to see. He reached up quickly to throw the switch off, picking up his mobile in a futile attempt to find a distraction whilst he waited. One quick glance at the screen and then his eyes returned to his rear view mirror to watch the near invisible Greg moving swiftly the short distance to his target.

Greg's trainers made no noise, only releasing a slight squeaking sound into the still night air in time with his brisk pace. Clear still nights were the worst – how he'd love some wind and rain, anything to mask his naked presence. A noisy, busy street was so much more anonymous. Fortunately he could detect no-one about to hear him making his approach except Greg himself. The street was entirely his and the knowledge helped calm him.

As he drew near and before pulling on his balaclava he chose his throwing position carefully. Far away felt safer, but the risk of a miss and the delay in having to try again was just too great. So he moved right below the lit window, double-checking the image on his phone to ensure it was the right one before taking a step off the pavement into the road, aware the drawn upstairs curtains hid him from sight of anyone inside. He tried to imagine the mysterious recipient, some unsuspecting soul getting ready for bed who any second now was in for the shock of their life.

He glanced swiftly in the direction of Matt and his getaway route, before steeling himself for the job in hand. Rehearsing the throw in his mind one final time, he drew in a deep breath and tightened his grip on his brick.

In a swift movement on went the balaclava, back went his hand tight round the chosen missile. A light went on in the next upstairs room. It almost threw him. Someone was up and about. He paused to reassess, then quickly decided no change of plan was called for. He'd come too far – it was now or never. Time to throw. The light at least told him someone was definitely at home. He took one last look up and down the street.

One good shot was all it took and Greg knew he wouldn't miss. The trainers were not only quiet, they'd help him run. He would need to be fast.

The brick rose and hit the glass full centre and the shattered shards cracked and splintered as they fell, some inside, others tinkling and crashing as they hit the hard ground below.

The brick and message had been delivered and Greg was swiftly into his stride, his heart pumping as he ran quickly away.

Hearing the noise, Matt was looking for his passenger, had started the engine and was eager to get going.

Job done, thinking they'd got away with it, they disappeared into the night heading back to Exeter.

5

It was late. Harry hung up his best suit carefully, knowing it would be needed time and again over the coming days. He made a mental note to make sure he bought himself some more ties, not something he'd worn many of in the past, but it went with the territory of being an aspiring politician in this Plymouth constituency. A tie, smartly tied, suited his new political image and would go down well with his community. He had always liked a sharp style. Much as he'd have preferred it otherwise, it didn't do to have open-necked or T shirts. To have a common touch connection required some stage management with appearance. He wasn't stupid; his role demanded he act the part.

Discarding his dirty laundry in the bin, Harry knew his Mum, as ever, would see it was dealt with for him in the morning. She'd always spoiled him – he told himself he had it made. He slipped into the bathroom and flicked the cold tap on and was about to brush his teeth, bending over the basin, when there was an enormous crash from his bedroom and the tinkling sound of falling glass. He wondered what had fallen over. Grabbing his dressing gown from the back of the door he hurriedly returned, worried that such a noise would have woken his parents.

The first thing that struck him, as he went back into his room was how fresh and cool the air seemed and he knew then that behind the wafting curtains there would be a broken window. Relief was his next emotion, knowing it wasn't his fault. He stepped carefully seeing shining shards of window glass on the red carpet. Cautiously, after switching off the bedroom lights, he pulled one curtain slowly to the side providing a narrow gap to view outside. Would there be anyone there?

Nothing and no-one came into view. They'd legged it, he guessed. He would have. It had to be dirty politics, he concluded, nothing like this had ever happened at home before. But who?

Leaning right out of the window to see further up the street, he spotted a white car pulling away at the end of the road, maybe with two guys in the front, but he couldn't be certain. By this time his parents were calling out on the landing.

'What's going on, Harry? You all right?' called his irritable Dad, his Mum murmuring something he couldn't make out.

'It's fine. Nothing. I'll deal with it,' he said quickly, trying to sound reassuring. 'Go on, get back to bed, Dad,' as he heard his footsteps approaching. It did the trick and all went quiet.

Then Harry had an idea and switched on his phone.

'Hi Cathy... Yes, I know it's bloody late. That meeting tomorrow morning needs to be now. My home's been attacked. The Muslims don't like my message. Call Cherry at the Evening News, come and take pictures of my parents and myself. We're living under terrorist attack. Even our own homes in Plymouth aren't safe anymore,' he said, before deciding to save the rest of what he would have to say until later. Just too bad his parents had gone back to bed, he mused.

Picking up his phone again, he then made a 999 call, asking for the police. He was quickly put through.

'Harry McNamara here, parliamentary candidate in the Plymouth Moor View by-election. I want to report a terrorist attack at my home, yes, a political attack.'

Looking down to ensure he avoided stepping on the scattered glass shards, he could now see that there was a brick on his bedroom floor, lying half-hidden at the side of his bed. He'd missed spotting it earlier. There was a paper with what looked like Arabic writing on it, tied round the brick with orange string. He still had his mobile to his ear.

'Sorry officer, a correction, it's definitely a religiously motivated political attack which may also be a terrorist one. Have you got that?' He paused before continuing.

'Are you sure about that, Sir?' the officer checked.

'There's no doubt about it. They threw a brick intending to hit me as I lay in my bed, just missed my head. It's covered with Arabic writing. Two guys I think, just legged it and went out the end of the road in a white saloon car. One has to ask why they hate us so?' Harry said, thinking fast, reasoning that it didn't harm his campaign if he embellished the details a little. Who would know he was in the bathroom? Since when had anyone ever been truthful in politics? To Harry's mind, useful news held the trump card.

The police promised to have someone round immediately. Though feeling tired earlier, the excitement and adrenaline rush that had taken hold of him led Harry to suspend his need of sleep for a while longer. His political campaign had just stepped up another gear. He instinctively knew events were again moving his way. He wanted to have the local press photographer and the TV reporters round as soon as possible, preferably whilst the police were still at his home.

As soon as he'd completed filling in the detail to the operator taking his 999 call, he made three more calls to get the press bandwagon moving. He also shot a short video of himself using his phone, hoping he looked like a staggering shocked innocent victim raising himself from his bed, horror struck at the damage to his window and his glass strewn floor. He had to be careful not to over play the role.

Finally, the shot closed on the half-brick with its message, Harry adding verbally, 'God, they just missed hitting my head. There's even glass on my pillow,' he said for good measure. The clip finished focussing on a particularly vicious looking shard Harry had raised from the floor to the pillow himself. These deliberately shaking and shocking video images might prove most useful later, he thought, wondering when the best time to release them would be.

Next he called a very sleepy Stu who denied he'd been woken up, when it was plainly obvious he had. Harry told him to smarten up and come straight over, an order he knew would be dutifully obeyed. He could hear Stu's new wife Penny mouthing off in the background as he ended the call. Harry smiled. There was a certain freedom in not having such attachments.

Our campaign's just taken off, he told himself. He couldn't believe his luck. They've just handed me a winning ticket. 'Bring it on. Bring it on,' he shouted out loud, only quietening as he realised his parents had by now, on hearing him making his calls, come back into his room and were awaiting his attention and probably some kind of explanation. His father looked puzzled at his son's emotional delight and wondered if he was all right. Harry sobered up and took control of the conversation.

'Look Dad, someone's had a go because I'm making a stand for what's right. I'm OK, I'm not hurt. We can get the window fixed, no problem. I've called the police. They'll be here presently. Leave them to me,' he told them.

'That's fine son, I'll get on to the window as soon as the police have gone. I've some board out the back. We'll need to sweep the glass first. Look there's even glass on your pillow, just mind yourself. I hope this is the last of it,' his Dad said, looking across to Harry's Mum who was visibly shaken and quite unable to take it all in.

'I'll go and put the kettle on. Expect the police will like some tea when they get here,' she said. 'We could do with some, since we're all wide awake. I don't know where this will all lead to, not sure politics has ever done this family any good,' she muttered as she turned to head off downstairs.

'Yeah, tea, great. Make sure you use the St George's flag mugs Mum. It'll help. I got them in for the campaign – they'll be useful now!' he added, ignoring her doubts as to his political ambitions. Harry, for his part, felt like he was on a high, buzzing with a cheerful wakefulness and sense of purpose that fed his ego. He would need to keep it in check.

The hours between 12.30am and 2.30am were fully occupied. Harry managed life in his dressing gown, moving between TV interview and police interview as if he were an experienced political animal, his team supporting him as best they could. By the time everyone had left he knew that breakfast TV would be full of the story, a story told as he wanted it to be. People would start to get frightened and they would see Harry as the strong man with the necessary robust policies to deal with it. After all, he'd told them, 'an attack like this on one citizen could be an attack on anyone asleep in their beds. No-one in Plymouth was safe anymore.'

So far as the police crime procedures went, he had no confidence whatsoever they would catch anyone. They'd talked to him about using CCTV to try and pick up a white saloon in the area, but admitted it was a long shot to think the perpetrators would ever be caught unless the police had a lucky break. They urged him to be vigilant about personal safety during the campaign ahead and asked if his party provided a security adviser.

Harry laughed out loud. He knew half the people who had nominated him were convicted football hooligans, the other half, former EDL, English Defence League members. What they didn't know about personal security between them was nobody's business. Nonetheless, Harry had the good sense to accept the offer of a specialist police constable coming to advise him on personal safety – no harm in that, he reasoned. He laughed again; the BFDP as a whole had just over forty members and less than one hundred pounds to its name. A Security Advisor! They must be taking the piss.

He politely showed the two police officers to the door, thinking that maybe the Chief Constable had sent her most useless local beat men round because of the stick Harry had given her over Stu Beamish's detention. No doubt she'd also told them to be careful, no-one wanted to be a victim of by-election shenanigans twice in as many days. Not normally one to bother much about security, nonetheless Harry double-locked the front door before making his way back upstairs.

At 3am, the house quiet once again, Harry fell into his re-made bed. His Mum had earlier made and cleared the tea, changed the bed linen and swept up before disappearing back to bed. For his part, his Dad had already placed a piece of temporary boarding over his window. Whilst his parents had been busy, Harry had kept out of their way downstairs deciding another beer was called for as he'd waited.

Once more back in his room, Harry turned off his phone, but not before setting his alarm for 6am. As he pulled his duvet up to his chin, he knew he was on a roll, the other candidates simply wouldn't know what had hit them. He couldn't wait to get stuck in again in the morning. How he was loving politics. It gave him a most welcome adrenaline rush; even so he knew he would sleep like a baby. Indeed by 3.10am Harry, much encouraged, was deeply asleep.

6

By mid-morning on Monday, 22nd May, all Exeter University students found a text message pinged to them from the Vice-Chancellor's office warning them to be vigilant during the current round of political campaigning in the South West as "students may inadvertently get drawn into situations from which it may be difficult to safely extricate themselves".

Apparently some students had been at the Exeter El Baraka Mosque two evenings ago when the police had been called. The university authorities claimed they "could not guarantee the safety of all students at all times and so all students are reminded of their personal responsibility for cautious and prudent behaviour. Students were to make their own health and safety and that of other students a priority".

There had been some escalation of tension because of the by-election in Plymouth, and indeed all colleges and universities in Devon's two leading cities, Exeter as well as Plymouth, had rapidly collaborated in an endeavour to reduce risks to all students.

In the meantime any concerns students had, in particular those with Muslim connections, were "advised in the light of the unexpected death of Imam Abdullah, to feel free to contact their tutor supervisors or call a help-line number the university were making available from today. Police Crimestoppers had also provided a new number for anyone who wanted to anonymously report concerns or suspicions they might have".

The student safeguarding gurus were running at full speed ahead, fearing the worst. In times when something like this happened, then experience showed that hate incidents on and off campus involving students tended to rise – best thing was to try and nip such risks in the bud.

Adam Taylor read the message out loud to his Omani fellow student girlfriend Raqiyah Nahari, before exclaiming, 'The nanny state has arrived in Exeter.'

'What's the nanny state?' asked Raqiyah, 'I've not heard that expression before.'

'Oh, you know, when those in authority start treating the rest of us like babies, telling us what to do, that kind of thing,' he explained.

'But it's good to know when there's danger, then we can avoid it,' she countered.

'It's over the top. An elderly Imam has died at prayers and it's been picked up by the right-wing party, that's all,' he said, turning off his phone.

'Adam, hold it, just look at this!' She pulled him across from the pan of pasta he was watching boil and thrust her mobile in front of him.

'You remember Harry McNamara, the football supporter hero when we were in Istanbul doing our summer placement, he's the guy creating all the fuss. He's leading the right-wing politics. He's an election candidate in Plymouth. This is so weird.'

'The very same, but that bloke looks too smart to be him, too over-dressed for Harry, in that suit.' He peered in more closely, 'Nope, I was wrong, you can see it's definitely him. Well I never,' said Adam staring in disbelief. 'Is this the guy stirring things up? Who would have guessed it?' He paused before adding ruefully, 'on second thoughts, can't say I'm overly surprised.' Adam didn't like any reminder of Istanbul. This was unwelcome news and he began to feel unsettled and ill at ease. It happened that way.

The pasta was done, the contents drained and shared between two bowls, a tin of tuna shaken out with the help of a fork to top and complete the dish. Adam passed one bowl to Raqiyah and the two sat down at the small kitchen table in their student house, quickly filling two glass tumblers with cold water from the tap.

The small Victorian terraced house had served as student digs for many years and the wear and tear was showing. There were marks on the walls, stains on the table and worktop surfaces, a grubby carpet. Still, the two, together with Bilal and Sophie, who had decided last minute to take up the second room, found the arrangement worked well for all of them, the house being near the main Pinhoe Road in Exeter and convenient for both Uni and city centre life.

The four students and housemates, all on the same course in Islamic Studies, had bonded well since their placement together in Istanbul at the end of the first academic year. The previous summer had turned out to be quite an adventure, albeit leaving Adam from time to time on medication to head off pending anxiety attacks. But, student life being what it is, things had very quickly moved on for Adam; bad times increasingly forgotten, better times to be had.

Adam had attended an autumn term of counselling with Inger Walker, the psychotherapist provided by Exeter University, finding it helpful to air his fears and park them up, to the point where he'd felt by Christmas he was able to say good-bye to her and they went their separate ways. This was all on the understanding that if Adam wanted to come back for any further counselling, at any future point, he had only to give her a ring.

Since the autumn he'd made only a couple of calls to Inger on bad days, but preferred to struggle on in recent weeks. Mental health issues definitely didn't get a sympathetic response from most students – Adam wanted to be clear of the taint, believing things would get better in time. His determination to be free of the stigma that went with receiving counselling support meant there had been occasions when the nightmares had been almost impossibly difficult for him to handle, something he kept under wraps.

Adam didn't like unexpected reminders of the time he'd spent in Istanbul and Harry McNamara was such a reminder, a part of those past events that he knew, even a year later, had the capacity to kick him off course. Harry was a link in the flashback memory chain that led straight back to that still earlier time when Adam was first kidnapped and held hostage by IS in Mosul, when on his gap year bike ride to Iraq, the summer just before he came to Exeter; almost two academic years ago.

The experience of being kept locked in a concrete cell, escaping and being caught up in Ali Muhammed's plot in London on Armistice Day, when he'd nearly died; and then, being caught up in Ali's later Istanbul extremism initiative whilst on a study placement, had left him scarred and traumatised. Harry, or Big Harry as everyone called him then had thwarted that part of Ali's terrorist attack planned for the Galatasaray football stadium and had come out of it an unlikely national and international hero.

'Big Harry. Well, well. Looks like he's come back from his near death brush at the hands of Ali's men. The report makes him sound like he wants all Muslims out of England; some of us go the other way,' Adam teased, trying to be light-hearted as he leant over and gave Raqiyah a pasta-lipped kiss. She pulled away.

'It's not a joke Adam. You don't know what it's like being a Muslim in this country. Mostly it's OK, but sometimes you feel you are feared, definitely misunderstood and at other times even hated. It's getting worse,' she replied. 'Someone like Harry McNamara scares me. England's so full of contradictions. One minute the bastion of democracy and human rights and freedoms, the next, giving Islamophobes like Harry the time of day. That misjudged Brexit referendum was a game changer. When I came here from Oman, I felt OK, safe-ish. Now, well, just for the record, I never know.'

'Hey, look at the media coverage here,' said Adam, pointing to his mobile. 'As of now, Harry's the one candidate getting all the attention. Maybe the university is not being so nannying after all. I'll need to stay even closer to you,' he said, again pulling her close. This time there was no resistance.

'That's all right by me,' she whispered smiling and wiping pasta from Adam's face with her thumb. 'We need to get the Uni bus in five minutes or we'll be late for this afternoon's lecture.'

They quickly dumped the bowls, cutlery and pasta pan into the sink on top of the unwashed plates and mugs from earlier, grabbed their things from the hallway and left the house.

On arrival at Uni they sensed a new tension in the air and when their Arabic lecturer began his class by re-reading the university student-alert text they'd been looking at together earlier, apprehensive faces, which included those of the many Muslim students, looked at each other wondering what would happen next. Perhaps, reflected Adam feeling anxious, waiting for the results of the end of year two exams taken at the beginning of May wasn't any longer the most important thing on people's minds.

All this was having a cumulatively bad effect on him. Raqiyah had picked up on this and kept looking over to check on him. She could see the anxiety, the frozen, rabbit stare in his eyes. He was somewhere else – distant. His fears were taking him over again. When this had happened before she had been there to help him and she knew she had got to get him to take his Quetiapine medication ready for such moments, it was just the thing for a crisis time like now.

'You got any of that medication with you Adam?' she asked, nudging him to get a reply.

'Yeah!' he said vacantly.

'Suggest you take a couple now,' she said quietly, passing him her bottle of water. He didn't move.

'Where are they?' she whispered. He blinked and looked at her.

'In my bag, I can get them,' he said.

As Adam reached into his bag, he suddenly began shaking, so much so he lost his balance, fell from his chair and crashed to the floor. Raqiyah was quickly down beside him, steadying him, speaking quietly to him as she had every time this had happened since Istanbul.

'Come on Adam, it's OK. Take a couple of these. It'll pass. Come on,' she coaxed as he squeezed a couple of tablets from the foil pack, Adam swallowing them with the help of the bottled water.

The lecturer saw that Raqiyah had things under control and resumed his lesson. He began to tell the class about choosing third year options. After Adam had swallowed the tablets, the effect of the Quetiapine was, as ever, pretty quick, his mood steadied and his fears gradually subsided, amazingly releasing him back from a dark place and into life once again.

After just ten minutes of sitting on the floor, Adam shakily re-took his seat. As he looked to the front of the class, Raqiyah wondered whether Adam would really be able to make it through to the end of his course next year. She knew that at times he was only just hanging in there. He never seemed able to concentrate for very long and he only got his academic work done in a rush at the last minute.

To her mind he'd given up his sessions with the university psychotherapist Inger Walker far too soon. A single term seeing her had not been long enough and a relapse like this served to show she was right. As the lecture ended and everyone began moving ready to leave, she touched Adam's arm.

'Adam, we need to get you to see Inger again. Things are going on in your head that are beyond me and you need to sort it out. Promise me you will, promise me,' she pleaded, 'promise me you'll see her soon.'

54

'OK, I'll call her. She said I could come back and see her again any time. There won't be a problem. What happened just now was because of Harry McNamara. It kind of reawakened a lot of things I thought had been put in the past. I'm surprised I was so bowled over. There was nothing I could do to stop myself. What happened a few minutes ago makes it clear I'm not yet free of past demons. Yeah, I'll call Inger, get an appointment.' He took his phone from his pocket as he swept up his bag and began making the call.

Raqiyah was anxious about Adam's mental state. She knew that his experiences of the past two years had taken their toll on him. Being kept in solitary by ISIS, living in fear of a cruel death, a perilous escape, being shot at, injured, then being responsible for saving his friends at the cost of killing the prime minister – how can anyone's mind process that kind of stuff without help, she wondered; and even then, how could someone ever live a normal life again afterwards?

It was then, with a sense of relief, she heard Adam confirm an appointment for tomorrow with Inger Walker. She trusted the woman. Inger's sessions with Adam seemed to help him, and she'd given him some useful exercises to do, not that he always did them.

As they strolled outside into the late spring sunshine, Raqiyah knew she liked Adam a lot, but it troubled her more than she dared admit seeing him fall apart as he had at the very mention of Harry McNamara. She hoped their relationship was strong enough to handle Adam's recurrent anxieties; only time would tell.

7

Adam Taylor considered seeing Inger Walker to be his private business. Now in his second academic year in Exeter, the time with his psychotherapist, provided for by the university for free ever since he'd arrived, was confidential. And he'd grown increasingly to trust Inger, despite her smart suits and rigour for time keeping. She seemed prepared to accept Adam just how she found him and nothing whatsoever had seemed to faze her.

The fact she never said much about herself or gave any inclination as to her own views on the matters that came up in conversation had been long accepted by Adam as part of the therapy deal. What he most valued from her was that she allowed him to be responsible for his own decisions and she made no judgement, even when he could see with the benefit of hindsight, he had decided badly.

But then, on reflection, had Istanbul really been a wrong decision? His Omani student friend Raqiyah Nahari had become someone very special to him as a result, they'd had one hell of an adventure and learned lots about Islam in the process. Big ups, big downs; right decision or wrong, events in his life had left him, as he described himself, all screwed up. It had, as ever, been Raqiyah who'd been there for him when yesterday's latest anxiety attack had hit him.

As usual, when Adam entered Inger's counselling room on campus she offered him a drink. He took a can of Diet Coke and settled himself in the easy chair facing her. Looking directly at him, she waited for him to speak. Today, he waited too. Why not? Besides, he needed to clear in his head, to try and order what he knew he had to say. The Quetiapine he'd taken earlier had got him to her room, now he needed to tell her what had happened and how he felt, but where should he start?

'I've had a bit of a crisis again, ended up a gibbering idiot in lectures yesterday afternoon. It was bad; I made an embarrassment of myself, ended up on the floor, a blob of quivering jelly. The tablets have helped me get by since.'

'Earlier this year you decided that you only wanted to call me if things got bad. You made a couple of calls, but overall, you felt you'd rather try and overcome your anxieties yourself. If that's still the case then something was triggered yesterday that tipped the balance the wrong way for you, yes?' she accurately surmised.

'Spot on. You know I still get nightmares sometimes and I find it hard to sleep properly. Things come back, especially at night, flashbacks. Well yesterday, the Uni sent out an alert to all students, you'll know about that,' he said.

'No, it passed me by. Tell me, what did it say?' she asked.

'You must know what's going on. C'mon!'

His counsellor shook her head.

'When that Imam guy died at Exeter Mosque a couple of days ago, it caused a bit of an issue. You see, the right-wing anti-Muslim parliamentary candidate Harry McNamara had challenged him to a live debate, and it was as he took delivery of the invite, he died. People say Harry caused his death. Whether or not he actually did doesn't matter, the Imam's death has led to loads of tension, on and off campus. That's what the alert to all students was about. When my

Arabic lecturer went over it in class, I felt, well, overwhelmed.'

'Oh,' she nodded understandingly.

'And I still can hardly believe it really is Harry McNamara standing. When I see him on TV – everything keeps flooding back. Yes, he's the very same Harry who was with us in Istanbul, well not with us exactly, but part of what happened there, a big part. He and his football hooligan friends stopped the Galatasaray Football Stadium terrorist attack. Unlikely heroes they were. The text to students tells us to be cautious, to be careful. Something bad is kicking off. Can I just get some water?' Adam was feeling dry mouthed, the Diet Coke didn't satisfy – he wanted to stand up and move around.

'Sure, help yourself, take your time.' She picked up a pen on her desk and started scribbling something down. She stopped as Adam came back to his seat. 'Are you OK to carry on?' she asked.

'Not sure, but I'll give it a try,' he replied, thinking he'd have some difficult explaining to do to Raqiyah if he ducked out of his therapy early. He sipped the water, taking his time before continuing.

'I get these debilitating anxiety attacks because of post-traumatic stress disorder, don't I?' Adam looked up and got an assenting nod from Inger.

'I thought I'd be able to get over it if I threw myself into normal student life and to an extent I think that's worked, well some of the time. But there are those times when I still suffer, like yesterday… and at night, I think I'm still a

58

psychological mess. I'm trying to be honest here Inger. Up to now, I think I've been trying to kid everyone, you included, myself too, that I'm well, over it, almost better. But I'm not, am I?' he said, pausing to look at Inger's attentive face. 'I'm coming to realise the psychological damage I've suffered is deep and lasting and I'm scared it'll drag me down; which is why I've come for help.'

'PTS, post-traumatic stress is commonly long lasting. You're right in saying that, but in my experience, how you see it, how you address it, and the support you have around you, makes all the difference as to how any one individual responds. In part it's up to you. There's no certainty around PTS prognosis in any individual patient. In your case, most of the time you see it as the glass half full rather than half empty and that has kept it sort of manageable.' She waited, letting Adam reflect on what she'd said.

'I just don't know. I'm not able to foresee what will trip me up. When I go down, it gets me by surprise mainly. I've got to try and live my life too; I can't shut myself away, wrapped up in cotton wool. But I have to admit I'm lucky, I've got good people around me; but then that's part of the problem.' He paused.

'I don't think I've told you yet that Raqiyah and I have been an item since we came back from Istanbul. She's great, pretty, attractive and clever; I like her loads, but thinking about her now is making me anxious. She's Muslim. You know already she was there, caught up in it all in Istanbul. She's really good for me. We so get on. But she's also a constant reminder of the past.' Adam stopped, looked into Inger's face and thought he could see a mind working away on what he'd just told her, but she said not a word.

59

'My Islamic Studies course was my idea. I wanted to understand Ali Muhammed's Muslim world better. His extremism is not something most Muslims identify with, certainly not in the UK. Ali was a vulnerable and no doubt exploited guy who had pressures put on him we can only guess at.' Inger nodded some more.

'I've really enjoyed being part of the Islamic Studies Department here, but the course has made me its prisoner too. It's part of the problem tying me to the past. My life is full of irreconcilable tension don't you think? As I'm trying to move forward I'm being dragged down. I can't see how it's going to get any better and that's what scares me more than anything,' he said, reaching again for more water. Inger leant forward to speak directly.

'I don't see either your relationship with Raqiyah or your study of Islam as negative in terms of your PTS condition. In fact, on the contrary. I share your initial assessment that both are able to positively contribute to your recovery.'

Adam was reassured by this and believed it to be true.

'I'm not saying you won't have any more knock-backs like you've recently experienced, Adam, but over time, these may well become less frequent and less severe. You can learn and adapt and as you've told me in the past, there are many ways you've exercised positive choices, even in the most challenging of situations,' she paused as Adam took in what she was saying.

'You know, Adam, even under immense pressure, you have a quite remarkable ability to respond with focus and determined courage. There have been times when even PTS hasn't held you down! And when it looks like it might, you rise to the challenge and meet it; try and head it off. I find that most encouraging and promising. Clearly the recent news about Harry McNamara and the death of the Exeter Imam, whether or not they are linked, has unsettled you. I'd like to offer to see you weekly, certainly until the end of term, to give you the chance to build some resilience in your life. It's work you'll be doing, not me, that's if you are up for it? What do you think?'

Adam knew that this was a good offer, but something inside him, maybe stubborn pride tried to make him turn it down and push on with his life under his own steam. Again, he felt he'd have to answer to Raqiyah if he turned these extra sessions offered for his benefit down, so he quietly assented. The counselling session wound to a close, but not before a further session had been booked for two days' time. He told himself that although attendance at the sessions bruised his ego, they really weren't too painful and might even be doing him some good.

As Adam left, his overall sense was he'd done the right thing. He felt a calm and peace about carrying on. After all, he told himself, life should just settle down again, get back into the familiar student end of term routine, now shouldn't it? However, the news images showing Harry's face were seared in his mind and his instinct told him that serious trouble was brewing and he struggled to contain his rising level of apprehension. He made himself shut the door to Inger's counselling room firmly and then tried to put a determined stride into his steps as set off to face an uncertain day, just double-checking as he left that his medication was in his pocket.

8

It was nearly 4pm, Wednesday 24th May, another warm and humid afternoon in the centre of Exeter. Clive Kone decided to give Adam a call. He'd been meaning to for a while but had yet to get round to it. It had been Adam who'd helped him make a fresh start by leaving London and who had enabled him to put personal space and a helpful distance between himself and the drugs and gangs world in north London that had been slowly but surely taking him over.

He still considered himself fortunate indeed to have escaped apprehension for a post office theft and work as a drugs courier, but a deal's a deal; and having agreed to help the authorities get the terrorist Ali Muhammed, he'd found himself given a precious lifeline. Even so, for his new start to be realised, to be made effective, he knew he had to get right away from London as soon as he could. In desperation, Adam, being the only person he knew and trusted living outside the capital, was the one he'd turned to for help; and thankfully Adam had helped fix things up for him.

After talking to Adam back in September, Clive had quickly found himself an access course place at Exeter College which would make good his educational qualifications shortfall, that is, if he applied himself to his studies, which he wanted to do for the first time in his life. The one year course would subsequently allow him to get on a nursing course the following year. That was where he was headed in his dreams.

Once offered the place there remained the not insignificant issue of where he was going to live and this is where Adam had come up trumps in offering him short term floor space in the lounge of his digs. Adam had had to discuss it with the others in the house first, but they'd all agreed to the temporary solution, though they hadn't told their landlord, and made it clear to Clive it was just a stopgap arrangement, something to keep quiet about so far as any enquiring minds were concerned, just whilst he found somewhere to stay for himself.

Now, several months on, Clive was sharing a room in a house with two other students from college. That very morning he too had seen Harry McNamara on TV and it was this that had prompted him to call Adam once lectures were over. Like Adam, he had been all too close to events in Istanbul the previous summer; and he needed to talk. Adam would understand why. Besides, it would be good to touch base with Adam again.

Seeing Harry in a smart suit as a posturing parliamentary candidate in the Plymouth by-election had proved an unsettling image, the more so, given the right-wing politics he espoused. To Clive's mind Harry looked like a football hooligan dressed for a wedding and he found it hard to consider Harry's political prospects with any seriousness. Even so it sent a shiver down his spine thinking about it. Racial hatred was a subject so raw and near the surface of life for him as an Afro-Caribbean young man, the very sight of Harry on TV was disturbing. Clive rang through, catching Adam soon after leaving his lecture, making his way toward the city centre.

'Hi Adam. It's Clive. How's it going?' he asked cheerfully. Adam hesitated briefly, wondering if Clive once again needed his help. Even so he liked Clive and was pleased to hear from him.

'Fine thanks. I'm with Raqiyah, walking back to the house after lectures. How about you?' Adam enquired.

'All's well. College expects us to get everything in over the next couple of weeks and there were some exams too – who knows? But all right, really, I'm all right. Hey, I'm in the city centre, had to see someone. Are you anywhere near? Have you got time to meet up? Be good to catch up,' he said.

Adam looked across to Raqiyah who could hear every word and she nodded.

'OK, how about picking up a coffee at the Giraffe in Princesshay?' Clive suggested. 'It's good and cheap if you take it away. We can sit around, chill somewhere nearby and as you say, catch up.'

'I know it. I'll be there in say, ten minutes. OK?' Clive said glancing at his watch.

They met up and once hellos and catching up, including questions such as 'How's that sister of yours, Kaylah doing?' had been satisfactorily answered, they sat clutching their drinks, sitting on a low wall not far from the shops.

'You've heard what Harry McNamara's up to now haven't you?' asked Clive.

'Yeah, and he seems to be getting a following. We were talking about him earlier,' said Raqiyah.

'Uni have issued an alert to all students to be careful. Not sure what it means, but it's left people feeling, well, a bit vulnerable,' said Adam, none too confident he really wanted to be having this conversation. So far though, what with the medication and sitting out in the open air, he seemed able to handle it for now.

'Same at Exeter College. Some twat even asked me if I was Muslim today, so he could have a go. I was in half a mind to say "yes" but he was bigger than me,' laughed Clive.

'That's all very well for you, but it's not so nice when you are a Muslim,' said Raqiyah.

'Sorry, that was thoughtless of me. But, going back to Harry McNamara. Harry is very hardline and lots of people want to hear what he's saying, even students. I think he came back from Istanbul with a personal vendetta against all Muslims, so much so he's the nearest thing to a scary right-wing extremist I've heard in a long time. People like him pick on one group, like Muslims, then next you know, it's people like me, who are black, he goes for next,' said Clive.

'I think what scares me most about him is that he seemed so convincing when he was interviewed, so in touch with what lots of people are thinking. You know I can actually see people swinging to support him,' Clive concluded

'Well, it's only early days in the election campaign. The big guns haven't come out firing yet and when they do Harry won't be left standing. I just can't take the guy seriously. You saw what he was like in Istanbul. He's just a yob,' said Adam. 'He'll never hold it together to gain the groundswell of support he'd need.'

'I once thought that, but I'm having second thoughts. He's polished up his act, smartened his appearance, and he's giving a clear message,' said Clive; 'he's dangerous Adam.'

'You could be right. The public's mood has changed. I noticed it when I went home to London in the Easter break. There's a lot more right-wing sympathy around than there was,' said Adam. 'Things have steadily moved further right than UKIP, that party we used to call the BNP in suits, but locally they've cuddled up to the Conservatives and lost their voice. I suppose that's left the door wide open to someone like Harry and his British First Democratic Party.'

'Some of my family won't travel to parts of Europe now because they say the right-wing politics are so scary,' said Raqiyah. 'I saw something on line about it. In Austria, there's the Freedom Party, in Holland the People's Party and in France the Front Nationale. They're all getting enough support to change things and get seats. Harry's going with the popular flow and he's not alone. He might just do better than you think.'

'I'm no politician, but do you think we ought to contact Harry and tell him he's got it all wrong. I don't mind finding out how to reach him and sending him a message. Would you be with me on it? I mean, he can't be allowed to get away with what he's saying unchallenged, now can he?' said Clive. 'He's not an easy guy to talk to, a bit bullish, but he could hardly refuse to see us, he'd remember who we were. He couldn't say no, now could he?'

'Count me out. I don't want to get involved. As I said, he'll be a side act, and then lose his deposit as soon as the main candidates get going,' said Adam, inwardly terrified at the thought of seeing Harry.

'Adam, I know why you might want to give it a miss right now, but I think Clive's on to something. I'd be quite happy to go along with you Clive to ask him a few questions. I think if he had both a black guy and a Muslim woman to deal with, between us, I think we'd make an impression. What can go wrong?' said Raqiyah.

Clive's eyes lit up. For a moment he thought of his father, Bishop Sam back in London and how he just loved public speaking and arguing with just about anyone. He wasn't like him, but maybe he'd learned a few skills from a lifetime spent watching his father that might just come in handy. He smiled at Raqiyah.

'OK then Sis. Tell you what. I'll track him down, call him, then get back to you,' Clive told her, his face lighting up at the prospect.

Adam felt himself getting anxious again. Although he hadn't wanted to confront Harry himself, the fact that Raqiyah was prepared to do so and put herself in the line of fire, was something he hadn't reckoned on. He now felt pulled to support her, be with her; yet so worried at the thought of squaring up to Harry, he didn't know what to think. In fact he couldn't get his words out and fell silent.

Clive told them Kaylah was coming down to Exeter from London for a weekend soon, bringing her baby Jacob with her. She'd started up an online jewellery business and this had begun to pick up. Still in the same flat the Israeli embassy had provided through Lena, she wanted to move on, find somewhere new to live and gain true independence. Her plans were to rent her own place by the summer. Their Mum, Shazee Kone had been helping a lot with Jacob's care.

'Maybe, sometime over the weekend, when Kaylah's here, we could all meet up again,' Clive suggested.

67

'That would be great,' said Adam, feeling he could handle this proposed social encounter a lot more easily than the one with Harry. So it was agreed that when Kaylah and Jacob arrived, they'd all meet up.

Clive then spotted one of his friends from Exeter college, after quickly made his excuses to Adam and Raqiyah he made off to join him, jettisoning his coffee cup into a street bin as he ran.

'Well, he seems to have settled down in Exeter. I envy him, he's always so cheerful,' said Adam.

'That's in part because you helped him, Adam,' said Raqiyah. 'Come on. Let's make a move. We might pick up some pizza on the way back. What do you think?'

It was agreed and they began wandering through the pedestrianised footpaths back to Exeter's High St with all its shops and crowds.

'Don't you think we're taking Harry too seriously by talking about going to see him?' asked Adam suddenly. 'You'd be encouraging him in his path, making him think people were listening to him. Wouldn't it be better to keep silence, ignore him? People like him just need the oxygen of publicity and they get a following, but if you block him out, don't give him any attention, he'll give up, won't he?'

'I wasn't thinking Clive would like arrange to see Harry in front of the cameras or anything. I thought we'd just see him privately for a conversation. I agree with you though; the last think I want to do is give him any support for what he's saying. Let's see what Clive manages to achieve. The meeting might never happen, probably won't. I still think it's

68

something we should try and do. Sometimes I think the point of being in this world is not just to understand it, but to change it,' she replied with a look of determination in her eyes. And that was the end of it, the matter dropped for now, but not forgotten.

Adam was beaten. Part of him accepted it easily for Raqiyah's willingness to stand up for herself, be independent and take on the world was one of the qualities he cherished most in her.

It took twenty minutes to get to the pizza take away near their house. Rick, in his orange peaked cap advertising 'Perfection Embodied' served them. The Perfection referred to the pizzas of course, but with Rick wearing the cap, the irony was profound. He looked younger than he was, like one of those spotty young people in the midst of adolescence. A student at Exeter Uni like themselves, he had been lucky finding this evenings only job, serving pizza.

It wasn't a bad job; many of the customers were fellow students like himself. They got on and Rick never skimped on the toppings. Rick had told Adam once he was from Leamington Spa and was doing a PGCE so that he could teach. As Raqiyah and Adam waited whilst Rick processed their order they glanced up at the TV screen in the corner. Samantha Snow was talking about the forthcoming by-election on BBC's Spotlight South West. Adam nudged Raqiyah to make sure she was following it.

There was Harry McNamara again. There had been shots of him visiting local schools, talking to children, and then the conversation took a different turn.

'I understand there was an attack on your home last Saturday night. What can you tell us about it? How did it make you feel?' asked Samantha.

'It was shocking really. A brick was thrown through my bedroom window by Muslim extremists. Just missed me it did. Shards of glass everywhere, even on my pillow. My parents were very shaken,' said Harry.

'Why do you say they were Muslim extremists?' she asked.

'The brick they threw was wrapped in pages of Arabic script taken from the Qur'an. The police came immediately and they're mounting an investigation. Thankfully none of us were hurt, but when ordinary British families are attacked in their beds at night as they sleep, then we know this country has let in too many migrants. Too many extremists have slipped in and it's time to stop them.'

'UKIP and the Tory parties won't say it, but I will. I will speak up for the ordinary citizen and if I'm elected I'll work to put a stop to immigration and will ensure that all Muslims are sent back overseas. Their way of life is incompatible with ours. The experiment has gone on long enough. We know the result – overcrowding, segregated communities, a massive drain on public resources, and not to mention all the extremist attacks,' he added.

'How will this personal attack on you and your home affect the campaign?' Samantha followed up.

'We don't give up in our family,' he said, 'like all true British people living in a principled Christian country, we stand up for what is right and see things through. When my friends in Plymouth invited me to stand in this by-election, they knew

70

I'd stand by my principles and fight and struggle until justice prevails.' Then lowering his head to speak more directly to the viewers, he confided with them.

'A personal attack on me and my family by cowards throwing bricks won't deter us. In fact it will make us stronger, all the more convinced to stand by the ordinary British person like you and me, to protect us, our white families and homes from the foreign invaders. We will make Britain safe again, a country to be proud of,' and with that final flourish the interview piece was out of time and Samantha passed over to the decorously attired weather forecaster to her side; the camera flicking across and away from the still smiling Harry.

Adam and Raqiyah looked at each other. What they'd seen was scarily slick and convincing. Harry was showing no sense of slipping out of the limelight. He was centre stage in this campaign. First the Imam's untimely death as he was given Harry's invitation to debate, now Harry under personal attack in a Muslim retaliatory strike on him and his home.

'Do you really think people will vote him in?' whispered Raqiyah.

'The way things are right now, they just might. Harry has stepped up a gear, improved his act,' stammered Adam. They barely noticed when their boxed pizza arrived before them and they set off for home in silence.

9

Thursday morning arrived and Adam was not so good. Raqiyah Nahari observed him, scared and shaking, popping his medication as he'd gone off first thing to see his psychotherapist Inger once again. Not since they were together in Istanbul had he been quite so bad. He must have made it to the Exeter campus by now she reasoned, otherwise she'd have had a call, or maybe not if he was really bad.

Her mind turned to an earlier conversation they'd both been party to. She was now half regretting the fact she'd agreed with Clive Kone so readily to arrange to try and quiz Harry McNamara as to his policies and intentions. In retrospect, twenty four hours later, she now thought with the benefit of a day's hindsight, her decision had been impulsive and risky. However, she didn't know quite how to say 'no' to Clive without him taking it personally. Part of her was also telling herself she was doing the right thing and it would all work out – she didn't know which voice to believe. It was all making her feel unusually unsettled. She was usually someone who knew her own mind she reminded herself.

It was mid-morning and Adam still hadn't come back from seeing Inger and she reckoned she'd have to talk to him soon about seeing Harry. Her apprehension rose. This could unsettle Adam still further. For her own part, Harry both made her feel angry and intrigued her. Just how could someone think the way he did?

Arguments she would put to him were already going through her head. Normally calm, he was winding her up – she knew it. She hoped she might put Harry McNamara on the spot, show him up for what he was, proving him to be an unthinking racist Islamophobe. She really wanted to do that and was surprised at how angry the very thought of meeting him made her feel.

Her mobile rang. Great, it was Adam.

'How did it go?' She quizzed.

'Fine. I've agreed to pop and see Inger each week for a while – I guess until the end of term. There's no magic bullet, Raq. I'm struggling with Post Traumatic Stress still; likely to be for sometime, but with luck and a fair wind, I'm sure things will get better. Inger knows her stuff. I'm free now. How about meeting up in town?'

Raqiyah judged that he seemed less agitated and they agreed on one of the small independent High Street city centre cafés, allowing half an hour to make their rendezvous.

Both were late by nearly ten minutes and began by apologising to each other. Seeing Raqiyah and taking her hand in his instantly relaxed Adam. They ordered drinks and sat down. Raqiyah sensed the time was right to talk about the plan Clive and herself had made to meet Harry, though she still wasn't entirely certain whether to go through with it or drop it. She decided to see how Adam would react before committing to the venture and finally making up her mind.

'It was nice to see Clive yesterday,' she began. 'He's obviously enjoying his time at Exeter College.'

'Yeah, suppose – he seemed OK.'

'What do you reckon?' the question left hanging.

73

As they took their drinks to a table by the window, she asked again, 'should I still arrange to go and interview Harry like he suggested, ask him a few straight questions to put him on the spot – or forget it?' she inquired. Adam had grabbed a muffin, calling it his late breakfast. They sat down, Raqiyah waiting on Adam's reply. She could see his mind was turning over what she'd said even though he was busy tucking into the muffin.

Rain had been threatening all morning, and big drops began to patter against the pane. Adam looked out. Then he turned to Raqiyah. He had the look of someone who'd made up his mind.

'It's your call obviously, but go ahead. You'd only disappoint Clive if you didn't. It doesn't need to involve me. Better it didn't, I guess. Keep me posted. I'm really interested to know what he's about.' And that was that. Raqiyah felt that she had been given the green light and in excusing himself Adam had extracted himself from any further direct stress. It felt like a resolution of sorts had been found.

The conversation quickly turned to the pressing matters of the day, like whether to attend the final lecture in the 'Geography of Islam' module that had been laid on as an end of year extra session for the really keen. It was scheduled to take place at 2pm. In the end, neither of them coming up with any bright alternative ideas, they opted to go. Adam felt that given how he'd been the last twenty four hours; a boring lecture might even prove to be of therapeutic benefit. The matter decided, there was still the question of how they were going to use the next two hours until then. A silence fell between them.

Drinks finished, Raqiyah said she was going to call Clive, upon which Adam decided he'd go and look in the cycle shop a few doors along while she did so. They parted.

It had been some time since Adam had been inside a cycle shop and once across the threshold all kinds of dormant senses were awakened. The smell of new rubber tyres was sweet in the air. He recalled Fred Striker's place in north London, making a mental note to call in next time he was home at his parents'. Home, he mused... he wasn't sure where that was anymore. Then his reverie was interrupted. An assistant asked if he needed any help, to which Adam responded by saying he was just browsing.

He really wasn't looking for anything in particular and his gaze moved from the new expensive racers being promoted for the summer trade, to the cycling community notice board. All kinds of rides were advertised, some bikes up for sale too. To his surprise there was a Marin bike like his, someone was trying to sell. How could they, he mused. His own bike was still his pride and joy, currently in the hallway of their digs and still in use almost every day. He really ought to try and get out on a ride with Raqiyah; now exams had finished maybe they would.

His eye spotted an open invitation team ride advertised from Exeter to Plymouth and back the following Saturday. The route over Dartmoor looked challenging as well as scenic. He took a photo of the advertisement using his mobile. It looked fun. Why not? He noticed a box of back issues of Cycling Weekly on the counter going free to anyone prepared to give them a good home and helped himself to three copies before leaving the shop to return to the café where he'd left Raqiyah.

'Success,' she exclaimed smiling as soon as he appeared, 'Clive's spoken to Harry and we're seeing him Saturday lunchtime in Plymouth. Harry was fine about it, Clive said. We're thinking we'll both go down on the bus together; bus is the cheaper option.'

'Good on you. Might take myself off on a bike ride Saturday whilst you're otherwise engaged,' he said, remembering the advert he'd just seen.

'Sounds good to me. How about we go over to Uni now and get some seminar preparation done before the lecture. I'm the one beginning to get anxious now,' she said smiling.

There was no answer to that. Adam knew he ought to do just the same – best to think of it as more therapy, he thought. Just what he needed, he told himself. With an OK shrug of his shoulders, they both got up and left, walking slowly up to Uni, the earlier rain having given way to a grey drizzle. The plans to quiz Harry and the rest of their day more or less planned out before them, life felt easier.

'You're always so bloody conscientious,' said Adam teasingly. It broke the ice, they both relaxed and laughed, though beneath the surface both were having dark premonitions of what might lie ahead.

10

Raqiyah met Clive at Exeter bus and coach station at 8am on Saturday morning. Clive, always a cool dresser, had smartened himself up to look as if he had an interview with the Queen. Raqiyah had chosen to bring a rose silk scarf to cover her head, a cool blue long outfit below. Their outfits made them stand out from the other passengers in jeans, shorts and T shirts. They looked an odd couple and heads turned.

'Look at us!' she exclaimed, glancing at their images reflected in the glass of a bus station shop window.

Clive looked bashful and Raqiyah had to laugh and then they both laughed. The day promised to be fun. A few minutes later and their bus pulled in. The driver let them on and they settled down for the journey. Raqiyah hadn't wanted to turn up at the meeting with Harry unprepared. The very thought made her anxious and she had a shortlist of questions and a clear steer in her mind of the direction she wanted their conversation to go. She was also quite determined to record the time with or without Harry's permission. She was surprised how quickly her laughter a moment ago had given way to less comfortable emotions.

'How do you think we should handle our meeting with Harry? You said he'd send someone to meet us and pick us up at the bus station in Plymouth. But he never actually said where we were having our meeting with him, did he?' she said, before adding, 'It feels kind of like he's controlling the shots, making an offer to us like that. I wish you'd never agreed to it.'

'That's politicians for you, controlling things. Mind you, with an election campaign in full swing, he'll be busy and he's got to find a slot in his busy schedule for us. We'll be in a queue, you wait. Most likely after someone wanting to stop all immigrants and before someone else wanting home rule for Devon. I expect it'll all happen at his constituency office in the city somewhere. We were lucky to get a meeting, and I don't think we have to read too much into being offered a lift from the bus station. We're just one small item in his busy day – be over in a flash.'

'You say, 'office'? Didn't know he had one.' Raqiyah's heart sank as she realised she'd overlooked something important. 'I'll just have a look at his website now and see what we can find out. There may be a blog or something so we can see what he's been up to, something besides what we've already seen in the media,' she said.

The bus was out of town and heading down the A38 trunk road in no time. Raqiyah produced some falafel wraps and a couple of orange drinks from the small rucksack she was carrying. Before they knew it they were admiring the rolling hills of Dartmoor to their right and the bright greens of Devon fields to their left. It was a good day for an outing, to be out of Exeter. Raqiyah thought of Adam shortly setting off on a cycle ride. He'd chosen a sunny day for it, the cycle ride would lift his spirits.

'Do you always travel so well prepared?' joked Clive, eyeing up the emerging picnic and interrupting her thoughts. She ignored the quip and passed him something more to eat and drink.

'Talking of preparation. We must get our heads round this interview. He's a politician, a dangerous right winger. He'll make us look a pair of idiots unless we know what we're about. Come on, we haven't much time, little over half an hour until we see him,' added Raqiyah with a sense of urgency in her voice.

Clive realised what she said was right and gave their conversation his full attention. Very quickly they realised a lot of their political thinking was not much more than what they thought Harry's Britain First Democratic Party suggested to their minds and that of their student contemporaries. Harry's website said a lot of things they had no view on at all and much of what he promoted was what simply sounded populist. On the key issues they wanted to pick up with him, namely racism and Islam, Harry had carefully written nothing more than suggestive outlines. They were less well prepared than they'd thought.

'I think we should just ask him straight out, lay it on the line, make him answer for himself,' said Clive.

'You mean, I say, "Did you come back from Istanbul a changed man or have you always seen Muslims as terrorists?" Something like that?' responded Raqiyah.

'Well, you won't be pulling any punches, but why not? Then keep asking him the same question, don't let him off the hook. Do it like they do on TV. Keep at him until he answers your question,' said Clive.

'And what about you?'

'Well I think he is a white supremacist. I want to know if he'll allow equal opportunities for people like me in his promised land. He wants all Muslims out of the UK, he's made no secret about that, but I want to know whether he's a racist and I'm quite capable of giving him a few true life stories of my own to see what he says.'

As they approached the outskirts of Plymouth, a large shopping centre, just like any other, greeted them. Then the slowing coach wound its way into the bus station before spilling out its full load of passengers. Standing in the aisle waiting to get off, Raqiyah had a growing feeling of foreboding. Should they pull out before it was too late? She was the only identifiable Muslim she could see, Clive the only black person. This would be no student seminar.

The reality dawned that she didn't have a clue what setting this interview was actually to take place in and they'd absolutely no control over events here on in. Plymouth looked different to Exeter; she was in a foreign land. Perhaps this was a huge mistake.

They stepped off the bus and looked round like lost children. A young white woman in a suit, ridiculously overdressed for a bus station thought Raqiyah, had spotted them. There could be little doubt she was not just a taxi driver, more a political aide of Harry. She approached them in moments; cornering them with a degree of certainty which told Raqiyah and Clive she was definitely there to collect them.

'Rita and Clive, that you?' she asked without a hint of friendliness.

'Raqiyah's my name,' a hesitant Raqiyah replied, irritated that her name was misinterpreted.

'Whatever, Rita, Raa-quii-yaah – makes no difference to me. I'm Cathy Nicholls, Harry's political advisor,' she said in a matter of fact, take it or leave it manner.

'Sounds interesting,' said Clive trying over-hard to be friendly, and earning a scowl of disapproval from Raqiyah. Even so, his ostensible show of interest lubricated the conversation into life.

'Sounds good, but it means I do anything he tells me, including running a taxi service when it's needed. Just follow me and try to keep up will you,' she said leading the way. 'He's got a busy schedule today. Everybody and his dog wants his time. He's always been a popular lad, but it's gone crazy round here the last few days now he's famous.' She paused, allowing a brief smile of approval to form before halting beside an old silver grey Ford Fiesta. The marked contrast between the decrepit car and smart suit caught both Raqiyah and Clive by surprise, they'd almost walked on past it.

'Jump in, excuse the rubbish. Too busy to clean it – my kids are not angels when it comes to cleanliness.'

Clive hopped in the back leaving the front to Raqiyah. With a roar the car pulled away into the busy Plymouth traffic.

'Where are we going?' asked Clive, looking around to try and get his bearings.

'White Horse,' she said. 'Landlord's closed the lounge off just for us. Friendly little pub. Harry's laid on beer and sandwiches for you. Must like you or something. Showing respect and Christian hospitality – that's what I admire in him,' she added.

After a short ride, the car spun into a pub car park and pulled round to the rear where there was a suited man standing by the back door. Arms folded he looked like a bouncer.

'That's Phil Potts, the Party Secretary. Like me, he's versatile too,' said Cathy; feeling the need to give some added explanation to her clearly bemused passengers.

They all climbed out. Phil moved across and nodded at Cathy enquiringly as if he needed assurance everything had gone alright. He looked Clive up and down; Clive wondering whether he was going to make a body search, frisk him for weapons or something, but the moment passed. For a fraction of a second Clive felt he'd been transported back in the blink of an eye to Will's north London gangland world. Phil had assessed these two students were no threat, though his face showed he was puzzled as to their presence. They followed him inside into a corridor where they were told to sit.

'You two wait here will you. I'll tell Harry we're ready for his next session. You'd better come with me,' Phil told Cathy as they both disappeared out the door leaving Clive and Raqiyah in the empty bar space. It was a brief chance for a private conversation.

'I don't like it Clive. He must know to put a Muslim in a pub like this, he's being provocative.'

'Come on, chill. Beer and sandwiches is only an expression – relax. Harry will be here in a minute, we'll have our chat and then we'll be on our way. He won't have time to give us more than a few minutes anyway. He must be so busy,' said Clive smiling.

The door opened and two people came in, neither of them Harry. One, a young woman, the other a guy with a camera.

'The name's Cherry Thomas, I'm covering the campaign for the local paper. Andy Stone here's a photographer. Harry invited us along, he's star rated his session with you two. Now let me check I got your names right, both students in Exeter aren't you?'

'We just came for a chat with Harry, it's nothing of interest to the public,' said Clive defensively.

'That's fine. Pretend we're not here. Believe me, everything Harry does at the moment is of interest, even that whiter than white brand of toothpaste he chooses,' she quickly replied with a laugh. They took up positions, standing either side of the hapless pair settled in their chairs. Each reluctantly spelled out their names as requested. These two were clearly not going anywhere without getting their story. Clive himself now had a growing sense of foreboding about the direction things were taking. To his mind they were trapped. Prospects didn't look good.

It took a further ten minutes before there was a commotion outside. Raqiyah had thought Harry to be inside somewhere, but in fact all the noise was heralding Harry's arrival.

Flanked by Cathy and Phil who must have gone to meet him, Harry in a sharp dark suit with neat shirt and tie looked so different to the football hero supporter of old, who they remembered from Istanbul, giving his impromptu press conferences. His entrance into the pub was polished. He had a natural, raw, assertive presence. A born leader, larger than life some might say; his domineering expression hid all feeling. Raqiyah and Clive were at a total loss how to greet him. It was his powerful blue eyes that captivated. Harry took charge.

'Please follow me to somewhere more private and more comfortable and please sit down. There's a tray of food and drink on its way. He nodded to Cathy who, once they had settled, looked back at the side-door, then opened it as a hassled looking young man from the other bar brought in a tray and set it down before them.

'That will be all for now, Matthew,' Harry said quietly as Matthew slipped back out the way he had come. Phil placed six pints of beer on the one table in front of them all.

'There's a round of BLT sandwiches on the plate. The British lunch of a pint and sarnies. What could be better? OK for you?' he said, clearly not going to take no for answer.

Raqiyah was seething. 'No thank you!' she said, her anger momentarily getting the better of her before she realised she'd played right into Harry's hands, who was already turning toward Cherry to make his point.

'Rejected hospitality again. No gratitude to be had in the Muslim population. You come as my guest. I generously provide lunch and you throw it back in my face. Is that how you want to start – with an insult?' Harry was stirring things, every poisonous word coming out from behind a broad chameleon-like smile. Raqiyah glanced across at Clive who was on the edge of his seat with rage. She quickly surmised that not only was Harry a difficult adversary to deal with, but she might have more problems still if Clive blew a fuse. Things could get out of hand and they had hardly begun. She worked to quell her rising emotions, to regain some control.

'No, I'm very grateful to you both for finding the time in a busy campaign to see us and for providing us with refreshment after our journey. You would find the same hospitality offered were you to visit my home,' she said with as much dignity as she could muster.

'Now, how can I help you two? We have about ten minutes,' Harry said, ignoring Raqiyah's reply and looking across at Phil who merely nodded. Though Harry had sat down to face the two, Phil and the others remained standing.

'I'd like to hear your views on racial equality, whether you think our current equality legislation goes far enough. Does it deliver a fair and just society for all?' Clive asked. Raqiyah was impressed at how well he had constructed his question, his earlier moment of passion having subsided or been suppressed.

'As you will know from our manifesto, the BFDP promise to deliver a fair and just society. But you will no doubt agree with me that there are significant obstacles in our path. There are people out there who claim to be members of our community but they are really parasites. Do you mind me asking, Clive, how old you are?' said Harry calmly, before waiting for an answer.

'Twenty,' said Clive, wondering where this was going.

'And do tell us what you've contributed to British society in your twenty years of life. Take your time. I'm really interested,' asked Harry, nodding in the direction of Cherry once more. 'Have you ever worked, Clive?' Clive felt caught out. He felt like he did when his father had a go at him.

'I'm at college, started last September, an access course. I want to be a nurse I think, well that's the plan,' he blurted.

'So you've never worked, never contributed anything. You're in your twenties now and have just become a student. And turning away from Clive giving him no chance to add anything further, 'and what about you, what are you giving to our country?' asked Harry, now standing right in front of the seated Raqiyah.

'I'm a foreign student at Exeter University. My family are paying large fees to give me a good education, fees which pay for the Uni, and help support the British economy,' she replied confidently.

'Don't they have universities where you come from then?' asked Harry.

'Yes, but not in the area of study I was interested in,' she told him.

'In my experience you are an unusual Muslim. If you don't mind me saying so? One who has turned her back on her faith, her people, her family. Doesn't the good book give women an honoured role in the home, which is why Muslim women in general don't need further education, isn't that right?' said Harry, looking at Raqiyah for an affirmative answer.

'No, not right,' she stammered.

'What's not right? Women are best honoured in the home or women don't need further education?' interrupted Harry, 'now which is it young lady?'

'Well, women are honoured in the home, but too few Muslim women go on to further education,' she said.

'Thought so,' said Harry cutting Raqiyah short, 'Islam is a backward religion, for the most part, and with respect, I'm sure your own family are different, but mainstream Islam is restricting the opportunities of women, imprisoning them in domestic servitude for the most part, and excluding them from the benefits of education in their own lands. Here in the UK, I want to see equality. Clive's right in mentioning equality, it's a British value we hold dear, and this means returning people who don't share our values to their own lands. Surely you'd agree with me – things need to be done, things need to change for the better in this country? Islam is a religion that needs to address many things and human rights, equality and fairness are, as you both say, pressing matters needing to be addressed.'

Raqiyah could see Cherry was also recording the conversation, no doubt the smile on her face betraying her delight in having another news item in the making. Her sidekick photographer, Andy, was busy taking shots. Raqiyah had put her mobile on to record the meeting, but felt everything said so far she'd want to delete. The intrusive attention of Cherry and Andy together with Harry's aggressive intimidating style had her flummoxed and she wanted out, knowing it had been a mistake to come and subject themselves to this. She looked across at Clive, whose face was again seething. She felt she needed to finish things, Clive once again looked about to blow. This was nothing like she had envisaged her conversation with Harry might be. She made one last ditch attempt to take back and regain some control.

'Do you remember when we were all in Istanbul last summer? What you did was very brave. You tackled three extremists getting ready to attack people at a football match. What I want to see is an end to extremism, don't you?' she said, hoping this would be a good angle to take.

'I'm glad you mentioned that. You and I both know that for extremists to get a foot in the door they need friends and supporters to help them. That's what was happening in Turkey. Mark my words that country will fall apart. There is an unstoppable factional Islamification happening there. For this reason we, in this country, are rightly wary of getting too close to Turkey. I've seen what it's like there, so have you.' Harry waited for Raqiyah to nod in agreement before continuing.

'In England the problem is different, it is the lack of integration by the Muslim community that allows young people to be so easily persuaded to become extremists. They show their lack of gratitude to their host nation by easily allowing themselves to become radicalised. While there remain families with young idealistic Muslims like this in my country, then we are all in danger, every last one of us. It makes perfect sense then to remove such dangerous families and their potentially radicalised offspring from our land. It is the only way we can make Britain safe. Don't you think we should try and make Britain safe, put Britain first, or are you an extremist sympathiser?'

Harry paused. When he saw his visitors were lost for words he added, 'Or, put it another way, can you offer us a better solution?' He said all this without raising his voice, delivering his question with a malevolent steadiness, blue eyes of steel above a mask-like smile. Harry felt pleased, he could see them crumbling before him.

'You want to extradite all Muslims from Britain. Your position is all built around fear. You're frightened of Muslims. I've seen your kind before. You're a playground bully, a football hooligan posing in an off-the-shelf suit. We made a mistake in coming,' Raqiyah spluttered bravely, now close to tears and feeling frightened.

'I'd just like our media friends to notice what is happening here,' interrupted Harry. 'In a busy election schedule I agreed to see these two young people who are, as it happens, non-constituents because I thought it would be helpful to air two or three key policy areas with people taking advantage of British Education. Clive here has never worked a day in his life. Who knows whether he ever will, but he wants equality. In my book, you have to earn equality. Spongers are parasites. You have to put in what you want to take out. Don't you agree?' This time he looked at Clive, but barely paused for breath before turning to look dismissively at Raqiyah.

'And this young woman Raqiyah, she's here from the Muslim world as a student because her own country doesn't provide her with a course. In fact they don't provide much for women at all. I want my constituents to note that I promise a different world, a better Britain, one where there are no places for shirkers to hide, no families for extremists to call home. I want a safe and great Britain again. Vote Harry McNamara and you'll see a better, safer, fairer world.'

'You're wrong, Harry McNamara, wrong on every count,' said Clive standing up from his chair. Phil reacted immediately stepping between Clive and Harry, blocking Cherry's and Andy's view of what happened next, as at the same time he buried a strong low punch into Clive's belly. This had the effect of tilting Clive even nearer toward Harry.

Harry stepped back, but Phil hit Clive on the side of the face with his fist sending Clive crashing toward Andy whose camera was catching everything.

'No! Clive,' yelled Raqiyah, as he fell to the floor. She got up to reach for Clive, but Phil kicked at her, his steel toe cap catching the side of her head and taking with it her headscarf. It was the last thing she knew.

'They attacked me,' said Harry, 'me,' he called out, as he moved backwards and was ushered out of the room.

11.

'What do you want me to do Harry? Call the cops? You can't be attacked like this and let them get away with it,' said Phil. Cherry had bent down to take a closer look at Raqiyah as she wasn't moving.

'Better call an ambulance first. I don't like the look of her. Think she's breathing OK, but she's out cold,' said Cherry. Clive was rolling and groaning.

Harry had to think fast. He didn't want the police, he'd had too much police contact in recent days. Then it came to him. Here was the chance to play forgiving victim. Besides, what politician hasn't had someone have a go at them? This wasn't serious, these were innocents abroad, but he didn't like the look of Raqiyah, and was scared that if she was actually seriously hurt it could totally derail his campaign in one fell swoop. Head injuries, he recalled from football matches, were so unpredictable – it put him on edge. Last thing he wanted was anything like this to throw things off course. Could spoil his day. Best get help and move on he concluded – no other option presented itself.

'Go easy in future, Phil. They weren't going to do me any harm,' said Harry quietly, 'they'd lost the argument, I'd got what I wanted from them.' Phil simply shrugged.

Then turning to Cathy, he called her to action – 'well what are you waiting for, call an ambulance, even if it's foreigners using the NHS again. Needs must,' he chortled.

With that Harry signalled to Phil to follow him; less than ten minutes and counting to get to his next appointment. The campaign wagon had to keep rolling forward. He turned and paused briefly as he strode toward the door.

'Sort it Cathy, then get them back on the bus and out of my constituency,' ordered Harry, finally leaving the room. Cathy nodded. She knew she had to deal with all the tidying up, as Harry called it. So far nothing had got totally out of hand and she'd been able to manage things.

The ambulance arrived to find Cherry and Cathy both trying to prop Raqiyah up, assuming every bit the caring and concerned role Harry expected of them; Raqiyah was now back in the real world, but still not properly conscious.

Clive was sitting up, looking worried, his hand on his cheek which sported a graze and a trickle of blood running down to his chin. No doubt it would swell up later. Familiar with street rough and tumbles in Edmonton where he'd grown up, he knew his knock was nothing, but he was more angry at the humiliation he'd suffered – the injury to his pride was the serious hurt. He turned to look at Raqiyah. Her face was very pale, her head tilted forward. He was fine, another scrape in a lifetime of knocks, but looking at Raqiyah he was worried, she needed medical help. He moved in between the women.

'Come on there. Just hang on till we get you out of here. You'll be OK. Ambulance coming,' he whispered caringly watching her eyes struggle to focus on him.

The ambulance arrived in minutes, a siren announcing its presence, tyres scraping on some loose gravel as it came to a halt at the front of the pub. A green-suited ambulance woman walked briskly through to where Raqiyah lay. She signalled to Clive with her hand indicating he was to stand back. After a cursory second glance in his direction on seeing the state of his face, she began checking her patient over. Then she swiftly signalled to her colleague.

'Need to get her in,' she instructed.

'Can I come with her? I'm her friend,' said Clive.

The two ambulance crew looked at each other. Cherry intervened and said, 'that would be a good idea' and Cathy simply said, 'I'll look in at the hospital later, see how you're getting on.'

Cathy then took the ambulance man to one side and whispered in his ear. Clive heard the response, 'not a matter for the police then.' He seemed happy with whatever he'd been told and Clive and Raqiyah were, without further ado, whisked off in the back of the ambulance the few minutes' drive to Derriford, the Plymouth hospital's A & E.

As they glided smoothly in front of the grey block building with its blue NHS 'welcome' board, Clive didn't for one moment like the look of Raqiyah, now paler than ever, who seemed to be drifting in and out of consciousness, her dishevelled head scarf pulled awkwardly back across half her face. She looked all wrong. The visit had been a total disaster.

12

It took four hours until Raqiyah was properly conscious, by which time a barrage of tests had been completed, with others still to come. Clive heard the word 'concussion' being used from time to time, but what he really wanted to hear was just how long it would take for her to get over it. No matter how many times he asked, no-one seemed able to explain what it meant to the two of them. About one thing he was clear, there was no question she'd be allowed out that evening.

Raqiyah, in a hazy, woozy world, had no recollection as to what had happened to her. Apparently the ambulance crew had been told by Cathy, who had "seen everything", that she had hit her head as she fell getting up to leave the pub. Clive, for his part, once he had wiped the blood from his grazed cheek, realised that, well, no one seemed to think anything had happened to him. The unexpected blow to his stomach had done no more than temporarily wind him.

When he overheard a nurse going through the medical notes with a colleague and the false story of a fall got re-told, and he heard it said that the students were found in a pub and maybe they had been drinking, Clive was angry, but decided now was not the time to pursue such matters. His priority was to see Raqiyah got medical help and got out of there as soon as possible.

As the early Saturday afternoon drifted into early evening, Raqiyah was beginning to feel more her usual self and was glad Clive was there. In the hours of waiting he'd recounted to her more than once the events of lunchtime – how they'd spent time trying to ask questions of Harry McNamara and how it had all ended so badly. She knew it had been a mistake to come. Both realised they had been set up. As her head gradually cleared, Raqiyah thought someone had better let Adam know what had happened, but then worried how he might react to the bad news. She didn't want to be the one to put another person in hospital on her account. In the end she told Clive to call him, to tell him they'd had to stop over in Plymouth as she was feeling faint. It sounded feeble and she added, 'Tell him what you need to, but just don't give him cause to worry.'

In the event, Clive couldn't reach Adam anyway, and then Raqiyah remembered he'd most likely be out cycling most of the day. She was pleased to think that he was doing something he'd enjoy. It was nearly 7 o'clock when it was Adam who called Raqiyah.

'Hey, you seen the news, what's going on? Are you two mad or something?' he began in a tone of agitated excitement.

'Sorry Adam, start again. What is it?' she said, puzzled.

'Just look at the links our friends are putting up on Facebook and Instagram, then call me back. My day, unlike yours, has been great until now,' and then Adam had gone. He sounded furious.

Raqiyah had a sinking feeling and it wasn't her painful head causing it. She felt she was a victim of something going horribly badly against her, a nightmare running away with itself. Clive was already on his phone. His eyes widened as his eyes scanned the stories, his fingers tapping as he scrolled down.

'Hell, no! They're saying Harry McNamara's surgery time was subjected to a deliberate attack. You and I apparently started a fight in the White Horse! Harry was forced to abandon his public meeting amidst fears for his own safety. It says here, the two alleged assailants were students from Exeter out to make trouble. No! No! – they're saying a Muslim woman encouraged her young black man co-conspirator to assault Harry McNamara. This has gone viral.'

'It's not true though, is it Clive?' Raqiyah quietly voiced.

'"The two students had planned the whole thing", Harry says, "though others behind the scenes may have put them up to it. The bloody nerve!"' Clive glanced at Raqiyah who was following his every word. He read on.

'"The two had gone to great lengths to see him, a request he'd graciously agreed to even though he was so busy and then the two used the privilege of the occasion to verbally and physically assault him. Fortunately, neither he nor anyone in his support team had been hurt, but in the mêlée the young Muslim woman had fallen and struck her head. Harry's team had immediately called for medical help." Look here, a photo too,' said Clive holding his mobile up to Raqiyah so that she could see it.

'"Harry McNamara doesn't want to press charges. He puts it all down to the excitement and enthusiasm of youth. At the heart of the students' quest lay a mistaken loyalty toward hard-line Islam coupled with a defence of sponging on the public purse. There are still people out there,"' he says, '"who want to argue for welfare benefits for undeserving people such as these two students. His political campaign on behalf of the good people of Plymouth would not be pushed off course by such incidents."' Clive looked to Raqiyah as if he were about to explode.

'Keep cool Clive. We need to think, give it time, otherwise we will both be answering police questions and who knows where that will lead. Can you call Adam back for me? Don't let him get too worked up. You know how he is,' she pleaded holding Clive's arm, 'and though I still can't see or think straight, when I'm out of hospital, Harry will be hearing more from me,' she said quietly.

Clive liked what he heard; it made all the difference and he had more than a little admiration for Raqiyah's show of fortitude in the face of adversity. A battle might have been lost but the war wasn't over.

'I'll call Adam outside, be back soon and for now I'll be staying over to keep an eye on you,' he added.

Standing between two parked ambulances outside A and E, Clive got hold of Adam, whose temper had cooled, and asked if he was ready to hear the full story and explanation as to what had happened. Over the next fifteen minutes he told it how it was and he could tell Adam was hanging on his every word, only occasionally asking for a point of clarification. Finally he added, very cautiously, that both Raqiyah and he needed to hold a council of war with Adam to work out how to deal with 'that lying bastard, Harry McNamara.' Clive was shouting loudly into the phone, quite unable to restrain his fresh surge of mounting anger at the injustice of it all.

Adam was surprisingly quiet at the other end and Clive started to get worried.

'You OK there Adam? Sorry I got a bit mad, didn't mean to alarm you or nothin'. You OK there?' he said with concern.

'No I'm fine, just chewing it over. Think you'll be back tomorrow?' Adam quizzed.

'Yeah. Don't you worry about Raqiyah. She's good, they're just keeping an eye on her, 'concussion' is what I heard. It's routine to keep an eye on a patient after a knock to the head they say, though if it were up to me I'd be bringing her back on the bus now. She's fine mate,' he said.

'Thanks, tell her I'll call later when I get back to Exeter.' With that he had gone and Clive headed back to the ward.

A few moments later he was back with Raqiyah, to find her now sitting in a chair, with colour back in her cheeks. Yes, he thought, she's OK and ready to go home.

'Adam's fine, you look a lot better now. Need anything?' he offered. She took some water but didn't want anything else.

Time dragged into the evening. Clive was allowed to sleep in a visitor's room chair. Finally, next day, after an age of waiting, a doctor doing her Sunday mid-morning round finally checked Raqiyah over one last time before pronouncing she was free to leave, but not without first giving a great list of do's, don'ts, and ifs. Then out of nowhere, as if on cue, Cathy sauntered in, looking this way and that until she spotted them. Their indecision at her unwelcome presence was interrupted.

'Come to give you a lift to the coach station,' she said. 'They let me know you can go. Harry wants to show no hard feelings, but between us, I don't recommend you come again.'

What could they do? It seemed churlish to refuse; even so they asked Cathy to give them a couple of minutes. She sauntered off to grab a coffee. Out of earshot, they agreed two things. First, not to say anything about what had happened, and second, to accept the lift.

When Cathy returned, take away coffee in hand, she was all charm. As they walked out of the hospital door, neither observed Andy, the photographer, snapping away for his next scoop. Blind to the next press release from Harry's office, they were taken to the coach station just in time for the next Exeter bus.

After dropping off her quiet passengers, Cathy didn't immediately drive back to Harry's next campaign meeting. She pulled up to make a mobile call. Notwithstanding the fact she knew Harry hated disloyalty and the people who went behind his back always paid a heavy price, this time she knew she had no choice in the matter.

The Circle had reminded her that her two year old little girl Etta, presently being cared for by Cathy's sister during the campaign, ought really to stay looking as beautiful and healthy as a delightful two year old should. They had even told her, and this made her shudder, where her sister lived and what Etta was actually doing whilst playing in her sister's garden that Sunday morning.

Cathy knew she had to make the calls they required. It didn't take long, and then she was able to continue on her way. This was bad, she was frightened, but like hell would she show it. The mysterious contact sounded so sinister, dark, evil even, she knew she was dealing with someone much worse than Harry McNamara, but despite the brave face she was putting on, she simply had no idea just how bad things could really get. How could she?

13

Clive fell asleep on the bus. He'd had an uncomfortable night in the hospital chair. Raqiyah was awake, now feeling none the worse for her head injury apart from a bruise to the side of her temple. The swelling was, thankfully, entirely hidden by her head scarf. Whilst on the bus, she'd made several calls to Adam and as they arrived and pulled to a halt, she spotted him astride his bike in Exeter Bus Station. He was looking in their direction, anxiety written across his face. Clive, now alert, was quickly up on his feet.

The two rejoined Adam, forced smiles all round. They decided to go separate ways, Clive excusing himself, reasoning to himself that three's a crowd, heading back to his room ten minutes away. Adam and Raqiyah linked arms awkwardly and walked slowly in the direction of the Pinhoe Road, each struggling to find words to say, neither wanting to be first.

'I need to tell you, there's been more,' Adam said. 'I should have said whilst Clive was still with us.'

'What now? Tell me, I need to know, Adam,' she said touching the bruise on her head, tender under her veil.

'There's a picture of you two leaving hospital earlier, being helped by Harry's political advisor. Do you know her? Name of Cathy Nicholls?'

Raqiyah nodded, looking flustered and anxious in the same moment. 'What's their take on that? We never saw any photographer, honestly.'

Adam looked at her waiting for more.

'Another set up. I've never felt so angry Adam, never in my whole life. I feel so naive, taken in, exploited, vulnerable and for the first time ever more than a little scared.'

Adam looked as though he'd not heard a word she'd said. Then he almost spat his words as they tumbled out – 'Cathy says Harry doesn't hold anything against you and that as a sign of his forgiveness, he wanted to help you get home safely and arranged a car to take you. They say you were really appreciative and it has made you rethink your views. In fact both of you are said to be really sorry for what he describes as "the prank" you pulled yesterday,' he added.

'Huh?'

'For what it's worth, I for one don't believe a word of it. Trouble is, I think almost everyone else will believe him. I'm worried that the university will pick up on it. We were told to be cautious and careful in that text they sent us last Monday. They might see what's happened as deliberate mischief making or worse. Well, too late now – we just have to see what happens.'

Raqiyah didn't know what to say and in a mood of shared despondency they walked silently and slowly, deep in thought, Adam pushing his bike with one hand and holding on to Raqiyah with the other. When they got to the Tesco Express in the Pinhoe Road, they both decided it was time to buy some food for later and the pressing conversation as to what to do about Harry was put on the back burner, to simmer quietly, definitely not forgotten, where it remained until late in the evening.

As night fell outside, having eaten a Pot Noodle each, they were chilling out in the lounge, making use of the old grey settee and moth eaten arm chairs. As with most things in the house, their landlord was saving costs in return for maximum rent. Raqiyah's laptop was playing a film quietly, neither of them really watching it when the conversation turned again to the weekend's events.

'I'm not going to let this rest, Adam. Harry really abused Clive and me. We walked into it naively, blindly. I've got to hand it to him, he was well prepared for us. All we did was have a five minute preparatory chat on the bus on the way down. We never thought politics could be so dirty. Harry used us, used me. He insulted Islam, he insulted the integrity of every Muslim, then he used us to help him promote his own hateful policies. I still can't recall how exactly I got hurt, but Clive is very clear and I believe him. The whole thing was like, like it was choreographed. It was such a bad place to be. How can someone like Harry McNamara get popular support? It can't be possible he'd ever be elected, can it? I hate him!'

Adam sat quietly, stroking her arm, listening to her as she talked and talked. She liked his attention and she knew he cared. It seemed as though he was coping with her story in his own way. Right now he looked fine, he seemed as relaxed as he ever was on the best of days. Maybe it was because he wasn't the one who'd been through it this time. Finally, he turned to her to speak.

'I believe you, and I believe in you. But what do you want to do about what's happened?' Then with his mind jumping this way and that, he was momentarily lost for words and sat back, watching her as she too struggled to work things out. It was Raqiyah who managed to speak first.

'We need to talk to Clive. I feel bad we just left him on his own this afternoon. He was amazing Adam. He looked after me, stood up for me. Stayed at the hospital. He'll be a brilliant nurse. He made light of his own injuries – he's tougher than I thought.'

'He's a big lad, he'll be fine. Grew up in north London, he'll be fine, trust me,' added Adam, wishing he had some of the resilience Clive had.

'No, you should have seen how they treated him,' her memory partially returning, 'he was really hurt. As he got up at the end of our meeting, the guy just punched him in the stomach – so quick. He fell forward and was punched again in the face, the same guy, Phil his name was. He was like Harry's minder.' She mimed the punches with her hands, first the left then the right. Doing that helped her to recall it now, exactly as it had happened.

'Every time Clive had tried to ask Harry questions, they just twisted it, turned it, wound him up and made him mad. No, don't get me wrong. He didn't do anything, I could just see his anger in his face. He feels really hurt, I know he does, and he was really kind looking after me. I owe him,' she said, pausing to look again into Adam's eyes.

'You've not answered the question. What do you want to do about it? Now is the time to look at your options and make your choices,' Adam said rather more firmly than he'd intended.

'Doing nothing isn't one of them,' she answered resolutely.

'Guess I saw that coming,' said Adam. 'So, you could go for something low key, like write a letter, put your side of things, make a few media posts of your own. Tell the truth. Maybe even write to the press. Call in a reporter like he did. Then you might feel better.'

'It's not enough. I don't know what to think about using social media – there's so much false news. People aren't interested in the truth. Why should they want to believe me? I get the impression people are lapping it up, believing everything Harry's saying – like they want to believe in him so much, they won't question anything he says or does.'

'Suppose you're right,' said Adam.

'I've seen what he's like and I can't let him get away with it. I couldn't watch him hoodwink the public and become their MP.'

'So what would be enough? Remember, you are still one angry lady. After sleeping on it, you might be calmer and more relaxed, why not let bygones be bygones and all that,' he said, not believing for one minute she would accept that, but hoping she'd allow things to calm for his own sake.

'I want us to call Clive over. Tomorrow will be fine. We'll hold a secret council of war. Harry doesn't play fair. Gloves are definitely off. We'll come up with something we can do to get back at Harry McNamara, disrupt his campaign, discredit him, that kind of thing,' she said.

'Are you sure? Lots of risks to what you're saying,' he said feeling apprehension and excitement welling in equal measure.

'One hundred percent!'

They heard Bilal and Sophie coming back from meeting friends in town. It was time to bring them up to speed on the events of the past 24 hours. After all, they'd met Harry back in Istanbul too. Fortunately, with their phone batteries running low, neither Bilal nor Sophie had looked at the social network stuff on Raqiyah and Clive, so from the start they were able to tell their own story and have it taken at face value. It was about eleven, pizzas were ordered from Rick's take away, delivered, and excited chatter lasted well into the early hours.

Though he was tired and it was very late, Adam found it hard to sleep. The rest of the house was quiet, as was Raqiyah beside him. She never seemed to have a problem sleeping. In the night he often liked to listen to her regular peaceful breathing. It was soothing, reassuring, comforting. The occasional hum of a passing late night vehicle could be heard outside, that was all. Exeter was a lot quieter than London at night, but even so Adam couldn't sleep well and tonight was one of those occasions when his mind remained alert and crystal clear.

What had happened to Raqiyah and Clive made his blood boil inside. Though he'd kept his own feelings as well hidden as he could, he was determined big Harry McNamara wasn't going to get away with what he'd done to his girl. She was up for getting back at Harry herself and he was determined he would be with her at her side all the way.

The more he thought, the more he knew these were uncharted waters, fraught with danger and a game that rekindled past memories was about to be played out afresh. Great care would be required, both in the work on a cunning plan and in its careful execution. They'd get the upper hand on Harry yet. No doubt courage would be needed, but when it had come to it, he told himself he hadn't failed where that was concerned, though how did this assessment squared with his panic attacks. Damn it, Raqiyah was going to get every bit of help he could give her, of that he had no doubt whatsoever.

As his wakefulness took him past 3am, gradually an idea formed in his mind. By 4am it was settled. At breakfast he would tell the others. Then he too was finally asleep and the whole house at peace.

14

In north London, PC April Cooper was feeling pleased with herself. She had finally been told she had a new police posting in the Devon and Cornwall Police, albeit it was only six months, 1 May to 31 October, temporary secondment to their regional Prevent Team. Nonetheless she was thrilled more than she dared reveal out of loyalty to her hard-pressed Metropolitan Police colleagues. Still young and relatively new to the police, this was also a good career move – she felt a dark cloud beginning to lift.

It had hit her hard when, the previous summer, her mentor and training PC, Bob Steer had been so brutally killed in a routine domestic call-out in Shrubbery Road, Edmonton. No-one could have anticipated that in making the call he would be shot dead at the front door of a drug dealer's flat. 6.15pm on Saturday 13th August was permanently etched on her mind.

That was when Bob had breathed his last; the bullet that finished him mercifully instantaneous, delivered like a coup de grace. It had entered the back of his head before exiting out through his forehead. Poor bastard. Why do the best have to be taken? she wondered. A day still didn't pass without her being distracted by his memory, but in a kind of way she felt she now owed it to Bob, as well as to her retired policeman father, to prove herself.

The autumn funeral had itself been hell. Her duty then, as Bob's closest buddy, had unavoidably catapulted her into the limelight, which was where she least wanted to find herself. In every press interview she had been the one ordered to sit at the same table as the leading Metropolitan Police officers. Then at the funeral, she had been asked to say a few words at the church service. All that was over six months ago, though it felt like yesterday. There was no doubt in her mind; news of a fresh start in the South West with a secondment to the Devon and Cornwall force was, in the circumstances, a dream come true.

Intelligence had recently come in that the newly announced Plymouth Moor View parliamentary by-election could turn nasty with extreme politics promising to enter the scene. Following the unexpected death of the sitting MP at the beginning of April, the local Chief Constable and Police and Crime Commissioner had already put out a joint letter pleading for calm and restraint as emotions had started to boil. No by-election had yet been called, but acrimony between prospective candidates had increased by the arrival of a new young right-wing politician on the scene, the parliamentary candidate for the Britain First Democratic Party. Since National Action had been proscribed by the Government as one of the leading extreme right wing groups, everyone was looking out to see who would fill the vacant space, perhaps the Britain First Democratic Party, the BFDP, was now the one to watch.

Early appeals for a more respectful approach had so far fallen on deaf ears, and outside police forces had been put on notice that additional help might be requested. April was one of three police officers with the specialist Prevent programme and anti-extremism experience making their way to Devon and Cornwall Police HQ at Middlemoor, located on the eastern outskirts of the city of Exeter.

The South West force had long been arguing the case that it was undermanned for dealing with counter-terrorism and/ or associated civil unrest. The Chief Constable had been outspoken in claiming her limited police resources could not get to a terrorist incident in parts of her area in less than an hour. However, someone in London seemed content to think a token temporary resource officer group of three people should keep them happy, for now.

In the first week of May, upon arrival in Exeter, April announced her arrival to the receptionist and was immediately met with a cheerful greeting by her new 'Skipper', who introduced herself as newly promoted Sergeant Emma Stirling.

'Glad to see you. A bit of experience from your part of the world won't go amiss down here in this sleepy Devon backwater. We need the extra help, believe me. Had a good journey down?' she asked warmly, her local accent pleasant on the ear.

'Yes, fine. Drove down late last night after finishing an early shift in Enfield. Get their pound of flesh the Met do. The M4 motorway was empty. Don't know what to expect here really. All I've been told is this election is already bringing out the worst in people,' she replied.

'That's true. First things first, there are preliminaries to sort, then I need to go through the usual induction protocol and procedures before giving you an initial briefing. I take it you have somewhere to stay?'

'Yes. Got a rented place sorted for six months on the new Cranbrook Estate just a few minutes from here.'

'Can think of better places, reckon they're building a slum for the future in the name of new housing. Streets are so narrow and chocker with parked cars, reckon emergency services will have fun there one day. Well, its new build, modern and nearby, I'll say that for it.'

Emma left April with a check list of things to do and she was shown to a workstation, given a login and password to use and was away. It took another hour and a half before Emma returned, the conversation turning immediately to policing matters of importance.

Once briefed, the following days passed quickly enough as April began to familiarise herself with the geography and organisational practices of the Devon and Cornwall force. She'd given a couple of talks on the work of Prevent, but in sum it had all been pretty quiet.

A couple of weeks later things changed. She'd only just arrived at her desk on a Saturday shift when Emma strolled over to say, 'You may have heard. It's had wide news coverage. We've had an Imam die at the Exeter mosque. Heart attack probably. That in itself isn't the problem. He died as he was interrupted leading evening prayers at the city's only mosque, at a point in time when he was being presented, wait for it, with a letter from the far right British First Democratic Party's agent Stu Beamish. The invite was requesting the Imam to attend a future debate with the party's Plymouth by-election candidate, Harry McNamara. The whole incident was witnessed by hundreds of people who were there.'

April sighed, knowing exactly how this could play out, but still asked, 'How has that left things?'

'Poised for trouble,' said Emma. 'Neither side is likely to calm down. The McNamara family home in Plymouth was attacked last night. It was only a brick through a bedroom window, no-one hurt, but there is a danger the whole campaign will turn very nasty. Was the Imam's death and the brick incident linked? Too early to tell. The popular mood is very tense at the moment. People are angry at the mosque. It wouldn't take much more than one further incident to happen and there will be serious eruptions of civil disorder.'

'There's more – this is strictly information for our team only. The South West Counter Terrorism Intelligence Unit are saying that GCHQ are seeing extreme right-wing messaging indicating interest in what's happening in Plymouth – its vague, but definite – that's all we need. That kind of thing sends a shiver down your spine. I'd say goodbye to your hopes of a more peaceful life in Devon right now, April. Looks like you timed your transfer down here just right! See you at the formal briefing later at 12:00 hours.'

Then with her smile now gone, Emma was off, leaving April wondering what might be coming her way. In truth neither officer had any idea what lay in store for them.

15

After a couple of weeks in Devon, April Cooper was feeling the beginning of some familiarity in her new surroundings. There was a more relaxed feel to police life away from London – not exactly sleepy, nor unprofessional, just a different local ethos with what she called a rural edge to it. Even Police HQ had wide open spaces around it, not hemmed in by other buildings as the police were in London's brick and concrete jungle. It didn't feel like the kind of place where things could go badly. The whole place had an altogether comfortable and soft middle England feel.

She was at her new police HQ desk. It was 6.30am on Monday morning 29 May. There was no noticeable late Spring Bank Holiday feel that she could discern as she opened up her computer. In her inbox she found a confidential e-mail from Rob Callaghan, the Regional Police Prevent Lead, saying Harry McNamara's election campaign of not yet two weeks was increasing local tension and worryingly gathering a much wider online interest.

April knew they had to monitor it, but discretely of course, for it wasn't acceptable for the police and security services to get too close to election candidates for obvious reasons. The Devon and Cornwall Chief Constable had already reminded all her officers to be careful. Without wanting to overstate his case, Rob felt the level of public interest and enthusiasm shown for this far right candidate, even for news items relating to Harry was seriously alarming – "unprecedented" in his experience, he said, and not a situation without a serious risk to public order somewhere further down the line.

He reported fully on the fact that over the two previous weekends Harry McNamara had advertised his robust anti-Muslim policy statements in local newspapers. The links to these were appended in case April had missed them.

From the way her governor expressed himself – she knew Rob Callaghan was a guy who just had to show he was boss. But he was irritatingly right too. Although she hadn't yet seen the articles he referred to, she knew she needed to read them as well. There was nothing for it but to start looking at them now.

Opening the files, she began skim reading Harry's rhetoric, noting how all the key words in his manifesto were carefully phrased and nuanced to stay just the right side of the law relating to the incitement of racial hatred whilst still having the effect of doing precisely that. She guessed he'd taken legal guidance – even so it was repugnant stuff.

Harry's treatment of a Muslim woman in Plymouth on Saturday, resulting in her hospitalisation overnight, had led to the call for a meeting of Muslim leaders in the South West, to take place that very Monday afternoon, at Exeter mosque, after midday prayers. Rob had told April he wanted her to get herself along – an experienced officer like her would know what to look out for, he wrote, and he wanted a full report on his desk by the end of the afternoon.

She was fine about that, glad to be getting involved at the grassroots where she much preferred to do her policing. It was too early yet to make calls to the mosque to get herself included, anyway in her experience e-mails to mosques were ineffective, it had to be face to face conversation to get anywhere. Meanwhile she pressed on with her reading to take a more thorough look at the links Rob had sent her covering the second weekend's stories.

The media link included pictures of the two Exeter students whose visit to Plymouth had sparked all the excitement. When she saw them she couldn't believe it – there were Raqiyah Nahari and Clive Kone, unmistakeable – two familiar faces from her days chasing down Ali Muhammed in London. Were they involved by coincidence, simply student voices getting heard, or was there some conspiracy behind it? All this really had her full attention now. The more she read, the more the stories written about them just didn't add up. These two were not the kind of people they are being made out to be, she thought. She was puzzled what to make of it all, but couldn't for the moment explain to herself why it so troubled her. To her mind this conundrum had to be resolved.

After an hour of total absorption in the coverage, she got up from her workstation and went to make some coffee. Perhaps she'd be able to gain a more coherent understanding by taking a moment away from her reading. Bob Steer, her first colleague and mentor, had always sworn by the importance of slowing down, taking some reflection time. She missed him and his experience a great deal; his untimely death was such a tragedy.

A few minutes pondering and she knew that she'd already decided she was going to catch up with these two and find out from them first hand what had really been going on, and she would do it today. Still not yet having much in the way of local knowledge of Exeter, she awaited the return of her Skipper who should, with any luck be able to help her get straight to the two hapless students at the centre of the weekend media frenzy.

She didn't have to wait long. Just halfway through her mug of black coffee, in walked her colleague Emma Stirling who April moved quickly to intercept.

Twenty minutes later, after discrete calls, using Emma's contacts at Exeter Uni and Exeter College, bingo! – Emma passed across to April both Raqiyah and Clive's mobile numbers and their address.

She glanced at the wall clock – for some reason all police stations seemed to have them, all identical – it was about being in an institution she concluded. It was still only a few minutes after 9am, far too early to call students and get a sensible response, so she decided to send an identical text message to both of them.

As she gathered her thoughts, she knew she wanted her texts to be totally non-threatening and yet be sufficiently attention grabbing as to give her the opportunity to talk to them as soon as it could be arranged. If possible, she thought, seeing them initially individually would help get her nearer the truth of the past weekend events. Raqiyah was in her sights first. She reasoned she'd probably get the most truthful account of events from her and then use the information to aid her subsequent questioning of Clive.

Satisfyingly, her phone almost immediately indicated a reply from Raqiyah with the simple message, 'Please give me a call.' She got straight back.

When Raqiyah picked up, she first told her of her Edmonton background, their shared stories in the Ali Muhammed extremism attack on London; and then of her recent transfer to the South West and in so doing hoped they'd remember her sympathetically. Even as she spoke she knew there was no way around the instant raising of barriers a call from the police invariably prompted. So often, in a job which relied on the public's information and cooperation, it was such hard work to win support.

Her instinct told her that far from bottling up, Raqiyah wanted to talk, could barely conceal her sense of injustice at Harry and the media's coverage of their plight. That confirmed to April that her initial reaction, her police instinct that the press story was all wrong, was spot on. Indeed, there was another story to be heard. Raqiyah had got something to tell her.

Her plan had been to see both in turn, Raqiyah at 10am and Clive at eleven, but that idea she now dismissed – she'd see them together. Raqiyah said she'd ring Clive there and then and would get right back with a time they could all meet.

Before meeting up, April decided to do some further reading around Harry McNamara's unexpected by-election campaign. She ought to thoroughly familiarise herself with the background. A few web and media searches and she had a growing sense of an increasingly bitter and polarised campaign. She hadn't been one for political interest, never read a party manifesto before in her life, but when she looked at what Harry's Britain First Democratic Party represented, she sensed a dark and divisive political direction which would only appeal to anyone with a grievance; people who were looking to scapegoat migrants and Muslims in particular. The generous promises made to local people were counterbalanced by scathing attacks on the main political parties for failing to deliver for the ordinary British citizen. Harry was "calling time".

She'd just finished when Raqiyah called. It was settled. They'd meet at eleven. Being new to Exeter, she had to ask Raqiyah where might be the most convenient place to meet up. In the end they decided on a café near the ancient Guildhall in Exeter's city centre's central High Street. Both Clive and Raqiyah could be there for 11am and that suited April too. She'd said she wouldn't be in uniform and just wanted to hear their stories – she reassured them saying there'd be absolutely no pressure from her.

For their part, once the meeting was arranged, Clive and Raqiyah had both begun to independently think this meeting might be a useful step on the road to formulate a way of getting back at Harry. They had nothing to lose and everything to gain in talking to April. It felt good to them both that someone was at last wanting to hear their side of things.

Clive was at the café first and found a table tucked to the side away from the busy serving counter. Raqiyah arrived on the dot of eleven, but April was nearly ten minutes late and apologised profusely. She explained she'd been kept waiting whilst trying to fix an early afternoon appointment. April's offer to buy drinks to make up was cheerfully accepted. All by now were in good spirits, anticipating this to be a promising, if not most useful meeting.

Both Clive and Raqiyah told their stories as they'd happened, both interrupting one another just to clarify or amend what the other had said. Pretty quickly April realised she was getting a truthful account of events and she responded by giving them the affirmations they were looking for. April now had a decision of her own to take. She should take these two into her confidence and give them the reason for her interest. After nearly an hour in their company, she did just that.

'I want to level with you two – explain what I'm doing down here. The thing is, I got a temporary transfer from the Metropolitan Police. Just started this month in fact. I'm part of a small group with a watching brief during the Plymouth by-election campaign. We're looking out for dodgy individuals, like extremists, who want to exploit the election for their own ends; and for any weaknesses in the community that might inadvertently lend them a hand. The last thing anyone in the country wants right now is to see increased tension or people's safety put at risk. So I'm here as an extra pair of hands simply to try and keep the peace,' she explained.

'I can see that,' said Raqiyah.

'I was sorry to hear about your colleague, the cop who was shot,' Clive ventured, remembering back, and thinking just how glad he was to be away from the guns and drugs world that nearly finished him too when he was in north London.

For some reason, the remark made April have to wipe a tear from the corner of her eye. Clive had no idea how much it meant to her to hear from someone outside the force that they too were sorry for what had happened.

'Thank you for that Clive, that means a lot,' she said. 'Bob Steer was a good man who never deserved what happened to him. He taught me so much and to tell you the truth, I wanted a move away from London for a while, away from all that violence, so when the chance came up for a transfer here I took it.' She paused, gathering her thoughts, before adding, 'I suppose the question you might have for me is, whether there is anything the police can do in the light of what happened to you and Clive in Plymouth over the weekend? I'm sorry to disappoint you, but If you were to make a formal complaint things might just have a result neither of you want.'

'We were both assaulted,' Clive said.

'But the trouble is, in spite of what you've told me, and I fully believe you both, there are witness reports to the contrary in the media, accounts that say you were the ones who started it. In fact it would be very easy for Harry to press serious charges against the two of you. If you take legal action, next thing you know, the police will be knocking on your door or worse, to question you. Do you see that?'

'We get the picture,' said Raqiyah, 'I kind of thought you'd say that, and I can see it now since you have laid it out so clearly. It's been good for us to have someone objective to tell about all this, and the best thing for me right now is that you believe us, don't you?'

'Absolutely, I can say I do personally, but if I were to give you an official or formal view, it would be to leave the matter wide open,' concluded April. 'What concerns me is what might happen next if a) you did take a case against Harry further or b) you got embroiled in Harry's politics again – it might go very badly for you.'

'What do you mean?' asked Clive.

'Well, you two felt strongly enough about the politics of Harry McNamara to go and see him and try to get him to justify himself. Is that the end of it? Will you be going to Plymouth again?' she asked them. They exchanged looks.

'We've both got end of academic year events to concentrate on for now and after results we're off by the end of next month. I think we're going to be pretty busy with student things and summer vacation from here on in,' offered Raqiyah. Clive nodded in agreement, though not believing a word Raqiyah was saying. He recalled, but had no intention of saying, that Adam too wanted to get back at Harry somehow. At that April said she had to be getting along. It was time to get back into uniform and show up at a local meeting, she told them. She stood up from the table, then stopped.

'I'm really glad to have caught up with you two and to have heard your accounts. Oh, one final thought for you to consider. If you were to make more of what has happened, then there's a strong possibility your university and college authorities might pick things up and disciplinary measures be proceeded with against you both. I'd sincerely hope that wouldn't be the case, but it's a real risk you should consider. You might even find you'd put your student places and futures in jeopardy. I pray it won't come to that.' She paused and gave each a kind smile, finally adding, 'Look, you've got my direct line number to reach me if you hear any more of what Harry's got going on, or if you want to tell me about anything else. Is that OK?'

With that April also handed each of them her business card before slipping out on to the pavement, into the throngs of High St shoppers. She thought that it had been a very useful time – and, as she had surmised earlier, Harry McNamara was definitely one to be watched.

Raqiyah decided they should stay on in the café until they had come up with some ideas of their own. Now the police weren't going to help them, they needed to find a way to get at Harry and they knew that they had only themselves to fall back on.

'Adam's with us, all the way, I spoke to him before I came out. So how do we get Harry back for what he's done to us?' Raqiyah ventured, airing her thoughts out loud.

'Serve him like with like, eye for an eye. I say, play the guy at his own game – meet false news with false news. Rough up his meetings.' said Clive. 'Can't we find something to say on social media that will undo him? Can't we get some students along to his campaigns to heckle and disrupt? I'm sure we can.'

'Hmm. Like the false news bit – best if we can discover something with some truth in it, something that'll be hard for him to dismiss. Let's play him at his own fake news game. I'm not with you on the violence bit – I don't like the idea of causing trouble at his meetings. Where might that lead? That sounds a bit unpredictable.'

The waitress came over and interrupted their conversation, wanting to collect their now long empty glasses. Once she had gone, Raqiyah, continued, 'Disrupting his meetings could turn out either way, for or even against us. Imagine, he could get more publicity for his own cause from what we do and that could play into his hands. We know that somehow he has the uncritical ear of the press on his side,' said Raqiyah, her head dropping as what seemed a promising idea bit the dust.

'Didn't mean real violence, just verbal stuff in his meetings, but yes, that would be harder to manage and keep under control. The thing is, we both heard what PC April said. We've got to be really clever about this. We can't risk exposing ourselves. Putting our heads above the parapet means the police, the university, my college and Harry's gang will be all over us like a rash. End of.' Clive drew his hand across his throat.

'That's true. I've also got to think of my family. I'm just hoping they haven't seen any of this. They'd be mortified if they saw me as part of any political trouble here and it would bring unbelievable shame if I messed up my studies. You're right – let's begin with the alternative story approach. I'd like to start doing some quiet information searching. I want to see what I can find out on Harry McNamara and his family. A guy like him must have a shady past. Why don't you do a search on student bodies, get talking to people, find out who our allies might be?'

Clive warmed to the idea. He too didn't want to risk his new start, lose his promise of a nursing degree place next year before he'd even started it. They went their separate ways. Raqiyah took herself off to the University library, finding a corner where she could work away quietly and where the speedy WiFi suited her fast searching pace.

Meanwhile, as April arrived back at Middlemoor Police HQ, she once again threw up on her screen the information she'd been reading earlier about Harry's campaign. This time she spotted a report of the incident at Harry's home in Plymouth.

It crossed her mind that not one of her colleagues had said anything about the report on the late night brick through Harry's bedroom window, and there was nothing flagging it up on her computer. She reached across to the desk phone and called the main Plymouth police station.

Helpful as they were, as she'd already guessed, they'd drawn a total blank and the matter was being quietly forgotten. Her Plymouth colleague expressed his unease at investigating the matter in the charged atmosphere of a by-election – 'unofficially my advice would be the best thing is to let the matter die, wither on the vine' he'd said. That wasn't April's view, but she didn't say so. 'All they'd had to go on,' he'd told her, 'was a vague description from Harry himself alleging a light coloured saloon car with possibly two occupants inside'.

Give him his due the Plymouth DS had nonetheless run through several CCTV recordings, asked around, done a door to door, asked for anonymous public calls, but nothing had shown up. They'd hit a dead end and unless they got an unexpected lucky break, that was it.

As April read the subsequent storyline in the media, Harry was still making out it was a definite Muslim attack, milking the event for all he could to suit his own purposes, though so far enquiries made hadn't found anything to confirm or deny Harry's opinion. She wondered if any forensics report had been sought on the so-called Arabic script piece of paper that had arrived through his window with the half-brick. Another phone call later she learned nothing had been done, though the Plymouth DS had the brick and message in a sealed evidence bag at the station. April at least managed to get him to agree to take a look at it and get the lab people to give a report. She knew she was clutching at straws.

When April returned from her meeting after her afternoon visit to the Exeter mosque, she sipped her stone cold coffee, pondering her day. She'd never liked Harry McNamara and she liked him even less after today. Sitting quietly provided the chance to reflect – strange that, she thought, to put a brick through a window with a definite Arabic text. It just felt that bit too easy to assume a Muslim was responsible. Instinctively it didn't sit right with her, like much else that Harry McNamara was claiming to be the truth.

Bob Steer had always said a good police officer listens to their instinct. She logged in her mind the dissonant overstated case of going to the trouble to tie Arabic text to a thrown brick.

It was late afternoon; she'd nearly finished her shift and as she began shutting down her workstation computer and collecting her things, she made a mental note of what she needed to pick up the next day, Tuesday. She knew she was already being drawn in deep. Harry McNamara was in her sights and she was glad of it. This was a new beginning, new work in a different place; the buzz today's work had given her, was even putting a fresh spring in her step for the first time in many months.

16

A couple of weeks in and Harry was very pleased with the way the early days of his campaign were going. The moment Alfred Carter, the sitting MP, had had his heart attack and consequential fatal road traffic accident, Harry had seized the day. Quietly talking to people in the following days, he had, by the beginning of May organised his emerging campaign team.

He was pleasantly surprised that this small election team were already so well organised and committed to the task. They were in two teams – door to door and online party faithful. Both were working with little need of his personal input. In addition he had a small core group around him – Cathy Nicholls in particular was thinking ahead all the time, carrying a key role in organising his election programme, planning forwards engagement by engagement, always gaining and building excellent media coverage. Harry was content, yet consumed by the cause serving political and personal ambition, though he never could tell which came first.

Since the first proper weekend of campaigning (after the candidates standing had been formally announced on 18 May) he'd seized the campaign initiative. Today he had no doubt he was still the front runner, even two of the opinion polls over the weekend were predicting a narrow Britain First Democratic Party win. A number of national media moguls were showing an interest at last, pointing to this by-election as a measure of the government's unpopularity. The thought made him smile. In fact more than once people had commented on his confident smile; he had the look of a winner, he told himself.

There were two things Cathy had asked him for a decision on. The first was whether he wanted to attend a public, Question Time style hustings event, to which all the other candidates had also been invited for Saturday week. It seemed a long way off, anything could happen in the meantime. Normally so decisive, Harry was uncertain what to do. He understood he was expected to say 'yes' and he instinctively knew the public would be scathing of him if he failed to engage. They required sparring politicians, but he was acutely aware he had little experience in the top flight, and even thinking about it undermined his normal ebullient self. He wasn't ready for that – yet. His answer was needed now, but for some reason, though Cathy had asked him twice, he still found himself holding back from making the necessary commitment. Indecision was a new experience and it unsettled him.

The other decision Cathy wanted was a strange one, and personal. True to her journalistic trade, Cherry Thomas had been given a lead from somewhere and she was now saying she'd quite like to do a "family story" on Harry, in particular bringing in his grandfather's commitment to local politics. Harry was more than a little wary. What did Cherry know about his grandfather that he didn't? Where had her information come from – he hadn't a clue. All she would say was, family stories and pictures went down well with the electorate – Harry wasn't convinced this was true in his case, but to be fair, Cherry had recently put such first class pieces up in the local paper, doing no end of good for the cause, that it would be churlish of him to refuse her this innocuous request.

In the few minutes Harry had before his next appointment, a businessman's breakfast event, he had no choice but to give Cathy the call she was waiting for. No problem with delaying the decision on the hustings event, she replied; but she thought he ought not to delay his "yes" too long.

Cathy thought Harry would be well able to take care of a hustings. If he said "yes" to her now; deciding he'd commit to do it, well, with a full week until the event, she'd plenty of time to bribe a few friends to be in the audience on the night armed with questions she'd given them that Harry would know were coming up. She wanted, as she put it, "to line up the ducks" to ensure the event turned up trumps for Harry. Harry liked the idea of a guaranteed successful outcome and gave her his undertaking to attend. 'I wouldn't want to be at something like that without knowing I was going to win before a question is asked,' he'd told her.

'No worries there Harry, I'll diary some space so we can talk it through,' she said confidently. Harry felt all the better knowing he could trust her to handle it. He quite fancied Cathy and wondered whether her efforts to please were driven by her desire for him – he wasn't sure. He decided this wasn't the right moment to try and find out.

'That other matter – Cherry's journalistic piece on my family background. What do you know about that? Where did she get her lead from? I haven't said anything to encourage such an idea,' Harry said. 'Where's she going with that one?'

'I was wondering about that myself. Tell you what, I might have a chat with her, find out more, come back to you – don't think it's urgent, just something she's working on to bring up at the right moment. We get something like this right Harry, then we give the people something they want. She has a point; the people need to know you, to vote for you. The family stuff will sit well alongside the strong policy stuff – know what I mean? Knowing your roots are round here, your political pedigree built around family, could be your trump card. The other candidates haven't got your local family credentials – it's a card we've got to play. Leave it with me. I'll start guiding her with some bits of information. I just need to ask, there's nothing embarrassing in your family is there? I need to know if there is,' she inquired, waiting for an answer.

'Don't think so. My Dad's always been a worker, running the local business, nothing dodgy there. He never talks about politics, never has. My Grandparents, they're all dead now. All straightforward, though I recently discovered Grandpa Michael McNamara had a secret right-wing side to him, but that was back in the 1930s.' Harry paused, thinking of the metal trunk he'd inherited and its mysterious contents, 'all that's lost in the mists of time, pre-history,' he added, thinking it prudent to let sleeping dogs lie.

'What do you know about him, your grandfather?'

'Not much really. Nice man. A family man through and through. It was Michael who built up my Dad's business, but he did seem to have a period in his life when he might have been one of Sir Oswald Mosely's supporters, but I don't really think that needs mentioning – bit too right-wing, pro-Hitler, to go down well these days. I find people still have a wartime view of Adolf – they've mentally not got over it, not grown up. I'm not sure anyone really knows about Michael McNamara's politics. Certainly it was a family secret, a taboo subject at home. I don't have a problem with right-wing sympathy being in the family history, it's nothing more than that, but all in all something I want you to treat with discretion. Best keep the pre-war bit under wraps. Sensitive issue in Plymouth, so much of the city bombed to

129

smithereens, and too many people with long memories,' he concluded.

'Just in case there is more to your grandfather's political life, I'll do a little fishing with Cherry. She may need a steer if she finds out something untoward. Can't be too careful, with polling day less than two weeks away. I'll keep an eye on her. She's been very sympathetic so far, likes your decisive style, a useful local ally. We can afford to stand her lunch, can't we? She and I get on. Leave it with me. Last thing we want are any unexpected skeletons in the closet.' It was agreed and Harry left it at that.

After Cathy had gone, Harry's thoughts of his grandfather were quickly forgotten as he had just moments to go through and rehearse his talk before his breakfast speech, which the Chamber of Commerce had organised for their regular monthly Tuesday morning meeting.

Harry was already thinking the occasion had to be another win. One businessman to another businessman was his approach. He knew what it was like for them. His Dad had given him some winning one-liners, stories too. He concluded, even before he rose to his feet, that whilst they were stuffing their faces with bacon and eggs, they'd soon be eating out of his hand too.

Phil Potts drove him there. It was time. The side door where he had been waiting to make his entrance was pushed wide open and he walked in. A tap of the table, and a polite quietness descended, the chatter died. He was introduced by the host, dismissed by Harry in seconds as just another woolly, bleeding heart liberal. As he stepped to the podium, his confidence was high, he could already see the audience's smiling faces and wondered whether he might get some party funds from them to boot. That would be icing on the cake.

Harry was getting into his stride when he noticed Andy Stone, the local press photographer at the back of the room, snapping away. Harry adjusted his position in relation to the lights and the photographer. More good press coverage in the offing, he thought.

As Harry settled into his speech, he used the platform on this occasion to ignore national politics, and chose rather to focus on the concerns of local business – taking in turn the anger felt at the rising council tax bills, the unfairness of the market, the failure, post-Brexit, to give business the confident culture in which to thrive. He tuned into the fears of a downward economic spiral making it harder to do business – something he maintained the main parties were doing nothing to address; he attacked local authorities for working against businesses and preventing expansion, smothering them with regulations. The very same businessmen who were finding themselves buried in mountains of red tape and unnecessary paperwork instead of generating wealth for the local economy. Layer upon layer he addressed their concerns and piled up their woes. As he looked at their faces, he could see they were listening, he had them.

Then, he began telling his attentive audience about his family's scrap metal business – how it had been built up in Plymouth from nothing, generation by generation. He added anecdotal stories which gave a utopian vision of a caring patriarchal family business where owners were also loyal supporters of their workforce and long-standing local philanthropists in their community. Harry even mentioned the contributions the family had made over the years to the

131

local parish church, whose eternal values of justice and tradition he himself had lots of time for.

Finally, Harry made some carefully worded pledges to prove his pro-business election credentials, concluding with the words, 'When it comes to business, only Harry McNamara can!'

Twenty minutes had passed in a flash. Applause followed, not everywhere, but enough to make Harry believe he'd won them over. As he sat down, his host next asked for any questions. Some returned to finishing their coffee and toast, others wanted their voices heard.

Three questions in, and just when Harry felt it was time to wrap up and move to his next engagement, an elderly grey-haired man at the back, sitting so quietly Harry hadn't noticed him until then, rose unsteadily to his feet. He looked a spectre from a former age, had traces of a military bearing about him, Harry wondering what line of business he could be in.

'Mr McNamara, Sir,' he began in a steady voice.

'Harry, please,' interjected Harry.

'I well remember your grandfather, Michael McNamara. He was a friend of my father. Seeing you there, the spitting image of Michael in his younger years, I can only congratulate you. He would have been so proud. You know, like yourself, he was a deeply political man. He cared about his country and spoke out against lily-livered left-wingers and unpatriotic spongers. He too was quite the political leader in these parts in the 1930s. Don't you think Mr McNamara, Sir, it's time for this country to rediscover its right wing tradition, time to vote in a strong far-right leadership, the kind of thing Michael McNamara believed in?' With that he promptly sat down.

Harry was momentarily lost for words. Initially, he didn't know how to respond. In a millisecond things had slipped out of his control and he needed to claw control back. He paused and shuffled to think on his feet.

This totally unexpected reference to his grandfather and his politics threatened to align him brazenly with an extreme right-wing agenda for which he was uncertain his audience were quite ready – one that many people associated with Adolf Hitler, an association he had personal but private sympathy for, but one he could not afford to allow to taint his nascent campaign. For one horrible moment, Harry felt vulnerable.

Being all too aware of how his projected persona must look, Harry smiled graciously, though disconcertingly for far too long, before re-stating his own manifesto headline policies and family loyalties, before thanking his audience, and being ushered out and on to his next appointment at the local Nursery. As he thanked his host and moved quickly to leave, he knew the elderly businessman's question, totally out of the left-field, had nearly thrown him into a state of political meltdown.

Quite what had that man been trying to do, Harry asked himself as he left the building with its now stale smell of bacon and eggs wafting after him. He re-entered the street and the safety this time of Cathy's waiting car, conveniently pulling up for him to step inside. If the man wanted to support right-wing politics, his question wouldn't have helped. No it was something else – then Harry knew what it was.

The man knew something, he wanted to get at Harry, unsettle him, test what Harry knew of something in the past. The more he thought about it, Harry saw deep down that something dark and unknown was reaching for him, and just now he had no idea what it might be or how to manage it.

Though he thought no-one else might have observed anything different on the outside, inside Harry had taken his first injury in the campaign. Something nasty was hurting, nagging at him, and what made it worse was that he had no idea what it was or where it had come from. His legendary control had begun to slip. Cathy noticed.

'You all right Harry? Look a bit pale.'

He ignored her question and stared straight ahead.

17

Cherry Thomas was only too happy to be offered a free lunch by Harry's Political Advisor Cathy Nicholls, even though it was nothing more exciting than the familiar interior of Harry's favourite watering hole, the White Horse. Still, it was nice to be feted; such treats were seldom offered journalists these days. After ordering Cornish pasties and white wines at the bar, they sat down in the window. Neither had very long, probably 30 minutes at the outside, so Cathy got straight to the point.

'Harry's interested in the piece you are putting together; he thinks it could really do him some good.'

'Can I tell you something in confidence Cathy,' she said, moving in closer and lowering her voice.

'Sure.'

'This hasn't happened to me before and it has come as something of a bolt out of the blue – a total surprise. It's not my usual sort of piece. I wouldn't normally have tackled a family article piece, I'm more current affairs, but I've been commissioned to write it, cash up front. The money's too good for me to turn down. Newspaper journalism is a mugs' game these days. Hardly any of us left doing it and the pay's rubbish. When something like this happens and money comes my way, then I have to consider it.'

'I totally understand,' said Cathy.

'But, I have to be very careful, especially when it's politics and the air is thick with dirty tricks,' she added.

'Don't blame you for being careful,' said Cathy, 'I'd be just the same.'

'You won't say, but this job came through to my e-mail. Bit odd really. It started with an innocuous enquiry asking if I was covering the by-election. I replied to say, "of course, see my articles," and they came back the very next day saying they liked what I wrote and wanted to pay me to write one on their behalf. I felt like ignoring them, but then the guy wrote to say he found writing difficult and it was my stock in trade. As he was getting older he'd like me to do it, and he felt able, very happy, to pay me whatever I asked, if I'd write the piece for him.'

'So what did you say? Yes?' asked Cathy.

'No, not exactly. I told him I'm very busy. So I gave a really high fee figure to write the article thinking he'd be bound to refuse and turn me down, take the matter no further, then that would be the end of it.'

'But it wasn't?' said Cathy.

'No, he agreed to my figure and unbelievably added a further 50% if I got it completed and published in our paper to his satisfaction by Friday this week.'

'Wow!'

'My editor will publish anything I give her, that's not the problem. My worry is, I just don't know who this Arnold Smith is and he won't tell me. Although he's not said anything, not told me what to write, I feel I'm being bought. I don't like it, it's really not me. Now I'm trapped – expected to deliver,' said Cherry, her head dropping into her hands.

'Have you asked him who he is or who he represents? He could be allied to a political opponent,' asked Cathy. 'It could explode in our faces. It could be a disaster for Harry.'

'Yes, sure did. All he said was, "Don't worry," and as a sign of his good faith he'd send me some useful material on Harry's family. "That should be enough to get you started," he told me. When he did that, my first thought was that I was being drawn into some kind of character assassination or worse. I didn't want to know. I wanted out.'

'But you've stayed with it. For the money?' said Cathy.

'No, I wouldn't do that. No, it was what Arnold sent me. There were pictures and articles about Michael McNamara as he was in the Blackshirts in the 1930s. Harry's grandfather was well, very prominently involved in the fascist movement here in the South West. No small fry either.'

'Is that a problem? Such a long time ago. I mean is this something, if true, that could damage Harry's campaign?' asked Cathy, feeling she had to get at the truth here before things went further. Cherry seemed to be telling her everything she asked, so she decided to press further to get the full low down. She did still wonder exactly how much Cherry was being paid, but that piece of information wasn't something that was going to be divulged and at the moment it was a red herring, not the real issue. "Big" meant over £500 in Cathy's eyes, and she pushed the pound signs to the back of her mind to concentrate on finding out what possible unexpected fallout there might be coming Harry's way from all this.

'I need to check it out with Harry,' responded Cherry. 'His Dad won't say anything to me. You can take that either way

137

you want to, but Harry's the only one who can clear things up, verify things for me. I still don't know, without talking with him, whether there is anything here worth writing about. I certainly won't want to give my editor some anonymously sourced uncorroborated story that might damage Harry. The next thing I'd know would be I'd be out of a job and the paper sued.'

Cherry went quiet before adding, 'This is really difficult – wish now I'd never responded, but he'd have found someone else, that kind do – there's lots of hard up journalists around, hungry for a story or some ready cash. You can make news anything you want to today. My only consolation is just that if they hadn't asked me, they'd have found some other willing gossip columnist or sleaze-ball. Truth is I need the money and I can't afford to turn away a possible scoop.'

'The Blackshirts were such a very long time ago. That's all history isn't it?' asked Cathy, following up a line Cherry had hitherto ignored.

'Not entirely. It's something of a dark secret here in the South West. You know, back then there was much popular support for Sir Oswald Mosley and his fascist Blackshirts. My source tells me Michael McNamara was a political adviser based in Plymouth, so he was more than just an ordinary member or mere local activist. A surprising number of local Blackshirts were arrested and interned in the war. I don't know about him. In fact I still don't know much about him – I need to do some more digging. Arnold's promised to send me more input.'

'History isn't relevant, doesn't count, as I see it. Not unless people here and now are moved by it and you've not told me anything yet to worry about,' said Cathy.

'They came to be seen as traitors, supporters of Adolf Hitler. To be a Blackshirt became something shameful. That's all I know, honest. So can I have half an hour with Harry, perhaps later today, to see what he knows, to check this out with him? No harm in that is there?' The pasties had arrived and Cherry filled her mouth.

Cathy didn't feel she could say 'no', even though her risk antennae was alerting her to a possible issue up ahead; at this stage it would be better if Cherry held her investigative conversation with Harry and she gave Cherry a nod of assent. To refuse would signal Harry might have something to hide. She did however win one concession that the draft piece would be run past Harry for accuracy prior to publication. That would be enough to see off any hares that might be set running by an ill-advised piece.

As Cherry dashed off, leaving half her pasty uneaten, Cathy knew she had to get to Harry before Cherry did. At least she had priority hotline access. She picked up her mobile and sent Harry an urgent message telling him to speak to her before talking to Cherry.

She watched Cherry through the pub window, saw her grabbing for her phone as she stepped into her car. Well, thought Cathy, if Michael is shown to be a right wing activist that could go in Harry's favour if it was handled right. She couldn't think of any other problem with Cherry's piece – and she was reassured it would be passed by Harry and edited to prevent anything libellous before seeing the light of day. Then she recalled her own worries and the threat to her daughter Etta. A thing too dangerous to share with Cherry, before pushing it to the back of her mind hoping and praying that nothing would happen.

As Cherry started up her car, about to leave the White Horse car park, she didn't pull away. Her phone had sent a pulse and she decided to check its latest message before heading off. It was a habit. Being first to a scoop meant always being a quick responder. She saw it was from Arnold Smith. Her pulse quickened. The enigmatic message simply read, "Michael McNamara was a traitor."

What, she wondered did it mean? What was Arnold Smith after? He'd promised more information, yet this was pejorative even dangerous stuff to start meddling with. Maybe there really was a newsworthy family story here, she thought, but this could be dynamite. The trouble was she wasn't sure what kind of time-bomb she was playing with, or whether it would explode in Harry's face or her own.

Whichever way she considered the situation she knew a true journalist like herself never turned down the chance of creating a good story. It might make her name.

18

It had been a busy day yesterday but, Business Breakfast apart, Harry had been totally energised by the rest of the day's political meetings. Although he hadn't known what questions would be thrown at him from one moment to the next, he'd risen to the challenge. He knew he'd always been good at thinking on his feet, rallying the troops; and after a good night's sleep, he'd woken early on Wednesday morning to start the new day with a spring in his step.

It didn't do, he told himself, to let himself go, and before doing anything else he stepped into the small training area he'd created at one end of his bedroom. He glanced at the bedroom window, now re-glazed, and told himself his parents needed to get a painter in. He'd remind them later.

Twenty minutes of pumping weights followed by a further twenty on his treadmill running, and then he was into a hot shower. The power-shower was so strong it hit his skin like pinpricks, but he counted this as just another necessary stimulation. He prided himself on being clean, smelling fresh, looking sharp, staying strong, looking fit – like a British bulldog. His life was a long history of self-preservation and it was essential he felt strong enough to take on the world – looking at himself admiringly in the full length mirror on his wardrobe door, he knew now he was ready. He'd allowed his hair to grow longer, giving him a welcome almost professional image. Bring it on he thought as the new day beckoned.

Dressed, breakfasted – his Mum, as ever laying out cereal and toast and clearing away after – Harry realised he still had one small space to fill in the day's diary. He grabbed his mobile.

'Cathy, glad you're up,' he said, hearing sleepy scuffling sounds in the background. 'I need you to call Matt Ashton, Chairman at Plymouth Rovers. Get him to see me at the ground later this morning, around eleven. I'll text you his personal mobile number. Don't stand for any nonsense, he owes me. You might need to remind him he wouldn't be chair without the Green Army's endorsement. He'll see me. I only need half an hour, and I'll need you to drive me there, OK.' It was a command not a question. Cathy grunted.

It had occurred to Harry that his football supporters were his natural constituency and he was in danger of overlooking what they could bring to his campaign. Their votes mattered. He'd ask Matt to give him a few minutes guest appearance time during half-time at the last match of the season on the coming Saturday, a so-called friendly. After the game the pitch would be ripped up and re-sown ready for two more years play. Since he was a small child, in fact as long as he could remember, the Green Army of Rovers supporters had been like his second family, Home Park his own back yard. Through his place at the club, he reckoned he must know not hundreds but thousands of people and in recent years he'd become their kind of unofficial spokesman.

People looked for strong leadership and Harry had shown himself able and willing to exercise it. He had built up for himself what he liked to call "respect". There was an official mantra about how things were run – all politically correct, but there was also the unofficial underground social network where he knew the real power lay; where things got done and where leaders were made or destroyed. That was his domain and he was king.

Harry was one of the old school. Though he had watched, even vocally encouraged the club to tackle racial prejudice, endorsing the 'Kick Racism out of Football' campaign, he did so whilst continuing to punch and rough-up any non-white players who came to the ground. From time to time he'd had to keep an eye on the new players they'd brought in, but by and large they'd kept a mainly English player team with no Muslims in the current squad. He recalled the number of surreptitious meetings the club had held with him and his real 'Green Army' in the dark corridors, toilets or streets outside, anywhere in the shadowlands where the CCTV or police weren't watching.

Harry had learned one important political lesson a long time ago – that the words one spoke up front served a purpose often quite disconnected from the actions one took where it mattered. Cynicism was the name of the game – fake truth the only game on. Why? Because he knew it worked – anyone his finger pointed at, well they wouldn't come to the ground again and the club would be pleased. Not because there were fewer Black, Asian or Ethnic Minorities , BAME's on site, no, they were too stupid to see that the racist chants reduced simply because fewer BAME's came along, they just thought their goody-goody policies were working – so it was win-win so far as Harry was concerned.

Yes, Chairman Matt owed him, who else made sure the fans kept coming, and the clinching card he had still to play was to remind Matt that only with the Green Army's support had the team just got themselves promoted.

Another thought then crossed Harry's mind. The recent end of season news of the club's promotion had done wonders for partnerships between the club and leading local institutions. Everyone wanted to share in the glory, final Saturday was going to be one big party. All the sponsors and partners would be fawning over Matt, and Harry therefore needed to be there too – their own parliamentary candidate – some of the success reflecting on him and his campaign. It would be an excellent move. He'd make sure Cathy got Cherry from the paper in on it and Andy for the pics too.

He grabbed his phone again, moved out of the kitchen, waving nonchalantly to his Mum indicating he'd finished his meal and the things needed clearing away. His Mum, in her tired looking apron, as drained of colour as she was herself, duly and silently obliged.

Harry called Cathy again, but her phone was engaged. Good for her, he thought, she was probably already calling Matt. Two minutes later he got through and she confirmed his appointment at the club was all arranged. He beamed with self-satisfaction.

'Got something else you need to do, Cathy. Remember at yesterday's Business Breakfast meeting that older guy, the one with the final question right at the end – the one who asked me about my grandfather Michael McNamara? I didn't see that one coming. One minute he seemed on message, an avowed right-winger, but the next minute he was taking the conversation into such hard line extreme right-wing territory I feared he might have done me harm. Who was he? What's his game? Can you ask around, find out for me, get a few contact details and let me know. It might need to come to a private conversation with him if he's looking to make trouble.' He detected a hesitation in Cathy before she responded, but let it pass.

'OK. I need to phone the club Secretary anyway to thank them for inviting you and go through half-time arrangements – I'll see what I can do.' With that she had gone.

Harry decided he'd better get his thoughts together for the first meeting of the morning. Cathy had arranged for him to call at the Mums and Toddlers' Group that her sister took Cathy's two year-old Etta along to. He thought he could just wing it there, no need for prepared speeches – a chance to get some nice pictures. Pictures convey their own winning truth, he thought, no need for words when it comes to adorable toddlers.

It was then he heard Cathy's car pull up outside to pick him up. There was a clatter of dishes in the kitchen, his Mum doing her usual domestic thing. He grabbed his suit jacket in the hallway, adjusted his tie in the mirror, smirked at himself with pride and let himself out. Cathy's face looked sad. She didn't convey the ambience of confident success and well-being Harry wanted to see in her and he told her so.

'Pull yourself together, Cath – we're on a roll, we've an election to win.'

Cathy realised what her face must have been saying and forced herself to smile.

'That's better,' Harry said, tweaking her cheek playfully, before turning his eyes to the road ahead. She didn't seem to like it, but touching her cheek triggered something in Harry and he thought that when this was over he ought to get closer to his political aide.

Cathy started up and they pulled away for the five minute journey to St Bartholomew's and St Mark's Church hall. She knew full well why she had been caught not smiling. She felt bad her sister was having to spend so long caring for her own child Etta, but Harry had persuaded her he needed her for the duration of the campaign and she'd had no choice.

He'd slipped her some money in her hand with the promise of more to follow and that was it. There was no going back. Still it would be nice to see her sister and to know Etta was safe, especially now.

For some reason, Harry had Stu, Phil, Cherry, Andy and herself all going to the Mums and Toddlers' group. It felt like overkill, but maybe with the none-too-veiled threats her mysterious caller had recently made, the more people she could count on being around the better. For Etta's sake she tried to find reassurance where she could. There was safety in numbers.

They pulled up in the church car park and walked the few paces to the hall where the group met. The high pitched noise of children playing excitedly inside could be heard even before they reached the door. After ringing the bell, there was an awkward pause as they, like anyone else visiting, had to wait to be let in.

Cathy's first glance around was to spot Etta and see for herself that she was safe. There she was, playing happily with some soft toys – not a care in the world. Some temporary relief comforted her. Harry was already working the adults, speaking to the leader as if they were old friends – it soon transpired they were. Being local and locally known was paying dividends. Harry knew that Jackie, the leader was a route to many more useful votes.

A short while later, Cathy turned to see Harry had picked up Etta who was happily smiling as Andy took pictures of them both. Alarm bells rang. She was paralysed as to what to do next. She couldn't tell Harry she didn't want Etta in his pictures, yet she feared Etta's innocent face being spread across the papers when she knew others in the shadows had their eye on her. It was becoming very hard to keep the smile on her face that Harry wanted her to wear for him. When would this visit be over? She longed for the time when this political enterprise of Harry's would allow her life to return to normal.

After tea was poured and Harry had milked the occasion for all it was worth, he finally waved his farewells, first bending down to address the children, who to be frank weren't very interested, but the photographer Andy was; then to the mums and leaders who seemed happy with what he had been telling them about promises of more funding and a better, safer future for local people if he were elected. Harry was leaving as he'd hoped, on a high.

It was then time to head to Home Park, Rovers' ground. This time they were in a convoy of three cars. Cathy let Andy and Cherry go ahead. They were followed by Stu and Phil, Cathy bringing up the rear of the procession. Not being a match day they were able to park close to the stadium entrance in the council run car park. Cathy nodded to Phil to sort out the parking tickets and threw him her car keys as she and Harry strode toward the ground's offices in front of the main grandstand.

Harry wished he'd organised a rent a crowd or something. The car park looked too empty and soulless as their small group strode across it – no suitable image in this, he mused. Too late to do anything about it now. Anyway he had a sneaking feeling this election was going to be won more through his tweets and use of social media than addressing baying crowds of potential voters. People didn't seem to do that kind of thing anymore.

There was fresh green paint everywhere, a green and white flag with a picture of the sailing ship the Mayflower, the letters PRFC for Plymouth Rovers Football Club, emblazoned beneath. The ship had taken the Pilgrim Fathers from Plymouth to America in 1620 to escape persecution in England. Harry's view, often voiced, was that those who didn't fit in had to get out – he had always believed the emblem to be the right image for the club and city. He made a mental note to refer to it in his later speeches.

Matt Ashton must have seen them coming. He was waiting on the pavement by the front doors as they walked toward him. Andy was busy snapping away as Harry and Matt shook hands and man-hugged like old friends.

'Come on in Harry, bring your friends with you,' welcomed Matt, patting down the windblown thin hair on his bald pate. 'What a great time for the club, ending the season with promotion, and thanks to you and all our supporters backing us through hard times and good, we've made it. Onward and upward, I say. Come in, come in. I know it's early in the day but I've some beer from one of our partners. We need to drink to your success too!'

The words were music to Harry's ears. This was going to be easier than he'd thought.

'Matt, I wonder if we might have a word,' said Harry, wrapping his arm over the Chairman's shoulder and guiding him to a quiet space as his friends gathered round the refreshments on a hastily erected functions table set out for them.

'On Saturday, being the last game, we need to make the most of the club's success this season. It would be doing me

148

personally a great honour if you were to allow me to stand alongside you before kickoff. I know I normally go in the stands but this time we need to show everyone we have worked together to get to where we are today. The Green Army have backed you as our Chairman and you have shown yourself worthy of our choice and I'd like to express, gratitude on behalf of all the fans publicly. That's OK isn't it?' Harry asserted, knowing that this request was easy for Matt to agree to, it signified nothing. Matt nodded.

'And tell me,' Harry added, moving on quickly, 'how many of our corporate partners have we got sharing the platform on Saturday afternoon? I do hope they'll all be there.'

'Oh, all of them Harry – civic, business, university. You name it, they'll all be there,' Matt proudly declared.

'Excellent, then that's settled then,' said Harry. Then he had a moment of inspiration, adding, 'Oh, and at half-time, on behalf of McNamara Metals I would like you to present with the team beside you, this year's Community Achievement Awards. Make sure your press guys are there – it won't take a minute.' Matt hesitated, this was unexpected, but it was the last game and as Harry explained how it might work, he soon relented and caved in.

Only then did Harry lift his arm from Matt's shoulder moving quickly to the door, calling out, 'Come, come,' to his surprised entourage who were only just getting into the refreshments laid out for them. Harry, having achieved everything from the visit he'd wanted, was already through to the outside and striding briskly toward the parked cars as the others finally caught up with him. He spied Andy, the photographer at work, he once again knew he could count on him to have caught all the best shots.

149

'Excellent result, Cathy. Put Saturday afternoon with the Chairman into the diary will you, and make sure you get a set of cups from the Sports Trophy shop in Cornwall Street – they'll do just fine. It'll work so much better if the awards are handled at half-time rather than tucked away in the Rovers's empty soulless conference facility. Need to have "MacNamara Metals" on them and "Community Achievement Award presented by Harry McNamara" and the date, "Saturday 3rd June" – and "the year"' he added.

'Got that. Yes? Oh, and you need to set yourself some time this afternoon to get my tweets and social messaging out. Call in on our media team, cheer them up and join up the dots, then get the message out about the Community Awards,' ordered Harry, not letting up.

'Yes, Harry. I'll get the cups sorted. Up to £100 all right? I'd already put it all in the diary,' said Cathy, 'because I've learned you always get what you want.'

Harry beamed and in return, for the first time that morning, Cathy gave a natural smile.

'Oh and don't worry about the messages going out, I know what you want to say. Andy will let me have a selection of the best pictures – trust me, job done.' Harry could have kissed her, but he didn't; one day perhaps.

Harry had never felt better. The two visits of the morning had been a triumph. Cathy knew how to tell it. Could anything go wrong?

19

For some while Raqiyah thought it would be nice to touch base with other Muslims at Exeter's Al Baraka mosque. She'd spotted an open invitation to a women's group on the notice board in the university's Islamic Studies block. The green poster announced the group met every Friday afternoon at 3pm. It looked to Raqiyah like it was mainly serving as a contact group for people from abroad trying to make themselves at home in Exeter. In two minds, she wondered whether it really would be worth the effort to put in an appearance.

Walking slowly back along Pinhoe Road on her own, the traffic noisily hissing by on wet roads, she observed there were lots of people about at the end of the afternoon. Strangely, she realised, she was walking as if she was not one of them and an unpleasant feeling of disconnect made her feel terribly vulnerable and self-conscious. This was something recent in her experience and she found it both unnerving and a little disconcerting.

She realised that of late she had been feeling increasingly marginalised as she walked around Exeter. People had looked at her, sometimes stared at her, even muttered things under their breath as they passed her by. No-one engaged with her, except at Uni, and then it was only people she knew on her course. Come to think of it, even they had been giving her more space – or was she imagining it? No, it was real enough, she concluded, and understanding this explained her hitherto inexplicable mood of growing despondency. This was something quite separate from her experience of visiting Harry McNamara, or rather additional to it.

A little support wouldn't go amiss in times like these, she told herself. She felt she needed to check out her own perceptions with people like herself, see how other women were feeling in these times. The contact group at the mosque increasingly looked a good place to start. She recognised it was probably her own pride getting in the way of her saying 'yes' to going along sooner. That and having to explain what she was doing to Adam, though she knew he wouldn't stand in her way.

In reality, last Saturday's visit to Plymouth had, though she'd not yet admitted it to Adam for fear of unsettling him, left her shaken. The savage blow to her head that had resulted in her spending a night in hospital was so unexpected. Nothing like that had ever happened to her before. She touched her head where the blow had struck, recalling the pain and still feeling a certain tenderness.

What had prompted such raw violence? The aggression was something she now saw as integral to Harry and all he stood for. Physical dominance and visceral coercion, worn like an item of clothing or badge of office – were picked up, and put on whenever it suited. Something inside told her this by-election had some way to go and things were only going to get worse, a lot worse. It was best to try and prepare oneself, finding and making more friends, keeping in touch, was a good tactic.

Her Uni course had another academic year to run, providing she got the necessary course credits and passed her examinations this year – here she felt herself to be on better ground, reminding herself that until now she had always passed every exam she'd taken. But how to stay safe in this country, and what if things changed, what if overseas students, Muslim students, were no longer welcome and had to leave? No, she chided herself, now she was surely getting ahead of herself, her imagination wildly running away with itself as she started to contemplate Harry's extreme policies?

But then when they'd all met with that police woman, April Cooper, at the beginning of the week, hadn't she left them with the feeling the powers that be were equally worried about what might be going on too? Raqiyah thought it inconceivable that by-elections normally warranted the attention of re-assigned anti-extremism police officers sent from London to the South West, now did they? Hadn't April been very attentive to everything they'd told her?

Once again, that could only mean one thing – things were not looking good – this was a by-election campaign set to be even nastier. The thought made her feel very uneasy – that settled the matter and she finally resolved to find out for herself what support there might be within her Muslim community – people she could turn to if things got really bad. No messing about, her mind made up, she'd go along to the women's group that coming Friday.

Lost in her own thoughts, the fifteen minutes spent walking back passed quickly. Wet through, she pushed open the front door and called out to see if anyone was in.

'I'm back. Anyone home?'

'Just me. Bilal and Sophie are working late at the library. I've been putting something together to eat. Fancy a chicken tikka, picked one up on the way back?' Adam countered. 'It's OK, it's kosher, I mean halal,' he added teasing. Immediately cheered by his presence, Raqiyah realised how hungry she was.

'Sounds good to me. I'll just change out of these wet things, then I'll be with you,' she said, pecking his cheek and grabbing a towel off the radiator as she strode briskly past him to go upstairs. 'I'll be down by the time you've served up. Smells fantastic,' she shouted.

Half an hour later, the meal eaten, they broke from snuggling up on the old sofa unable concentrate on watching a film. They both got up and moved to the kitchen sink. Over washing up, as Adam washed and she dried, it was then she decided to broach the matter so preoccupying her – she determined to tell Adam of her plans for Friday.

'Adam, I saw a notice advertising a women's group at Exeter mosque – thought I might go along. They meet on Friday afternoons from 3pm. Well, I'd like to give it a try, go along once, see what it's like, who's there, whether it's worth bothering with. Might get to know a few people in the few weeks left of term.'

'Sounds a good idea. Do you think they'll be meeting in the community rooms rather than in the worship space itself? Do you remember when we went to look round, that place where they served refreshments to all the students visiting from the Uni Islamic Centre, those rooms at the back? My guess is you'll meet there,' said Adam.

'Maybe… I'll find out when I get there. You know you go and see Inger Walker from time to time, well I think I need some female friends who can give me a bit of support in these uncertain times. Last Saturday in Plymouth was not good. Shook me up more than I realised at the time.'

'I wondered how long it would be before you were ready to mention that. It's been on my mind ever since, but I didn't want to make anything of it for fear of upsetting you.'

'This is so silly. I didn't want to mention it to you for just the same reason,' she said, drawing closer.

'Look we're done in here. Let's go down the pub just the two of us. I think I feel ready to hear more about what happened last weekend if you're ready to tell me. Pub therapy has always worked for me!' said Adam with rather more outward certainty than inner conviction warranted.

The rain that had been falling all day had eased, pushed away east by a lively breeze. The two set off arm in arm, heading away from town to end up in Henry's Bar on the corner of Mount Pleasant Road. It was fairly quiet in there this evening, mainly locals drinking, but a few students too – no-one there they knew. Ordering a ginger beer and pint of draught bitter they found a table to themselves.

'You know, you really are someone special Raqiyah. You're so thoughtful and I just don't know what I'd have done without you this past year,' began Adam, holding his pint in two hands, and looking unusually serious as he stared into his beer.

'Fourteen months and ten days actually,' she said, 'gazing up from her own ginger beer.

'You're amazing – you're counting! Suppose from the moment I arrived as a late student in year one you and I have always been friends, more than friends,' he added.

'I'd never have expected to have met you and well, last summer we had more excitement in a relationship than most people see in a lifetime. A summer in Istanbul never to be forgotten.'

'Or repeated,' Adam quickly added. 'Some of it was a nightmare, but you stood by me when I was in pieces.'

'And now, I want you to stand by me,' she said. 'I don't feel this country is safe for me anymore.' Raqiyah thought what she had said sounded all the more shocking for having been voiced out loud.

'Is this because of what happened when Clive and you went to see Harry?'

'In part, but it isn't just that. You can see the way things are going in politics here. People seem quite unafraid to voice their prejudices, things they'd normally have kept hidden under the thin veneer of respectable British society. Well, they don't hold back any more.'

'Yes, I've noticed things are going all the wrong way. I've begun observing how people have begun looking at us – as if they question we should be together. Apart from Harry there's nothing else specific to report is there?'

'No, nothing's happened to me exactly, but being so visibly different, wearing a headscarf, albeit colourful and modern, makes me a ready target for anyone who feels like it – and there are people out there who feel like it. Being a woman too – I see a mixture of pity and hate sometimes. They think I'm a victim yet they also fear me or hate me as if I'm someone from a different planet – a threatening species, an alien.'

'Yeah, but it's not so bad at Uni, is it?'

'You say not, but I've noticed things changing there too. There are calls to ban religious attire in lectures, check out and even ban visiting speakers, that kind of thing – things unheard of before. Anyone who looks like me is suspect – I never felt that before. People try not to let it show, but I'm no longer imagining it, it's true.'

'It's hard for me, a white bloke, to judge. OK then, go along on Friday, it would be good to see how some of the other Muslim women are finding things – might even get some useful information about what's happening in the Muslim world locally – you must feel so isolated from the main stream mixing with only students and being on campus so much of the time.'

The matter was decided, Adam said he'd use his time the coming Friday to take himself off on another cycle ride, maybe on the scenic estuary ride cycle path from Exeter down to Exmouth.

Another round of drinks was ordered and they settled down to chat about what everyone else was doing – while beginning to wonder what they might do over the summer. With no placement obligations, both thought a holiday spent somewhere peaceful and hot would be ideal.

As they discussed various venues, first in Europe and then further afield, they realised that things were changing overseas too. Recent elections and terrorist incidents had left a legacy of Islamophobia and right-wing politicians claiming the public space. At the same time, ordinary people were being made to feel afraid, were looking over their shoulders at anyone different. The world was changing, it was getting hard to find somewhere safe to go on holiday, let alone somewhere to feel comfortable at home. Once again their conversation was becoming increasingly gloomy.

Their thoughts turned to the Middle East, with maybe a trip to Oman and Raqiyah's family, but that started to make Adam fearful and neither of them really knew how Raqiyah's family would take to Adam. Much to Raqyiyah's disappointment, Adam couldn't face the idea. The frustrating conversation was going nowhere and they both agreed they'd see what some of the other students had in mind. Neither knew what Bilal and Sophie had planned – it would be good to ask them later. Those two had been as much an item since last summer as they were. They all got on, so why not a holiday together? That was as near as they got to resolving the matter, but nothing could be settled, and everything was left hanging there.

Their drinks long finished it was time to think of heading back. Pushing the pub door open they started walking toward town and their digs.

The streets had quietened down, though there was still a fair amount of traffic heading in and out of town – blue fronted Stagecoach double-decker buses, smart cars with well-to-do occupants cocooned from the cool night air, and the occasional cyclist – Adam trying to check out what make and model each one was riding as they sped past. Raqiyah looked upwards hoping to see the stars, but the city lights killed that idea. As they moved away from Henry's Bar, she nestled comfortably into Adam's arm and they ambled homeward-bound together.

'You know we've not discussed my plan to get back at Harry McNamara,' said Adam suddenly interrupting the quiet.

'Harry's like, like representing all that's going wrong, isn't he? He's appealing to all the anti-Muslim, anti-foreigner feeling he can. He's stirring things for all he's worth.'

'And what's scary – people are actually listening to him. He was the first item on the news earlier. You know what, I couldn't even tell you the names of the other candidates he's standing against.'

'When I was cooking, that's when it came to me – the idea I had wasn't my own. I was watching a replay of what happened through the use of social media in the American Presidential elections – how people were able to undermine political candidates. It was so funny what people were able to do and I imagine quite annoying to be on the receiving end. I thought it might be fun to do it too. You remember when the new president was supposed to be signing some important papers, someone put round that image of him with crayons and a colouring book. If we could put some images around on social media of Harry – making him look small and ridiculous, playing up his character weaknesses – mocking his gangster-like appearance, his football hooligan background, his coming from a shady scrap metal business family – those kind of things, it could hurt him,' suggested Adam.

'Like using an image of Harry being a patient in hospital and having to have treatment from a Muslim doctor?' butted in Raqiyah, rising to the idea. 'Could paint a picture of fear and horror on his face, but underline how essential to the NHS foreign doctors and nurses are. Or even his parents going into a care home run by overseas carers – imagine his face!' They both laughed out loud.

'Sounds good to me. Bilal's good at this kind of thing. He's got contacts. Let's talk to him and Sophie when we get back. We need someone who knows what they're doing, and we need to be very sure there are no kick-backs on us this time,' said Adam.

'Don't like the mention of kick-backs.'

'Sorry. Come on, nearly there.'

They were almost at the door, Raqiyah groping around to get her door keys out of her bag, when a lad accompanied by two other guys and a girl, called out from across the other side of the road. The lad had spotted them, stepped forward and hurled a comment in their direction.

'Oi, weren't you the turd who had a go at Harry McNamara down in Plymouth last week?' He'd tilted his head as if it were an official enquiry and his friends began smiling at the prospect of some fun. The girl hung back.

'Think you got the wrong people,' Adam rejoined, but Raqiyah's frightened response, dropping then retrieving her keys from the ground, only fed the baying gang who wanted blood.

The door was open, they moved quickly inside, slammed it shut, only to hear a moment later what sounded like solid footwear kicking hard against it, banging and reverberating it against the frame. Would it hold? They waited, too scared to move.

'We know where you live, time to go back home if you know what's good for you,' the same voice rasped. After a moment listening, both were much relieved to hear footsteps retreating down the street.

'Come on, let's get another drink,' urged Adam, 'they've gone.'

They withdrew into the lounge, closed the curtains carefully to ensure they couldn't be seen from the street, switched on the TV and cuddled up to each other for comfort, with occasional pauses as they glanced at the shut curtains and listened warily for noises in the darkness outside. It was night.

20

A well-organised gathering in France behind him, and now back in East London, Carl Reynolds had just taken a call from The Master. He'd been told things were moving too slowly for The Circle and there were fears that a loss of momentum might cost their current rising star, Harry McNamara, the prized parliamentary seat they were after.

So Carl, their trusted lead local operative as well as useful administrator, was being sent west, having been told precisely where to inject a little energy in appropriate places. "Your'e to prod here and there and make things move for us," and he'd been told precisely what he then had to do in a tightly written set of accompanying orders.

Orders read and understood, Carl knew this was what he was good at. The Circle had been cutting its teeth in recent elections in France, Holland and Austria and been delighted at the noticeable shift to the right. Local operatives had played their part, with varying degrees of success, now it was Carl's turn. He was heartened at the progress overseas, but what really mattered to him was what happened in his home country – England. This was the big one so far as he was concerned. A man who bored easily, once he'd been set a task, it was as if someone had switched on the ignition to fire his engine deep inside.

His efforts the weekend before last to organise a brick with a message thrown through Harry's window in his Plymouth home had only met with partial success. Harry had taken the bait as they thought he would and he'd made the best he could of the opportunity to blame local Muslims, but as the Master assessed things, that brick had not sufficiently raised the temperature or galvanised local feeling to back Harry.

There was as yet no discernible mood swing, just rumblings of discontent across the constituency. Polls weren't reliable, it wouldn't do. Carl knew his orders meant taking things to the next level, injecting more fear. One domino falling needed to be followed by the next until a gathering momentum took everything down.

Once again Carl had spent the morning carefully packing away his things in his London flat before walking to the lock-up where he kept his black Range Rover. His great fear in life was to leave any forensic evidence in his flat that the authorities might use against him at some future time. Cleanliness had become an obsession and any dust, hairs or marks were assiduously removed as the place was scrubbed. All incriminating material was bagged and meticulously carried off site for safe disposal.

This flat, that no-one ever visited except him, was in effect his clinically clean office, and a second flat in Tower Hamlets was where he lived with a different identity. There he relaxed and allowed himself to function more normally; the 'office' as he called it, was his private domain. A life in the military as a young man had established his organisational habits and set in motion his subsequent pattern of life. He knew it always paid off to be meticulously careful to the last detail.

This time he was wheeling two small suitcases of equipment out to the car with him, his brief to 'turn the Plymouth Moor View by-election campaign toxic'. It was annoying him that the cases were so difficult to steer, swerving from side to side, slowing his progress. He made a mental note that he must change them once this mission was over.

Thinking to himself, he knew exactly what toxicity meant. Success in far right politics depended on fear – and there wasn't yet nearly enough of it in this by-election. Things were going to change. He'd see to it. Blood, sweat, fire and tears were needed.

He knew fear had to be carefully administered in the right places, targeted precisely to polarise communities and deliver the voters into a safe pair of hands – Harry McNamara's hands, though as yet Harry didn't know it.

It would be for the best that Harry didn't know until it became absolutely necessary to reel him in. Carl had read up on Harry. He thought him naive, at best a foot soldier, predictable and plodding. Yes, Harry was thinking in the right direction, but what political awareness, what political experience did he have? None! He was a pawn to be pushed forward on the chessboard and if necessary sacrificed. Maybe he'd prove himself to be the right kind of stooge to do The Circle's bidding in high places – the choice wasn't his call and in his view that remained to be seen.

It had taken a couple of days to get the items he needed together, to inspect each in turn, drive out to Epping Forest one night, practice some long range angled shots, just to be certain everything worked; himself included. He'd been glad no late night dog-walker or jogger had spotted him.

He'd then packed a black SIG Sauer German P226 with a small cache of double stack ammunition magazines into the glove compartment of the Rover. A brand new SIG, no previous owner – he knew many people would love to have access to such a quality tool. The Circle preferred to use its European sources for its equipment – there never seemed to be any problem getting good weapons, or for that matter disposing of them safely afterwards.

His first case contained anonymously sourced clothing – a three-quarter length dark grey jacket, a pair of Cabela hunting boots for silent movement; all fitting him perfectly and to be disposed of afterwards. These had been sent to him by parcel post from sources in Europe, arriving on the 20th of April – a nice present to mark the Führer's birthday. The second case – well, he merely nodded to it out of respect for its explosive content, anonymously sourced, though explosives were never that anonymous – had made its way from eastern Europe, a gift from "new friends". The third case was already secured in place in the back. Three cases in all – explosives, snipers rifle, clothes and personal items – all now safely stowed on board.

Carl was glad to be on his way. Sat Nav on, he headed west, taking the clogged artery of the M25 round to the M3 and then the dual carriageway to the south-west, the A303. The first part of the travel was one long frustrating drag, the traffic grinding to a halt every few miles, especially as he passed the Heathrow junctions on the M25 to the west of London, so he put on his earphones and switched on Mozart's piano concertos to close himself down, to calm his disposition as he drove in a personal bubble of musical distraction.

Two hours later and well clear of London, he decided it was time for a stop and pulled into a small service area. Checking his phone for the latest messages, he saw he'd been forwarded some further instructions. Quickly scanning his new orders he sent an agreed single word of acknowledgement. Once inside the boxy cafe, he ordered a latte and danish pastry. He sat himself down to look more closely at what was expected of him. After a second slow read, he took a moment to think things through, then to play it over, rehearsing his actions time and again to test them out for any potential error.

He knew they'd never leave him to decide a full mission for himself. Command lines all radiated out from The Circle. The Master carried ultimate authority and never let up in his need to control everything and everyone. Carl knew he had always been good at following orders and had an impeccable reputation for seeing his missions through. It was his great gift, tireless energy for the cause, coupled with attention to every last detail. That's why he had been chosen, that and the fact he had no emotional attachment – no-one in his life, no family, no friends. He was a loner and preferred it that way; so did they. They understood his grievances – the way he'd been treated; he was seduced by their promises and comforted by their regular cash drops into his bank account.

As he read, Carl sipped his hot Latte. It burnt his lip. He cursed quietly. The pain stimulated a smile that crept across his face as he understood what was being asked of him. Unexpected, the thought came that he quite fancied himself as a latter-day John Tyndall, John the one time 'Führer of Notting Hill.' In Tyndall he saw a guy who stood up for Britain and steered the right into mainstream political life back in the 1960s through the British National Party, then later the National Front. All this he'd done well before the EDL, UKIP and all the softies that followed, whose only legacy was to collectively lose their way. The Circle learned from past mistakes and maybe in him they had found their contemporary John Tyndall.

Carl loved history and his mind turned to the lessons he believed had to be learned from those early days. With immigration into Britain gathering pace in the 1960s, a golden opportunity had presented itself to the right wing – their failure to take the initiative then was painful to recall. The theft of the right's clothes by Margaret Thatcher's party had been later repeated by Theresa May.

It was now time, Carl truly believed, to push politics to the extremes and only a campaign of fear would deliver the population back into the far right's hands. Only then would Britain be united and great again.

A series of escalating attacks were all that would be needed – and what others might call innocent, ordinary people – well they would do very nicely as battle casualties, collateral. This was, after all, Carl told himself, total war and himself a serving soldier.

It was inconceivable now, having come so far, they would fall at this hurdle. Unlike in the past where the one-time fear of Jews or the later fear of black or Asian immigrants didn't worry the average British person unduly, except when the occasional riot rattled their cages, today it was different, the Muslim extremist, well they could be painted in much more terrifying vibrant colours – everyone and anyone could be their victim. It was timely and possible for everyone to believe how evil they were – today, it would only take a little fuel on the fire to set the world alight.

Carl pushed what was left of his coffee to one side and left the table with a determined step. He jumped back in the Range Rover and glanced at his watch. No-one noticed him, just another unmemorable customer, as he left the tasteless anonymous boxy service station behind, sliding into the line of vehicles, rejoining the traffic going west.

Easing up through the gears, he reckoned there was ample time to get within striking distance of Exeter before nightfall. He didn't feel tired, only a surging drive within, compelling him on, coupled with an unswerving belief in The Circle's vision and mission for England and the world beyond. He'd no doubt his time had come. The world would finally come to respect the name of Carl Reynolds.

21

Cherry Thomas was pleased. She'd got an interview slot with Harry that evening at his house in Ham Drive, Plymouth. She thought it promised to be the right kind of relaxed setting to get him talking. Having not told him what it was about, she'd rather assumed Cathy might have done that already. The story really shouldn't be a big deal – easy money.

It was six-o-clock, Thursday evening, when she pulled up in the typical drab suburban road. The earlier rain had eased, everything seemed damp, a muggy humidity embalmed everything in its grip, the south westerly air still heavily laden with moisture. This time of year the days were stretched out, long, light lasted.

Harry himself opened the door with a smile.

'Knew it would be you,' he said, standing aside to let her in.

'Let's go through to the front room,' he said not waiting for a response.

'Mum, pot of tea, will you – there's two of us,' he ordered, his sharp dark suit with ironed creases giving the scene an almost bizarre, comic, military air. There was a quiet murmuring response from somewhere in the back of the house. The two dropped into the comfortable chairs, an open newspaper strewn coffee table in front of them, as if someone had been searching through, then given up.

'Harry, I wanted to ask you about your family. I think this is a story that the public would like to hear more about. It's a matter that politicians take different views on – some keep

169

family totally out of it as best they can, others bring in the family side. In my experience, where it's done well, it can be a decisive advantage in a campaign.'

'Yes, I know. You can count on mine being in.'

'Can you tell me the family story. When did the family first come to Plymouth? I assume they did come from outside – McNamara's an Irish name isn't it?'

'Family tradition is we're descended from the Vikings, the hounds of the sea, they call us. And yes, you're right, from County Clare in Ireland – a proud family who provided strong leadership. My mother's family, they're from Plymouth as far back as we know, true Janners, local people, every last one of them.'

'When did the McNamaras come to Plymouth?' asked Cherry, 'you don't mind' she added, as she began recording their conversation electronically; Harry nodded his assent as the machine was proffered.

'Grandpa Michael McNamara left for England to make his fortune. Lived in Liverpool to begin with before moving south to Plymouth when the recession of the 1930s made life there intolerable. He knew a bit about metal and was taken on at first as a rag and bone man, door to door collecting – bit like a Steptoe's apprentice. Done with a horse and cart in those days. His lucky break came when the guy who employed him became ill and died. Michael got to carry the business forward himself. It was the metal side of it that took off – call it an example of a recycling business if you like,' he added with a smile.

A little tap at the door was followed by Harry's Mum delivering a tray with the tea and biscuits. She made a quick exit, before Cherry could call out thanks; noticing Harry never even bothered to acknowledge her, let alone say thank you. Mrs McNamara was invisible to him, taken for granted – even his slave, she observed. Cherry shuffled in her chair uncomfortably, she felt she had just shared in something vaguely indecent. Harry, oblivious to her reverie, reached across to the traditional brown teapot and began to pour. His mind was on his story.

'Through good fortune, hard work, taking the opportunities that came his way, Michael was the one who founded and then built McNamara Metals to what it is today – a successful Plymouth company contributing to the local economy.'

'Michael, like yourself, had an interest in politics didn't he?' Cherry ventured. Harry fidgeted slightly and hesitated, a nerve somewhere had been touched.

'Yes, mm, that's true. I guess some people still remember him for it. His main interest was his business. He never stood for MP or anything.'

'But he did take on political responsibilities locally – he had a political heart?' Cherry added pursuing her line of enquiry.

'Yes, I remember him telling me stories from the old days. He believed in local people taking local control. He didn't like outsiders, people in Bristol or London having too much say in running things here. "They don't understand us," he always used to say. "Local socialists are always seeking to undermine and ruin local businesses," was another of his favourite lines.'

'So he joined the blackshirts, didn't he?' followed up Cherry.

'Yes. In those days that was the only right of centre, sensible, available option. The Blackshirts were very popular in Devon. They struck a chord with what local people were thinking in the years before the war. Grandpa Michael had a natural instinct for local street level politics and proved himself to be quite a talent. The party needed people like him with his ability to organise and then recruit new people to the cause. Personally, I recall him as a quiet, caring man, passionate for what he believed in, a brave man too – someone who'd stand up to the fists of the socialists if he had to.'

'What happened?'

'What do you mean?'

'Well, he never pursued politics, never took it further – it fizzled out, didn't it? Did he lose interest or something? I can't find out anymore about him in our newspaper's archives after 1935 and that's well before World War 2.'

'You probably know more than I do. All I can tell you is that the Grandfather I knew and loved was a good man, successful in business, passionate in politics and when he died a few years ago, the family realised they had lost its patriarch. I'm afraid whatever political secrets he might have had, died with him,' said Harry, trying to sound convincing while making a mental note to himself to find out more to make sure he wasn't caught out later by some unknown ugly surprise from the past.

'Did your Dad, Patrick McNamara, pick up the mantle when Michael laid it down?'

'No. They're very different. My Dad's consolidated the business – that's where his heart is – total respect I have for him. He's made sure he provides for his family. He'll be in the factory now – works all hours – never wanted to get involved in politics – "political shenanigans are not for me", he always says.'

'Did your Grandfather inspire you, Harry? Into politics I mean?'

'Yes and no. He gave me a belief in grassroots politics – the importance of the voice of the ordinary man. But, what fired me up most was my trip to Turkey last year. I realised we can't let our politics at home be dictated by what happens abroad. Islam is a real and present danger to our way of life. I stared the terrorist threat right in the eye – I saw the dark evil there in their minds – evil to get at us, and I'm determined it shouldn't happen here in Plymouth. Ordinary people need to be involved in politics and make their voice heard, their votes count, be part of the great defence of everything we hold dear. I say "choose or lose" – too many people don't choose and they'll be the losers.'

'The rumour I heard was that your Grandfather turned traitor to his politics in the end,' said Cherry.

'Where did you hear that?' countered Harry darkly.

'Just something I picked up,' she answered vaguely, 'may have been that all right wingers got tarred with the same Hitler supporting brush. What do you think? Did he see what was coming? Did he get into something poisonous and then got out of politics, or did someone know something and push him?' Cherry knew she was clutching at straws and had no evidence yet to back up her line of enquiry, but she had nothing to lose. It was worth a try.

'Hmm. Could be. Need to stop it there for now Cherry. Got what you wanted? Pass what you write past Cathy before publication and I'll see if there is anything further I can let you have for your story. Think the public will like the piece? I'm sure Cathy can also dig out some photos for you too.' Harry got up from his sofa chair, clearly signalling the interview was over.

'Thanks Harry. This is such a help.'

Cherry was shown the door as Harry then quickly disappeared upstairs. His mind was racing. Not for the first time in recent days had he been caught on the hop, it had also been suggested at the Businessmen's Breakfast that his grandfather Michael was a traitor – he needed to get to the bottom of this, the last thing he wanted in the middle of his campaign was for a skeleton in the cupboard to be found.

Harry knew he had a local library meeting in half an hour – and for the first time he felt the pressing demand of the campaign left him just too little thinking time, too little chance to plan ahead. Time seemed to be accelerating toward a polling day just a week away and past demons were clamouring at the gates. Could he hold them off? Could he continue his populist surge to the finishing line and take the glory?

Harry went upstairs to change his tie. In his room, he glanced at the metal chest containing his Grandfather's things. No time to look at them now, to go through them carefully again to search for clues.

Everything was beginning to feel like it was moving all too fast, yet where it mattered, in terms of keeping him on the front pages, he was there. Yet he feared he might slip down the polls, as a crucial weekend in the election run in approached and a library meeting probably wouldn't cut the mustard. One's media profile as a politician was a volatile mix – either surfing to the top with a heady popularity or a depressing no-show. He knew he needed another lucky break, another piece of good fortune to come his way.

He had an instinct for knowing where he stood in people's eyes and he was feeling worried. Something had to change or everything would pass him by and like Plymouth's morning sea mist evaporate away, he'd end up being a forgotten man.

In spite of his honed instincts, little did Harry know that behind the scenes there were forces at work for him – his campaign was going to be given a very big helping shove in the desired direction; none of it of his own making.

22

People at GCHQ Cheltenham, the government's listening centre, don't do 'twitchy', but when information leads come together to hint at a pattern, even though it doesn't fully reach a threshold for action, a decision has to be made by a senior officer whether or not to follow it up. It was a crucial piece of decision making, and wrong calls easily made.

This particular Friday morning, the night shift handover report to the day team, omitted to flag up that a set of linked encrypted phone messages passing back and forth in Europe might have a bearing on the safety and security of people living in the South West of England. That decision, to overlook what might make any of the more experienced spooks at GCHQ 'twitchy', would prove to be a bad decision. They'd missed their moment, and unknown to those charged with protecting the people, they'd inadvertently allowed The Circle to stay ahead of the game.

The previous evening, Thursday 1st June, Carl had arranged to stay in a small bed and breakfast on the coast road just outside Exeter, a quaintly English Devon village called Newton Poppleford. He was staying next door to a pub, the Cannon Inn, where he chose to take supper after first checking in at the B & B. There were a few other people about, whom he assumed from their appearance and demeanour were touring visitors like himself, and just a handful of locals. None bothered him, he preferred it that way.

He always felt more at ease with himself when on a mission; it was about having something useful to do, like it was when he was in the army, his life taken care of. Nothing was worse than those months after discharge when he didn't belong anywhere and felt totally lost. That was when they found him and gave him a job. He'd never looked back. He belonged once again and life regained its meaning. So many of his former colleagues had, on leaving the forces, either turned to a life as a mercenary, fighting wars they didn't believe in, or found themselves sleeping rough, or even worse hitting the bottle to escape the realities of civvy life. His destiny could have been any of those possibilities, a waster – could so easily have been him – but he'd been lucky. He'd been found and saved.

Supper over, he decided to have a whisky, just the one. It would help him sleep. The tumbler was brought to him by the cheerful middle-aged waitress at The Cannon – a double shot, with ice. It soothed his still coffee-burned lips, applying a malted and peaty tingle as it slipped down.

After settling his bill, he walked the few yards back to "Field's B & B" and using the keys he'd been given, climbed the stairs up to his room. Putting the "Do Not Disturb" sign on his room door knob, he sat at the tired looking table with its selection of glossy tourist leaflets about Bicton Park, Escot House and other local attractions on the Jurassic Coast. His first instinct was to push them to one side, but then he thought he needed to appear like someone taking a holiday break, he chose a selection of leaflets and threw them on his bed. He took out his phone. Here was his entire office and he settled down to work.

Calling up his Spread Sheet on his Smart phone, he glanced again over the plan of campaign. All the prior months of planning and meetings that led up to the window for action had been deleted, removed, cleansed from its memory. Remaining entries began on 1st April, when he had had a job to do on the brakes of a sitting MP's car, thought to be enough to give a man with a notoriously weak heart a heart attack. He smiled as he considered that mission to have been a notable success. Only the weeks of the current mission from 1st April to Thursday 8th June, polling day, were retained. With his thumb on the screen, he scrolled across to Friday 2nd June, tomorrow.

He considered the real action in the political campaign to be only beginning the very next morning – what he liked to call his own mini-Beslan mission. He knew it did him good to go through, time and again, what he had to do, imagining his way into the mission step by step, until finally reaching the exit strategy and allowing himself to regroup.

Carl often wondered why criminals were so careless, as if wanting to get caught. He had no intention of dying before time in a shoot out, in some premature glorious martyrdom whilst the cause was still incomplete and The Circle would still need him. If only more of them worked like he did, approaching illegal activity with professional business-like military minds. Then, like him, they'd get away with it – they'd achieve and political targets would be realised.

All the equipment he'd brought with him in the two cases, were for now secure in the locked boot of his four year old Range Rover; a car with additional anti-theft security features he'd personally fitted. He felt self-assured, reminding himself that in his all round professionalism he'd left nothing to chance.

He opened his phone again, this time to look at an Exeter city centre street index – but no ordinary list this. He'd been provided with a map showing CCTV coverage, including the location of cameras, each marked with a red dot. He'd got someone to ask an innocent public access question of the local authority as to the CCTV coverage of the city centre and the official had posted him a document with maps appended. There was always the risk it wasn't fully up to date, but that was a small risk he'd have to run with.

Back in London he'd been glad to have a wide screen laptop which had enabled him to eye-scan the route he would need to take to avoid detection. He'd gone over his route and what he would do several times. The route was now imprinted in his memory. Having replayed it over yet again in his head, he changed into his boxer shorts and white T-shirt, went to the bathroom, before lying on his back on top of his bed waiting for sleep to come. Even after whisky it rarely did.

Following their weekend meeting near Calais, a small sub-group from The Circle was overseeing their own by-election campaign from a secret national HQ in Leytonstone, NE London. A self-imposed social media and phone black-out with their colleagues in Europe for over a week had kept contact to a low level; it not proving possible to eliminate all communication. European members were, as GCHQ had discovered, still talking to each other, but the London end, being out of the loop, gave listening ears the impression they were not currently functioning or had closed down for now.

In reality, communications are harder to kill than people, and The Circle were exposed. They were trying their level best to hide the fact a mission had gone live. There were currently three people sitting in the London HQ awaiting news from Carl – staying together as task group until Carl had done his job. There was little more to be done by The Circle except explore other possible opportunities that might be offering themselves in an extremely promising political period in Europe. The Master, one of the three, didn't much like travelling across from his luxury west London flat to join his team, but he accepted there were personal security benefits in operating away from home.

Carl breakfasted, settled his bill, and jumped in his Range Rover, a red early morning sky in his rear view mirror. He slid into the building traffic heading for Exeter. It could hardly be called a rush hour, but it was busy as he'd hoped for – offering the chance to enter the city boundaries unobserved.

By 9am he had found himself a parking meter in a CCTV camera blind spot not far from Southernhay. The slight rain suited him as he pulled his hood over his head, pushing up a large black brolly to further hide his presence. To all appearances, he was an ordinary looking business man, trundling a smart dark suitcase, heading toward the professional offices of nearby law firms and accountants. He soon reached where he was headed and paused to scan his surroundings. His were the cold, hard, empty eyes of a seasoned campaigner.

The city's historic medieval Guildhall, the present building dating from the 15th century was the country's oldest, yet still functioning civic building of its kind. Located at the heart of Exeter's modern shopping centre, it was currently, as it regularly did, playing host this Friday morning to a party of visiting school children; this particular class having made an early start from Exmouth Community College. Their coach had dropped them nearby and they were making their way in a noisy line toward the ancient double wooden doors under the stone portico entrance. It was there, as the teacher was checking in the excited party, trying to do a head count with the uniformed Guildhall steward, Carl's moment had come.

Walking through the group, he was unobserved as he left his case propped up against the back of the door. He turned and exited the way he had come. He looked every bit like just another one of the accompanying adults with the group. Seconds later he was once again on the opposite side of the road, hidden under his brolly and walking briskly away from the area and back toward his vehicle.

It was only as he was climbing into the driver's seat that he heard the muffled sound of the explosion and, as he pulled away, he could see a column of grey smoke against a now orange-grey sky rising above the buildings opposite. He smiled. It was now up to the men in London to play their part. There was no need for him to send a confirmatory message – they'd know soon enough.

As Carl put on his vehicle's radio, it was only moments later that a news flash was broadcast saying there had been some kind of explosion in the centre of Exeter and casualties were feared – it was too early to say whether it was terrorist related. Bus traffic through the pedestrian area was being diverted and an emergency major incident plan was being put into action. A phone number for concerned members of the public was provided. The reporter made comment of a recent city centre hotel fire and hoped this would not be as serious. Carl smiled again, knowing how wrong the reporter would prove to be.

It was time to head to Topsham, sufficiently far away and up market so as not to attract attention. He'd booked ahead for lunch at the 18th century Salutation Inn and decided that before checking in at Plymouth later he'd take himself for a walk down the Exe estuary after leaving his vehicle discreetly parked minutes away from the Inn. His first job was done.

Back in London HQ, the team of three following Carl's progress sent a single encrypted e-mail message that was received in a flat in Brussels. It was then recomposed, encrypted again and relayed twice more before finally a message was sent, purportedly from a Syrian website to Reuters news agency in New York saying that IS had succeeded in carrying out an attack in Exeter, UK and it wished to praise its local operatives for their daring and courage in serving the cause of the caliphate.

GCHQ Cheltenham also picked up the final message from Syria, and this time they did react when they intercepted it. However, by the time they had thought it was possibly genuine and sent messages through to MI5, MI6 and the Counter Terrorism Unit command, Reuters had already told the world the devastating news of an IS explosion with numerous casualties, many believed to be school children, at Exeter's historic Guildhall. Devon was now the uncomfortable focus of the world's media.

23

There's nothing worse than seeing the anguish of parents facing their worst nightmare – anticipating, then enduring the suffering and loss of their precious children. The TV screen moved between showing traumatised anguished and tearful faces and what remained of the front of Exeter's landmark Guildhall, the building which had survived Hitler's blitz. It had collapsed in on itself and debris lay strewn across the street, stone and wood at crazy angles, everything covered in dust and shrouded by grey smoke. Flames were licking at the rising grey smoke, crackling as they did so. It was a scene from hell.

Emergency crews were making their noisy way into the cramped scene, deafening alarms and sirens were sounding in every direction, the narrowness of the street amplifying their noise intolerably for survivors and bystanders alike. The confined space meant crews were jostling each other to try and get access, desperately trying to find a way into the interior of the building, but being turned back at every point, either by rubble, smoke or fire. Fire crews and emergency service personnel endeavoured to do their work; no-one fully having the measure of what had occurred or sure whether further explosions were yet to come. The ongoing pain of not knowing dominated emotion and thinking in these first hours.

Casualties lying on the pavement and road were being attended to and then lifted on to stretchers, moved into ambulances, blood pools on the wet street marking the ground. Disfigured bodies and limbs were left where they lay, sheets being found to cover them from sight. Whose small body was that one or that? – the pain in not yet knowing whose son or daughter this was. A convoy of ambulances was already forming, stretching in a sinister queue back down Fore Street, with still more police vehicles and fire engines trying to approach, squeezing past each other ever so slowly.

The police tape flicked and twisted, a blue and white contortion, rising and falling in the breeze at various points across the High Street. It had already broken and been re-tied as emergency personnel passed one after the other underneath the fluttering boundary, a makeshift marker between heaven and hell.

Two officers were now trying to tie more tape at a distance to drive back onlookers and camera voyeurs, shamelessly gathering like hyenas round a kill. Someone else already had a camera drone bouncing almost uncontrollably in the windy corridor of the High St, moving jauntily into its vantage position high above, in and out of the rising smoke – perhaps it was official – from the fire or police service. As yet more tape was being hung up, the wind caught it, whipping it savagely – it was but a flimsy barrier between the curious and the caught, the watchers and the purposefully engaged.

Harry was watching it all as it happened, at a safe distance, live on 24 News. Shocked at first, he quickly felt adrenaline coursing through his veins, a rising anger surging within. He wanted to hit someone or something. Gripping the arms of the easy chair in his front room, he calmed himself, taking control of his thoughts.

He wondered whether this 'major incident' would lead to the by-election being called off, but thought not. He was angry at the unknown 'bastards' who were threatening his chances. Then, surprisingly quickly, just as a claim of IS involvement came through on TV, he realised his campaign had just been given his longed for golden ticket. His mood changed and he smiled.

Harry grabbed a pen and a notepad from the nearby coffee table and quickly began jotting down some thoughts as they tumbled into his mind. Five minutes later, as his eyes lifted once again to the TV with its endless re-run news on loop feeds, it was time to ring Cherry Thomas. Harry needed the media, whilst equally loathing and respecting it. It was like some untamed beast that had to be constantly fed bad things to keep it alive. It didn't do good, it came alive with the evil.

'Cherry, seen the news?' he asked.

'Yes, looks very serious. They're saying there are deaths and numerous casualties. Rumour is, a party of children – a nightmare! I can't imagine what the parents must be going through.'

'How soon can you pick me up?' asked Harry ignoring her assessment.

'Err. What have you in mind Harry?'

'A quick trip up to Exeter. I know it's way outside my future constituency... don't ask. We should get there in under the hour. How soon can you be here?'

'OK, OK. I'll be there in ten, maybe fifteen minutes. We can talk in the car. You can tell me what you have in mind then.'

Harry ended the call and jumped from his chair. He punched the air, crying out, 'Yes! Yes!' and reached for his suit jacket. He pulled off his green and black tie. He needed his totally black one, the one he last wore at his grandfather's funeral.

'Mum, Mum, get me my black tie. Like I need it right now. Off out, something's come up.' A door closed somewhere and footsteps could be heard ascending the stairs to Harry's room. As Harry self-groomed in front of a mirror in the hallway, his Mum soon appeared, black tie dangling over her arm.

'Here you are, dear. I hope your day goes well. It must be so exciting for you. So proud of you, really,' she purred, before disappearing back into the kitchen. Harry's Dad had already left for the yard, a big movement of scrap to send to China he said. That was where he always was these days, thought Harry. Never stops working. Sometime he must tell his Dad to get a life.

Sooner than expected, Cherry's car announced its arrival outside with a double toot of the horn and Harry stepped briskly out, slamming the front door behind him.

'Morning Cherry. Can you get live news on that thing?' he said pointing to the car radio.

'Yes, sure,' she said, reaching across to switch it on. 'How are you today Harry? I guess you want to say something about what's happening in Exeter, though I'm surprised; it's outside your patch.'

'When it comes to public concern, I don't do boundaries. I want the people of Plymouth to see I care and that I want to do something about these things. What happens in our neighbouring city could happen here in Plymouth too. You still got a contact in BBC Spotlight?'

'Yes.'

'Can you call them up on your hands-free and tell them we're coming up to Exeter, we'll be at the Guildhall.' It was an instruction, not a request, and she nodded as she began to make the call.

Within the hour, and by taking a circuitous route, they finally pulled into the public car park at Mary Arches, Exeter and began walking together toward the Guildhall guided by the sound of all the action and the acrid taste of smoke in the air. Cherry was on her phone again to the BBC. She'd once had a bit of a thing going with one of the outside broadcast news crew. Reckoned he should come good.

'It's sorted, a camera crew are on site already and will fit you in. We'll find them in the High Street, on the east side, about four hundred metres away from the Guildhall. It's about the only point one can still get within sight of the Guildhall. They're pushing everyone back.'

Harry pulled his notes out of his pocket and scanned them to refresh his memory before putting them away. He checked his tie was in place and slowed his walk to a more statesmanlike pace. A hurrying policeman cast him a puzzled glance.

'You can't go down there, Sir,' he said, lifting an arm.

'Harry McNamara's the name. Where's the Chief Constable?'

'Don't care who you are, who you want to see, you're not going down there, Sir. Move this way,' he said reaching to take Harry's elbow.

It was at that moment Harry spotted the film crew just ahead and filming his way.

'Thank you officer. I'm with the BBC. Would you like to join us for the interview or have you something you ought to be doing?'

Seeing the cameras, the officer hesitated, looked back toward the Guildhall and hurried away. Harry seized the initiative whilst he still had it, a reporter reaching out an arm to pull him further into camera shot. Harry didn't wait for any introductions. The cameraman was clearly already filming, it was time to act.

'Harry McNamara, party political candidate in the Plymouth by-election and here to show solidarity with the good people of Exeter. What you feel, we feel. What you suffer we suffer. Where's your Labour MP? I don't see them.' Harry made a demonstrative glance up and down the street, to let the viewers get the point – the camera following his gaze – 'they aren't here – they don't care – they don't know what to say'. He paused as if he were contemplating the impact of the dreadful scene.

'Can I say that we have an unfolding tragedy here in Exeter, a terrorist incident at the very heart of this community. An attack on the symbol of our democracy as well as a massacre of the innocents. It makes me so sad that ordinary men, women and children can be attacked in such an evil and indiscriminate manner and I offer my heartfelt condolences to the victims and my praise to the emergency services doing their best. We've watched tragedy unfold in other cities on our TV screens. Now it's our turn in the South West,' Harry paused.

'Look at this,' he said, sweeping his arm across the still smoking panorama of destruction. 'First, I felt shock and sadness, but now I feel anger and rage. It shouldn't be allowed to happen!' He pulled out his ironed white handkerchief and feigned a tear, wiping the corner of his eye. 'There will be homes where children will not be coming home tonight and our hearts go out to them.' Harry paused as if emotion had taken hold of him, before apparently collecting himself and once again looking straight to camera. It was neatly and convincingly done.

'The mainstream political parties are failing us. They've let these evil-doers in, they've cut the policing budgets until there's no-one left to protect us, and they haven't got a clue how to tackle these repeated attacks that are killing our families and terrifying our people.'

'Let me tell you what I will do if I'm elected MP. I will see that police and security budgets are not cut like they've been sliced and diced this past decade. I will put more beat officers on to the streets and I will make sure that everywhere we can call upon armed response officers at a moment's notice – when we need them.' He raised a hand and beckoned toward the camera confidingly.

'Do you know that across the whole of our police area there is only one armed response unit, and where was it when we needed it? – not here until far too late.' Harry was none too worried if this was true or not, no-one from the police with their cautiously released press statements later in the day would be going to contradict him. His tone moved from compassion to one of visceral anger.

'Let me tell you what else I will do. I will get every person who is suspected of supporting terrorism rounded up and locked up out of harm's way. Not only has this government been closing local police stations and slashing budgets, this government has also been closing down RAF bases, naval bases and army sites right left and centre. There's no shortage of space to lock away these murderers. We've plenty to choose from – it's time we placed any Muslim sympathisers under lock and key. I want to see us, the British people, are protected and safe.'

'And that's not all. Do we want them here at all at our expense? No, never! Never! The time has come for us to expel undesirables. For too long open frontiers have been abused. It's time to send undesirables back to where they belong. We have a right to live in peace and a right to choose who we offer our hospitality to.'

'What about human rights, Harry? The kind of thing you are suggesting means turning our backs on international laws and agreements designed to safeguard individual freedoms. This country can't simply lock people up or outlaw them, can it?' asked a reporter stepping into Harry's space. His editor back in Bristol had whispered in his earpiece that what Harry was saying might be interesting and wanted the fire stoked.

'Human rights need to go hand in hand with human responsibilities. Isn't that right? The generosity of the British people has gone too far. How can it make sense that anyone who has tried to go to Syria, Libya or any other terrorist den in the Middle East or north Africa should have the right to come here. They shouldn't – it's too dangerous! The politicians don't get it. Attack after attack on decent families and they don't get it. It's time to pull up the drawbridge and support one another against attacks from outside. It's us or them, us or them! You or me!' and he dug his forefinger firmly into the reporters chest forcing him back, 'Get it!'

'We've over 13,000 foreign nationals languishing in our jails at our expense – these places are hot beds of radicalisation. We need to cleanse our prisons, disinfect them. It's time to clean them out. In the past such people were made outlaws, expelled from decent society. Let's cast them out, put them abroad and reintroduce capital punishment for the most serious evildoers. Make no mistake this is a war. War on terrorism and all who support them, and I for one am not afraid to take the fight to the enemy. Look around, friends, I still can't see a single one of your so-called party leaders standing here with you. We need leaders who will lead the fight.'

Two heavily kitted out armed policemen appeared and started shouting at anyone near them, edging ever closer to Harry and the camera crew. Harry adjusted his position to ensure the camera caught them as well as himself. 'Do not doubt for one minute', he confided again into the camera, 'this is war.'

'Get back, everyone back, run, move, move. That's you,' one said, pointing at Harry. The interview was over and Cherry and Harry began to retreat away from the crumbling facade of Exeter Guildhall as more debris from above crashed down into the street. There would be no chance of close up interviews with anyone here now – Harry had stolen the moment.

Harry walked slowly with dignity, pulsing messages into his phone, his Twitter feed alerting the world to the hopeless political stupor that had led to the present situation.

The camera man was still filming as Harry glanced up.
'Look at this,' his finger jabbing at the mobile screen in his hand. A final comment – 'The PM doesn't care enough to do

anything. Apparently we don't need to worry – bullshit! Of course we need to worry. Are you with me? Are you with me?'

24

April Cooper had been scrambled into action the moment the alert came through. Every available officer, whatever their normal duty, was sent into the city centre – she'd hurriedly dressed in appropriate yet cumbersome gear and was carrying all manner of equipment. She and her police minibus, now full to bursting with adrenaline fired officers on board, roared out of the station yard and into the road, siren wailing.

Moments later they were there, pouring out onto the street being told to keep people back and calm whilst the specialist teams, including bomb disposal, did their job. How do you keep people calm when children have been blown to pieces – crying, hurting, mutilated, terrified, traumatised along with those around them? April had to steel her resolve.

She looked around to see what protection was immediately available to their own team – just one armed officer with their group. Another concern she had was the fear that there might be further explosive devices. She knew this was in everyone's mind though no-one seemed to own it – time for brave faces and comradely solidarity.

A few paces and April ended up standing outside an optician's, a few yards east of the Guildhall, the chemical pungency of acrid smoke fouling the morning air.

An hour later she was still there, left to watch an empty shop, her colleagues up and down the road doing similar things. Occasionally some news bites reached her. As the hours passed, tensions began to ease and the boredom increased. Time slowed. She began to reflect on events.

There had been no warning, no alerts from Counter Terrorism nationally – nothing in the early morning Prevent team briefing. That made it feel worse, more terrifying, a failure in her world. Having some control, some handle on terrorism made it more manageable somehow. To have had nothing... The unpredictability of the attack, the rumour mill alleging many, many children amongst the casualties somehow made her feel the police were to blame, for failing to keep the Queen's peace. They'd let themselves and those whom they served down. It made her angry, frustrated, sad and she scraped her boot on the ground in annoyance. It was hard to find any encouragements, any hope.

Glancing at her mobile in the shop doorway she could see a media picture emerging, and there was that man again, Harry McNamara, making political capital out of it all. She couldn't resist playing the clip on the news channel. It sent a chill through her veins. Whilst she agreed, she wanted to see more police and an end to austerity tied budgets, a stronger political lead and hot beds of terrorism dampened down, she couldn't believe that what Harry was offering was the way forward. This guy was scary, she thought – his politics those of Attila the Hun. She slipped the phone back into her pocket.

Seeing Harry on film was alerting April that something deeply unpleasant was happening. She couldn't quite put her finger on exactly what it was, but she and her colleagues had talked in the minibus about a discernible shift in public opinion taking place. People had had enough and there was Harry, who had somehow caught the popular mood and was using it to his own ends. With a feeling of sad resignation she knew he was going to find people getting behind him as views polarised and hardened in these now desperate times.

The past voice of reason and calm was slipping away; perhaps it was already no more.

Then she remembered the very reason she'd been called down to the South West from London was because the by-election campaign was thought to be upping tensions – how right they were! Now she knew that not only had tensions increased, but they had a full scale major terrorism incident running alongside the political campaigning – a toxic mix set to turn the campaign, polarise views, the public mood becoming more ugly by the day. She wondered why the local Prevent lead Rob Callaghan, or indeed her Sergeant Emma Stirling hadn't been in touch – it wasn't a good sign.

Her quiet reflections were interrupted, a sergeant strode towards her, April in his sights. She thought he looked set to give a verbal update on the explosion at the Guildhall, but it soon transpired that wasn't it.

'OK?' He didn't wait for an answer, before adding, 'They need you back at HQ pronto. All Prevent Team are being assembled for a meeting at Moorside. Get your skates on. Car's on the corner, now.' He pointed to a waiting station car.

'Yes, Sir, right away,' she replied, walking away.

'Run officer, run. Not the time to be slovenly,' he barked, his anger at the situation they were dealing with raw, acerbic and on the surface, eroding his normal professionalism. She wondered if he had a young family.

Picking up speed awkwardly in her heavy kit, she climbed in the back of the waiting car. Unexpectedly she found herself sitting alongside her Prevent colleague Rob who looked at her as if she might be able to tell him what was going on. She simply said, 'Your guess is as good as mine. Thought you'd have heard something.' He nodded nonchalantly. The rest of the journey passed in silence.

Back at the station, they took their pick of any one of the many empty meeting rooms, grabbing coffees as they waited. The biggest room was being set up to run the major incident investigation. It was twenty minutes before their own room was fully complemented with the regional force's Prevent officers, some of whom April had never seen before. A couple of other people had come in as well as two sharp suited spooks. An inspector finally joined them, took charge and gave a short briefing.

'This one's different. That's about it. There's no intel, no whispers, no CCTV yet, nothing that can help us – bloody thing had to have been professionally done – no easy leads – no people to lean on yet who can tell us anything – nothing at all any which way we look. Can't tell Joe Public that, and it's early days. We might get lucky, but don't count your chickens. Has anyone a grain of comfort here?' He glanced round the room at the silent blank faces hoping for something but with a face resigned to the fact they had all nothing as yet to go on.

'Thought not. While we wait for SOCO, for forensics on the explosives, CCTV analysis and for any witness material of merit to come up with anything, what do we have? Anything? Come on, the world awaits your collective wisdom,' he said with bitter sarcasm. This time there were a few halfhearted shrugs, but still nobody spoke up. April couldn't keep quiet.

'Sir, what about the claim from IS, that they were responsible? I know they usually lob these "we did it" claims in, whether or not they actually did anything, but what do we know? Also, if it was professionally done, then do we know if any Syrian or other returning ex-fighters have shown up on the radar? And what are the early guesses as to the type of explosion – what are people saying?' she asked. The Inspector nodded across in the direction of the shorter of the two guys in suits.

'Sir, it doesn't fit,' he said before turning to face April. 'The Inspector's right, the claim has been fed to us, but this time through a different track, the route carefully hidden, but definitely not the usual route. We don't know why that is, can only make guesses. This incident is different. Speaking personally here, off the record, I doubt it's IS. Further, despite what people say, that we don't watch suspects – so far as we know there are no returning war experienced IS suspects running around this patch. Can't give you anything on the explosive used yet.'

'Could it be that someone might want us to think it was IS, to suit their own purposes? We shouldn't rule anything out here,' replied April.

'Spot on. Can't rule anything in or out.' he said vaguely.

The Inspector looked lost for words, before adding, 'This means we've got to sharpen up, do some professional policing so we notice what is important. We must miss nothing. We're to work collaboratively, keeping one another posted on anything we suspect, anything out of the ordinary, even if it's PC Cooper here, using her grey cells for the first time,' he said mimicking her London accent, trying unsuccessfully to inject a little humour.
'Is there nothing our friends at GCHQ or MI5 have to offer us? Apart from IS, any other chatter you've picked up – come

on you're supposed to be on top of this, spill the beans?' he pleaded, having a second attempt to find something out.

'Only more questions at this time,' the taller guy interrupted. 'Patterns and gaps in patterns, all the stuff which says to us, as Rich said, this time isn't the normal – so our advice to you local guys would be this – first, be open to who might be behind this, it might not be who you first think of; and second, be prepared for anything to happen, even more of the same. Whoever is doing this, and we are guessing, well they are better trained, better prepared, better hidden than usual and as yet giving nothing away. We don't know whether it is a single individual or a group. Hold all possibilities in mind. That's the best I can advise.'

April felt she had to speak up again.

'We've got a by-election in Plymouth and this explosion, the deaths and injuries of school kids, is going to have a huge public impact. It's unlike any of other terrorist acts in London that I've seen. The deliberate targeting of kids has crossed the Rubicon. There's one parliamentary candidate in Plymouth, well to the right of centre, who was there at the Guildhall very quickly this morning because he knows it. The possibility this by-election could turn toxic was why I was moved from London down here.'

'Yes, I saw him,' said Rob, 'He was fiddling while Rome burned – using one fire to stoke another from what I could to tell. We could do without that right now.'

'As far as I can tell, Harry McNamara's making political capital from all this. What's happened is likely to make some people very angry and Harry McNamara is going to stir and stir such divisions in our society; he could make the Miners'

Strike and the Poll Tax riots look like teddy bears' picnics. Prevent is supposed to be about making our communities resilient to extremism, but what I fear is that what has happened might fatally undermine all we are seeking to do. Shouldn't someone speak to him, possibly all the parliamentary candidates to tell them to moderate what they say? Otherwise, Harry McNamara will make our job impossible to do.'

'Plymouth's not Exeter. You might be right, we'll have to wait and see. But I'll tell you one thing, no police officer, no matter the rank, is going to be telling politicians what to say or what to do in a by-election – that's out of the question. The Chief Constable has already had a call from the Home Secretary asking her to explain her conduct in relation to events at the Exeter mosque. What I want all of you to be doing is getting into the community more, talking to people, helping them see they have to act within the law, that's the limit to what we can do on that front,' the inspector said.

Emma whispered in to April's ear, 'Good thinking, April, nice questions.' To be given some praise lifted her.

The meeting was about to break up, but as the inspector took a call, he signalled that everyone should remain where they were a little longer. This had to be important. They watched and waited as they listened to a one sided conversation. He dropped his phone to his side and turned to his colleagues. The inspector nodded across to the taller of the two men in suits.

'Our friend from London is not just a pretty face – things have just got worse, much worse,' he said putting his hand on April's shoulder. 'News is just coming in from Plymouth, of gunfire in the city centre. It's an attack by an as yet unknown number of assailants, at the Drakes Circus Shopping Mall. There are many casualties. A least one weapon's being used. My God, we will need the army to help us. All our Devon and Cornwall Police resources are now up here in Exeter, including our armed response unit. We've left Plymouth to fend for itself! God help them! Meeting dismissed.'

The inspector ran from the room once more clutching his mobile to his ear, the officers looking blankly into each other's faces wondering what this new turn of events would mean. The South West had suddenly become a very dark place.

25

Adam and Raqiyah made their way walking, without haste into the city centre on the Friday morning; Raqiyah determined she was going to meet with the women's group at the mosque in the afternoon, and the plan was to do some window shopping before then. Things were definitely in wind-down mood at Uni and there was a party that evening they'd decided to go to. It was about time – time to let their hair down, relax a little. They needed to pick up a few things to take along – bottles, snacks, these were the understood price of entry. They were going to wander into the city centre – chill out.

They were still in the Pinhoe Road heading toward the centre when they realised something wasn't right. They popped into a local supermarket. Back outside again, there was no doubting a weird silence hanging in the air and there were fewer people on the street. A distant wail of sirens punctuated the air, and it gradually dawned that something was up. Adam looked up at a slow moving helicopter scything its way along, moving sideways just above the retail area rooftops. Its spinning blades pulsed shock waves. As his eye followed it, he spotted the column of smoke rising into the sky from the city centre.

'Think there's been a fire,' he said, his arm raised in the direction of the smoke. Raqiyah tapped her mobile into life and quickly found the latest news bulletins.

'Oh no! Look! They're saying there's been a bomb blast, at the Guildhall. "Expect fatalities", say the police. A party of school children were visiting at the time. Looks bad, really bad, Adam.'

'What shall we do? We could change our route to avoid the High St, cut round the back by John Lewis's, head straight to Uni now.'

'Doubt we're going to be allowed much further along the High St – bet it's all cordoned off further down. You kind of wonder what the scene is like there, whether it's truly as bad as the media say, or whether it's being hyped up – fake news and all that.'

'Well, we need to go in that general direction, but I doubt we'll see anything, we won't be let anywhere near, you'll see,' said Adam.

The two set off, the small rucksack on Adam's back now filled with the party fare. Just a couple of minutes later and they could see the High St was indeed closed. Adam observed the people around him – a mix of curious onlookers heading one way and the fearful watchers looking for a way out.

They slowed and paused briefly at the blue and white tape stretching across the High St from the bookshop to their right to the multi-story retail fashion store to their left. The police officer standing looking at them from the other side eyed them suspiciously, taking a step in their direction. Some yards behind the burly officer there were several people making up what looked like a TV camera crew who were being escorted down the High St in their direction and away from the explosion.

As the group approached, the policeman moved another step toward them and grasped the tape ready to raise it and let them exit. They watched as the news team moved rapidly toward them, clearly not welcomed by the police where they'd been, now being driven still further back by two escorting police officers within yards of where Raqiyah and Adam were looking on.

'That's Harry McNamara, in amongst that lot,' said Adam pointing.

'Time we slipped off to the right then and moved away from here, come on,' replied Raqiyah.

Adam turned, only to hear his name called out. He froze.

'Adam Taylor, isn't it. Oh my god! I'd recognise your face anywhere,' called out Harry, his loud voice well practised at reaching across a crowd. He was drawing nearer with every step. The camera crews were still filming, Adam, now a rabbit in the headlights, didn't know what to say, what to do.

'Adam,' he said more quietly, knowing he had his attention. Turning to the camera, Harry added, 'this is Adam Taylor, the young man who saved his friends and killed a prime minister.' Then turning back to Adam, 'What brings you to this part of the world? And more importantly, what do you make of what has happened in our High St this morning?' Harry's words hung in the air. Adam was saying nothing.

As he waited for Adam to speak, he finally recognised who he was with. 'You again! Raqiyah Nahari, my student interrogator. Don't tell me Adam, you're a student here and you know this young woman?'

'We're both students here,' said Raqiyah taking the initiative.

'Have you searched his bag officer? I mean this man's with a Muslim sympathiser. Do you know what he's got there?' The camera crew started to take steps back away from Adam. Adam remained frozen to the spot, unable to move.

'Can you put that bag down on the ground please Sir, there in front of you,' the officer said after momentary hesitation. Everyone was jumpy, and the officer's eyes showed he was trying to think fast. Adam wasn't moving.

'Adam, put the bag down, please,' said Raqiyah. However before she had barely got the words out the officer had thrown Adam face down on the ground, knee on his spine and began pulling the bag from his back, but quite unable to get the straps off Adam's shoulders. 'Back everyone, back, he shouted. 'You too miss', he said looking at Raqiyah.

'Adam, Adam,' gasped Raqiyah, hardly able to get the words out. The officer began talking into the radio in his one hand whilst nervously fumbling to pull the bag's zip with the other. With a tug, the whole rucksack fell open and cans and bags of crisps tumbled out on to the pavement. Another word in his radio, and the officer got up, standing back from Adam who remained prone on the ground.

Raqiyah stepped toward him, then another step and put a reaching hand out to touch him. The officer, having finished his call, pulled Adam none too gently to his feet. 'You need to do what you're told Sir, save everyone a lot of trouble.' He stepped back to recommence patrolling his tape boundary.

'Adam,' Raqiyah said softly. 'Adam, its OK.' The expression on his face was a combination of pain and terror, a faraway look in his eyes. She put her hand to his cheek and stroked it. Adam's eyes moved and softened as he connected with her. 'You OK?' she asked.

'Yes, yes. What the fuck did he do that for?' said Adam.

One of the other officers from the camera escorting party stepped forward.

'Now, Sir, language. We don't want any trouble here. We've got enough on today. Spare a thought for what's happening. Suggest you get up and make off before my colleague changes his mind about your wasting police time. Next time, be a bit more cooperative – it's the best thing to do, Sir. Now move on, move on.'

At that he took hold of Adam's arm, shoving him away in a single movement, leaving Raqiyah to gather up the rucksack and its contents strewn across the pavement as best she could. Adam still shaky, rubbed his lower back, checking the bruised areas of his arms and shoulders as he slowly moved his feet.

As Raqiyah finally zipped the rucksack closed, she lifted her head to spot Harry now standing a little away, but looking across in her direction. He was still talking into the camera and as he watched her, she was sure there was a smile in his eyes. Glancing away, she wondered what poisonous bile was even now coming from his mouth, and knew her first priority, rather than confronting Harry, was to get Adam and herself out of there, and find somewhere safe, as fast as she could.

Grasping the rucksack in one hand and Adam in the other, she discovered that deep inside she felt a hatred for someone else she'd never experienced before. In response to what had happened to her and Adam, she wanted to hurt Harry badly, to watch him bleed, see him suffer, make him die. It shocked her to find herself thinking it didn't overly concern her that she was nurturing such raw hatred for a fellow human being. Harry needed to die.

—

26

'Adam, take one of these,' Raqiyah urged once they were down the hill away from the scene. She'd pulled out Adam's Quetiapine pills from the side packet of the rucksack, 'No, take two,' she said judging him to be having one of his more serious anxiety attacks. She offered him one of the soft drink bottles from the back pack in her other hand. Adam did as bidden, standing and leaning for support, his back to a wall.

'Wasn't expecting that,' he murmured after swallowing as instructed.

'You OK, not hurt or anything?' Raqiyah asked.

'No, nothing but bruises I think. Like I just fell off my bike!'

'And you've done that loads of times,' said Raqiyah, beginning to relax.

'Why don't we head down Bailey Street and then up to one of the nearby parks, Rougemont Gardens by the castle or maybe Northernhay.' Adam merely shrugged in agreement, and they set off slowly, with each step the incident on the High St slipping further behind them, but their feelings of fear and confusion stayed.

It always amazed Raqiyah how quickly the Quetiapine took effect. By the time they were in the park and taken an empty wooden bench seat for themselves, Adam was talking freely again.

'Being in an open space always makes me feel better,' he offered. 'That Harry McNamara is an unpleasant piece of shit,' he added, 'nasty comes naturally.'

'When he pointed at my bag, like I was some suicide bomber, he orchestrated the part of frightened bystander to perfection, I couldn't move. My mind was somewhere else. In Istanbul it was Harry who jumped those terrorists, this time he got the police to jump me! When he called me a "Muslim sympathiser", it was like I was a member of some anarchistic antisocial revolutionary body – even a terrorist myself. Did you see that policeman's eyes. He was scared – of me! What's the world coming to?'

'He did it because of me,' said Raqiyah, 'because you are my friend. He instantly saw who I was and that was it. He made the policeman go for you – I'm sorry for that. If I hadn't gone to Plymouth to interview Harry with Clive last Saturday, none of this would've happened.'

They sat close and chatted for several minutes, then gazed across at the still rising column of smoke above the city centre.

'People are so jumpy because of that,' said Adam, pointing at the sinister smoke cloud drifting across to obscure the morning sun. He opened his phone to see what the latest news was.

'They're saying it's another terrorist incident and to expect significant fatalities, but not releasing any details. Wait. Something else is happening in Plymouth at the Drakes Circus Shopping Mall. Gunfire. More casualties, fatalities there too. Police in Devon have asked the army for help with an ongoing gun battle. People in Plymouth are being told to stay locked indoors for their own safety until it's over. Looks bad – so many of these attacks – where next?' He thrust the mobile away in his back pocket. No sooner had he done so, then Raqiyah's phone began to ring and Adam wondered whether he had accidentally called her as he put it away. She answered it anyway.

'Yes?' Raqiyah saw the number was "id withheld" and didn't volunteer her name. 'Who is it?' Then she confirmed her name to the caller and she was quiet until the call was over. Finally, she looked up, tears in her eyes, she couldn't help herself. 'It's the university – they want me in – that was the Vice-Chancellor's office. Want me to keep this confidential – want me in immediately – for two-o-clock. Only suggestion they had was that I look at Section 5 of the General Regulations for Students, the bit about, "bringing the name of the University into disrepute." They wouldn't say anymore, it wasn't something they'd discuss over the phone.'

'Did they say what specifically? It must be a mistake? That's unusual. You need to check it out,' said Adam, concerned to see Raqiyah so distressed.

'No, but they were clear on one thing. They said it was a personal conduct matter, needs to be dealt with face to face.'

'Is it to do with Harry McNamara do you think?'

'Yes. I can't think of any other reason.'

'You've nothing to worry about. You've not done anything wrong.'

'But you hadn't done anything wrong and look what that policeman just did to you! And I'm a Muslim! Don't you understand?' She was getting stressed herself.

Adam realised, felt and understood in that instant all the tension that had been building in her in recent days and weeks.

'Look, we'll deal with it. I'll come with you. I'll help you. You'll be allowed a friend. Don't let them get to you. You can tell them what's happened. Can't think it'll be much more than giving you some words of advice about being careful who you mix with, that kind of thing, you'll see.' Adam's aim at cheerfulness was falling on deaf ears and he felt helpless, with nothing he could say to lift her spirits.

Raqiyah's phone rang again. She answered it warily, relieved to see it was Sophie on FaceTime. She held up the phone so that Adam and the park were in shot before speaking.

'Hi Sophie, you OK?'

'Yeah! Yeah! Shopping trip's off – city centre's closed. Where are you? Looks nice.'

'Rougemont Park – we can see the smoke rising from where we are sitting.' She turned the camera accordingly.

'Raq. Had a visitor just now from Uni wanting to speak to you. Bit off-hand, strange. Wouldn't say about what. Just thought I'd let you know. They are trying to reach you about some meeting – they wondered where you were – all a bit odd – thought I'd let you know.'

'Thanks. They've reached me. Just taken a call. Got to see them at two. Tell you about it later. Catch up with you two this evening at the party. Have a fun day!'

With that Sophie had gone. Raqiyah knew now for certain the call from the university was no hoax, it was desperately serious.

Raqiyah put her phone on to the live news stream hoping to find out the latest, only to see Harry McNamara talking to the camera again. 'Adam look, look,' she cried. Adam leant across raising a hand to shade the sun from the screen.

There was Harry in the High St, exactly where they had been not half an hour earlier. Then to their horror they realised the filming was from the time they were there and from when they had come into shot. Then, the whole incident was played before their eyes, this time with Harry's evil verbal gloss in silky newspeak words explaining what was taking place in the way he wanted the world to understand it. The clip ended with the policeman on Adam's back wrestling with the rucksack, the camera crew jerkily moving away, all the while Harry commentating, upping the ante, ensuring anyone listened to him, and together understood that the familiar world of the shopping street had to be seen as a terrifyingly harmful place.

'These are dangerous times. We need to watch who is befriending Muslim sympathisers. Often it's students who think violence is a justifiable way to protest. I say we cannot tolerate this any longer if we are to be safe in our own country, on our own streets, in our own homes,' concluded Harry before the picture switched back to the smoking mess that was once Exeter's magnificent medieval Guildhall and the desperate efforts being made to try and save still unaccounted for children.

Raqiyah looked at Adam with fear in her brown eyes. She wondered how they were going to get around the streets safely themselves without harassment or worse. She glanced anxiously around the park, a few minutes ago a safe place to relax, a place of refuge, now potentially a place where they might be attacked. Though it was almost empty of people, she felt watched and so very vulnerable.

They began walking together, Raqiyah wondering where she could go; where could she hide? She looked at Adam, the Quetiamine having taken effect, coping well again as if nothing was wrong, but moments ago, a frozen traumatised shadow of a being. This was not her idea of how student life was meant to be, just where would all this end?

27

Carl loved it when a mission was in full flow, running on track, his adrenaline level at maximum, his alertness that of a wild animal on the hunt. He'd strategically parked his black Range Rover on the top level of the Drakes Mall Shopping Mall Car Park. Few people had bothered to park beyond the more convenient lower levels, but he was reassured to find there were enough cars around the entry point to the department store to allow him to park anonymously. Even so, he hated the sense of exposure to the sky, the feeling of easy entrapment and the distance he had to cover to get to the car park exit. These risks, he reflected, had all been taken into account, with nothing arising last minute to cause undue alarm, he just need to calm and stay on task.

Here at the top, there seemed to be no-one about. For now he could do as he pleased and if anyone did come by they would have little cause to look his way. He'd need to keep half an eye on the door to his left just in case.

To Carl's eyes, the Drakes Circus Shopping Mall looked monstrous as well as prematurely jaded. Little more than a decade since it had opened to great acclaim, he thought it resonant of every tired city shopping centre he'd ever been to. He detested such places – somewhere for poor lost souls to wander in, a kind of purgatory; and today, he smiled, there would be ghosts to add to what he saw as the ever-shopping living dead. He recalled from somewhere that Drakes Circus had once gained celebrity status for winning the Carbuncle Cup for crimes against architecture. Indeed it was a deadly place and he would ensure it would be ever remembered for that very reason.

For Carl, the Mall complex, with its nice clear access routes, built as part of the city's redevelopment programme, looked just perfectly designed to serve his purposes. Having a clear exit route was his first priority, for he had no death wish, no desire to be apprehended or worse still, get – shot, well not yet any road.

The Circle's vision for a better world, a truly great Great Britain, was something he wanted to see into reality. Then, as a faithful trooper, they would give him, reward him with, everything he ever wanted. Then he wouldn't need to hide in the shadows and could take whatever house, whatever woman, whatever liberties he desired. They'd see he was happy, they'd look after him, the Master had promised.

He stepped outside his vehicle to look briefly over the car park parapet; the metal fencing provided sufficient space to fire between as well as offering him virtual personal invisibility from below. Satisfied with the target area, he noted that nearer at hand he was also totally hidden between the fence and his vehicle for the task ahead. He reached inside the rear door of the Range Rover, pulled at some plastic sheeting and poles. They were slightly awkward, but he was fit and strong and after one final glance around he pulled them all out on to the concrete.

The thing that pleased him most was that in his calculations he had meticulously planned everything from the opening scene to his final escape route. His quick glance reconnaissance had shown him nothing had changed since his visit to check things out back in April. The long narrow Mall below, shop entrances either side to left and right ran away from him, maybe for over a quarter of a mile and it was satisfyingly well crowded with shoppers, oblivious to his presence high above them. He was thankful all the careful timing and choreography he'd endlessly rehearsed in his head since his earlier visit, did not need to be changed. All was just as it should be.

His vantage point was far enough from the killing field not to draw attention in his direction, and he was sufficiently elevated behind the late morning sun to have a gloriously commanding view of the Friday shoppers. He'd calculated he could take a goodly number of unsuspecting targets before the rest had taken it into their heads to run for cover. This should be fun, he thought.

He began guessing how many he could down cleanly in the space of five minutes, before reminding himself this was not a sports competition. His sniper's rifle was always slightly awkward to move quickly from target to target, so he estimated conservatively something upwards of ten, maybe twenty if people didn't realise quickly enough what was happening. He was pleased to be using his familiar sniper's weapon, not some indiscriminate rapid fire automatic machine gun. It mattered that he would try and take people out cleanly if he could, but had to admit that hadn't been the case back in Exeter.

He knew that at some future point, the place he'd chosen as his base would be discovered. An aware off-duty military person doing their Friday shop, and in Plymouth there would be many, could cut down his firing time. Later clever forensics, analysis of bullet trajectories etc would finally point exactly to his lair. It was irrelevant; all being well he would by then be long gone. He would outwit them all.

Ensuring once more he was alone in the corner of the rooftop car parking area he hastily erected his free-standing screen, supported by the poles displaying a professional touch of his

215

own making with the words "Plymouth City Council" emblazoned on the sheeting. Having walled himself inside his white cocoon, he knew no-one would come inside to see what he was doing.

Next, he began assembling his long sniper's rifle. In practised movements it clicked and locked smoothly into place, the telescopic site finally being adjusted. The silencer would also help to delay discovery, but with additional wrap-around modifications of his own he'd also brought with him, he hoped to further baffle the sound of each shot to little more than a quiet burp.

He placed his rounds of ammunition on a small raised folding stand next to the rifle now on its tripod, its tip pointing down at the Mall through the fretwork of open architecture and wire fence that composed the car park's ornamental facade. He was ready. All had been done in minutes without a moment of forensic carelessness. Feeling in his jacket pocket, he found his mobile phone. Ensuring it was still switched off so as neither to indicate his presence nor interrupt his aim, he leant forward to peer down on the unsuspecting targets below.

He had time to quickly observe his quarry. The pattern of people coming into view intrigued him. The numbers he could see changed so very much, the clear targets one minute numbering forty or more, the next barely five or six. It was when he saw a larger group of shoppers arrive simultaneously he took an opportunity not to be missed. Some of them were pushing pushchairs. Maybe they all knew each other in life he mused, now they would know each other in death. He adjusted the position of his small metal and canvas folding chair. It had a swastika stitched into the weave – the only symbol of his deep affiliation to the cause he carried with him. He hurriedly mounted his killing throne.

How to choose who to shoot was never a problem for Carl. He took his shots in a slow arc moving from left to right and then back again, weaving further and further up the street before heading back to the foreground to finish. At the end of his first arc right, he counted fourteen successes, every one a clean kill to the head. Moving back to the left, and further away, people had begun to move, aware of something, but not yet sure of what, and fewer opportunities presented themselves.

He only counted a further five hits and two of those were body shots which felt less professional. He began swinging right and bringing the shots nearer to him again, his eyes scanning the scene below. Now the cries and yells were reaching him, and it was becoming more difficult. Some wary eyes were scanning the buildings, none looking directly at him. He needed to check his car park lair to be certain he was all alone. It was time to stop.

Quickly and with practised ease he urgently put away his kit, finally rolling up the protective plastic shield. In his haste he was not able to get it wrapped small enough, so he resorted to bundling and stuffing it in the back. The tinted glass windows would hide it. Gun dismantled and packed methodically back in its bag, he finally threw in his chair before climbing into the driver's seat.

Quickly moving away, circling ever down through the car park's levels toward the barrier exits at street level, he grasped the exit ticket poised to insert it, to ensure not a second more to delay him. This was the pinch point, waiting in a short queue at a barrier to get out, to get free. He had to control his impatience as precious seconds were added, the driver of the car in front putting their ticket in twice before the barrier lifted.

Then it was his turn. Timing judged to perfection, only seconds remaining on his exit ticket and he was out in the morning sunshine, driving anonymously in Plymouth's busy lines of city traffic.

Looking for a parking spot out of range he began thinking to himself that an afternoon in the Barbican quayside area with all its tourist cafés, arty shops and sailing boats, even a boat trip would be just the perfect way to stroll and unwind, before checking into his hotel that evening.

Looking at his watch he calculated it wouldn't be more than minutes before all the emergency services started piling into Drakes Circus Shopping Mall, now a safe distance behind him. He'd done his job, society had got payback. Exeter was ablaze, Plymouth in terror, it was time for a beer with maybe a whisky to follow.

28

The street closures were making the return to Cherry's car tedious. First, it had been a long walk away from the car park down Exeter's High St in a large semi-circle. Then, more precious time had been lost with an unexpected encounter. Harry thought he could well have done without this further altercation with Raqiyah, but had to laugh to himself at Adam, the ready victim for a spectacularly successful piece of street theatre that had so easily been set in motion. The idiot!

As they made their circuitous route back to Cherry's car, he could see it all, played over again in his mind, as if in slow motion, Adam flying to the ground as the policeman, right on cue, had thought he was a terrorist. Now, he asked himself, who was the bigger fool – Mr Plod or stupid Adam? He couldn't help himself, as he laughed out loud, and as he did so looked across to see Cherry's puzzled look on her face, wondering at what she took to be his inappropriate good humour.

'It's nothing, really, nothing,' he said, forcibly calming himself down.

Eventually, back at Cherry's car, humour gone, he felt a growing sense of impatience getting on top of him. He urgently needed to get back to Plymouth and valuable minutes were passing, a key moment slipping from his grasp. For Harry, timing was everything. He felt the empty pit in his stomach as a stunningly good advantageous opportunity was just drifting away from him and he could do little about it. If things were kicking off there in his own patch and he wasn't bloody well there, his opponents would have a field day. He hated the thought of his election victory slipping from his grasp.

'Step on it, Cherry dear, will you. Any news on that mobile of yours? Mine's got no signal.' She threw her phone in his lap with more force than intended, as she grabbed the steering wheel in one hand and the Citroen's gear stick in the other. Soon to be MP or not, this Harry McNamara was beginning to annoy her, and his "dear" thrown in for good measure was almost more than she could take.

'It's switched on – take a look yourself. I need to get back to Plymouth too you know; I've got to get material back to my editor – you're not the only one up against it.'

'Hurrumph!' he countered dismissively and began scrolling through her mobile phone's news stories, pausing now and again on anything that looked interesting. In some Twitter feeds he began to see the latest newsfeed as to what was happening.

'Hell! Like I say, put your bloody foot down girl, we should have got away sooner. Come on! There's been a terrorist gunman at work at Plymouth's Drakes Circus Shopping Mall – reading between the lines, lots of fatalities. Why do the main news people never tell it how it is? Always the same, start with just a few, one, maybe two casualties, then let the public down gently as they gradually up the numbers ever so slowly over the coming hours and days. What do the media take the public for, mugs?' he said forgetting himself for a moment.

'I'm media,' Cherry replied curtly, 'and I'm not your "dear" and I'm not your "girl". Tension was building between them, the air now sparking. So much so, Harry became aware of it, and then he went quiet as two thoughts simultaneously crossed his mind. The first, that he quite fancied her when she was angry; the second, he need to be careful and keep Cherry on board.

He stopped himself. This wouldn't do, he needed to calm his impatience, he thought. Right now he needed Cherry's allegiance, he needed to restore things to a happier footing. After all, she couldn't be expected to fully understand what was at stake here.

'Present media company excepted, of course,' he returned with a smile. 'Let's just get there and find out the truth and let the people have it straight this time. I make the news, enough of this fake news stuff. I'll tell them just how serious it is and what we need to do. People don't want wishy-washy liberal sentiment at times like this. They need leadership,' he countered. 'I believe you can write it as it is. You're the best journalist around!' His flattery fell on deaf ears.

The rest of the journey south was mainly in silence, but for Harry, still unable to fully restrain himself, periodically asking if the car had any more speed in it. Eventually, they were dropping down the sloping dual carriageway gradient bringing the outskirts of Plymouth into sight. They filtered left off the main road, to join the slowing city traffic Harry once again beginning to fret out loud.

'Fuck it! When I get elected, I'll make sure the road planners are the first to get the bullet. What the hell have they done with this re-mixing of the traffic flow except to make everyone fucking later than before. Idiots!' he shouted in total frustration, banging the dashboard hard with his open palm. Cherry just looked straight ahead, assessing the stresses of the day were taking their toll on Harry. He was becoming volatile like some raging bull.

Drakes Circus Shopping Mall was just visible as they rounded the last roundabout and swung left. Then they were in one long stationary line of traffic, blue flashing lights and emergency service vehicles milling around like startled ants, policemen standing in the road talking to frustrated drivers with wound down windows. Whichever way they looked ahead of them, it was clear they were going no further.

As Harry gazed ahead, the giant flat brown ice cream wafer shapes, shielding the shops beyond from sight, so acclaimed as an architectural triumph a decade ago, looked like forms without meaning in Harry's eyes. So much of Plymouth, destroyed by Hitler's Luftwaffe in the last war, had seen that destruction only eclipsed by what was erected as post-war architecture in its place – bloody boxy shops, tarmac, paving and instantly forgettable concrete forms everywhere.

In the waiting, just for a moment Harry recalled the magical skyline of Istanbul, spied from the Bosphorus, whilst he was there the previous summer. The memory of Mediterranean hues of dazzling blue skies, mesmerising cityscapes, in a haze of kebab smoke. The reminiscence confused him briefly, before he corrected himself to the grey vista now in his gaze. He really shouldn't be thinking the Ottoman architecture, built by Muslims, might be thus compared with his own city – he couldn't explain his illicit thoughts to himself. It was enough to jolt him back into the present, he needed to get out of the car and walk.

'See you later,' he told Cherry as he stepped out of the car, pausing only to announce his departure. At this latest act of unpredictability, she lifted and dropped her hands on the steering wheel in evident frustration, before turning her head to make a 180 degree escape manoeuvre. When she looked again in the rear mirror, she could see Harry was already striding briskly to the heart of the action. Damn, she thought, it's so hard to get a good story, realising that she'd need Harry as much as he needed her.

Harry forgot Cherry as soon as he'd left the car. The grey day felt clammy to his skin, but he was not going to shed his jacket – a sharply cut, clean self-image was everything. It got him places.

It took ten precious minutes before he encountered his first policeman. Harry slowed to take in the scene. The officer had a roll of the ubiquitous blue and white tape and a very wide street across which to place it. There must be a warehouse full of the bloody stuff, thought Harry. As the hapless policeman tried to fasten his tape he was constantly being interrupted, mainly by people trying to get away from the shopping area, but also by the gusty wind, so his attention was continuously being distracted. This suited Harry who chose his moment carefully. He'd been to enough football matches in the past when he'd had to get past patrolling policemen. This officer's mind was on too many other things – piece of cake.

Less than a minute later, Harry was three buildings beyond the tape and that much nearer his desired destination. Even if the officer saw him now, he knew he wouldn't leave his station to chase him. Harry with the arrogance that came all too naturally to him couldn't be bothered to turn his head to check.

Harry spotted the ruined Charles Church, now preserved as the city's war memorial. Like the smouldering Guildhall in

Exeter he'd left behind but an hour ago, this ancient building too had once been a smoking fire, its heart ripped out by explosion and flame. Inside it today were the 1,200 inscribed names of Plymouth's civilian war dead. Plymouth seems to have war memorials everywhere, he thought. That kind of number, a mighty 1,200 corpses, thought Harry – well that really was something worthwhile to get worked up about. The present losses just didn't compare with the past.

He reasoned that the deaths of most of one school class, a number of teachers and adult minders, taken together with the shoppers shot here at Drakes Circus, that was, well, really sad, especially the kids, but in the greater scheme of things, not something he ought to allow himself personally to get too moved by, he told himself. His feelings had to be kept in check here. A sense of proportion would help him manage things. What had happened in Exeter and now in Plymouth were just fortuitously timed minor incidents in the greater role of history that might be significant enough to help him swing an election win. He must keep focused, he told himself, his thoughts always in danger of running away with themselves.

Soon he had covered the final few yards to the point where he could see there would be little chance of getting any further. The emergency service definitely rules who goes here, he noted.

Wondering briefly what to do next, his heart warmed as he spotted familiar faces among the film crews and reporters gathered before him. It was time to get in on the action and no policeman could stop him now. He spotted small groups of emergency service people clustered and crouching over motionless human forms lying on the pavement. So this is it, he thought, I've made it to the heart of the action – panic over. He adjusted his black tie and smoothed his hair with the palm of his hand before announcing his presence.

'It was Sir Francis Drake himself who said, "England expects every man to do his duty,"' he bellowed, loud enough to cause the media scrum to swing toward him. They turned as one, like the city's seagulls at the sight of bread.

The move caught two approaching policemen unawares and they slowed, allowing Harry, in that instant, to place himself securely centre stage. He could tell by the look on their faces they'd recognised him, and they'd hesitated because they wouldn't risk any further claims of police interference in a by-election. The signs were that obvious.

'Come over here,' he called the nearest of the two officers, wrong-footing him, leaving him surprised and apprehensive. Once in the full gaze of the media, he was like a rabbit in the headlights with no safe escape route. Harry put an arm round his shoulder, their two faces too close for the policeman's comfort. The policeman wasn't sure whether Harry's arm pinioned or embraced him – any which way, Harry had him.

'We rely on the bravery of our city's emergency services at times like this. I've just come from Exeter's Guildhall and I've seen the sterling work the emergency services are doing as we face these latest crises, these attacks on our British sovereignty and way of life. I want to see our police given all the resources they need to protect us. No austerity, no cuts, and definitely no police cuts on my watch. Thank you officer.' Harry let the officer go. Such was his relief, he almost fell away.

'Sir Francis Drake called upon us all in the face of threats from overseas to do our duty, and following the example of the brave people of those days, I call upon the people of Plymouth today to be strong and pull together in these dark times. In time of war, we know how to behave here, and we will show the scum who attack our own what we are made of. Listen to me. Mark my words. There will be vengeance for the taking of innocent lives. There will be no hiding place for these vermin.'

Harry raised a telling forefinger as he added, 'there will not be a stone left unturned as we seek you out. We will find you. We will bring you to justice, and if I am elected in these coming days, I will make sure we have penalties that fit the crime. Death for a death. Capital crimes demand capital punishment. It's what we the people want, nothing less.'

One of the reporters interrupted Harry, 'we've had a sniper, some sharp shooter taking the lives of innocent families this morning. People simply going to work or going shopping, even taking children to school. An elderly lady on her mobility scooter, a policeman first on the scene. How does that make you feel?'

'My first thoughts are with the bereaved, those who will have lost loved ones today, the homes without a mother, without a much loved child. It grieves my heart to see these things happen here. But the tears of grief shouldn't blind our eyes to the truth of what has happened. Failed government policies caused this. This city's politicians have allowed our beloved city to become a so-called dispersal centre for the terrorists of the world – every month for two decades, thirty or more people whose backgrounds have never been checked out, have been allowed in, to live here, hidden like germs among us. These people take our housing, use our education, health and public services, rob us of our taxes and everywhere grow like an infectious disease in our midst. How do they thank us? – by killing us. None of us can feel safe.' At that moment Harry gazed up at the surrounding buildings. 'Even now, they might be planning to take another shot. I could be in their sights even as I speak to you.' The media crew were already on edge and began looking around anxiously.

'Do you think we ought to move out of danger officer, out of sight?' one of the reporters asked the other policeman. Before he could cut short Harry's news conference, Harry himself had other ideas how to keep things rolling, and turned to take another question he could see a long haired younger reporter waiting to ask.

'Hold on Harry, that's a bit rich. We're proud of our city offering a welcome. Aren't you one of them, Harry?' he said, stepping forward whilst pushing a microphone right in front of Harry's face.

'Sir Francis Drake was right – it's all about duty, the duty all of us bear to one another. It's what we expect, nothing less. You shouldn't be asking me that question, no. It's one for the politicians who framed this failed policy, who let them in to come and harm us. Ask them whether they're proud of welcoming terrorists. Incidentally, where are they? I don't see any political leaders here right now. Where are they when they're needed? I'll tell you where they are– they're hiding. They're ashamed of themselves. They know now what the people think of them and their policies. They are rightly frightened of the people.'

A stretcher bearing party hurried by, one of the party saying, 'this one's alive, make way, clear a path.' The media pack moved aside and back. Harry, though, seized the moment and moved forward, arrested the party's progress, gaining just enough time to place his hand on the prone victim's arm. As he strode alongside he said, 'stay with us,' whispering loud enough of course, for the watching media to catch his every word.

As Harry leant down there was, to his shock, a sudden reaction by the prone form. A jerk and twist, his arm flinging out. In consequence he fell from the stretcher, his face now exposed and facing Harry – a pulsing bloody mess; from his shattered lower jaw he emitted a guttural scream and a simultaneous gurgle erupted from what was left of his lower face. The stretcher bearers tried to bring some professional dignity to bear as they bent to try and retrieve their patient from the pavement.

At this the nearest reporter recoiled, his recording device flying from his hand bouncing on the hard ground, like a stone skimming on a pond before it came to rest several paces away. The small press group tried to register what had happened. Was it another shot that had caused this sudden further horror?

Then there was pandemonium. No-one knew which way was safe, no-one knew where to run. Eyes stared, bodies as if glued in place, but desperately needing to be moved. Then people were scattering, different directions, jostling one another, crouching, running for the nearest doorways, anywhere to get off the street. Fear, panic enveloped everyone. People pushed and fell. The press group then tried to reassemble in the shop doorway opposite.

Only Harry and the stretcher case remained. Harry's heart like flint spotted opportunity in this. He remained looking at the now silent young man on the ground, reflecting what he should do next. In the seconds that followed, he moved in to help the bearers and helped heave the injured man back where he belonged, on the stretcher.

Harry could feel no life in this now still man. Getting him to hospital wasn't Harry's first concern. His eyes had followed the reporters with their camera and he could see them watching him from the safety of the building opposite. That was where he would direct this medical group.

Forcing his presence upon the two ambulance personnel, he grasped the side of the stretcher and commanded them to follow him – then with a determined hold on the direction of travel, he walked slowly and uprightly like some hero from a war film straight into the pointing lenses. He was giving his constituents the hero they were looking for.

Harry knew it looked better if he kept all his smiles on the inside for now. This little scenario was a political candidate's gift. A city like Plymouth with its proud military history was certain to elect him for this. Once in an area considered safe, he let go, the puzzled bearers looking around them as to where they should go next. Meantime Harry's gaze was on the future, to a campaign he considered all but won.

29

The Master didn't rely just on one operative. He had a growing task force. Most were not what he would call team players, and in his control of them, he liked, so far as it was possible, to observe the silo principle – no one person knowing what another was doing. It carried the added benefit of considerably cutting risk to the organisation's security and it kept him safe. He reflected that Carl was a good ex-soldier to have on board, but the current campaign in the South West needed something added, something really special and for this, Steve Collins was the man.

Steve had served on HMS nuclear submarines as an engineer, finally ending up with colleagues at Rosyth in Scotland waiting for the next posting, the one that never came. Within a month he'd been signed off – discarded, made redundant – it came as a bitter body blow to him. It was in that period, told to go but not yet gone, that he took some leave he had to use up and went down to London for a long weekend. Whilst there he was picked up and taken to The Circle's Personnel Chief who had hired a room at the Grosvenor Hotel in Buckingham Palace Road. It was The Circle who were able to offer a very jaded disillusioned naval officer a much better future.

First though he was told to take a 'holiday' in Egypt – a trip as much about testing him out as equipping him for what The Circle needed from him. Given the right paperwork, no questions were asked when he reported to the Egyptian Naval HQ in Alexandria. He was there to learn about limpet mines, especially the Egyptian limpets as modified by the CIA for use by the Mujaheddin in the Afghan War. They carried the right Middle Eastern signature.

Being an engineer serving on submarines it was important he understood everything there was to know about the danger limpets posed, and anxious to take foreign income, the Egyptians were only too happy to take a foreign national with excellent references on the week long course.

Steve's background was Belfast. He'd seen the navy as a way to escape the Falls Road estate with its Catholic gangs and rampant anarchy. If people thought the Good Friday Agreement had brought peace to Northern Ireland, they hadn't told his neighbours! The trouble was he hadn't found the fulfilment he'd hoped for in a career in the navy, and now they were about to cast him off, like they did the ships on which he'd served – neither being thought of to be any serviceable use any more.

The Circle soon learned that what Steve liked was order. He lived a very self-disciplined life. It was easy, being single and with few friends. A girl-friend in Glasgow understood he was a serving officer in the navy and was happy to see him whenever he visited. He had a brother he hardly had any contact with in Brisbane; a man with few ties – perfect.

Disillusioned with society, he'd have loved to have seen someone take control of his estate back home where he grew up and still had a flat. He'd have been the first to applaud anyone who could bring the estate's villains to heel. He'd long since lost patience with the Royal Ulster Constabulary – chicken livered, anything for a safe, quiet life. There had to be, he hoped, some way of bringing about a better future. A bit of a loner he had begun searching on line, when off duty, for any groups or causes that might offer him encouragement. He wasn't someone who could just sit on his hands, he needed to do something.

Some websites and chat rooms he visited seemed only populated by nutters and he'd steered clear. One day, he'd happened upon one of The Circle's many sites and he'd used the "contact us" key to start up a conversation. It was this that eventually offered him the Grosvenor Hotel Meeting. All he had had to do was fill in a fairly detailed questionnaire. Yes, he was still a serving Naval Officer, but hell, he very soon wouldn't be and he went so far as writing down "they could go to hell." So he'd filled in the form as The Circle had required and posted it to the "Personnel Chief".

The course in Egypt had been, to be frank, not overly interesting and he had failed to see its relevance – orders were orders after all. He'd done everything they asked of him and got the attendance certificate to show for it.

Once back in England he had been called back in mid-May to a second meeting at the Grosvenor where this time he was interviewed more formally by a man who simply called himself the Personnel Chief and a woman he referred to as his deputy.

Steve himself wasn't stupid and realised that he was being drawn into a network. Strangely, he found he didn't mind and was comforted going along with things. They seemed to value him and what he might be able to do to help bring about a better world and offered him an opportunity to demonstrate the skills he had learned in Egypt and put them to good use.

'First of all, do tell us what diving experience you've had, what you are capable of. And, did the Egyptian course provide the promised Scuba Instructor training?'

'Yes, that was one of the weaker elements. We have to do a lot of diving working in subs and we get much better training in the RN – better facilities, better trainers, better equipment. Can't say they taught me anything new there. I can dive with my eyes shut – literally!'

'It's not so pleasantly warm in British waters!'

'On that point I totally agree. Springtime in Alexandria is perfect for diving,' he added.

'That's good to hear. And on the technical side...' Then rather to Steve's evident horror, the Personnel Chief placed a sinister looking metal object on the table in front of him. Meanwhile, the deputy at his side was scribbling away on her notepad quite unperturbed.

'Now Steve, a little test for you. What do you see?' he was asked.

'Where did you get that?' asked Steve in surprise. He didn't get an answer.

'What do you see?'

Steve leaned across to take a closer look.

'Egyptian make limpet mine, used most successfully by the Mujaheddin to attach to Russian trucks rather than boats in the Afghan War. This one looks like it dates from that time, manufacturer's details here,' he said pointing them out. 'Wait, it's been modified. This one will withstand water penetration for a limited time, maybe two weeks. Also, this model of timer is a more recent addition, hopefully more reliable than the earlier ones. Much more easy to prime, won't go off when placed, can be set for any time to detonate, look I'll show you.'

Steve reached across and quickly pressed the electronic control touchpad. 'It's now armed and will explode in thirty minutes.' The tension rose in the room and looks were exchanged. 'No worries, one can cancel the order, like so'. The red lights went out, to the evident relief of the two sitting opposite him.

There were more questions, then the showing of a short promotional video. It wasn't particularly well done so far as Steve could judge, but the message was clear – a new societal order able to deliver a utopian national state could be established if those committed took the opportunities open to them. It lasted maybe no more than three minutes. There were more questions, then the two on the interviewing panel, for that's what it was like, nodded in agreement – they'd been suitably impressed. The Personnel Chief spoke.

'We will have new orders for you shortly, a posting for which you will be amply rewarded. This organisation runs on a code of strict military discipline. We expect orders to be followed exactly and if not, we can be very punitive. We find it works. Stick and carrot – it's very simple. We don't do namby-pamby – we get things done.' There was some discussion of terms before the session concluded and Steve found himself back outside on a London street.

It was almost a month later when Steve was in the pub at Rosyth, killing time with equally disillusioned colleagues, that the expected call finally came. He stepped outside into the Scottish rain to take it.

'We know you like to visit Glasgow in your Volvo estate – Novotel, Bath Lane, isn't it? Can you please do so this coming weekend. Do as you usually do, arrive Saturday night, return on Sunday evening, but this time park the car on arrival in the nearby Ibis Hotel car park. You're familiar with it?'

'Oh yes, of course.'

'We will be delivering some equipment and placing it inside your car. It would help us if you leave your car keys on the driver's side front tyre. You'll find them there when you go to leave. It's in our interest and yours that you don't try and observe the transfer of goods to your vehicle. You will also find an envelope on your driver's seat. It has your orders and a cash contribution toward any expense you may incur. We pride ourselves on being discreet.'

'Right, OK,' replied Steve, partly caught by the surprise of the call, but also perturbed that they knew his plans and probably who his girl-friend was. Well, he reasoned, if he stayed on the right side of them he had nothing to fear. However, the thought of having something useful and exciting to do when his future otherwise looked bleak, action in a worthy cause, lifted his negative mood and he added cheerily, 'I'll be right on to it,' before signing off.

It was the last weekend in May when he made the journey east from Rosyth to Glasgow. It took just under the hour in the fading light, heavy rain falling in a grey shroud, misting everything, draining colour from life. He called Carrie to say he'd arrived and would be with her shortly. In the few minutes it took him to walk from the Ibis Hotel car park round the corner to the Novotel, he cursed at how wet he'd got.

Still, he was overdue some welcome leave away from Rosyth, different only in that this time Carrie and he would be using taxis to get around Glasgow's pubs and night life. He'd have to explain why – a little white lie came to mind.

30

Calls were coming in from desperate police colleagues in Plymouth, calls to speak to anyone in the Prevent or Counter Terrorism team. April Cooper ended up as police switchboard's default first point of call. She wondered whether everybody else in Prevent had battened down the hatches and hidden themselves more effectively. Who wanted something like this to show on their watch? Regional teams were fine, she thought, so long as what kicked off happened where the team was based, but here she was, in Exeter, and things were now kicking off in Plymouth. She'd never even been to that city. They were all clamouring for intelligence, anything to go on to help them nail what was happening and she had nothing to tell.

It was with some relief April was then corralled by the emergency response team into providing extra police personnel in Exeter's High Street where, by lunchtime, the curious as well as local shop and business staff were getting over their first terror to come back and enquire when they might resume normal life. Time and again she politely instructed them to go away, to return to what had been designated the safe zone, but on what basis it had been so called, she had no idea.

Enquiries answered to no-one's satisfaction, she was then detailed away from the public facing front line to find herself located next door to the still smoking remains of the Guildhall. Acrid and inescapable uncertain smells assaulted her nose. Ghostlike forensic officers in hoods and masks were disappearing inside. Looking up, she couldn't believe the words she read above the foodie outlet where she was standing, adjacent to the Guildhall. Incongruously, it read – 'The Turks Head'.

Her third mobile call of the morning came in, this one from a sergeant on a Plymouth street, someone clearly trying to hold a telephone conversation whilst giving orders to the multi-agency emergency personnel dashing between many victims. As he spoke, the ghoulish screams of seagulls interrupted their conversation. A Sergeant Gaskell wanted to know what April knew about local terrorist sniper threats. She told him the blunt truth, 'nothing', and after an expletive he hung up on her.

Ten minutes later her radio called her up again. This time it was the command inspector in Plymouth. She stepped back into the Turks Head doorway for a quieter space.

'Yes Sir, April Cooper.'

'We've a situation here in Plymouth and I need your take. We've had one sniper or more, using a vantage point above the Drakes Circus Shopping Mall, taking out shoppers and anyone in sight. It's been like a turkey shoot. Bodies all over the place. Best guess he was up somewhere high. Must have escaped the scene now, shootings stopped, but we don't know for certain and everyone's looking over their shoulder wondering if they're next. Presently we're looking at upwards of eighteen dead. Clearly this is a skilled marksman with a professional weapon and a military take on the situation. We have not had a single lucky break, so it's all down to routine policing graft now. I called thinking maybe you can help us with something?'

'Nothing directly, Sir. We've been concerned in recent months at the hundreds of IS returning fighters leaving the Middle East – you'll know about that. Since the collapse of the caliphate adventure they've changed tactics. Attack us where we are by whatever route remains open to them. Well, we know some are finding their way back into Western Europe, several hundred undoubtedly coming to Britain. Could be that one or more of them have had their sights on Plymouth – but actually, Sir, I've got nothing to back that info up with.' She heard a grunt at the other end of the line before continuing.

'We've had a bomb attack here in Exeter earlier today. Undoubtedly the two incidents are linked, but whether the same group is responsible, well I couldn't say, it's too early. We really haven't got any lucky breaks here either. No reports have reached me of any sightings of the perpetrators, nor have I received any intelligence as of now and it'll take time to get the CCTV images and mobile call analysis in.' Her voice died. She didn't have anything further to say and what she'd already said sounded, in hindsight, as so much bullshit. Having nothing sounded no better for dressing it up. It felt like playing cards and looking at your hand knowing you were losing the game come what may. The thought depressed her.

'And that's it. Nothing else?' the inspector said politely, if disappointingly.

'Yes, that's it. And no, Sir, nothing else. I'll let you know as soon as, when, if, I hear anything further,' she said lamely.

'One other thing. I'm faced with a difficult decision here – Rovers are playing at Home Park tomorrow afternoon – can you offer me anything as to whether or not the match should go ahead?'

'Sorry Sir, there's nothing I can help you with there at this point in time. Maybe something will come up before then to help,' she said forlornly.

With that the inspector had gone. April hesitated before stepping back out of the shelter of the doorway into the street. She wanted to gather her thoughts. It was easier to do so whilst remaining out of the line of sight. There was an empty pit, not just hunger, gnawing away in her stomach.

These two incidents left her feeling useless, bringing nothing to help, having not a crumb to offer her information-hungry desperate colleagues. This time the police were on the back foot and more difficulty would come when, once the public had overcome their initial shock and were wanting the police to explain their impotence, by then in the febrile atmosphere of rising public anger, looking for someone to blame – if not the perpetrators, then the police would do. She wondered why so often those in blue were the fall guys.

Then, unbidden, in the shadows, she felt PC Bob Steer's presence beside her. It made her feel tearful, but she held herself together. She knew he couldn't really be there, and she'd never believed in ghosts, but her mind needed to find some grain of comfort and the virtual presence of her past mentor, colleague and friend seemed to do that for her. Now Bob, in all this crap, what would you have told me to do? she asked herself.

He'd probably tell me to take a deep breath, insist I walk the whole thing through more slowly and give it time. Oh yes, and he always said, trust your instincts above everything. In that instant she wished this experienced copper hadn't left her. Hearing him speaking to her in the shadows wasn't enough, and yet it was enough. She definitely felt a fresh calm descend and her mood lift. Her own father had been a good policeman, and like Bob, they had both told her time and again that she would be a good one too.

April remained there standing still where she was, but now she stood more upright and felt taller. She carefully scanned the scene, slowly letting her eyes take in afresh what she might have missed in the haste of the morning so far. She stepped forward back on to the pavement again to get a better view of the scene.

The emergency services personnel, fire, ambulance and police were moving like hurrying ants, moving left and right, disappearing into the black hole that once marked the Guildhall's double door entrance, as others emerged from the dark, blinking into the light. Their was understandable anguish written on many faces.

Slowly, that was what Bob said. She looked left, then right, noticing the several routes, any one of which the bomber or bombers may have taken to get to their target. There was no news yet that it was a suicide bomb, so they could have exited the same way. Footpaths opposite offered one possible route, taking only a few paces to place their explosives and escape. Side streets a little further off offered another possibility. She made a quick call to her Police HQ to ask after the precise location of local CCTV cameras and then she knew where to look.

Only one walkway was unguarded, Martins Lane, a Cornish Pasty Shop Advertising board on the pavement marking the narrow entry off the High Street. It couldn't be more than fifty paces through to the multitude of access routes the other side.

Ignoring her orders to stay on the High Street, she moved right away from her post outside the 'The Turks Head' and into this pedestrianised way, taking her past a jeweller, a pasty shop, the Ship Inn and out toward Exeter cathedral.

Walking its length she observed there were no obvious CCTV cameras. It was so narrow, shop fronts and walls hemmed her in on both sides, only a corridor of grey sky in the narrow air above. At the far end, the entrance portico to a tiny old church had a small raised area of pavement – offering a precious sales pitch to a Big Issue seller. Once there she bent and pushed under the blue and white tape which another woman PC was guarding. She was through milling with the shifting watchful waiting crowds the other side.

April stopped again, to wait, to look, to listen, ignoring an enquiry from a man in a suit who wanted to get down Martins Lane to his office. Turning, she glanced down at the man sitting on a blanket with his Big Issues. Why was it, she wondered, that "Big Issue" sellers have dogs? The man and his dog filled the small set back area – a precious place for people in his situation.

The man had noticed her the instant she'd eyed him, if not before – he still had a large wad of "Big Issue" copies to sell and looked at the passing pedestrians with almost desperation to do some business. She wondered whether it was his addiction or the events of the morning hitting his sales that were hurting him most. Walking slowly toward him, wary of his dog, she decided to squat down at his level before speaking.

'Excuse me, Sir, can we do a deal?' she whispered, being sure she spoke loud enough that he'd hear. The man turned his head in expectation. She had his undivided attention.

'What's that?'

'Have you been here all morning?'

'Well, yes, and every day. Get here early, nowhere to sleep, catch the workers coming in, my best customers.'

'Splendid. Then I wonder if I could help you sell your remaining Big Issues. How about it?'

'Sure, sure,' he replied not knowing where this conversation was going, his face full of wary suspicion.

'If you tell me the story of your morning, starting from when you arrived, I'll buy all your stock.' She paused letting the possibilities sink in behind the man's still attentive eyes, before adding, 'all at full price. I'm not asking you to do anything other than give me five minutes of your time. Just tell me about the people who came by, heading toward the High Street and maybe back again. Can I sit down? Doesn't bite does he?' she asked as the dog began to face her as she got nearer.

'No, no problem. I heard what happened. Them poor kids. I'll tell you anything I can that might help.'

April realised the man already second guessed what she was after. He was nobody's fool and he had street wise craft running in his veins. She was close enough to him now to see his teeth were bad and his skin scabby and patchy.

'Talk me through the morning and tell me who passed by. Where do you want to start?'

'Give me a tenner to start me off.'

April pulled her pocket wallet out and pressed a folded ten pound note in his open hand, making sure as she did so, the man could see the other notes she was retaining.

'I'd do it for free, but I have needs to think about, know what I mean?' She nodded understandingly. 'Don't want to waste your time. I'll cut to the chase. We're both busy. What I say now I'll never repeat to anyone again. I don't do police statements, courts, all that kind of thing. Can't.'

'No problem,' she said reassuringly, though knowing it not to be true.

'There was one stranger who stood out. I know it was him. A stranger, not a shopper, not a business man. Looked at me strangely when I called out, like he feared he'd be me in another life. Some people react like that. Looked military to me, like the homeless ex-military men do out on the street. There's enough of 'em. You can't shake the institution of the forces, like a smell it is, carry it everywhere, advertising their presence. Your man was military.'

'What do you remember? Tell me how he looked and what he did,' she asked gently, trying to look calm and comfortable on the hard pavement, now inwardly excited by what he was saying.

'Dark smart outfit. Black shiny shoes. I see everyone's shoes. That's sure military give away that. They can never resist shining shoes. An obsession it is. An addiction. He was carrying a dark briefcase, no, tell a lie, it was a black suitcase he was carrying, by the side handle. It was odd from the moment I saw it. The case was heavy, I could tell. I like to know what people have, it's in my interest to know. It was precious to him. His hand gripped it tight, white knuckles, big hand, fancy ring, Nazi thing.' He stopped and laughed out loud. 'That's poetry.' He looked across at April for a reaction. She was looking at him, and he was hopeful he'd get his money from this copper.

'Fancy ring, Nazi thing,' she repeated smiling. 'What's that then?'

'Two angled SSs, small but unmistakable etchings on his ring. Nothing wrong with my eyes. See a lot from down here other people wouldn't notice. People write us off, don't notice us, rush by, but we notice them. Our lives depend on it. Well, he went down there, looked at me strangely when I called out, too much on his mind, I'd say,' he said, raising his arm, loosely waving it in the direction down Martins Lane from where April had just come.

'Some minutes later, maybe as long as fifteen, he came back. No case this time, only his black brolly, and he was moving quickly. Strange, all wrong, a fish out of water – noticed he was going the opposite way to everyone else – yes, a fish swimming against the morning tide.' He wiggled his hand, fishlike, as if April hadn't caught on.

'He was leaving the city, everyone else was coming in. Never looked at me, he did, but I saw him. His mind was preoccupied – that sort never notices the likes of me. Went down there.' This time with his "Big Issues" pile in his lap, he lifted his other arm and signalled down past the cathedral. The man looked in the direction he was pointing and fell quiet.

'Describe him, can you?'

'Smart, face straight from an army text book, squarish jaw, fit I'd say. Yes, and he stood upright, like he had to. Can't remember any more, but he'll be your man.' His hand

245

grabbed and then offered the "Big Issue" pile to April as if to conclude matters, but she hadn't finished.

'His jacket, or as you'd see from this level, his trousers?'

'Grey, dark trousers, definitely not blue. A kind of felt, dark grey, three quarter length jacket, smart. Not second hand.' He stopped speaking. He had nothing more to offer.

'Thanks. Really helpful. You always here?'

'Yes. Took ages to get this pitch. Don't want to lose it.'

'Here. Take this, and keep the "Big Issue". And thanks, thanks a lot,' she said meaning every word and passing another ten pounds into the man's grateful open palm.

April forced herself back to her feet. It must be so uncomfortable sitting down selling like this, she thought. The man's dog gave her a parting growl, before the man cuffed it into silence.

Two minutes later she had returned to her post outside "The Turks Head". No-one seemed to have noticed her absence. She knew she had precious information and had to pass it straight on.

Stepping back into the seclusion of the darkened doorway she made the call. The only change she made was to protect her source. He was simply referred to as 'a witness on the street'.

31

Harry's mother didn't often complain, but this particular Friday evening she wanted to know why Harry hadn't called to let her know what time he'd be back. It was very hard to keep a meal presentable, she told him, when she had no idea when he'd be stepping through the door and she wanted to watch her favourite soap on TV. If he still wanted the pie and mash it was being kept warm in the oven, as for herself, it was late, she was tired and heading for bed, but not before giving him an update on her own day.

'You've been on TV all day you have,' she told him. 'And the phone here hasn't stopped ringing. I had to call your mate Stu to come over and help take the calls there've been so many. He's left you a note somewhere. You'll find it. I might do your cooking and cleaning, but I can't do the secretary bit as well. You've become a right celebrity, can't say it's a good thing, too disruptive if you ask me.'

'There, there. Take yourself to bed, Mum. We all have to make sacrifices for the cause. Where's Dad?'

'He went up ages ago. He's had it up to here with all this election stuff. Be glad when it's all over, he says. Of course he's really pleased it's going so well for you, proud of you he is, but he says he won't let it interfere with his life. He's keeping the home fires burning, minding the business. We'll still have to pay the bills when all this is over with. He's very tired. Goodnight, dear.'

'Goodnight, Mum.'

Harry made his way into the kitchen. His Mother had left a couple of bottled beers on the kitchen table for him, a plate and cutlery out ready for his supper. Grabbing a tea towel, Harry reached into the oven and grabbed the metal tray. He hadn't realised how hungry he was and quickly devoured the over-cooked fish pie and mash. He left everything on the table knowing his Mum would clear it in the morning, then grabbed the beers, before making his way upstairs to his room.

He saw Stu's list of the day's calls lying on the bed, then eyed the now mended bedroom window and could see it had been freshly repainted, the slight odour of paint annoying him. They could have left a window open, he thought, as he dragged the curtains closed.

Hanging his jacket up, he flopped down on his bed, his mobile in one hand as he grabbed the TV remote in the other. The TV news channel murmured quietly, nothing new attracting his attention. There was catching up to be done. The few outstanding messages and e-mails on his mobile could wait. He posted another Tweet, resolved it would be his last one for Friday, and was startled to see just how many thousand new followers he had picked up in the course of just one day. He tapped out a post about expectation and doing one's duty, echoes of Drake's words once again coming to mind.

Then he picked up the open notepad on his bedside cabinet. It was Stu's writing, his message taking. Good old Stu, left him an update on all the calls he'd taken. A star marked anything Stu had thought was important. He cast his eye quickly down the front page and then flipped through the several sheets of notes. My, he had been busy. Only one thing caught his eye and Stu had underlined as well as starred it.

There'd been an anonymous caller, a man promising a generous helping hand to guarantee the campaign the success he felt it deserved. A large donation to the party would be made, but there was a condition, a meeting would first need to be arranged, between just the two of them, privately. He'd call again in the morning, at nine sharp. It sounded promising, but such calls, thought Harry, couldn't be relied on to deliver. He'd seen enough broken promises in the course of this election already, enough to fill the trunk at the end of his bed.

With his feet resting on the trunk, his thoughts turned again to his grandfather. For some reason he didn't understand, the very presence of the trunk, saved from the skip, containing the few possessions he had of his late grandfather, lifted his spirits. It was as if he knew his grandfather understood him and the election battle he was fighting. It was time to go through some of the remaining items inside, the things yet to be discovered. What better way was there to put the busy day behind him?

Harry swung his legs to the floor and placed his beer on the bedside cabinet before reaching to open the metal trunk. The lid fell back with a loud, unintended, metallic clunk. Reaching down, he pushed aside one of several bundles of the fascist news letter, with the headline banner title, 'The Western Fascist - The West is Best.' He'd look at those later.

Right now he was curious to discover what else there might be tucked away amongst these bundles of browning papers all tied up with ribbon. Some official looking envelopes looked interesting. Retrieving them, he carefully shut the lid, kicked off his shiny black shoes and lay back on the bed, his head on his pillow, and began fingering through them. He

249

could see they were all identical envelopes, each addressed to Mrs E McNamara, his grandmother.

The red ribbon bow undone, he released the top letter. It contained a single sheet. He pulled it out and held it up. To his surprise, it was a letter on prison stationery from Brixton Prison. Much more to his amazement, it had been written by his grandfather Michael to his grandmother Elsie. There was a prison censor stamp on the top, alongside which someone had initialled and put the date in pencil – 23 June 1940. Gripped by what he was holding, he read the pencil written letter slowly, holding the letter to catch the light, to help him decipher the smudged and ambiguous words; he so wanted to read it aright.

My dearest Elsie,
I hope you are keeping well in these difficult circumstances and not getting too much grief because of me.
I find myself detained under Defence Regulation 18B because some civil servant somewhere thinks I am 'capable of prejudicial acts against the state.' You above anyone truly know, I love my adopted country, but I can't say a lot, everything is subject to the censors and it is only now I've been allowed to send this.
The British Union of Fascists, well we dropped the Fascist bit some time ago, we've been continuing with our 'Peace Campaign' best we can from inside, though in reality we're pretty well shut down. Our members, not so long ago in their many thousands, have disappeared like swallows in winter. It's the end for the BU I think. Many of our old friends don't like the new Peace Campaign policy.
You won't believe this, how ironic life is. Now that I've fallen out with the man, I find I have Sir Oswald Mosley sleeping under the same roof as myself, but we have not yet spoken. If we did meet, I think we'd only argue, so it's probably just as well.
Reckon Cable Street, back in '36 was the beginning of our undoing, rightly so. It was after that debacle, many blackshirts, including

250

myself, thought again about our politics. I made the mistake of sticking with them, hoping for peace with Germany, when deep down I knew the BU were no good. Where does hating people thought to be different ever get us? Before Cable Street I never realised people's eyes could be so full of ignorant hate. All I wanted was to make the world a better place. A bit of national pride and belief instead of apathy could have done a lot for us.

I'm OK, get my ration, but nobody likes us. Hoping soon to make my case to be free and come home, but no-one is rushing to listen to the likes of us, so may be a while yet. It grieves me not to be around to help you in these times and I fear for your safety. Don't worry about me, I'm good. Look after our darling baby, young Patrick's a lively one.

All my love to you both,
Michael

Harry was spellbound, gripped by what he was reading. Wow, his grandfather had been imprisoned for his fascism and interned in the war. He'd done his duty. This was a family secret, something no-one had ever talked about. Harry felt confused. He turned the letter over in his hand. It had to be genuine.

He lay back, still clutching this one letter, the others he put down to one side to be read at another time. He couldn't help but cast his eye down the letter again, but this time what had niggled him on first reading shouted at him on the second.

Michael McNamara had fallen out with Mosley in the end, but looks like he was disillusioned with the cause well before that, he thought. I'm not surprised he fell out with Mosley – the man was a maverick, more show than substance. He glanced up at the poster still above his bed and the more he thought, the more Mosley looked like some pantomime character. It felt depressing to think his grandfather had ended up a loser. He'd sold out on the fascist ideal – that was such a shock, even a betrayal. Perhaps that was why no-one had told him, that and going to prison, that's why his Dad never engaged in politics; the shame and ignominy of it all. It all made sense to him now.

Then he remembered the question hurled at him so unexpectedly at the end of the Businessmen's Breakfast meeting earlier in the campaign. What had the man said? He, Harry, was the spitting image of his grandfather. Recalling Michael personally as an ardent right-winger, he saw Harry as offering the same kind of leadership needed today. But this letter tells that Michael had a change of heart, he fell out with Mosley and the Battle of Cable Street was the watershed moment though he took his time to see it. Was Arnold a fascist or anti-fascist? What did he mean calling Michael a traitor?

Though it seemed like a different age, it was in fact only the previous evening Cherry Thomas had interviewed him here at home about his grandfather and then thrown a bombshell saying she'd heard he was a traitor to the blackshirt cause. Maybe she'd heard something from someone after all. She never revealed her sources, nor did she substantiate what she had alleged, but the letter in his right hand confirmed, if true, her story. Harry shuddered at the thought that his grandfather had betrayed the movement in his day and it unsettled him to have his beloved grandfather's character so besmirched.

He was tired, it had been an exhausting day. Beer and food were having their effect and he needed to sleep, another busy day of electioneering awaited him on Saturday morning. A welcome outing and useful publicity at his second home, with the Rovers match in the afternoon. Then, in the evening a hustings meeting had been arranged, his first chance to counter his political adversaries in live debate – the thought left him feeling unusually uncertain of himself.

By now the call to sleep was winning. Throwing his grandfather's letters back in the trunk and quietly closing the lid, he resigned himself to the overwhelming pull of sleep when he could dream dreams of his own.

32

April needed to act. She knew she had vital information, but how to tell it to sceptical colleagues? Would she be believed or worse still, be ridiculed? Already she and her Prevent team had given no warnings of what was to come and since the incidents, she'd offered no clues as to who the terrorists might be; now she had information which, the more she thought about it, could be seen at the station as completely the creation of one of the least reliable witnesses this new transferee could have found. Nonetheless, her instinct was telling her this was important and impelling her to act. So she called up her Prevent lead, Rob Callaghan. Although she'd found him to be a decent enough guy so far, this, she thought, will test things.

'Hi Governor, April here. I've just picked up some new information that ought to be fed into the investigation.'

'Source?'

'A man on the street, on the one pathway to the Guildhall, a route, to my eyes any road, not obviously covered by the local authority's CCTV.'

'I'm listening, and for the record, as you know, this call is being recorded – ready to feed in?'

April told the story as she had been told it, omitting only the identity of her informant. After she had finished, he politely thanked her, then asked an obvious question.

'When everyone thinks it was Muslim inspired extremism, unless this guy is a white revert, this goes against the tide – tell you the truth, not what I was expecting, but it's just that which makes it sound a lead worth following up. There's been so little for us to go on so far, in spite of an appeal to the public for any information they can give us. Counter-terrorism has, between ourselves, been useless. What you say is as good as it gets, we'll follow it up.'

'Thank you Sir.'

'I'll get the people on the street to get straight on to the local shops where your sighting was made. We've already picked up the CCTV from the High St shops in the vicinity, the guys are looking at what we've got right now. I'll get them to go back over it again and look for the guy in a three quarter grey jacket with a hand held dark case. Shouldn't take long, we've already isolated and captured the critical time frame. People often forget retail outlets and other places have CCTV too and more often than not it's pointing toward the door and may just catch our man with a case and a brolly.' He paused as if thinking.

'I want you in on this April. We should be able to seize any new CCTV footage in that pedestrianised passage and get it back here within the hour. But I want you back here too, pronto, report to Gold Room on arrival, right.'

'Yes Sir, right away.' April felt a mixture of relief and apprehension. Her instincts told her that she'd done exactly as she should, for the moment her source hadn't been compromised, but there was still the anxiety that what she'd been told was in reality nothing, a dead end that might come back to ridicule her and the Prevent team in the eyes of her already disappointed colleagues.

Before leaving her 'Turks Head' position, she told the commander in the High St she'd been ordered back to Gold

Room at HQ. He was so preoccupied, he hadn't noticed her earlier movements and temporary disappearance and cursorily waved her off. She quickly found a waiting car in Southernhay and was driven away at speed the short ride back to base.

In a room of maybe as many as thirty people, the Gold Room operational centre was a hive of purposeful activity. All were beginning to try to assemble the foundations of a major investigation, building from the tentative facts around the scenarios the case suggested, trying to bring a semblance of meaning and order to the morning's as yet unexplained attacks. A live TV news channel occupied a screen next to an adjacent live police screen. Whenever they wanted, they could link the two.

Gold Room was insulated from the mounting public fear outside, guarded against media intrusion. As she entered, she immediately spotted her sergeant Emma Stirling, bent over a screen, who simultaneously eye-balled her and waved her over. She pointed in front of her.

'Cornish pasty shop, even they had CCTV – police motorcyclist brought it in – look at this.'

It was a surprisingly sharp image and April studied it intently like a woman possessed.

'Can we move the clip forward and back, slowly, real slow. I want to check. There, there, focus in on his hand. See, see that is exactly how my contact described him – a hand with a silver ring with a Nazi SS etching.'

'The etching's a matter of conjecture – it's too grainy too see. But I want you to see the next clip. It's the clincher. See, same guy, eleven minutes later, comes back the way he came, but without his case, only his brolly. I've had our explosives boffins assess what they think the mix was for the Guildhall explosion and give me its size and weight – it's possible – the case fits. At this point I want to move two doors away, to the public house camera.' There was a pause. Then as the next clip rolled, the man's side on face came properly into focus for the first time. The square chin. Quite possibly ex-military, thought April.

'This is the best image we have of him so far. Doesn't match anyone on our files yet so far as we know. Search is ongoing. I've already sent out for a requisition of all other possible private CCTV footage – might give us more, but what we have is very useful.'

'But can't people refuse to hand CCTV over?' said April, worried at not being able to find out more.

'Not a problem, they always cooperate. Either they give us the tapes or they watch us march off with their entire system. I've never known anyone refuse to cooperate when the facts are explained,' she said with a knowing smile. And to be frank, everyone is so upset at what has happened they want to help.

'I need to know more about your informant,' said her sergeant as they stepped away.

'Can't tell you officially, he won't testify, just call it street talk I picked up and followed up,' she told her – that seemed enough to stop any further questions for now.

'Well, a word of advice. Inspector Rob might ask for more on your source – it's his call. But be prepared. He's talking to counter-terrorism at the moment, but keeps looking in to see what we've got.'

In the lull that followed, and with, as yet, no sight of Inspector Rob Callaghan, April wandered over to the coffee making area, a hastily set up table, and poured herself a mug of welcome coffee. As she stood, pondering the situation, she reflected on the direction things were taking, wondering what she should do next. She then moved to gaze upon a white board, centrally placed on which various scribbles, boxes and lines had been made. Her Sarge, Emma came across to stand beside her.

'We're using what we've had from you already. The images we have, they've been forwarded to counter-terrorism; we're also looking for facial recognition, and the profilers are on the case too. We'll get this bastard, children on a school trip to the Guildhall, how low can they get?'

'Is anyone thinking what their strategy might be? I mean two incidents, got to be linked don't you think? I can't see anything that's come in of any use from Plymouth yet.'

'It's desperate there. Not safe, not even sure if the sniper is still taking people down. All our searching and intelligence here doesn't suggest there were more devices planted in Exeter, but in Plymouth it keeps getting worse, twenty one casualties so far. The parliamentary candidate, Harry McNamara, had got himself back there pretty smartish. He was talking to the press and making the most of it. Look, when bring your coffee and give me a hand viewing the other CCTV tapes we've got, two eyes are better than one.'

As Emma moved back to her Gold Room workstation, April hung back. She'd had a thought. The reason she had been sent from the Metropolitan Police to Devon was because of Harry McNamara and the pending by-election, now only just days away; she wondered whether there was some kind of a link between what was happening and Harry? He had certainly begun to swing the voters behind him if the polls were anything to go by and increasing public fears were only going to serve his cause.

Every time she checked the news, there he was, his extreme right wing message no longer barely disguised. Harry seemed to be milking every opportunity to stir up xenophobic, Islamophobic reaction. Public sympathy was undoubtedly sliding in his direction, but none of this had a real connection with these two terrorist incidents, or had it?

For now, April kept her thoughts to herself, she'd already trusted her instincts once today, that felt like enough.

33

Saturday morning and Harry woke with a start. Hell, he was still fully clothed and his mouth tasted sour and dry. Pulling himself off his bed, he glanced at his bedside clock, then calmed himself. He chided himself, he'd let himself go, a slip he didn't want to repeat – still no harm done this time. He stripped off and threw on the power shower. Ten minutes later he felt a lot better. Still naked he began lifting some weights in front of his full length mirror, convinced by his athletically good looks and strong barrel-chest frame he hadn't let himself go too much.

Physical exercises completed, he threw his dirty clothes from the bed to the floor for his Mum to pick up later, found himself a fresh outfit, shirt and tie, and looking immaculate to his eyes, he was ready for the new day. Throwing open his bedroom door, he yelled out.

'Mum, top of the morning! Coffee in five.'

He only pulled his door closed again once he heard movement downstairs – when he knew she'd heard him. Picking up his mobile, he hurriedly plugged it in to charge up, realising he'd forgotten to do so overnight and he'd never get through the day with it unless he gave it a good hour before leaving the house.

After double-checking his day's programme, he realised he'd need to grab an hour to properly brief himself for the hustings to be held that evening at the civic centre. Cathy's efficiently laid out campaign diary spreadsheet showed the Archdeacon of Plymouth was offering himself as honest broker, an unbiased referee to chair proceedings.

Thinking about Newsnight and Question Time on TV, the only real debates he could recall having ever seen, and then only rarely, Harry knew he'd have to step up his game for tonight. He laughed out loud as he thought of the rings he would run round the hapless Archdeacon – a dove among hawks. This evening wouldn't work with sound bites alone, he needed to win arguments in the political arena, so he was reassured to see a team effort, a council of war already in the diary for this morning to line up the ducks. He hoped his mates had put some serious thinking into it, but he knew it was up to him to shape everything, pull it all together.

He began calling up his troops, just to remind them they were expected, flicking on his TV as he did so. He wanted them all at the house by ten, not messing about and drifting in late as they would do if left to themselves. He set about issuing the "Team Harry" summonses even as he watched the extended news live broadcasts from outside Exeter Guildhall and Plymouth's Drakes Circus Shopping Mall. Yesterday had been the South West's "Black Friday" – so they were describing it. It made miserable viewing, except for Harry.

He'd just finished making his calls when his Mum tapped quietly on his door, before walking in with a tray – coffee, boiled eggs and soldiers, all neatly in place, complete with ironed linen cloth and a napkin in Harry's personalised silver ring. Ignored, she left it on his bedside table as another call came in. Who was this? – caller identity withheld. It made him hesitate, but as he reached for his coffee, he decided to take it anyway.

'Harry McNamara?' said a male voice, enquiringly.

'Yes, speaking. How can I help?'

'We've been following your campaign with great interest and have decided to offer our help.'

'Most kind. We need all the support we can get. Thank you,' said Harry, now reaching for his first soldier and looking to dip it in the soft boiled egg. As he listened to what the mysterious caller said next he didn't get it back to his mouth and yellow egg dripped on his bedclothes.

'There will be news in the media tomorrow that will make it clear that renegade IS returnees together with active local Muslim support were behind yesterday's attacks in Exeter and Plymouth. We thought you should hear this news from your friends before the media get it and get all excited. I'm calling to tell you we'll help you have the chance to be one step ahead of the political furore that is about to follow; and of course one step ahead of your political rivals.'

'Are you sure about this?' Harry said, thinking he needed to be persuaded.

'I'll send you the statement that IS are releasing in the next ten minutes. We intercepted a pre-release copy. Our concern is that there is an appropriate political response to these developments and we are convinced that amongst all the candidates standing, only you, Harry McNamara and your British First Democratic Party can provide this.'

'Of course,' said Harry.

'We want to support you in your constituency and in our country's hour of need. I've been asked to personally call and meet you face to face with an outline of the support we are prepared to offer and present you with the first in a series of monetary gifts to finance your political work. I assure you it is very generous and with absolutely no strings attached. I tried to call yesterday and apologise for the urgency, but are you free at 11am?' There was quiet as Harry tried to quickly assess what was being offered and manage his diary plans.

'Yes, I should be able to bring my earlier meeting to a close by then or very soon after.' Harry was beginning to feel uncomfortable. The man wasn't asking him the usual questions – his e-mail, his address…

'I'll call at your home. I know where you live,' said the man, the way he said the words almost sounding sinister to his ear. Harry felt a sudden chill in the air, but dismissed it as nothing than early morning blues after his chaotic start.

'Who are you?' Harry remembered to ask, trying to get a grip of a conversation in which the man had not introduced or said anything about himself or who he represented.

'Time for that when I knock on your front door. Call me Carl,' he said, and then he had gone.

Harry looked down at the egg on his bed and lifted his head and his voice – 'Mum, you'll need to bring up a cloth,' he shouted before turning his attention back to the stories on the TV.

A few minutes later and he knew from what reporters were saying that nothing was being said about who was to blame for yesterday's terrorist attacks. Apparently the police were keeping a lid on what they knew urging against unwarranted speculation in order to protect their lines of enquiry. Too many times in the past, information had been released early which then hampered subsequent investigation.

Over the next half-hour Harry found himself glancing at his e-mail inbox whilst keeping half an eye on the TV. Then, as his party colleagues began to arrive, the promised e-mail from Carl dropped into his inbox with a disconcerting ping.

Staring at it sitting there, he realised the path of his campaign had suddenly got more complicated than he had anticipated. Control was slipping away from him and he didn't like it.

34

Saturday morning, just after 9am, Adam and Raqiyah were lying in bed side by side, awake, silent, and both lost in deep thought, the events of the past twenty four hours weighing heavily on both their minds.

'Want a coffee?' asked Adam suddenly, getting out of bed and moving off toward the kitchen. 'We need clear heads and there's a lot we need to talk about.'

'Yeah I was just thinking the same. OK, I'll take mine black, not too strong, mind,' said Raqiyah pulling herself into an upright sitting position, readjusting the pillow behind her head.

When Adam reappeared with two steaming mugs five minutes later, they looked at each other – there was still sunshine in both their eyes and they each recognised it – somehow that helped make everything bearable. Adam passed Raqiyah her coffee and placed himself back beside her. She was the first to speak.

'Yesterday was so unreal. We need to untangle what actually happened. We ended up in town just after an explosion at the Guildhall, and then in an unexpected fracas with Harry McNamara, the result of which was you ended up on the wrong side of an argument with a policeman, a situation Harry totally set up,' she gently recalled in a soft voice.

'Don't remind me. I still feel humiliated by the experience. I walked right into that one. What do you make of what happened in Plymouth, those shootings after the Guildhall explosion?' asked Adam, trying to move the conversation on.

'I think they've got to be linked. When did anything ever happen like this before, let alone two attacks in the South West on the same day? No, the two are connected,' said Raqiyah staring into her coffee.

'Do you think that IS have got a nearby cell, an operational terrorist outfit? There have been warnings for months that returning IS trained westerners will be infiltrating Britain to return and wage war on home soil now there is no future for them in the Middle East, with the Caliphate finished, done for. No-one's saying anything on the media – it's as if the security forces and police haven't a clue, or they're keeping their cards close to their chest as they hunt the perpetrators down. Guess they don't want to alert the people they're tracking. What do you think? Have IS got in under the wire?'

Adam paused and took a sip of his steaming coffee. 'When you went to the mosque, to the women's meeting yesterday afternoon, what were they saying, they must have talked about it? Surely?'

'It was my first meeting with them. There were around fifteen women, most like myself; students or migrants feeling in need of contact with others who understood the world of Islam we had all left behind. Actually, it was very supportive and helpful. There's something to be said for a strong sisterhood.'

'But did they say anything useful? I mean about what's going on in society – yesterday – what did they think?' asked Adam.

'Their afternoon programme was very structured, overly so if you ask me, and it was only when we broke for refreshments we talked about it; even though it was obviously the one thing at the forefront of everyone's mind. The women who'd been in Exeter longest, the ones more in touch with the mosque leadership and trustees, they were as alarmed as the rest of us. The question was asked, not by me, as to whether there were any radicals linked with or even visiting the mosque.'

'Are there?'

'None of them thought there had been anyone unusual around and were saying the men folk were as fearful as they were as to community repercussions against them for what was happening. To tell you the truth, ninety per cent of the conversation was about what all this meant for their own safety and the security of the mosque and their families. Someone suggested setting up a hate crime reporting and monitoring centre at the mosque, but no-one agreed to do anything. I told them about the abuse we had coming back from the pub the other night,' Raqiyah added smiling, 'though I didn't say we'd been to the pub.'

'So no obvious worries of possible links with terrorists so far as you could tell. They could be wrong of course, but assuming they're not, that means there could be another explanation for what is happening. The options are – a highly disturbed individual, like a mentally ill guy who's left the army with a grudge, or a splinter IRA faction, or a right winger, or a policeman who's angry with the Home Secretary or ...' Adam extending six fingers to illustrate each possibility.

'Now you're being ridiculous. What usually happens is that someone likes to claim responsibility for it.'

'Well, no-one has, have they?' Raqiyah's voice was rising, 'Even if they did, they'd claim it was them anyway and you can't believe them – why should we?'

'Whoever's done it, for whatever motive, they're helping Harry McNamara top the polls and head straight for parliament. Now who would want that? It would be too far-fetched to think the terrorists and Harry are working together wouldn't it?'

'I don't know. Extremists aren't too fussy about who they side with, so long as they can polarise society and get a reaction. The more fear and panic, the more reaction, the more instability, the greater chance they have of success – it's their only way,' she calculated.

'Do you think these attacks are linked with the election? It's a thought, isn't it? Harry is an evil right wing extremist. We know he doesn't care how low he stoops to further his cause. He's just like the other lot, IS. I feel exactly the same loathing for both,' said Adam.

'But he's right wing, extreme right wing Harry is, and he couldn't be responsible, we saw him in his suit. And he was in Exeter when things kicked off in Plymouth, we saw him.'

Things went silent between them; this unresolved puzzle gave the bedroom a claustrophobic feel and Adam began to feel uncomfortable. He'd got better at identifying when anxiety attacks were coming on, so he began to do some slow breathing, calming relaxation exercises. Raqiyah saw what he was doing and reached to take his hand. They sat quietly, side by side, for maybe ten minutes or more. It was Adam who spoke next.

'Though we can't place Harry in the terrorism, someone who sympathises with him, someone who wants to see him elected, could be trying to swing things his way. If they were, the tide is certainly moving in his direction.'

'Maybe we need to have another chat with April, what do you think?'

'Good idea, I'll call her,' said Adam, reaching for his mobile. It took a minute to find her number again, but once found, he immediately called it. She picked up.

'Hi April, Adam Taylor here. Been thinking, having ideas. Any chance of Raqiyah and I meeting up with you for coffee again? It's nothing definite, just want to share ideas we've had and we'd like to talk with you again.' He heard April hesitate at the other end.

'Sorry, I realise you must be really busy at the moment,' he added.

'No problem, I'd like to,' she said, 'How about same place as before, at 11 o-clock. I'll call you if I can't make it. I have to go, see you then.'

Adam turned to Raqiyah. She looked sad, even tearful.

'What is it?' he said, putting an arm around her.

'The meeting at the university. You know it got cancelled yesterday because of the chaos, well they called me again last night. It's now going to be held on Monday. I'm terrified they might send me home. The Vice-Chancellor's office told me again to look at Section 5 of the General Regulations for Students, the bit about, "bringing the name of the University

269

into disrepute." I have. I think they can do what they want with me. I think they'll make me go, especially after what happened yesterday.'

'We'll fight them together. You've stood by me, you're allowed a friend. Before we go and see April, let's look at the regulations together and then ring the Students' Union about representation.'

'I hadn't thought of that – the Students' Union. I'd be interested to know what appeal process might be open to me and whether I might finish my course. It's so unfair, so totally unfair,' she said rather more loudly than she usually did. She immediately telephoned a friend in the Students' Union and told her what she was facing. The possibility of support didn't sound very promising.

It was eleven exactly when they arrived back in the High St, entering a café just yards from the barricaded section in front of the Guildhall. A little way off they could see police officers guarding the site from the crowds of curious spectators and other investigators; people with clipboards or cameras in hand and white suits as uniforms. There were still two fire engines quietly parked in attendance.

They spotted her. April was not in uniform, had a coffee already and was sitting at a table with two empty chairs. After they'd picked up their own drinks, they joined her. Adam was surprised how easy April was to talk to. She was the kind of person one naturally wanted to confide in her, it surprised him. Soon they had shared their ideas, views that April listened to extremely intently.

'I can't tell you how the investigation is going. I'm sure you understand that, but what I can say is that what you are telling me has many resonances with one of the many lines of enquiry we are making. My own role is as part of a reinforced Prevent team, that's to help stop people being radicalised or prevent groups or mosques from becoming vulnerable to radical infiltrators or ideologies. I see myself as working with people in the community. I'm not counter-terrorism – using intelligence to break down doors and intercept extremists, all that kind of thing. I see myself as a community policing person, hope that's clear?'

She got nods from both.

'But when something like yesterday happens, everyone gets roped in to build a team to catch the suspects, whilst reassuring the public that life can go on normally. I've even got to be part of the duty football match team down at Plymouth Rovers' ground this afternoon. In fact I've really got to be going, but look I think what you've told me is really helpful, it opens up some interesting possibilities as to what lies behind recent events. We'll talk further, soon,' and with that she got up from the table and dashed outside.

'What do you think? I kinda think she thought we were on to something. If anyone can, she ought to be able to see the links we are talking about,' said Raqiyah.

'I agree. I think we leave it with her now. What else can we do?' Raqiyah assented. They'd finished their drinks and Adam was looking at his phone.

'Want to go to the match she mentioned? Forgot to mention Bilal and Sophie have invited us. They're pressing for a decision. There's a student coach, leaves at 1pm?' He could read reticence in her face. 'See it as part of your Adam led integration programme,' he jested, 'come on, try a game, it's only football. They want us to come.'

'I thought in England football was more serious than anything else,' she retorted, as they both agreed to give Bilal a call to see if they'd still be able to join them. For some reason they decided to call and see if Clive was also around. A few minutes later, everything was fixed. Clive was coming too, and all five had their afternoon out finalised.

Leaving the café, turning away from the Guildhall, they began wandering back. It was only then Raqiyah wondered whether she'd made a wise decision to go back to Plymouth. She touched her veiled head where the bruise still felt tender and though she didn't want to show it, her inner apprehensions grew with every passing minute.

35

Harry opened the e-mail Carl had promised. Before opening the single attachment, he decided to click on the name 'Carl' to see what e-mail address he had sent it from. It gave nothing away. It came from a Dutch server address, after a meaningless letter and number e-mail name tag. He opened the attachment; quickly skim reading a diatribe from IS addressed to the unfaithful non-believers. The short message declared that the infidel would suffer at the hand of the jihadists – the fight for the Caliphate was not over, the march to triumph and ultimate victory would be theirs.

As Harry scanned the text he remained unconvinced by what he read. It didn't persuade, it was just empty hyperbole, hollow rhetoric, words from nowhere. Yet he couldn't deny there had been an attack in Exeter and shootings in Plymouth – perhaps it was true. Who was he to judge? Well, this Carl guy had some explaining to do when he came at eleven. He decided it was prudent to keep the e-mail and mystery visitor to himself for the present and switched his attention to setting an agenda for the more pressing matter of his imminent meeting with his three party colleagues.

A thought lifted his spirits, for he knew that his campaign had made impressive inroads on the position of his political rivals. Hadn't these terrorist events, whoever was to blame, played right into his lap? But wasn't it also true, that it had been entirely up to him to make political capital from it – the others had been wrong-footed and shown themselves to be out of touch.

He decided that there was still more advantage to be taken and in offering a consistent hard line anti-migrant, anti-

Muslim platform, backed now with pledges of substantial additional funding for the police, he was convinced he could gain even further political gain. He could feel people were frightened and wanted a charismatic strong leader to deal with the threats they now faced. It suited his natural style.

A few minutes later Harry opened the front door. Stu arrived first. His eye fell on the phone call list Harry was holding, the one he had left out for him the previous evening, glad to see Harry had indeed picked it up. Then Cathy and Phil almost immediately followed and strode in alongside each other, leaving Harry thinking they had got their heads together beforehand – he couldn't work out whether that was a good thing or not – he'd have to wait and see what they came up with. He opened the front room door to call to the kitchen.

'Mum, be a dear and get these good people something to drink, would you. Orders please,' demanded Harry, turning to his colleagues, before shouting, 'Four coffees, two black, two white. Can you find some biscuits? Not sure they'll all have had breakfast,' he jibed.

'Welcome everyone. I've got another meeting, a private unscheduled session with a possible financial backer of our campaign in an hour's time. I think he'd prefer to keep his anonymity, so I'd like us to finish before ten to eleven. We should be able to deal with business before then. Short meetings mean we focus down and work harder.'

'I've got two things to check through with you. First, this afternoon's match and half-time community award presentation – that's been your bag, and Cathy, I'll need you to brief me on that. Second, we've got the first big hustings tonight in the Plymouth Council Chamber. Phil, I know you've been over there and spoken to the Archdeacon who will be chairing it – but I need to have some intelligence on the format, before I can begin thinking through how to play the likely questions. I'll need to hear from you Stu. You read things well on the ground and I need to connect with the people on the ground tonight, people watching and reporting need to hear everyone cheering for us.'

The drinks arrived, silently produced on a metal tray by Harry's Mum who backed away and quickly and wordlessly disappeared. Harry couldn't quite work out whether his Mum was an embarrassment or a help on the occasions.

A lively conversation followed at the end of which Harry felt confident that the day's events would be his for the taking. Mindful that the number of active campaigning days was dwindling fast, he asked Cathy to come up with a revised diary plan to make the most use of the time that was left to him. It was then he realised that Phil and Cathy had indeed met earlier as she handed him a draft schedule for him to look through and give her feedback on later. Harry could see Phil's ideas permeating the programme. No harm in that he thought, and he lifted his head and thanked them both, praising their efforts, before ensuring they all left promptly at ten fifty.

In the few minutes he had to wait until Carl arrived, he felt distinctly uncomfortable. He sensed an unsettling power play at work which he hadn't got to the bottom of. Carl was not straightforward, Harry's nose, his sixth sense in noticing these things never failed and his antennae were humming in warning. He knew he had to be on his guard. Greater politicians than he had been undone by a wrongly judged offer or a dubious social acquaintance. He was glad it was private.

Moments later, Harry had come to a decision. He decided, not really knowing why, to call his Mum and tell her she was to stay in the front room whilst his next visitor came to see him. She asked if it was all right if she cleaned the silver whilst she sat in, it had been a long time since it was last done. Harry grunted. She took that to be a yes and scuttled off to find polish and cloths.

At precisely eleven, the front door bell rang. He let his Mum answer it as he glanced quickly round the front room to carefully choose where best to sit and where he would place this mysterious visitor, Carl.

Carl came in, the man had presence and stood in front of Harry's favourite arm chair before Harry had a chance to direct him. Harry was immediately wrong-footed, but let it pass. Carl, after all, had something to offer, including a gift to his campaign. When his Mum followed him into the room, she resumed her polishing as if they weren't there. Harry offered Carl the choice of tea or coffee. Carl declined. His Mum's attention returned to her polishing, Carl looking at her with a hint of amusement. He turned back to Harry, now instinctively feeling he didn't much like this man.

'Nice to meet you at last, Harry McNamara,' offered Carl cooly. 'I haven't much time, so I'll get straight to the point. Your election campaign is going well and attracting a building body of support – congratulations. It's all heading in the right direction, some say turned a corner in local politics, and will even cause a major upset.'

'Yes,' interrupted Harry, also choosing not to sit down, not wishing to be at any more a disadvantage than he felt he already was. Harry watched as Carl proffered the large white envelope he was carrying.

'Here's an anonymous ten grand donation to party funds. No receipt needed, no acknowledgment, no audit trail, just for you to do with entirely as you wish – of course it's given in a spirit of our trust in you.'

He passed the envelope to Harry, who took it, feeling the wads of notes inside, but with a sense of deep misgiving, knowing control of the situation and much more was passing from him to this stranger as he did so. Being bought off felt cheap. He had no doubt that in that second a boundary had been crossed, a threshold he couldn't name, and he knew inside himself there was no going back.

'Great, thanks, no worries, pass on my deep gratitude, I'm sure you'll let me know who to write and thank and if they need more from me,' he said, passing the envelope straight to his Mum who'd stopped her polishing and was looking up.

'Hold on to this for me. More party funds,' he said cheerfully by way of explanation, knowing immediately his Mum could see straight through him and didn't like what she saw. As ever, she said nothing to her son. She simply put the envelope on the sideboard, pushing it out of the way with her cleaning cloth as if it were so much more dirt.

'They will need more,' Carl added. 'We're both men who understand there is no such thing as a free lunch. But, I'm sure it will all feel very natural, make perfect sense. It'll only be what you really want anyway – for our mutual benefit. You may not have realised until now, the British First Democratic Party has friends all over, in the UK, yes and also across the world. You've made a name for yourselves as a party of our time, you've successfully made a connection with your people in their need and set a clear vision for a better, purer world and we all like that, like it a lot.'

'Don't mind if I ask, but who's the "we"?' Harry asked, but Carl carried on, apparently without noticing Harry had spoken.

'Don't expect you realise what a positive impact you've had, Harry, but you have, and that's why I'm here, here to help. My people are impressed, and they expect to see your campaign pick up further still in this election end game and anticipate you will get elected. During the election process and when you get to parliament you will need more party help. No offence, but your Cathy, Stu and Phil are local grassroots; they won't do London, national politics, it's out of their depth. But that's where we can help – people, funds, office, flat, expenses account. You name it, what you need, no problem. You've earned it Harry, it's like, you've almost made it, but not quite.'

Harry didn't recall telling Carl his party colleague's names. 'What do you mean, "not quite"?' he replied.

'I'd like your dear Mother to go busy herself. I'm sure she has things to do. There are some things I need to say before I leave, but only to you, if you understand me,' Carl said, turning to Harry's Mum and rather than offering her his hand, just appearing to do so, he made a gesture that unmistakably said – it's time for you to move.

In truth she didn't want to be there and she required no added comment from Harry as to what to do next. She got up and without a word made her way to the back of the house. In her absence, Harry was left feeling strangely vulnerable. He felt even less secure as Carl proceeded to put gloves on – such a bizarre action.

'What a nice lady. In fact what a nice set up you have here Harry. Your Dad running the family business, a reputable firm, doing well I hear, employing a lot of local people, and such a solid set of accounts. But you know, how quickly things can change, Harry – in an instant. Think of those poor people in the Guildhall – boom!' His raised voice made Harry unintentionally take a step back. 'Good life, bad life, even no life – life's so fickle. Think on it Harry.' He paused, his dark blue eyes looking coldly into Harry's face, before continuing.

'Think nearer home Harry, think of the sniper yesterday at the shops. Pop, Pop – Pop, Pop,' he said almost spitting out the words. Harry noticed for the first time that as he spoke Carl's body language accurately mimicked the professional soldier sniper pose. In that second, Harry knew Carl had inadvertently slipped up, given something vital away. Harry glimpsed it and that fed his confidence just when it was almost at rock bottom.

'I like a military man,' said Harry, his words driven by instinct.

As the words came out he immediately recognised the slightest change in Carl's demeanour, a flicker in his eye, as if some slight irritation had distracted his line of thought.

'Who were you with?' Harry quickly followed up, trying to take some control.

'That's classified, the less you know… just focus Harry. You're not stupid. Think about the impact on your campaign of recent events. You're the winner, Harry. The attacks aren't over yet, believe me. Boom, Pop, what next? How about something even bigger?'

'What?' said Harry in puzzlement, beginning to realise the concerted terrorism campaign was deliberately enacted to serve his own political cause.

'Come on, you know what the score is. You know what terror and fear do Harry. You know the lessons of history – it's all about power. Those who exercise it take control. This is all about you and, like I said, our efforts together.'

'You know what this is Harry?' He pulled out a pistol from inside his jacket. 'I'm sure you do. It's loaded. And you'll know what this is too?' He pulled out a silencer and clicked it in place. 'And you'll know what I mean when I say I'm not messing about Harry,' he said menacingly. Harry wondered if this Carl was mad and began fearing for his own safety. He was rooted to the spot, powerless, his pulse rate soaring, standing, waiting. This was beyond a scrape on the football terraces or jumping a couple of Muslim geezers in Istanbul – this was dealing with the devil and all his works.

A step forward and the muzzle was cold on Harry's temple. He heard as well as felt the knock of the gun against his skull. 'Now listen carefully, Mr Harry McNamara. I don't mess around. I need you to know that we're counting on you. The stakes are high, so high we will destroy you and all you hold dear should you fail us. But don't read me wrong, the rewards are really what we all want. Isn't that so? I'm sure you want that too. Do we understand each other?'

'Absolutely,' Harry said, 'we understand each other.' Harry realised this could be no more than show so long as he played along with Carl and his nerves began to settle.

'Good,' said Carl stepping back, removing the silencer and putting his weapon away. 'It is so important you understand the full seriousness of this election and just how much is being invested in it. Your right wing friends will go to any length to ensure your victory. Believe me, nothing is too much. Just be sure you stay on message like you are doing and as events around you drive the voters into your hands you hear them, you welcome them, and you offer them the homeland they deserve. Time I went. Discretion's the name of the game Harry. Total discretion, and look, don't worry about how you can contact me – I know where you live.'

With that meaningful remark, Carl turned, his gloved hand reaching for the door. 'I'll see myself out,' he said, and in an instant he had gone, leaving Harry cold, numb, hopelessly compromised, and for once in his life feeling totally not in control of his own destiny.

He sat down. Told himself to take a grip and took a deep breath. He'd been in fixes before. There were things to take from this, the powerful friends, the money, the offer of political support and help; but big negatives too – a downside that could prove catastrophic.

Like a poker game, the stakes were high, it was winner take all. Maybe he had only to win and things would be all right. And Carl, he was right. Events were indeed moving his way. The attacks were turning public sentiment, his chances were building, he just might be able to do it. Now though, he couldn't risk losing. It was no longer an option. The door in his present life had been closed, only the future could save him.

36

Carl thought it had gone well, clinically well even. He'd done as The Circle required and had left Harry McNamara knowing who was boss and how things stood. Harry was hooked, and whenever The Circle wanted to, they could reel him in. It was so much simpler if, in order to gain compliance, he didn't have to engage in any further unpleasantries by upping the stakes. No, Harry understood how things were, he was sure of that.

His black Range Rover had been parked up hidden from view from the house. No risk in anyone making clever links. He turned the final corner after a two minute brisk walk, and as he did so, experience told him he was being followed. Not unduly bothered by the development, he used a window opposite to check out his suspicions. There was indeed someone, a woman, clutching a file under one arm, a mobile pressed to her ear in the other. More than likely it would be one of Harry's people, he surmised. He walked on without varying his pace, passed his vehicle, quickly thinking through what options lay open to him. Flight or fight?

He spotted a lady pulling a shopping trolley behind her. She'd just left her house, pulling her door shut, locking it, but not her porch door which had tall green house plants in it. The woman didn't look back. Confidently he walked up to her porch, pulled the door almost shut behind him and dropped quickly down amongst the greenery out of sight. He listened. His follower approached. She stopped at the driveway, confirming his earlier suspicions, then continued past. He heard her footsteps recede.

With years of military training behind him, he judged the moment to exit to perfection. His follower thought she had all the information she needed as to where he allegedly lived and was no doubt relaying it all back to Harry. Carl had a choice to make – whether to let her go back with her erroneous address that would lead Harry nowhere, or send him a lesson. He chose the latter.

Retracing his steps quickly to his Range Rover he assumed his follower would take a definite route along a couple of streets back in the direction of either Harry's place or the main road. He had to act quickly and purposefully without undue haste. The last thing the situation needed was further untoward attention in his direction.

Powering the Range Rover round the first two corners he spotted her. She still had her mobile to her ear. Perfect. She was oblivious to his coming. He checked his mirrors. Nothing – not a car in the road, not another pedestrian except the woman with her shopping trolley ahead and she was not looking his way. A final check and he accelerated evenly and just before he should have passed her he mounted the pavement and hit her, with an initial thud, followed by a jolt as she went under first the front and then the back wheels, before instantly at the next driveway pulling back on to the road again.

That'll do it, he thought, as he moved away, glancing as he did so through his rear view to see her twisted form, still and prone on the tarmac. She'd be lucky if she survived that he concluded and even if she did, what she knew wouldn't lead anywhere. She worked for Harry, of that he was now certain, and by the time news of her little accident filtered back to Harry, he would know, if he didn't already, just how high the stakes had been raised.

Carl never saw the lady with the trolley turn and go over to Cathy. She saw Cathy's mobile on in her hand. Her daughter had one of those mobiles. So she picked it up and spoke.

'Hello.'

Harry heard her voice. He had been hanging on the line since it had gone dead. He'd heard the sound of a vehicle approaching, the sickening thud and then the silence and guessed what had happened. He rightly anticipated this was a passer-by come to the scene, an elderly woman.

'Get an ambulance,' said the old woman, 'whoever you are, get an ambulance quick, to Watts Park Road.'

'I know where you are,' said Harry. 'I'll call them now and join you,' and he cut the call.

Before he dialled 999, Harry reflected for a moment. Cathy had told him she'd acted on her own initiative. She had followed Carl when she saw him leave Harry's house, because she thought it was in the local party's interest to know who the mysterious benefactor was, even if Harry didn't. Harry had got annoyed with her for it, they'd argued, but nonetheless she had been honest with him in telling him what she'd done and his curiosity was such he wanted to hear where Carl had gone and what she'd discovered.

In those last few minutes she'd told him everything she knew and in the end he'd thanked her, he needed to keep her on side. They'd just begun talking about the afternoon presentation at the Rovers ground when it had happened – bang – then silence.

If he called 999, he'd be implicated. If he didn't call 999 they'd soon come knocking anyway. They'd soon trace the mobile calls, and her call to him would be the last one, the one that would bring the police asking him unwelcome questions. He decided to call 999 anyway, on balance he'd come out of it better if he did, but he wouldn't ring now.

He'd had a better idea. Dashing out the door, he ran to get to the scene of the accident. It was only round the corner. He'd phone from there. It would look better. He'd call from there. Running the last few steps to the lady crouching over Cathy, Harry asked if he could help. He watched red blood trickling from Cathy's ear forming a widening pool. The old lady passed him Cathy's mobile. He surreptitiously slipped it into his pocket, then called 999 using his own phone.

It took six minutes for the ambulance to get there. She was pronounced dead at the scene. Harry meantime had made a number of calls, including one to Cherry and Phil. Press coverage of what had happened was needed. He had already posted some Tweets. The news had to be managed. Ten minutes later, Harry was feeling things were getting back under control. It was only when the ambulance had taken Cathy away, the policeman sent to the scene began asking questions.

Harry described how he had been expecting Cathy to call and see him, so he'd stepped outside to see if she was coming, only to find an accident had happened in the street. He himself had made the 999 call. He was thanked for his assistance and a short while later he walked off back home, Cathy's mobile still securely in his pocket.

As he shut his front door behind him, it suddenly hit Harry for the first time exactly what had happened to Cathy. Carl had brutally killed her! Harry's life was getting overly complicated – he had some really serious problems to deal with as well as win an election. He'd have to be extremely careful from here on in and what was he going to do without Cathy? Were the wheels about to come off his campaign?

37

Home Park was unusually full. Without much else on, and a grey day, it seemed like it was the only place to be for entertainment that Saturday afternoon. The football season proper had already finished on a high, today's friendly being a nice way for satisfied fans to meet up, Rovers having again moved up in football circles, the whole city currently basking in the favourable shadow cast by their team's success.

Adam's group going to the match had swollen to nine, various friends finding they too were just hanging around at the end of the university term. Finding the Uni coach full, they'd travelled down to Plymouth in two cars, courtesy of the extra friends who were lucky enough to afford them. In return for offering lifts the two drivers had had their match tickets paid for by the others. It seemed a fair deal.

Burgers, pies and chips in hand they made their way into the ground. Piped music was playing, trying hard to set an upbeat tone as people made their way to their seats. En route, Adam grabbed a match programme only to discover that half-time now featured community award presentations, given by none other than prospective MP Harry McNamara. That guy certainly got about!

He decided that he wasn't going to show this to Raqiyah, walking beside him, well not just yet – he needed to know how to handle it first. He tried to tell himself it shouldn't amount to much, a quiet recognition of some community causes in the short interval at half-time. Concluding it had to be low key, he began to feel better about it and when they sat down it was then he pointed out to her the item in the programme. She simply raised an eyebrow with a nonplussed, 'well, what do you know?' expression and to Adam's surprise that was the end of the matter.

Immediately prior to the kick off there were additional security announcements followed by a minute's silence in memory of the victims of the previous day's two terrorist attacks. It added a sombre note to an otherwise festive occasion.

Adam also noticed there were numerous police as well as stewards placed around the ground, and those were the ones he could see. It all gave the occasion an edge, when no one felt fully able to relax. No doubt this extra added security was in the light of yesterday, mainly intended to reassure people. As he looked at just how many there were, all wearing protective body vests and helmets, he thought the overall effect more sinister and threatening than one inspiring confidence. Strangely, sight of the uniforms reminded him of his time in Istanbul the previous summer. For him such high numbers of uniformed forces indicated a serious underlying level of threat.

All this was soon forgotten once the match itself had got under way. The referee's whistle at kick-off banished all other thoughts than the match itself. The atmosphere was cheerful and included the kind of ribald banter he had not heard since he went down to the Spurs ground with his Dad when younger. 'How many Exeter fans does it take to change a light bulb?' called out one guy. 'Both of them,' yelled back another, to huge guffaws. It all lifted his spirits and he found himself joining in the good humoured, sometimes cutting criticism of players and match officials alike.

At half-time, the score was two goals apiece, and the players and officials headed off the field as a small platform was dragged on to the pitch in front of the main stand where most of the supporters were sitting. A speaker system was also wheeled in place and two microphones on stands placed centrally.

From the right a military band marched on and came to a halt, finally dividing their forces equally, to come to a standstill either side of the platform. A posse of people in suits and fine dresses strolled up, local worthies who attracted more sarcastic comment from the fans. They came over with the chairman of the club striding to the fore.

The chairman, Matt Ashton, in a bright red blazer, was ready to lead on the formalities and start proceedings. Adam looked for, but couldn't yet see Harry. Then there was a brief fanfare and the chairman stepped forward to address the crowd.

'Good afternoon, one and all. We've had a brilliant season and yes, the players did the work on the pitch, but without you, the supporters, cheering them on through thick and thin, we wouldn't be here today. It's not about me, though I did choose our best players! Nor about our owners, well they did put their hands in their pockets for a few quid and put money and confidence into the club when it was needed. No, it's about you, the people of Plymouth who have stood by us all the way through – thank you!' There were cheers and catcalls before he continued. At the far end of the ground, the Exeter fans pretended this event wasn't happening.

'One man and his family in particular have done much for this club, and you know who I mean.' Then there were cheers, loud cheers, that caught Adam by surprise.

'And it's my pleasure to welcome to the platform Harry McNamara, long time member of the Green Army and loyal supporter of this club.' The band struck up by playing the opening lines of the well-known hymn tune, 'Jerusalem'.

As the music died, heads turned, and from the far end of the pitch Harry made his appearance standing on the back of an open back Land Rover, with the Devon and Rovers flags flying side by side from poles set at each rear corner of the vehicle. They looked splendid as they caught the breeze. The Land Rover was surrounded by an echelon of red, white and blue Minis and two open top Jaguar e-types bringing up the rear. The stadium loudspeakers broke in with the music, "Always look on the bright side of life" as the procession moved ever more slowly before finally pulling up to drop Harry at his podium place.

This was brilliant theatre, thought Adam, and the ground responded by bursting into rapturous applause. Brilliant, but unsettling and Adam and Rayiyah began to feel exposed, the mounting pressure to join in hard to resist. Harry for his part appeared to be smiling, a man at ease among friends. This was his power base, at home with his mates.

'Big Harry! Big Harry! Big Harry!' rang out the chant round the ground, until Harry raised an arm to gain quiet.

'Friends, I'm most grateful to our chair for his kind words of welcome. We've come a long way as a club and he's been a great chairman, right on!' Harry made a show of back slapping and leading applause. More cheers.

'But my task this afternoon is to present community awards to those who serve our community with tireless energy and commitment, the unrecognised people of Plymouth who give of themselves and make our community what it is.' The ground quietened.

'But before I can do this, I have to tell you that we live in a time of unprecedented threat to our community and our way of life. Yesterday we witnessed attacks, here in the South West, upon our democracy, our shoppers – ordinary decent people, men, women and children. They were cut down without mercy. For too long our good nature has been taken advantage of and it is time to say enough is enough. We won't let you do this to us, we won't let you invade our land, we will stop you taking our wealth. We will end your exploitation of the public services we have paid for, for our use. Our British good nature has been exploited by your killing of our people. It must stop.' Harry hung his head at this point and Adam couldn't believe that Harry might feel something akin to tearful emotion.

'Bloody crowd manipulation,' he whispered in Raqiyah's ear, only to be rebuked by the man next to him with a, 'have you no respect?' Adam bowed his head submissively. As he looked around again, the whole ground was silent as if in some collective stupor. The spell of the moment was broken by Harry himself.

Before Harry resumed his speech, Adam heard a man explaining to his young son that the vehicles had only been allowed on the pitch because it was the last match of the season and the turf was being ripped up and re-sown after the game.

'I decided to stand in the by-election because I believe in our city, our country and its people. I was born here, grew up in Plymouth, the Green Army is my family. Here is my second home. I did not decide to stand as a candidate lightly because I hate bloody politicians – charlatans every last one of them!' he shouted. At which there were more cheers.

'I decided to stand because my friends here urged me. "You're one of us," they told me, and so I stood. Little did I know that Muslim extremists would try and derail the very process of election. Little did I know that it would come to this – terror on the streets. But you my friends know how we need to deal with these scum. We need to send them back, scurrying to their desert caves. Let me say it loud and clear. We don't want migrants here!'

Someone near Adam called out, 'Let's hear it for Harry,' and cheers erupted all round until there was total uproar, with much cheering, hand clapping and the thumping of boots on the terraces. Harry again broke through the noise, playing the mood of the crowd, turning them his way. They were liking this.

'Last year some of you know I got caught up in an attempted attack on our England team when they went to Istanbul. An attack on any of our lads is an attack on us all.'

'Harry's a hero,' someone called out.

'No Muslims will build their mosques in my constituency if you elect me. No Muslim will be able to stay here if I can find one single boat to ship them out in. I'll make sure of it, they'll all leave. We'll flush them out into the open, we'll send them running to the beaches, we'll burn their bridges.'

'And their homes,' a young guy shouted from somewhere in the stand behind. Adam felt Raqiyah press close – they felt surrounded. This was bad, very bad.

'I promise you this,' added Harry waving his fist into the air and holding it there. 'We will take back our country and we will make it great again. You know what to do, you lazy sods, get out and vote me in.' At which there was mirth and laughter, the mounting tension in his speech gone.

'But that's for another day. This afternoon I'm here to make awards to the best of our people,' and the remaining period of half-time was given over to the making of three awards to community representatives, Harry being helped by the club team captain in making his presentations. Thankfully, thought Harry, the absent Cathy had got all the detail organised before her unexpected accident.

Then, duty done, the band playing once again, Harry climbed on the back of the Land Rover Defender and he and his cavalcade had gone.

As he exited the stadium, Harry's thoughts turned from the success of his afternoon club appearance to the more problematic campaign management issues his one political advisor Cathy's sudden loss would mean for his campaign. He recalled her lying there in a pool of blood on the pavement. Well, it's only five days until election day, he concluded, I can cover the gap she's left. I'd liked her, fancied even, sad what's happened, but I've got to put it behind me. Life's too short to get sentimental.

Meanwhile, back in the stands, Adam felt Raqiyah holding on to him tightly. He looked at her ashen face, her fearful eyes.
'How do I get out of here?' she asked him quietly. Adam knew there was no way out, a tide was turning, they were trapped at the ground, it was neither safe to go early nor safe to be there at all. He too had felt the power in a massed

crowd of people driven by fear and hate. He knew his own anxiety levels were rising and tried to manage them.

Only if their own group appeared to go along with the jolly atmosphere, if they acted as one with the crowd, could they hope to feel safe. Dissembling remained their only option – they became as one with the other football supporters, they couldn't be seen to be doing anything else.

Harry had done it to them again. It was as if life was being drained from them, but slowly by degrees.

38

Saturday afternoon and April Cooper was at the Rovers' ground, having been given the only slightly more interesting task of being inside the stadium rather than traffic duty outside. She found herself assigned to observe a wedge shaped area of the main stand. Police don't watch the game, they face the other way and watch the supporters, looking for any sign of unusual or potentially criminal activity that might catch their eye. Not that April was interested in football as a sport anyway.

Most of her watch she had been left entirely to her own thoughts and time had dragged, but when half-time arrived, she was awoken from her stupor when she heard Harry McNamara's speech-making. With every sentence she felt a rising concern. It felt as though he was directly wired by his words into the mind of the crowd, so connected it made her shiver inside. Harry was getting away with being more right wing than anyone she had ever heard.

It was the nearest thing to idol worship she'd witnessed since she attended a live pop concert as a teenager. This however was idol worship of a different order, a popular adulation requiring not just devotion of all present but an unquestioning assent to every word Harry uttered.

Was this incitement? she wondered. Had he overstepped the mark? She thought so, but it wasn't her call. What made her shudder was the animal-like response of the crowd, like a pride of lions scenting a kill.

Harry was the main reason she'd been moved as an extra Prevent resource from the Metropolitan Police to Devon just weeks ago. Hearing him speaking, she understood exactly the direction his campaigning was taking. His words taken together with yesterday's attacks made her absolutely realise her bosses had been right to send in Prevent and alert counter-terrorism. Maybe they had not done enough. What was happening here was no mere UKIP pandering to anti-migrant sentiment, this carried the potential of something altogether nastier and more violent. Harry was stirring up deep inner prejudices, dividing them into people like us and people who were wholly other, those upon whom all negativity was projected.

Recent events were serving only to further endorse Harry's cause and so far as she could see, he was milking it for all he was worth. If the crowd's response was taken as a poll, this man was heading for political victory. My, how she hated him and what he stood for.

As Harry's entourage left the pitch at the end of half-time, she had the opportunity to talk to a colleague on the adjacent detail. He was a new rookie PC, a babyface, keen to share hot news, he felt it did his status good, she thought.

He told her that there was some news coming in about a fatal road traffic accident nearby. It annoyed her that because she'd been preoccupied with her own thoughts, she hadn't yet picked up on it herself.

Did she know Harry McNamara had made the 999 call himself, from a street near his home to report a vehicle and pedestrian incident? The thing was, her colleague said, and this was the strange bit, news was coming in that it was Cathy Nicholls, Harry's campaign Political Advisor. She was the alleged victim though it hadn't been made public yet.

Didn't she think that rather unusual? And even more unusual that Harry himself had made the call? It sickened her to hear her colleague speak in fawning tones; enjoying the sense of mystery he was spinning around the case, he was full of admiration for Harry.

'And to think he knew and was still able to deliver a blisteringly good speech,' he added. April's heart sank further as she realised that even her colleagues were now seeing Harry as the saviour from all their problems.

April agreed with him only to say that it was indeed surprising to hear Harry himself had made the call. She made a note to herself that she needed to contact the investigating team once back at the station. Her instinct told her this was no coincidence, but for now she couldn't think where the connections lay. Bob would have said, give it time, so she resolved she would too. After thanking her colleague and sharing a few further pleasantries required from the situation, April returned to her observation point.

The second half passed without incident. Apart from the over enthusiasm of an alcohol excited fan whose friend was trying his best to keep him under control, there was nothing else that caught her eye. She didn't want to get involved in a time consuming pointless arrest with lots of paperwork and a station desk, who would definitely not be pleased to see another drunk in their lock up when there was so much else on. She moved a few paces away and pretended not to notice.

An afternoon at a football match was not her idea of productive policing, but needs must, she told herself. All the while though, she had that nagging feeling in the back of her mind that there were more important things she needed to be getting back to.

As the game finished – with a full-time draw leaving neither side happy nor disappointed – it was time to watch people leave; the match stewards taking a lead shepherding their flock.

All was going smoothly until she noticed to her left some agitation. It was enough for her to call it to her immediate colleague's attention and together the two began moving toward what showed every possibility of becoming a more serious crowd disturbance. The knack was to use a speedy presence to discourage, disperse and assert control before anything worse could happen.

When they were but a couple of rows of seats away from the target group they could see the source of the trouble. A small group of supporters were being corralled and victimised by several rough looking characters. They were spoiling for a fight and April could see their minds were calculating whether they could still get away with throwing a few punches before exiting.

Finger waving and chants of, 'fuck you foreigners' were being repeated. It was turning ugly and movement to the exit had slowed to a halt; there now being a danger that others sensing what was happening might come over to watch, or worse still, join in.

April called up more colleagues on her radio for back up and began to step forward. She didn't think the two of them would be enough. The ground stewards had counted the odds and had begun to move back, away from the trouble they thought might be coming and in so doing had slowed even further the exit of other fans away from the scene – April really didn't want to be caught up in this. Then she saw the cause of the commotion, Adam and Raqiyah and those she took to be their student friends.

'Adam Taylor,' she called out loudly, 'bring your friends over here. The rest of you keep moving. You move!' she directed forcefully, pointing at one young man in her sights. Adam recognised the welcome sound of her voice and began to move in her direction as he was told.

The authoritative direct personal commands took the gathered gang by surprise and they had not expected their targets to move toward the police. 'And you,' she said, keeping the initiative with herself as she pointed to another guy who looked like a ringleader, 'you're on camera, so keep walking unless you want to get yourself nicked.'

His hesitation was enough to turn the situation. April felt relief as she spotted three more of her colleagues approaching; the situation regained, everything was back under control.

'Is your middle name trouble, Adam Taylor?' she asked him with a twinkle in her eye.

'Thank, thank you,' muttered Adam, shaken but still in control of himself. 'Never been so pleased to see a policewoman in my life.'

'Thank you. I was so scared,' echoed Raqiyah, pulling on Adam's arm.

'Let's see you safely on your way. What brought that about? Want to tell me?' asked April.

'No doubt in my mind, it was because of what Harry said at half-time. It's as if he gave permission to every racist to stop holding it all in. They saw Raqiyah and Bilal were different and went for them first.' Bilal and Sophie were hugging and comforting one another as he spoke, Sophie with tears running down her cheek. 'We just tried to stay calm, keep together. Nothing we could do.'

The five officers got them to wait with them until the crowd had all but totally dispersed and the ground almost empty before asking them how they were travelling home.

They then escorted them back to the two cars, easily identified, parked alone in a now near empty car park. They piled in, eager to get away from Home Park and back to Exeter. They'd had a lucky escape.

As they headed north, they all realised the world they once knew as safe had fundamentally changed and it wasn't safe anymore.

39

April arrived back at police HQ in Exeter long after her shift was supposed to have finished, but she felt impelled to catch up after her football duties, to find out all she could as if everything depended on her. She knew she was probably being irrational, but truth to tell she had nothing to go home to, only an empty flat.

The visit to Home Park had been deeply disturbing, as if something evil had stirred in the society she had always taken to be liberal and fair-minded. She grabbed a coffee from one of the many refreshment stations and then walked over to the Gold Room. She could see it was as ever a hive of activity even before she stepped inside.

She still had Harry McNamara's call to the police reporting the death of Cathy Nicholls lodged in her mind as no mere coincidence. The key period in any investigation was the first few hours and she didn't want to let more precious time pass before asking a few questions of her own. In her Prevent role she could legitimately bring left field enquiries into an investigation, things other officers might not consider appropriate to ask.

First though, she needed to know who was on the case. She saw her sergeant Emma was still around, head down at a workstation monitor. No doubt she'd been ordered to work over. April approached her and asked if she'd like a coffee.

'Some water would be nice,' said Emma, pleased to see her colleague.

'I'll get some,' April said, observing the tiredness in Emma's eyes. On returning two minutes later, she asked casually how the investigations were going.

'Complex. Two major incidents in parallel. Thinking here is they are definitely connected. Grey man, well that's his name in here, he's shown up on two more CCTV clips. Growing feeling is that whoever he is, he's our strongest lead and it's hard to see him as IS. Yes, we've had an alleged IS claim, but counter intelligence and GCHQ Cheltenham are saying the claim has too many oddities about it to ring true. Current assessment is we're dealing with some kind of right wing or maverick attack.'

'I heard that there had been a hit and run involving Harry McNamara's Political Advisor, Cathy Nicholls – what do we know?' asked April.

'Oh that,' said Emma dismissively. 'Only that Harry made the call. It clearly wasn't him. He was walking to meet her, found her where she was hit when he was looking for her. She'd almost made it to his house. An older lady was there already with the victim, she was walking to the shops with her trolley. Nothing suspicious so far as the team on the ground can see. The woman says she heard the car but cannot say what it was. Looks like a car lost it, took her down, and the driver for whatever reason legged it. Death was mercifully instantaneous. Another hit and run maybe. Could be no insurance, over the alcohol limit, on drugs, who knows?'

'Where's the body?'

'Body's down the mortuary, Coroner's office want the forensic pathologist to work out what they can. Post mortem should be in soon. We have the scene of crime SOCO examiner's report. It was SOCO who wanted the full post mortem. He said there were no skid marks, which he thought unusual, with no CCTV as yet, no witnesses either, he wasn't happy. Given the scene of the incident, it's hard not to think there might be more to it, but what? A conspiracy theorist might say she was deliberately taken out, but why? Internal feuding – we've no evidence of that, no proof, no witnesses, nothing, in fact nothing at all to support such an approach…' Emma ran out of ideas.

'What was she doing there?' asked April.

'Think you'd better ask the investigating officer Nick, he's just in. Like you he was sent to Plymouth to help out, he's sitting over there.' She pointed out a tall lanky guy using her raised glass of water as a signpost. April strolled over to talk to him. Introductions were needed, the two had never met before. April took an instant liking to the man. They sat down next to each other and she told him the long story, why she was there in Exeter, her work detail, her day.

'But what I really wanted to hear was your take on the Cathy Nicholls death. What did you make of it?' she asked.

'Sometimes it helps just to say it how you find it – so off the record, if you've got five minutes, I'd like to share the evidence – truth to tell, it doesn't stack up. It doesn't carry the ring of truth. Must be more to it than we know. I'd be interested to know what you make of it.'

Nick outlined the case, from the moment of the 999 call to the first on scene officer's report, finally to the SOCO's call for the Coroner to be involved.

'I was there at the scene pretty quick. I took it in, followed up the hit by a driver who failed to stop initial line of enquiry, began writing it up, but as I came away, I just had that feeling I'd missed something important. Now I'm sure of it.'

'Oh?' questioned April.

'It won't look good on me, but I later realised I'd never looked into exactly why Harry McNamara was really there in the first place and how he ended up reporting it. We'd all been given the third degree about not interfering with the by-election candidates by the Chief, it was only when he'd gone, saying he was off to make some community awards at the Plymouth Rovers Ground I realised I had been easy on him, I'd never asked the questions I should have done.' He paused to think.

'Then there was what the SOCO said about lack of tyre marks, no evidence of avoidance, slowing down – no screeching or skidding noise that neighbours should have heard. That tells me like, it had been deliberate. Two other things about her – where was her phone? She should have had one on her. We did a fingertip search when I thought of it and unless it's been picked up – it's vanished. And now look here, I just got hold of this.' Nick pointed to the screen.

'Her phone signal record shows her and her phone located at the scene, having earlier left more or less Harry's address, then making an extended call to Harry McNamara as she walked along these two streets. There's no signal since – either it was damaged in the impact or switched off, one or other. Harry never mentioned he'd just left a meeting he'd had with her at his address, never mentioned the subsequent call to him, or the reason she might have been returning to his home – it doesn't add up. Harry's reaction was odd too, as if it was something incidental, he showed no emotion, his mind was elsewhere. Enquiries with her family have drawn nothing. They're distraught. By all accounts, well-liked local woman, single mum, no enemies, had thrown in her lot with Harry's campaign.'

'I was at Home Park when Harry made the community awards. He never mentioned or showed any indication he'd suffered such a loss. What was the relationship between the two?' asked April.

'Not discussed. But if it was up to me, I'd be on to that too. But everyone here's treating him with kid gloves, frightened he'll cause them trouble.'

'So where's the investigation going next?'

'I'm back here to get a report on it done for the Chief. Given the political sensitivities on this one, it's not my call.'

'Did you hear what Harry McNamara was saying at Home Park? Did you see the reaction he got from the crowd? I hadn't realised how far right things had gone. I didn't for one moment expect him to be welcomed like a hero. Nor did I expect to hear so much hatred. I even thought we could have had him for incitement, but I guess that won't happen given, as you say, "the political sensitivities". We ended up having to protect people leaving the ground. It was supposed to be a friendly – the hatred Harry McNamara spouted made my hair stand on end.'

'Which raises another question.'

'Which is?'

'Will anyone be doing any profiling of Harry McNamara? He's the nearest thing we've got to a suspect – I'm convinced he knows more than he's letting on. That Cathy was in his house only a short time earlier that very morning. We need to know how that earlier meeting went – but I doubt we'll be allowed to get into that. Something smells, but it's now up to the Chief – that's what she's paid for.'

'Good luck with the report. Sounds a difficult one, and for what it's worth I totally share your misgivings,' said April, thinking it was time she got back to her own Prevent agenda before heading home.

'One final thing?' asked Nick as she was already moving away.

'Yes?'

'In your Prevent capacity, is there anything I'm not hearing, any connection I'm not making? It's not every weekend we have two major terrorist incidents in the immediate run up to a bitter by-election campaign and one of the candidates loses his political advisor in mysterious circumstances. Am I missing something?' Nick asked. April's heart missed a beat. He was thinking along the same lines as herself. She wasn't imagining the scenario, it was the right thing to think.

'Nick, I've got no evidence that's been passed to me that you've not heard already, but I have a police officer's instinct. When something smells bad in my experience it is because it is – our problem is finding the evidence and getting the conviction. I came back here, when I should have been back home with a gin and tonic. I came in because like you, things don't sit easy, they just don't add up. I can start imagining things, but that's probably going to take me off track. What we need are more facts. We had one lucky break on the first terrorist attack, an ID, a mystery man we subsequently caught up with on CCTV. What he did has only served to further mobilise Harry McNamara's following. What I keep asking myself is this – was the attack or indeed attacks, were they intentional – designed to help Harry? Is there any connection?'

'Hold on. Hold it there,' he said excitedly. 'Give me five minutes to finish and send this report and if you're up for it and we're both off duty, we could have a drink, fool around with ideas too far-fetched for the facts. At least chill out after a long day. How about it?' he almost pleaded. She didn't hesitate in her reply.

'OK, why not? I need maybe fifteen minutes here. Meet you then, main reception foyer,' April said, feeling she would enjoy some sociable like-minded company. It won hands down over drinking G & T on her own.

40

Adam and Raqiyah were pleased to get safely away from the football ground. The event had kicked Adam's anxiety levels sky high, his never far away post traumatic stress condition again reawakened. In the crisis of the impending attack in the stands he'd been fine, his adrenaline kicking in, but as soon as he approached the safety of the car, he'd involuntarily withdrawn into some dark place, deep in his mind, no longer able to engage either with his surroundings or his friends.

This time, with no medication on him, by the time he was in the back of his mate's car with Raqiyah, he was in something of a vegetative state. Raqiyah tried her best to stay calm herself as she soothed him, stroked his forehead massaging his temple and explained his symptoms to his concerned companions.

Raqiyah was in two minds whether to take Adam to the hospital accident and emergency department as their travelling companions advised, but in the end she decided it would be best if they got him back to their digs in Pinhoe Road first – the medication he had left there usually worked. If it didn't, A&E remained an option for later, she reasoned. Besides, she had no wish to return to the hospital she had left not a week ago – the staff there already had negative views of her.

On return to Exeter it took two of them, one on either arm, to get Adam, head down, into their house. Bilal and Sophie were not yet back, so it was just the two of them.

Thankfully, soon after taking his Quetiapine, and by seven in the evening, Adam was, much to Raqiyah's relief, more talkative and back with her. A corner had been turned. They decided on a home-delivered pizza and a quiet evening in. There had been more than enough to cope with that day.

As they waited for their pizzas to arrive, Raqiyah decided to check her e-mails, having neglected them all day. There was only one that caught her eye and she dreaded opening it. It was sent from the university, the Vice Chancellor's office.

It could only be about one thing, the pending disciplinary measures being taken against her for what had happened in Plymouth a week ago when she had gone to see Harry. Only a week, it felt like a lifetime.

The communication was as she had guessed, but it was with some surprise and relief she read that the disastrous prospect of an imminent ignominious exit from the university with no degree and a humiliating return home to Oman had radically changed.

The already once postponed meeting, rescheduled to Monday because of the terrorist attack, had now been postponed indefinitely. The reason given was that following representations made on her behalf, and her previously unblemished academic and disciplinary record, the matter was not being proceeded with at the present time. She didn't understand it – representations made? She herself hadn't made any.

'Adam, Adam, listen to this,' she said cheerfully, gaining a raised eyebrow and immediate attention. She read through what she had been sent.

'Brilliant!' said Adam, 'but what does "following representations made on your behalf" mean?' he asked quizzically.

'I can't think. Wonder if it was my friend at the Students' Union?'

'Give her a call – at the very least to tell her the latest.'

'I will,' said Raqiyah, immediately scrolling up her number and making the call.

'Hi, it's me, Raqiyah. Guess what! They've postponed disciplinary proceedings.'

Her friend at the other end seemed to know all about it. She said she'd been to the Vice Chancellor's office straight after their earlier conversation. The VC was there in person which was both unexpected and fortunate and she'd laid it on the line what the implications were of what he was doing. 'He and I sort of get on,' she told Raqiyah.

'What do you mean, "laid it on the line?"' asked Raqiyah.

'Sometimes the university acts as though it is in a glass bubble, totally removed from the real world. The VC needed to understand what kind of political campaign was going on and how it wasn't advisable for the university to be drawn into politics at this point in time. I also reminded him that we have an ongoing summer campaign to recruit more students from Oman and the Gulf, and wasn't it rather short-sighted to initiate a disciplinary measure against a respected student from that part of the world with a hitherto unblemished character and whose influence could entirely undermine the university's ambitious targets for foreign student numbers. Had he done the sums?'

'That's a really good point,' interrupted Raqiyah.

'What clinched the argument was the university's naivety as to relations with its Muslim students and Islamic sponsors. When I started talking about Islamophobia and the reputation of the university being besmirched as anti-Muslim, he suddenly saw the light and dashed into his office to get his PA to write to you and the disciplinary board members. That was it, you're off the hook.'

'I owe you, I owe you. Oh, thanks such a lot,' cried Raqiyah, bringing the call to a close.

She explained what had been said to Adam who seemed to take it all in, and then Raqiyah, quite unlike her usual self, burst into tears, and it was Adam's turn to offer comfort. It was at this point, as they were clinging on to each other in the hallway, the doorbell went to announce that the pizzas had arrived. Grabbing plates, cutlery and a drink they adjourned to the shared lounge as Adam flicked on the TV.

'I can't believe it!' said Raqiyah, laughing and smiling radiantly. I'm so happy. I feel so relieved.'

'Me too. You know what, you're really bad for me. Wherever you and I are together we get into scrapes. We go to Istanbul – what was that – the nightmare or adventure of a lifetime? We go to a football match – end up having to be rescued by the police. What are we? How is it life has dealt us such a hand? If it didn't scare me so much I'd say life's a ball!'

And then they both started laughing, pointing at each other, rolling around, hysterically letting go. It was uncontrolled release, on Adam's part the medication removing his anxiety, on Raqiyah's the burden of past days lifted from her shoulders. It was a short-lived euphoria.

The next moment there was Harry McNamara on TV, being introduced to the invited audience; a live broadcast of a hustings meeting from Plymouth with all three parliamentary candidates was about to commence.

The Archdeacon in the chair was explaining that the absent UKIP candidate had chosen not to contest the seat, urging his supporters to switch and vote Conservative.

Their mood changed and as they ate pizza together on the tatty settee, they were glued to the programme about to start.

41

Harry was about to be driven to the hustings debate by Phil Potts. They hadn't had a chance to talk since the events of the morning. Harry sat in the front passenger seat and clipped on his seat belt. He was unusually quiet.

'Can't believe it, Harry. Cathy gone, no wonder you're quiet. We were all together one minute, then she's... she's gone,' said Phil. 'Have you visited, been in touch with her family yet?'

'Go there now will you. Hustings can wait,' ordered Harry, warming to Phil's suggestion and annoyed with himself for not seeing the opportunity earlier. 'Got a camera with you?'

'Sure, always have, but it's not the time for pictures, Harry. They'll be upset.'

'Make sure people know what a grieving family is, will you. Get the images I need, they're suffering, people need to see them, they won't object. I want them, I want everyone to know I care,' said Harry. 'We'll only have five, maybe ten minutes max, hustings won't wait. It'll be long enough.'

'What do you think happened, Harry? All she said to me when we both left after the meeting with you was, "I'd love to know who Harry's secret visitor is". She was so supportive, Harry, nothing was too much trouble. Not exactly accident prone was she, and the street where she got knocked down, can't see it, really I can't. Never known anything like it. This kind of thing could really unsettle our campaign, even lose us the election.'

'Not if I have anything to do with it,' interrupted Harry brusquely. He gave Phil a look which decidedly closed the matter.

Harry proved to be all charm and sympathy at Cathy's home where her two young children were sitting quietly on the settee watching children's cartoons on TV, her parents having come over to mind them. They explained they didn't know what else to do except try and keep things as normal as possible – hence the children's channel. Harry disturbed their blank looks as he stood between the kids and the TV.

'Hi kids, how about a high five for Harry,' he insisted. The two leapt to their feet and delivered the high fives. Whilst standing, Harry grabbed and squeezed them both in an embrace. One began to cry but Harry didn't let go. He swung them round and then both were crying. The spin stopped when he had both clutched close and was facing Phil with his mobile camera. Harry knew the shots he wanted were in the bag.

'My deepest condolences,' said Harry with a doleful face, turning from the children to address their grandparents. 'Cathy was my right hand. Whenever I called, she'd come at a moment's notice and never spare herself in the cause. Only today she was arranging my meetings. When I win, I will make sure she's never forgotten.'

Then Harry was out of the door, Phil trailing in his wake.

'I didn't think you were going to be that quick,' said Phil.

'I need the best image of the grieving kids on social media within thirty minutes. Can you do it? You know how you can make pictures connect. That's what you need to do now.'

'I'll need a few minutes when we get there,' said Phil.

'Look, I'll go in and leave you in the car. There'll be five minutes of nothing as people are introduced and rules of engagement are pronounced. But I do need you, or better still, Andy to get some shots in later when I plan to raise the temperature. OK with that? – Good,' he said without waiting for Phil to reply.

Harry adjusted his tie when they pulled up by a policeman guarding a door entry.

'You can't park there, Sir. Oh, sorry, didn't see who it was,' the policeman said, aware that a crowd of Harry's supporters were enthusiastically pressing round the car having spotted who it was inside.

'At ease officer, he's only dropping me off,' said Harry, 'but I will need my car and driver available afterwards.'

'Well, just use that space right there, I'll personally keep an eye on it,' said the policeman smiling and trying to make good his earlier faux-pas.

Harry noticed Cherry standing beside the main entrance doors. After acknowledging the adulation of his fans, Harry strode over to her and whispered in her ear, 'Phil has something for you – a scoop, just for you. Will you be around for the debate?'

'Wouldn't miss it. I still haven't run the story about your grandfather Michael yet. It's written. I'd like to pass it by you first. Can we catch up after?'

'If you're in Phil's car when I leave, we'll meet up then. OK?'

'Sure, Harry,' she said as he disappeared inside, concerned ushers glancing at watches, their final candidate arriving just seconds before eight-o-clock. Harry noticed the pressing crowds, some people without tickets clearly unable to get in. It was gratifying how many were sporting the red, white and blue colours showing BFDP support.'

That was something the other candidates hadn't understood, observed Harry. Working out what to say wasn't half as important to the campaign as setting the atmosphere, and the presence the candidate created. They still didn't get it, people weren't interested in words anymore, they were interested in an emotional connection.

Harry arrived as the long awaited celebrity candidate, the one everyone was talking about. The others sitting and waiting already felt annoyed at this late incomer, finding themselves all the more frustrated as Harry took his time to make his way to his seat like a true statesman.

Finding his seat he could feel the disgruntlement of the other candidates. Those looks lose votes, they were losing out and at that point were powerless to change a thing. Harry smiled at them, then looked beyond them and to the cameras aimed directly at him.

The Archdeacon of Plymouth, chosen as a non-political neutral chair, looked round as if someone would help him to know when to start. Unfortunately, he was on his own and though he tried not to show it, rather out of his depth. Harry had stolen all the opening images, without a word being spoken.

Archdeacon Peter Chapel was desperate to have the chance to outline how proceedings were to be conducted and to take back a measure of control. It would reflect very badly on the church if he were unable to ensure fair play. He found it somewhat irritating to have Harry McNamara give him the nod to proceed. He could see Harry himself was feeling entirely comfortable. Harry, for his part, already believed it would all go his way and since a youngster on the street he instinctively knew how to work a crowd to his way of thinking.

If to begin with people thought Harry was quiet, well he was. He let the other candidates talk about jobs and the economy, the nation's future relations with Europe, and how their own political leaders were endorsing their campaigns. Harry yawned. The Archdeacon asked Harry if he would like to comment from time to time, and was mystified as to why Harry wasn't using the opportunities he was being given. Harry declined again. He had his own rules.

With barely ten minutes left to the hour long debate, Archdeacon Peter presented Harry with the moment he had been waiting for. In an effort to be fair, he had closed down the other speakers, telling them they had had their chance. People wanted to hear from all the candidates, and what would Harry like to say? For the first time that evening, everyone and the cameras turned toward Harry. This was his time. He began speaking quietly, his audience having to listen to catch his words.

'Thank you. All of us this evening are mindful of the attacks on Exeter's Guildhall and Plymouth's Drakes Mall Shopping Centre. I would like to express my condolences to all affected and pay tribute to our emergency services who have toiled under dangerous and difficult circumstances to save lives and care for the injured. Yesterday, I visited both sites and spoke with people in the midst of these attacks. I know Exeter is outside Plymouth, but when an attack like this occurs, hearts need to rule before heads, care put before before political boundaries.' Harry paused and turned to address the panel.

'For the record, I didn't see the other candidates make an appearance, or show any sign of human concern or compassion. What is also significant is this – as I have listened carefully to their policies this evening, well-meaning no doubt as they are, neither of them were prepared to grasp the nettle and address the issue that concerns us all most – what to do in the face of attacks on our security and safety. The other candidates have nothing to say.' There was some effort to intervene to his left, but Harry quickly raised his voice to cut off any attempt to overrule him.

'The threat to our families by migrants, by returning and home grown terrorists is self-evident and I have made no secret of my party's policy to repatriate such people and to increase resources to our police and counter-terrorism forces to bring the perpetrators to justice. We need to do this. How many more need to die before we wake up to the reality of what is happening?' Harry looked around. People were watching him and hanging on his every word.

'This evening our party is prepared to offer a further policy measure to help safeguard Plymouth lives. It is not something we offer lightly and will not be undertaken without great care to protect human rights. We propose the immediate use of internment camps to contain those identified as extremists, those we need to take off our streets until they can be repatriated.'

'And how will you do that?' asked the Archdeacon, his impartiality slipping as he fired a question to catch Harry out.

'We need to see some of our disused naval, air force and army bases used for this purpose. We cannot continue to let returned terrorists from the Middle East, who are armed and dangerous roam our streets and attack us at will. We need to take steps ourselves. Internment is the only measure that a humane and decent civilised society can take to remove the threat from our midst.'

'No, No, No,' the Labour candidate, Pamela Dane called out, peering over brown circular spectacles. 'It would be unworkable. Every ethnic minority person would feel threatened and could be swept up.'

'Then what do you propose?' asked Harry calmly.

'We would spend more on public services, especially the police, and on that we agree with you. But we would not have a dragnet in which all our good citizens of whatever faith and background get swept up and imprisoned.' But her plea was falling on deaf ears and her words died on her lips.

'The people of this city want action. They want to be safe. I know what it is to be attacked by Muslims. In Istanbul last summer, I saw what can happen first hand. We need action and thorough going measures taken under firm and decisive leadership.'

Someone called out, 'Our Harry's a hero!' Harry recognised the voice, he'd remember to thank him later.

'Please, please,' called out the Archdeacon, flapping a hand up and down in a wing like gesture meant to silence the audience, but Harry ignored and over-rode him.

'Today I had one of the most difficult things I have ever had to do, to visit the two children of a young Mother cruelly killed on a Plymouth Street. She was our party's Political Advisor, Cathy Nicholls. Her kids were inconsolable, in tears. Cathy grew up in this city, as did her parents. The police are looking for her killer. Terrorists don't like the stand my party is taking and we are putting our lives on the line. It would not surprise me if Cathy died because an IS sympathiser did not like our party's response to the weekend's incidents. They use vehicles like killer weapons – we've seen it in London and in Europe, and now I believe we might well have seen it here too. But let's not be hasty, let's not jump to conclusions. Let the police do their job. Our concern is to see Plymouth is prosperous and safe for its people. That's our vision and we believe it's what the people want too.'

There was hearty applause, the first of the evening. Time was running out. The Archdeacon looked down at his watch. Harry seized the moment to press on.

'This afternoon I was at Plymouth Rovers' ground, Home Park. I'd been invited to make some community awards to some of the unsung heroes and heroines in our community, people that you, Mr Archdeacon, would be proud to have in your church. I believe your MP should be as much about encouraging a caring, happy society as it is about keeping everyone safe. If I am elected that's what I promise to do.'

At that the Archdeacon began summing up the evening. He asked the leader of the local Chamber of Commerce to give a vote of thanks to the candidates. It was meant to be even handed, but Harry's father had reminded him of the metals contract he had with McNamaras and in his comments he mentioned being present at Harry's speech to the Businessmen's Breakfast and how well it had been received. The Archdeacon glowered knowing he was powerless to intervene and then it was over.

As Harry stepped outside, having spent more time than the other candidates pressing palms in the foyer, he spotted Phil and Cherry in conversation. He joined them.

'Excellent, Harry,' exclaimed Cherry. Phil has given me the story and the pictures from earlier. The one of you with the two children ought to go forward for an award. Andy was here taking pictures for the paper and he also got some great shots of you in the meeting, leading the debate. The idea of internment has certainly grabbed the social media – look! Everyone's discussing the idea. You've stolen the limelight again! Congratulations!'

'The momentum is with us,' said Harry. 'Did you want to come back to talk about that piece?'

'Yes, if that's all right, Harry.'

'Let's go!' said Harry to Phil. 'We're all busy people.'

42

The Master sat at his heavily ornate genuine Louis XIV table in his west London flat which served both as his work desk and thinking space. It was now Saturday evening on 2nd June. By safe and circuitous routes, he had received regular update reports from Carl Reynolds who seemed happily expediting his orders and moving from one project to the next as they all had hoped and believed he would.

Things were so much safer when only one operative was at work, he thought, the risks so much more manageable. Now he was thinking about his second – the risks upped. It was now some weeks since the weekend meeting in Calais when plans had been given the final go-ahead and with the by-election now only days away, it was time for him to sit down and take stock of the evolving situation. Too much hung on this rare opportunity, another may not present itself for a long time.

He knew it was bad for his health, but he lit up a cigar from the box facing him. At least he took one less often these days. The sight of the coiling smoke always calmed him and helped him to think. He had got to where he was today only by taking the utmost care about everything and by being utterly ruthless when the need arose. Carl Reynolds was on his mind, Carl his foot soldier and secretary, a useful functionary, nothing more, whatever he himself might think.

Pulling a piece of white paper across the table toward him and reaching for his fountain pen, he began to think in pictures. He drew concentric circles to represent Devon, a bigger one for Great Britain and a still larger one for Europe. He thought it too ambitious and overreaching at the present time to bring in America and Russia, though friends and allies were already at work there. An X marked Plymouth.

Next, he drew small vertical rectangles to represent people, like characters in a play he was producing. Each were labelled. A big H for Harry, a C for Carl, an S for Steve, and a big P for Mrs Plod – the Chief Constable of Devon and Cornwall Police supposedly investigating things. Then he drew five stars, a large one with a G for Guildhall, another with a D for Drakes Mall, a third one with an Su for submarines and then two smaller stars – an I for one dead Imam, and finally one, with a CN for Cathy Nicholls. Both I and CN had been unexpected.

Then he sat back and drew on his cigar, the smoke twisting and winding in white clouds between himself and the urban view from his window. The trouble with the antique chair was that it was hard and angular and uncomfortable. He corrected his posture before leaning forward over the paper before him.

Then he started writing a column of letter Qs. Against the first he wrote the question, 'How far is the tide turning Harry McNamara's way?' Then he wrote underneath, 'How on board with us is Harry?' Then, 'What might lead to things unravelling before election day?' And so the list went on all in copper plate neat writing. As the questions came to him, he added them. Then it was questions about resourcing and disposal that filled out the bottom of the sheet.

He felt pleased with the progress made and on balance believed Harry would have his parliamentary seat, but was frustrated that the level of fear and polarisation had not gone far enough. There had been some good fortune – the death of the Imam at Exeter Mosque, an opportunity he'd been gratified to see Harry had fully utilised.

However, there was still a chance that British decency, fair play, toleration and love of the rule of law would upset his plans. There was still the risk that the election would be postponed, but even as he thought it, he discounted that possibility, tapping the star marked S for Steve as he did so.

It was thinking about Carl that had made him anxious. It concerned him that Carl had taken one step beyond what had been ordered. He had acted on his own initiative to kill Cathy Nicholls.

Carl had explained what he'd done in his latest briefing, but the Master had felt unconvinced by Carl's argument, in the end certain the death had been an unnecessary act, an added risk. He had no issue with the killing itself, these things were part of exercising power, he'd ordered many deaths personally, but this one left him feeling less in control of the mission. He'd always utilised Carl because he saw something of himself in him, a man looking for a cause, a man who needed a role outside the military institution, a man quite prepared not to play by the book and who shared the vision of a new society, the one they were going to build for everyone.

But to kill Cathy Nicholls, for what? For using her sense and walking down a road to follow him. Carl had surely many options open to him and had chosen badly – why hadn't he simply lost her or even confronted her?

Another option was to let her see him and report back to Harry. After all, Harry was sucked in now, what would he have done when she told him? Nothing! The killing was poor judgement, Harry was theirs already, it wasn't necessary and it wasn't authorised.

Carl's action had further widened a police investigation that now had a third opportunity for a lucky break, another path they could use to track Carl and The Circle down – that wouldn't do. He wondered whether Carl had come to the end of his usefulness. He was mindful there were other, more promising and younger people who were keen to serve, well able to fill his place. In response to Muslim extremism, new resources were coming forward daily. He would need time to think this through.

First though, it was personally up to him to release the message that tripped the final part of the campaign into action. He reached for his mobile phone, scrolled down and pressed "send" a pre-arranged coded message instantaneously pinging into Steve Collins' waiting inbox.

For this remaining task, Steve would know what to do. He had little doubt he would succeed, but then what was to happen to Carl, the problem he began with?

He blew another cloud of cigar smoke up above him and watched it disperse as it tracked up; he liked old flats with high ceilings, they had a certain grandeur.

As he followed the smoke, swirling around in invisible currents of air, some caught the draught from the window, and as it did so, an idea came to him.

He got up, screwed the paper he'd been working on into a long spill, and using his cigar, blew a flame that caught and consumed it.

Holding the paper as it burned, he carried it over to the fireplace, dropped it in the hearth and poked the ash until it was an indecipherable scattering of black dust. People had to accept dying for the cause.

43

Adam and Raqiyah were at home watching Harry on TV, and the hustings broadcast had just concluded. They pushed their empty pizza boxes onto the coffee table and Adam reached for a couple of cans.

'It's just like watching a soap, but it was real. He's unbelievable! Harry makes up a story that people fall for. He's a total fascist! A bloody right wing extremist who will do anything to take power. Look at what he did to you in Plymouth! Look what he did to me in the street! He has no scruples. What else might he have done we don't know about? How can someone like that possibly get elected?' asked Adam.

'He's good at what he does though, isn't he?' replied Raqiyah. 'Look at how he used Cathy Nicholls' death to win sympathy tonight. Look at how he got audience sympathy by visiting the two terrorist sites and offering sympathy and solutions. Being good at what they do is how people like him get elected.'

'You met her, Cathy Nicholls, didn't you? Wasn't she the one in the car who came and picked you up when you went with Clive to see Harry in Plymouth to ask him a few questions?' Adam recalled.

'Yes. I didn't like her much, but I wouldn't wish her dead. She'd got a young family. Her old car was full of detritus, kids' drawings, soft toys, mess. She had family.'

'I think every time something horrible happens, Harry doesn't seem very far away, and you know what they say about smoke?'

'What?'

'There's no smoke without fire. Fire, that means bad things, are never very far away. I mean, Harry must have something to do with it all. There must be a link,' said Adam, but he said so without really knowing whether it was true or where to take his thoughts next. Then he remembered something.

'You know I want to get Harry back for what he did to you last weekend. Well I haven't forgotten, it's just I haven't come up with the right thing yet. Anyway it's a good thing to let ideas stay with you a week rather than shoot from the hip in the heat of the moment, isn't it? I was talking about getting a social media campaign going to discredit him, getting Bilal and a few friends with IT nous to help me, but we're running out of time and I'm wondering if we can't do something more effective.'

'Like what? Burn his house down!' said Raqiyah.

'No, No – sorry, thought you were serious for a minute.' He smiled. 'No, why don't we try and counter his campaign by doing a goodwill event, something that shows Muslims are supportive of society rather than a threat to it. We could talk with your new group at the mosque – I don't know, offer tea and chat in an open day here and at Plymouth Mosque – anything to break the hate cycle.'

'I don't know. I can't risk my studies again,' said Raqiyah.

'Come on. We wouldn't need to be in the front line. It wouldn't lead to trouble – it's a good thing. Look, there's loads of young Muslims who will hear a call to defend their mosque, defend their community. They'd all sign up to a good idea. Tell you what, when April the policewoman met with us in the café she told us what she does – all that Prevent stuff. Reckon on that basis, we might persuade her to help us. Police support and backing has got to be good. It doesn't have to be directly about the by-election campaign, just about promoting good relations. It might just open a few people's eyes to what's going on. Harry would hate it. We could bring it to his attention, nothing more – send him a few flyers about it. Don't think it would undermine him. He'd hate it and there would be nothing he could do about it. Look I can get Bilal to help with the publicity side, can you talk to your new friends at the mosque, do a bit of social networking and find out what we can about supporting Muslim brothers and sisters here as well as in Plymouth. Come on, give us a smile, this is our chance.'

'Why not? It's not as though we're doing much except hanging around waiting for term to end.'

Whilst Adam tidied the food packaging and empty cans into the kitchen, Raqiyah began making calls. One call soon led to another and another. She asked Adam to fetch pen and paper, and a full hour and a half later, it was covered in her writing. Adam had peered over her shoulder once or twice and made a few conclusions of his own as to what was happening from hearing one side of a conversation. In the end his impatience couldn't be contained any longer.

'OK, before the next call, I need an update. Sounds like you've got a positive response. Please, please give me the heads up on where you've got to,' Adam pleaded.

'You're right! The women's group were keen to hear what I had to say and signposted me to a couple of the mosque trustees, the ones who really decide things both here and in Plymouth.'

'Not the Imams then.'

'No, their task is liturgical, prayers, that kind of thing. They don't control things.'

'And what did they think, the trustees?'

'They were up for it. They said there had been such an increase in race and religious hate crime over the past week they were desperate to do anything that might help, and they wanted to see something happen soon. They'd been thinking along similar lines but hadn't yet come up with anything concrete. I suggested both mosques hold an open afternoon when people come and sign a book of condolence to express their solidarity with the recent victims of the attacks, and hospitality, tea and so forth could be freely provided along with people prepared to tell the story of our community and answer questions people might have about Islam. They really were very keen. I've been invited tomorrow morning to Exeter mosque. He said I could bring you along too!' She reached for him playfully, grasping his hand in hers.

'I feel this is the right thing to do. Muslims like me need to step up to the mark, take responsibility for engagement, not keep a low profile, hiding beneath the minarets,' she added.

'It's parapets, not minarets,' corrected Adam. 'Thinking about that hustings event, I'm going to call the Archdeacon of Plymouth tomorrow. He seemed ill at ease with what was going on. Bet he'd like to get the churches supporting the mosques for a goodwill event. I'll call him and see. Nothing to lose. That sounds like Bilal and Sophie returning,' said Adam turning toward the sound of a key in the front door. 'We'll hold a campaign meeting right now.'

They were talking excitedly until one in the morning, by which time everyone was wholly committed to the cause and excited at getting one back at Harry. Their thinking was further strengthened by the idea that students from the Islamic Studies course and the university's student Islamic Society body might be persuaded to join them. Then there was an interruption as Bilal read some news coming in on his mobile.

'There is something big going on at Plymouth Docks right now. People are being evacuated from houses and premises in the vicinity. That's all it says, but I don't like the sound of it.'

'It's happening again. Anything we try and do may be too little too late,' said Adam, holding his head in his hands, believing Harry to have outfoxed and outplayed them once more.

44

April hadn't long been home when she was called up. She was very tired and had been hoping for some sleep. Luckily it had only been the one gin and tonic with Nick and she was up to driving and reporting in as ordered. It had been nice getting to know Nick and she hoped they might repeat the experience of a drink after work. They'd exchanged mobile numbers and that had cheered her. Her social world needed to rise from rock bottom.

To be called up late in the evening after just getting home from a shift was unusual. It hadn't happened to her before, so something must be up. As she gathered her things and left her rented house on the Cranbrook estate, she hastily switched on her car bluetooth and called Nick.

'Sorry to call you Nick, but just wondered if you had got the same message as me. I'm on my way back to HQ. Something must be up – heard anything?'

'I'm doing the same – driving in as we speak. They are busy lining up transport to ship a large contingent of us to Plymouth asap. Someone called me to say the naval base is a target, and this time it'll be a joint operation – the military have been called in. News embargo's in place, so it must be very serious. Didn't expect to have the pleasure of seeing you again so soon,' he quipped.

'Me neither,' she replied, and he'd gone.

Parking up at the Middlemoor HQ on the city of Exeter's outskirts, she was amazed at how busy it was, cars emptying officers who were all hurrying in one direction. Lights on everywhere. The building was humming. This is major, she said to herself, her heart pounding as she hastily joined her colleagues. Large white buses were pulling round in a line, no doubt to carry them all south. She noticed that even police reservists had been brought in.

Once inside, briefings for so many were handled a group at a time in different rooms. Frustratingly, April learned little more as they were simply told to board the waiting buses when further information would be provided. She heard someone mention Plymouth naval bases' decommissioned nuclear submarines as the latest terrorist target. Fears of an Armageddon came to mind. Still nothing for it but follow orders. Her colleagues were either talking in whispers or not at all. It was a strangely subdued atmosphere, one she'd not known before. Is it like this when a country is at war? she wondered.

It was only a matter of minutes before the coaches left one by one, each escorted front and rear by cars with blue flashing lights, not that there was any significant traffic blocking their path. As soon as the coach picked up speed on the motorway there was a call for quiet and a brief statement was given by the senior officer sitting at the front. He was in a sombre mood.

'Right, listen here. I can only tell you what I know. We're going to Plymouth. Can't say when we'll be back. I don't want you all phoning loved ones – it's a sensitive operation – outcome unpredictable, so keep your phones off, and that's an order. Clear?'

'Yes Sir,' came the group response, before he continued.

'A major operation is underway to clear people from their homes and businesses in the docks facing area of the city –

Devonport, Millbay, and Stonehouse areas amongst others, moving them to sports halls, community centres, churches, schools, wherever we can. It's about getting them well away from the immediate area. We're joining the hard pressed officers already doing this.' He paused as the coach lurched left before regaining its steady course.

'We've received intelligence that one or more of the nuclear submarines awaiting decommission in the harbour have been compromised. We only know this to be more than an idle threat because we have detected one live explosive device attached to the reactor area of a sub.'

'Is there any risk to us from exposure to radioactivity, Sir?' called out one officer.

'If you will let me finish, I'll come back to your question later. Reports in suggest most people are proving cooperative. No-one wants to leave their home late on a Saturday evening, but there is good compliance. We reckon there are several thousand people needing to be moved, and we anticipate some opposition to the idea. Orders are everyone is to be taken. We've been told by the Home Office that in these circumstances we are not to take "no" for an answer. Everyone has to be moved with or without their cooperation. You understand me?'

'Yes Sir,' everyone intoned.

'On the question of risk to yourselves – indications are that there is no undue risk to yourselves in doing this. No-one is certain what will happen over the coming hours. Whether there will be a detonation of nuclear material creating a dirty area and risk to all in it, who knows? Experts are on the site and are monitoring this aspect of the incident. Just to reassure you we are transporting specialist kit in separate vehicles.'

'Just a bit of background. Over the past three or four years, Her Majesty decided she doesn't require so many nuclear submarines on active duty these days and so there are now upwards of a dozen rusting hulks left sitting there, been there years, no-one doing anything about them, with local people periodically getting worried at the risk they pose to their health and that of their families. Subs have been queuing up since 2002 to be decommissioned. To my knowledge there are still at least eight with nuclear fuel on board because no-one can find a waste disposal solution – it's been a fairly quiet, managed nightmare for everyone until now. No doubt when the shit hits the fan, someone will say, there we are, we told you so. In the meantime we have to go in to sort out the mess they've left us. Don't be surprised if we all return home glowing green.'

'How much radioactive material is there, Sir?' asked someone.

'Upwards of twenty five tons, which isn't hard to find out, and is why I'm in charge and you're not.'

A period of pensive silence followed.

'We've a city of a quarter of a million people sitting on a nuclear time bomb and now someone has started the clock ticking, literally. We've been told that some of the nuclear material will be released consequent upon an explosion in one of the subs. The military experts are going to take some time to make a thorough check of all eight subs. News is, they've already taken one viable limpet mine from a sub at 7pm this evening. It was found on one of the most recent

336

subs to be mothballed at Devonport, HMS Tireless. They expect to find more, but the clock is ticking.'

Plymouth looked different to April as they approached in darkness. Twice they were overtaken by Military Bomb Disposal Vehicles heading fast for Devonport Docks. As she gazed out of the coach window it was clear an exodus in the other direction was beginning – vehicles were exiting the city in significant numbers as if it were rush hour, panic clearly written in people's faces.

The nearer they got, the more she wondered whether she would be leaving the city alive. Never had she felt her life threatened as it was now. She looked back inside the coach at the faces of her colleagues – shadows, flickering in the passing street lights, but she could read nothing from them except resignation. It was all in the line of duty.

The coach struggled through the narrow streets before it pulled up in James Street beside three vertical towers of high rise flats. They sat and waited. To April, the modernising garish facade panelling, a green design on a white background looked like a giant hypodermic dosing poison down into the ground, perhaps an inadvertent symbol of life in the area.

After ten minutes sitting and waiting, their commander broke off from his radio conversation to announce they were to begin by clearing Tamarisk Tower, the middle block standing right before them. All three towers, along with the surrounding housing near Devonport were, he told them, particularly vulnerable to any radiation leak as all were immediately situated down wind and the closest part of the city to Devonport docks.

In pairs, each pair was to take and clear a floor at a time. They were to send residents down to the front door – once outside they could take their own cars or wait for public assistance to remove them to safe areas.

'The order is we are to only clear those nearby areas downwind of the docks, I'm waiting for a full list of addresses to be sent through. As soon as this block is cleared I want you all back here inside the coach – then I'll let you know where next.'

To April's eyes, there was an evident lack of organisation, things were being done on the hoof. It was not a recipe for a smooth operation. She was in the fourth pair off the coach; the two looked at each other, both knowing this wasn't going to be easy. They also understood it was going to be a long night before they were done.

45

Carl had booked himself into the Invincible Hotel, Plymouth weeks ago. He'd located it easily enough as he turned the corner from the Citadel into Lockyer Road. It was conveniently sited overlooking the green expanse of the Hoe. Carl didn't think he'd seen a place with quite so many war memorials as this particular historic piece of public park. There was even one directly facing the entrance to the hotel.

After passing some hours driving out of Plymouth toward the moor for a spot of walking where a Range Rover most naturally blended into the environment, he'd returned nearby late on Friday afternoon and parked up to view the Hoe, watching people come and go for an hour. A busy spot with lots of tourists, he'd every confidence he'd mingle unnoticed. Then he'd checked in. They were happy enough to agree to his request for a room overlooking the Hoe. He always liked to be able to see what was going on.

His arrival at the Invincible Hotel had gone almost unnoticed and he could tell people were preoccupied with what had been happening in the Shopping Mall earlier in the day. He couldn't help but notice the news feed TV in the reception area telling of a major man-hunt currently underway, and there were pictures of the homes of local Muslims being raided. He smiled as he took his pass key and made his way up to his room on the second floor. Then he phoned down to room service for something to eat, instructing that they knock on the door and the meal be left in the corridor outside where he would collect it.

The room wasn't bad for a small hotel, functional and modern, the decor inside in the usual hues of whites and greys. The window gave him the view he'd wanted, looking out across Lockyer Street toward the Hoe. He set his case down beside the bed and then lay down, his eyes fixed on the ceiling. Not a bad result these past twenty four hours, even though he said so himself, not bad at all. He permitted himself the luxury of a beer from the minibar to celebrate.

A tap on the door, a clatter of tray and crockery, footsteps moving away. He got up and collected supper, a rump steak, chips and peas – just perfect. Sitting on the side of the bed, tray on his knees, he tucked in. A mission success was just that, everything that lifted his spirits. He thought The Circle would be celebrating with him as the news fed back on the progress made, plans fulfilled. Harry had the perfect storm in which to rally support and win. Harry would be certain to stay on side now that his political advisor had signed off.

What else needed to be done, but for Carl himself to make a quiet return to London and keep below the radar until the heat died down. As he reflected back, he couldn't think of one thing that had gone wrong; he reached for a small bottle of red wine to have with the steak.

He'd finished his meal and it was still light outside. Connecting to the WIFI he immediately took an unusual e-mail. It had to be from the Master, though as he would have expected, it didn't give any indication as to the identity of the sender. He read it carefully, then again.

Carl, we have an extra job for you to do before leaving Plymouth on Sunday. An ex-military guy is on your tail and will need to be silenced. He poses a very serious risk to the wider mission. Attached is a photograph of him. He is already nearby and will be waiting on Plymouth Hoe by Smeaton's Tower at 8pm Saturday evening in the hope of getting a lead on where to find you. He must be silenced as he waits there, he is a threat to us all.

Then get clear, return to your hotel and continue to celebrate our impending triumph. This is an order. Suggest you stay within your hotel room whilst in Plymouth to reduce risk of your discovery. Stay on guard at all times. You must send back the message 'Silenced' to confirm the kill. You will of course be appropriately recompensed for this additional last minute task when you return to London on Sunday. Regards, M

Carl was perturbed, on edge. It was so last minute. He looked at the e-mail's attachment, a photograph of his target – an unmistakeable face. He glanced at his watch. The tight time line, twenty four hours, made him sit up sharply and make some quick calculations. He had to think this through. Looking at the two empty beer cans and an empty wine glass, he regretted that he had prematurely celebrated the weekend.

He didn't sleep well on Friday night and on Saturday he watched the news endlessly repeating before him. Time stopped still. The daytime slipped slowly into a dull, grey, wet evening. That suited him, for there wouldn't be many people on the Hoe at this time of night.

He needed to get outside, to reconnoitre and find a suitable lair where he wouldn't be disturbed, within good eyeball range, allowing for a safe exit. He reached for his case, opened it and checked his rifle over, reached for his cleaning kit, placed a single shot, rolling the ammunition over and over in his hand. Then, after another glance at his watch, he quickly put everything back in the case, slung on his three quarter length great-coat, pushed his pass key into his pocket and left the hotel.

Outside the front door he made his way very quickly on to the Hoe, following a solitary path to the massive form of the Military War Memorial. He looked at it as a possible base, deciding it's solid structure offered him excellent cover. However a clear shot at someone standing at the foot of the red and white striped Smeaton's Tower was not possible from there; the mown lawns falling away too steeply hiding his target from view, and his heart sank as he realised he'd have to move still further from the edge of the Hoe and sanctuary in order to get his shot.

His eyes lit up as he spotted another stone memorial just ahead, between him and the Tower. Close to he could see the black shape of Sir Francis Drake atop and an ideally placed pile of black cast iron cannon balls to the right – he'd found his spot, the perfect cover.

He turned to see that he had a direct route back to the security of his hotel just a few hundred metres away. He felt uncomfortable at the thought that he was shooting from a point where all around the best and most honourable of English military were remembered. For a brief moment he thought he could hear their disapproving murmurs coming through the misty murk. Not every military name will get etched here he thought as he settled to the task before him. Again and again he played through what he had to do before finally opening his case at the last moment.

Gradually he felt more at ease about his mission – a final look at the watch, only seconds until eight-o-clock. He assembled his weapon quickly with polished ease, stroked his ammunition as he slotted it in place, and then searched the scene for its recipient, screwing his eyes into the wind coming in from the sea.

There he was, wandering back and forth, looking for his contact. No-one else there. A lost man. Carl noticed he walked with poise and bearing, every bit a military man. It took one to know one. A glance around 360 degrees – all clear. A final check of the swirling wind direction, a tiny adjustment, target's heart in the cross hairs – damn his swirling coat.

'Pop!' – target hits the ground. The gun hastily repacked, the bag grabbed, then a brisk walk taken back in the dying light to his hotel – mission accomplished, just a one word e-mail to send – 'Silenced'.

Carl did not observe a young man called Greg Ward feeling with his right hand the front wheel of a nearby Volvo to retrieve some keys, clutching a bottle of what looked like orangeade in his left. A minute later the Volvo drove past Carl as he turned right to head into his hotel. Neither noticed the other.

Greg had been given his own orders, he recognised the format and this time had been even more generously paid. He was to take the car and torch it. Greg couldn't think of an easier way to earn a thousand pounds. He had no idea why he was being asked to do it, but with that kind of money he didn't give the job a second thought. He headed toward the Devonshire Dockyard, always quiet on a Saturday night, a parking lot reserved for employees and contractors; it would be empty and just the place to torch the car.

Greg couldn't understand it. It was all wrong, they couldn't be looking for him, surely? The streets were full of police officers hurrying about, directing people – some kind of manhunt? It made it hard to concentrate on his driving.

When Greg finally got to his destination, the car park was a parking yard for white coaches, some with waiting police teams on board. Police everywhere he looked. No, this was something else, not a place for him to hang around. He hesitated, not certain what to do.

Then he was spotted by a patrol car, it followed briefly, but they appeared too preoccupied about other things to be worried about him. What should he do? He had had his own orders to obey, there was nothing else for it, so pulling the Volvo hard round across the car park exit, he opened the plastic bottle of orange fluid and poured. He sprinkled petrol over the front and rear seats before leaning in the driver's door cautiously he finished the job with his cigarette lighter.

The blaze quickly took hold and Greg slipped away into the shadows.

46

A thin elderly man leaning into the wind looking to the ground just in front of him, walking his black labrador, found Steve Collins lying prone, bleeding into the wet lawn at the foot of Smeaton's Tower. He took out his phone and called 999 asking for an ambulance. It took a long time to get through, and after he'd explained the situation and had been told an ambulance would be on its way, he was asked to examine the man in front of him.

Gently rolling him on to his side he spotted what looked like a bloody hole in the man's shirt, from which a steady flow of fresh red blood was running. On advice, he took his own jacket off and pressed it into the wound to stem the blood loss, and then he waited for what seemed an age. In all this time the lying man didn't move, but the man caring for him thought that he might still be alive.

After nine, maybe ten minutes, the ambulance could be heard approaching and with his free arm he waved to attract their attention. His dog was getting restless. A transfer took place, the professional ambulance crew beginning a series of checks, one of them getting straight on to the radio to call for police back up.

'Looks like a shooting, he's taken it in the upper abdomen, very close to his heart. We need to bring him in, but we need someone here now.'

A police car arrived very quickly. The scene was assessed and quickly contained, and after a few questions the man and his dog were moved into the police car to be taken as soon as a second car arrived for video interview at the nearby police station; his dog pacified under one arm he carried his now bloodied jacket rolled up under the other.

Steve Collins was lucky to be alive. The wind and rain of a grey dusk, together with his swirling coat, had resulted in the sniper's bullet passing through him, but vitally missing his heart by millimetres. The pain and then the loss of blood had led him to faint, but amazingly by the time he was on a drip in the ambulance he began to come round. He had a police officer and an ambulance man beside him.

'What's happened to me?' he asked to their surprise.

'You look as though you've taken a bullet to the abdomen. Don't worry, lie still, we'll have you in hospital very shortly.'

The police officer, going through Steve's wallet, looked up to ask, 'Are you Steve Collins, Sir?'

'Yes,' Steve groaned.

'A serving Royal Navy Engineer?'

'Yes.'

'Do you remember what happened to you?'

'I was waiting to meet someone, then a distant noise, a gun – I know what a gun sounds like – maybe a sniper. Didn't see a soul. Threw me back, like a punch. Will I be OK?'

The policeman nodded to the ambulance man to take over, whilst he grabbed a rail, stood up and whispered into his radio. The word 'sniper' changed this incident entirely and he needed to let Gold Room know. Call made, he turned back to Steve.

'I need to ask you one or two more questions, Steve. I'm hoping you can be of some help here,' he said.

Steve nodded.

'Where are you stationed?'

'Rosyth, Scotland.'

'What were you doing here in Plymouth?'

'I've nothing to say, Sir,' Steve stuttered.

'How did you travel here?'

'Car, my car,'

'Where did you leave it, Steve, somewhere nearby?'

'Lockyer Street, yes, near the Hoe.' Steve's eyes closed and the ambulance man looked at the policeman as if to say that was enough. But the policeman was fired up, he'd been in Drakes Mall Shopping Centre that morning and afternoon, he'd seen the victims, and he knew he was on to something here, though he wasn't sure what.

'Can you describe your car? – someone will need to pick it up.'

'Volvo estate,' and Steve whispered the registration, the officer jotting it down in his notebook. He stood up again and resumed his earlier radio call. When he next looked down, Steve was white, eyes closed, a continuous bleep sounding from a monitor. The ambulance man jumped up.

'Back, back. Keep his airway clear, whilst I do CPR. Just do it. Looks like a cardiac arrest.'

By then the ambulance was pulling into the A&E at Plymouth's Derriford Hospital. As it slowed to a halt, there was already another police team waiting there for them. Steve Collins was supposed to have died, but if he lived, he was now a major lead for an investigation desperately trying to chase down who was responsible for the South West of England's weekend of terror. The police were impatient to ask this surprising lead more questions. They wanted him to come round – hypothetical links between Rosyth and Devonport were already forming lines of questioning.

Meanwhile, furious calls were being made to know more about who this Steve Collins man was, and why someone had wanted him silenced – because of what he knew, of that they were already certain. Another lead to follow, perhaps it was the lucky break the police so desperately needed.

47

As Phil drove Harry and Cherry back to Harry's place, Cherry checked her phone for messages.

'My God! Harry, news is coming in of another major incident, this time at the docks. After a warning was given, allegedly by IS, a primed explosive device was found attached to one of the nuclear submarines awaiting decommission. They're saying it's been rendered safe, but an undisclosed number of other explosive devices are being looked for by bomb disposal teams and divers. The fear is we could be looking at a nuclear incident – a so called dirty bomb scenario.'

'My God, a third incident, what a day! Anything else?'

'Police are beginning to move nearby residents away from the most vulnerable areas whilst an urgent search is undertaken. People are being told not to panic and to move out as instructed.' Harry and Phil listened in silence.

'Why the hell hasn't Stu phoned to let me know?' exclaimed Harry. 'By the way has anyone seen him? Everything's kicking off. Fucking polling day on Thursday? Where is he, the twat? He'd better have a good explanation.' he blurted out, immediately rather regretting having let his image slip.

'Calm it Harry,' said Phil, 'You need to think about this latest bit of news.'

'We've had pieces in the paper for years warning of the danger these dumped nuclear subs pose to us. No-one in government was prepared to talk to us. We've got more nuclear waste here lying in Plymouth's naval scrapyard than anywhere else in the UK. All we've ever heard from Ministry of Defence officials were excuses about nowhere to process the nuclear waste. Reckon they will try to get it to Sellafield one day, but progress is too slow, it's been a catastrophe in waiting. People living near the dock area were especially worried, people with kids mainly,' said Cherry.

'Well, they were bloody well right!' said Harry, his mood none the better. Here he was stuck in a car, heading home, when where he really needed to be was down at the docks making political capital.

'Change of plan,' Harry suddenly announced. 'Glad you two are on board, a man with a mobile to take pictures and a script writing journalist. Perfect! We're going down to the docks. Next left, you idiot,' he instructed Phil who wasn't paying attention to the direction taken. Harry had spotted an opportunity, he needed to act now. He went quiet to think things through. Whatever Stu was up to would have to wait until later.

The traffic was heavy in the other direction, away from Devonport and Stonehouse.

'Look, people are fleeing the area, Harry,' said Cherry, taking her video cam from her bag. 'Do you think it's safe to go in there?' Harry ignored the question, eyes fixed ahead.

'Anything on chat lines, Twitter feeds,' asked Harry. 'Need to know what people are saying, what's going on,' he asked, placing his own phone in his hand in preparation for his own latest Twitter posting. He counted on his belief that political winners use social media sound bites. He waited so that he might actually send it from the dockside, so people knew he was there, with them, alongside them in their hour of desperation. There were more votes in this, he could feel it.

'Bit faster, can't you,' he urged Phil impatiently.

They headed toward a nearby tower block being emptied of its occupants by police officers. Many were waiting anxiously for the convoy of buses commissioned to take them to places of safety. 'We'll go over there,' he said, pointing to the waiting group of families clutching bags and cases, forming a despondent straggling line down the street.

Harry felt his rosette, corrected his tie, was glad he had his smart suit on. Then he spotted Stu, he was helping his brother and probably his brother's relatives out to the pavement.

'Over there,' said Harry, no further explanation needed. He stepped from the car and immediately caught Stu's eye. Harry moved toward the waiting evacuees and Stu stepped forward to intercept Harry. He knew he could expect a rebuke for neglecting Harry, but family needs had come first.

'Hi Stu, do me a favour, get your folks to chat with me for a minute. Bring them over here, it's a better shot, slightly in front of all the others,' Harry said directing things.

'OK Harry.' Stu turned and went back to confer with his family who seemed to be nodding in agreement.

'His chance to redeem himself,' said Harry as an aside to Cherry, his eyes fixed in Stu's direction. 'Time you chased up where the nearest camera crew is. Must be one around. Call Andy – there's news in this. Come on! Come on!' he chided.

'Harry, there's more news,' Cherry said, tugging Harry's sleeve. 'A shooting victim has been taken to the Derriford,' she said as she simultaneously tried to contact a local TV news team.

'Domestic, or what?' asked Harry, still watching Stu, now engaged in an animated conversation. It was half a minute before Cherry answered him, but not the question he'd asked her.

'You've all the luck, Harry. Camera crew are in this very block, but the police have told them to leave. Should be coming out in five.'

Harry smiled, the familiar phrase of Hannibal Smith in the A Team, 'I love it when a plan comes together,' crossed his mind. Turning back to the shooting story, Cherry looked up with more news.

'Oh, no domestic this. Twitter says man shot by a sniper on the Hoe!'

'Then we'll go to the hospital next,' said Harry. Once he saw the camera crew coming out and Cherry moving over to engage them, he caught Stu's eye and beckoned over his family group. He could tell Stu had done his thing, got them ready for him, nicely lined up. He might forgive him if this comes off, he thought.

All set and ready to roll. Harry took two paces toward Stu and into concerned politician and hand-pressing role.

'So sorry to hear you are all having to move. What's going on? What are you being told?' Harry asked.

'They banged on our door and told us to get out in two minutes. We've literally got what we can carry. It's chaos in there.'

'Sorry to hear it. Why the urgency?'

'Because our politicians have done nothing about making safe the nuclear subs dumped here in Plymouth. Our local authority, our MP's accepted them. We warned them. They didn't listen to us. Now we're all in danger and we've got to get out.' Great answer thought Harry as he smiled knowingly at Stu for lining up the answers.

'Where are they taking you?' followed up Harry.

'We haven't been told. No-one seems to know. It's chaos here.'

'Is there anyone from the local council to tell you what they've arranged?' asked Harry.

'You must be joking! It's Saturday night. They're all out in posh parts of town, they don't care about us. We're the forgotten people. Our tower blocks are neglected by them, they're unsafe as it is, they aren't going to show their faces down here.'

At that point a double decker bus pulled up, it was out of TV shot. The transport was for them and Harry thought he might lose his golden moment with Stu's family. He wasn't quite ready to let them disappear.

'I promise you one thing,' said Harry. 'On Thursday we have the chance to change things round here. I'm with you. I'm with you,' he cried as the camera moved to follow Stu and his group dragging their possessions over to the impatient crowd now swarming around the waiting bus.

'Right Cherry, Phil, Stu's forgiven. We're going straight to the hospital. Tell the camera crew, Cherry. I think they'll follow. Tell them there'll be some action there.

Turning on his heels, Harry led the way back to Phil's car. Phil cursed as it took three attempts to start, but once going, it didn't falter. Negotiating the heavy evacuation traffic fleeing north and east delayed their journey, as did crossing the east west A38 trunk road. It took a full forty minutes to get to the Derriford's A&E department. Harry insisted they drop him at the entrance.

The rain was falling again, it could pock-mark his smart suit, and image, as Harry well knew, was everything. Time alone was time for inspiration. Right now he was tired and feeling in need of some respite. He'd promised a news story but the promise was based on instinct rather than fact, he knew he had to manufacture something. He looked up as he saw Phil and Cherry hurrying through the rain, running towards him. He had an idea. It was now nine forty five on Saturday evening. The camera crew was waiting in the reception foyer. Once Harry had his colleagues alongside him again, he was set.

'Time to make an entrance,' he said, moving inside.

The duty receptionist had seen Harry arrive and had called security as well as her manager. This was out of her league. Word had quickly spread through the hospital grapevine that they had received another sniper victim that evening and she had been told to send for help if needed to deal with unwanted visitors. It was needed now.

Harry took to the floor, occupying the best position. He gave the camera crew a nod and a wink and then things were live. It was precisely two minutes past ten and he knew he'd still catch the ten-o-clock news with live coverage.

'I'm full of admiration for the work done by the medical staff at our local hospitals over the weekend as they have had to contend with serious Islamist terrorist incidents. What's more remarkable is their selfless devotion as people have come in from rest days and leave to help provide care. Let me be the first to say a huge thank you on behalf of the people of Plymouth.' Harry paused.

'I'm here this evening for another reason. Tonight there has been a further sniper victim brought here, to A&E, and I have come to visit and wish the patient well.'

Harry turned to find a hospital manager had, as he'd anticipated, come to join him.

'Sir, I'm delighted we have someone from the hospital with us. I was only saying how full of admiration and gratitude we all are for the work you and your team are doing.' The man was wrong footed, a camera close to his face.

'It has been a difficult weekend, but we are doing well. As you know regular bulletins are being issued as to the condition of the victims.'

'Yes, but what can you tell us about the person shot this evening, by Smeaton's Tower, the very symbol of our proud city?'

'I really can't tell you anything about the man's condition,' he said plaintively.

'So it's a man and he hasn't died,' said Harry, looking at the man to give him more.

'The police are with him,' he added.

'As a victim or a suspect?' fished Harry, wondering whether he should have said what he did.

'Umm, you will have to ask the police. The ward is protected by the police and I've been told not to issue any information. We will have to leave it there. I'm sure the Devon and Cornwall Police will release some information in due course.' But Harry hadn't finished.

'Would you say it was normal practice for patients to have a police guard? So far as the surviving patients from this morning's attack at Drakes Circus Shopping Mall are concerned, do any of them have a police guard?'

'Well, no, but…'

'So this patient is different. He's someone the police might think is involved in some way?' pressed Harry.

'I really have to leave it there, thank you,' said the hospital administrator, clearly keen to get off camera shot, knowing he had said way more than he should. Harry turned back to the camera to sum up.

'I want to end where I began with praise for our hard pressed and dedicated medical staff, and to express my best wishes to the patients here. But coming here tonight has alerted me to the fact that the police have more to tell us than they are currently revealing. They have a victim of sniper fire, a man. They haven't said who it is, this man who was shot near Smeaton's Tower earlier tonight, someone, given the level of police protection and interest, who might have insights into who these terrorists are. I for one want to hear from the police just how their investigations are going. I'm sure the people of Plymouth do too.' Harry was raising his voice, speaking directly to his viewers.

'We, the people of this proud yet suffering city, the victims of these incidents and public policy failure, need some answers from our politicians – where are they tonight? From our Chief Constable to the CEO of Devonport Dockyard – where are they? We, the people of Plymouth deserve better.'

With that Harry was pleased. Things couldn't have gone better. He looked at Phil. No more to be gained by staying here. Hospital security staff were getting ready to throw him out – he didn't want to give them the pleasure. It was late, visiting patients for bedside photos could wait until another day.

As they got back into Phil's car, Harry recalled something. He decided he didn't want to go over Cherry's article tonight – it could wait. 'Look Cherry, just ping me over the draft article you wanted to discuss. It's late. I'll look at it tomorrow. Phil, just drop me home. I can hear a steak and kidney pie and chips calling! Then I'll crash out, I'm all in,' he added feeling exhausted but also cheerful, if not positively elated.

48

It was Sunday morning and the sky had cleared. It promised to be a fine June day with lots of warm sunshine. No one in student accommodation gets up early on Sundays, and this house was no exception. Adam was the first to stir. Anxiety didn't lend itself to sound sleep patterns and he awoke with a fuzzy head after a broken night. Raqiyah, next to him, was still sleeping, purring softly, oblivious to the call of the new morning.

Adam liked the beginning of the day. Its quietness reminded him of those days on his bike cycling across Europe in his gap year, those early starts, the adventures. He could still only cope with thinking about it for short periods before he became too stressed, but he had to acknowledge early mornings were generally a good time.

He spotted the coffee cafetière and looked in the fridge for a bag of coffee grounds, cooled to retain freshness. Kettle filled, he put on the TV as he listened to it purr and crackle into life as it began to heat up. The continuous live TV news coverage was about an evacuation of Plymouth dockside, of residences and commercial properties. Even the naval areas were being cleared of personnel.

The reason was given in the rolling red headline breaking news banner with its white script. It told of an unknown number of terrorist Improvised Explosive Devices or IEDs planted on nuclear subs in Devonport dockyard. It was another incident in a terrible weekend and the potential consequences this time were far reaching. Talk was of panic and alarm and what to do if there was a leak of radiation. A road traffic bulletin explained that exit routes for the city were all clear after earlier severe congestion. Relocated families were shown temporarily bedded down in a sports centre.

Next a weather map and an inappropriately cheerful presenter. She showed the prevailing wind direction for the next ten days, and in historic footage of the 1986 Chernobyl disaster mapped coloured balloon shaped areas downwind indicating the different levels of expected radiation in the event of an explosion. It didn't look good, with Devon facing a Domesday scenario. Whatever the wind forecast, Adam noticed, the docks area and the adjacent Stonehouse Estate, immediately to the east, were always shown beneath an ominously glowing bright red colour.

Kettle boiled and coffee made, he grabbed two mugs, added milk, and carried them in one hand, the cafetière in the other, to perch on the side of the bed next to Raqiyah. She woke, glanced at the time on her phone, groaned, muttered 'eight thirty' but then smiled as she caught the scent of fresh coffee.

'Just been watching the news. Areas adjacent to the Devonport Docks in Plymouth are being evacuated. Because of possible explosions on nuclear subs awaiting decommissioning the cause. No one's saying, but popular thinking is that IS are behind this like the others. Where will it all end?' asked Adam.

'We can't stand by, do nothing, with these attacks on innocent Muslims,' answered Raqiyah. 'We must do something. We were really getting fired up with some good ideas last night. Let's get going, lots for us to do. I'm so energised by the belief that ordinary Muslims must step up and do something – I did a list on my phone. Let's grab some toast and then make a start. Pass me a coffee.'

An hour later and Raqiyah and Adam felt they had achieved a great deal. Bilal and Sophie had emerged from their room by this time and together they shared plans and updates. Calls kept coming in from the women in Raqiyah's Mosque group whom she had begun calling the previous night. They were wholeheartedly supporting her enthusiasm, and without Raqiyah having to do anything further they had planned a tea at the mosque event scheduled for both Exeter and Plymouth for Monday afternoon and early evening.

'I think we need to get the men more on board,' said Adam. 'They'd like to think they could defend their communities, especially the younger ones. In the face of the Harry McNamara's of this world, they'd warm to the idea of taking a stand. Are you up for helping do this Bilal? I mean it would need to be totally peaceful, non-violent, no weapons or anything like that. They're more likely to listen to you than to me.'

'I've not done anything like this before, but I know one or two people. Give me a couple of hours,' and he disappeared back in his room to make calls in private and without disturbance.

By lunchtime, plans were really taking shape. Adam had had a lucky break in trying to reach the Archdeacon of Plymouth. Although hesitant at first, a local Vicar, desperate to show goodwill when he heard what Adam had in mind, had been prepared to give him the Archdeacon's mobile number, and at the third attempt Adam had got through.

'Hello, Archdeacon. My name's Adam Taylor. You may have heard of me, I don't know. I was the young guy who got kidnapped by IS in my gap year as I cycled across Europe, then had the misfortune to be at the centre of events when an

IS attack occurred last Armistice Day. I'm now a student in your part of the world.'

'Yes, of course. How are you doing? Are you enjoying your course?'

'I'm fine and the course is good thank you. I saw you live on the TV at the hustings event yesterday,' said Adam.

'Not my best day – all very difficult, lots of messages since, not all happy ones I'm afraid.'

'I'm phoning to ask for your help. We're facing a bit of a crisis in inter-faith relations as a result of the recent terrorist incidents here in the South West and some fellow students and I, Muslim as well as Christian, well we thought an open community invitation to tea at the mosques in Exeter and Plymouth would be a good idea. I wondered, with your help, if we could get some support from the churches – to promote integration, goodwill. I'm afraid it is all rather short notice, Monday afternoon and early evening...'

Ten minutes later, Adam turned to his friends beaming. 'Got him,' he said, thinking of Harry in his sights, his friends however thinking of the Archdeacon.

49

April would have liked a day off, but all leave was cancelled and they were looking ahead to working mega shifts. Some were glad of the overtime, she wasn't interested in that – some breathing space would do her good, but the excitement of being involved in active policing kept her going, happy to be where the action was. The Home Office had agreed to meet any additional policing costs.

A short sleep on the coach back to Exeter at 4am, home five fifteen and she was back in the Gold Room Saturday morning at ten. Nick caught her eye. He was sitting at his screen. She thought she would speak to him directly before reporting to her skipper, Emma.

'Morning Nick. How's things?' she enquired moving in close.

'Long night. Little sleep. Big workload,' he replied. 'And you?'

'Much the same,' she said.

'Hey, you might be interested in this. Nothing further yet on the Cathy Nicholls hit and run, but there was another unusual death last night that's taken priority. It's not strictly my case, but the form is this. A sniper's bullet, matching the bullet type and gun used to kill people in the Drakes Circus Shopping Mall, was what was used to shoot an off-duty Royal Navy engineer at Smeaton's Tower yesterday evening – a male, Caucasian, name of Steve Collins.'

'What do we know?'

'He's down from Rosyth – reason for being here not clear – up to no good if you ask me. Our sniper definitely wanted to take him out. Thing is, the sniper missed. It was windy, raining, an early dusk. He's injured, shot right through, but below the heart and with luck he should make it.'

'What's the story?'

'Let's leave to one side the probability this same sniper wanted this man dead for a moment and consider Mr Collins' car.'

'His car?'

'Yes. He came down here in a grey Volvo. He said he'd left it in Lockyer Street, but someone deliberately took it down to a parking lot near the docks and tried to torch it.'

'Tried to?'

'Accelerant was used, so the Fire Investigator tells us – petrol probably. But whoever tried to set it alight hadn't reckoned on how many police were on duty down there last night. Some of our guys off the coaches and out of the cars were straight on to it, tackled it with fire extinguishers. Now here's the really cool bit. The front seats were badly burned, but the boot of the Volvo estate was more or less undamaged. Guess what was found inside?'

'You tell me.'

'A diving wet suit.'

'Not so strange if you're in the navy or if you're having a seaside holiday,' she said smiling, knowing there was more Nick wanted to tell her.

'No, but if it is an Egyptian model wet suit fitted with a give-away limpet mine carrying plate on the front, it does make you think doesn't it!' He paused to let April take it in, as she fell silent, wide eyed at this news.

He continued, 'It's a puzzle. He could have been out diving around the nuclear subs. He probably had the know-how, or he could have assisted some other person or persons unknown. And Egyptian equipment – that suggests links with Muslim radicals perhaps.'

'What more do we know?'

'Either he did it or someone who had got to him did it and then they wanted to silence him – saw him as a liability. Counter-terrorism are screaming at the military police and at GCHQ for urgent intelligence. Don't know any more.'

'I'm flabbergasted,' said April. 'I'd better report in to my Skipper. Thanks for the heads up, Nick. See you later,' she said, strolling away, letting her hand rub across his shoulders just enough that he registered her touch.

As she walked across the busy Gold Room floor her mobile rang. She could see it was Adam Taylor, so she walked quickly outside to take his call, waving as she did so to Emma to show she was on the phone.

'Adam,' she said.

'Hi April. Wanted to say thanks to you and the police for getting us out of the Rovers' ground safely yesterday afternoon. Thanks from us all.'

'That's OK, thanks. Nice of you to call.'

'Just wanted to run an idea past you if you have a moment. We, that is Raqiyah and I and our friends, we were wanting to work with the mosques in Plymouth and Exeter to have an open to the community 'tea' Monday afternoon. The mosques like the idea, we're going to ask the churches for their support too – they seem a likely ally, pro inter-faith, etc. pro good community relations, that kind of thing.'

'Sounds good to me, but be careful, there's a lot of tension out there. Keep me posted how it goes. I'll make sure the local community beat officers know it is happening when you confirm the arrangements. Must go, thanks, and have a good day.'

Back inside Gold Room, she finally caught up with Emma who looked drained. April wondered if she herself looked any better. People were running on adrenaline and strong coffee fixes.

'The army are being brought in today to work with us to keep a cordon sanitaire operating around the threatened dock area. Dogs are being sent in to see we didn't miss anyone last night. We don't have the resources in the police and when COBRA met yesterday at the Cabinet office they approved the continuing use of the military. Our guys will still be sort of in charge though, it's mainly about keeping people away from their homes for now, until all the devices have been rendered safe.'

'How many have been found?'

'Seven so far. We reckon there's probably one more on the remaining sub yet to be checked. They were planted by someone who knew exactly what they were doing; going for the most vulnerable point nearest the subs' nuclear reactors. Anyone moving out of the water, would most likely have been seen by the navy guards on watch. This had to be done by one or more skilled divers. We can't assume there's only one more, but there's a definite pattern to how they have been laid and no penetration of the sub interiors has been detected – so there's some optimism we might have this one under control.'

'What do we know?'

'Egyptian made limpets, fuelling speculation of an IS link. They had to be armed and set by someone who had been out there and trained – apparently priming and placing them is not as easy as they make it seem on films, and they can easily be detonated by mistake or if tampered with. Navy Bomb Disposal are the bravest of guys.'

'Were they primed?'

'Yes, all set for nine-o-clock tomorrow morning, when most of whatever naval workforce we've got left is on shift at the base.'

'So the clock's ticking to find and disarm what we think is the last one?'

'Yes. It's a better picture than we were looking at last night. I saw you talking to Nick. Did he tell you about our mysterious sniper hit diver man, Steve Collins?'

366

'Yes, but I'm puzzled – he's a man of contradictions – how does he fit in?'

'Counter terrorism have been in touch. We think he was turned. Not sure by whom yet. Someone will be going through his comms. He had a mobile on him. He's been serving on nuclear submarines for years, but was about to be decommissioned like his sub and it was common knowledge he wasn't happy about it. He isn't able to talk yet, but he will, he will. MI5 report he took a flight to Egypt recently and did a week's course in Alexandria. Apparently the Egyptian authorities are so keen to work with us on counter terrorism, they can't tell us enough. They're saying our man Steve Collins actually completed a training course in Alexandria recently, with a diving module, a course which figured significantly on Limpet mines.'

'But the questions are – who was behind him, grooming him if you like and who shot him and why?' surmised April.

'Maybe they wanted him dead in case he talked. That's often the way. So we know either he had something useful for us, or they needed to silence him for their own reasons.'

'And his killer, he's still out there, a professional sniper.'

'This was a single target, a single shot, and no accident. The target was deliberately chosen, and the miss was a slip up, reckon because the weather was bad making the shot risky in the first place. This man in hospital could be the lucky break we've been waiting for,' said Emma.

'And who's behind what's happening?' April asked.

'Trained IS explosives and snipers have infiltrated the UK as their campaign in the Middle East has collapsed, that much we know. After each of the three major incidents we've had these messages claiming to be from IS, but GCHQ Cheltenham are still saying they think they are suspect, they're not all they purport to be, leaving open the strong possibility it's someone else.' Emma went quiet for a moment, time to think.

'I want you to start your shift talking to our Prevent colleagues, double check what we've heard through participants in the Channel programme, what messages we've had come in from anywhere as to risky individuals or vulnerable places. We need something helpful, and it'll probably emerge only after hours of sifting through data, doing what we're good at.'

With that Emma moved away and April sat herself down. Once signed in to her temporary workstation with her personal ID, she began making the calls. An hour later and she knew she had nothing. She had begun by talking to her opposite numbers in the West Country forces, then took a coffee break. As she charged her mug, she thought of the Metropolitan Police she had so recently left. It felt like an age ago. The investigation was an excuse to talk to some of her old Prevent Officers in London. On returning to her seat, coffee steaming beside her, she rang Sally Fergusson in Islington. They'd stayed in touch ever since passing out together after police cadet training at Hendon.

'Hi Sally. April Cooper here – it's business not pleasure I'm afraid, but we must catch up sometime.'

'Hi April, good to hear from you. Everything seems to kick off wherever you go – remind me not to ask for appointments where you are,' she joked.

'I'm just making routine calls to Prevent colleagues to listen to what people are picking up on the ground. No stone is being left unturned in this investigation.'

'You mean the investigation isn't going anywhere yet,' she replied.

'You could say that. So what is bending your ear Sally? Anything of interest you're working on?' There was hesitation on the line.

'Could be nothing, but what's happening is exciting all the extreme right wing contacts we know of here in north London. They can't restrain themselves, want to tell me they see Harry McNamara as speaking for them. He's a certain bet to get elected they say, and a new right wing government only a matter of time. I can't put my finger on it, so it's just my instinct, but their enthusiasm has the feel of being orchestrated, someone or somebody more like, is behind the scenes pulling the strings, firing them up. They are more buoyant and confident in their own repulsive way than I've ever seen them before.'

'I've heard Harry McNamara speak. He's scarily unsettling. He's got a big following and all the attention is on him down here. With local fears sky high, he plays into that. I've never known a community to be so polarised. I took a call from a couple of people earlier who are trying to organise the local mosques in the South West to open their doors to the public – I sense the Muslim community's fears in the face of what's happening. I've got absolutely no intelligence that IS radicals are at work on the ground here, and the investigation is currently just throwing up puzzles,' said April.

The call over, she wondered whether she had anything worth reporting to Emma, but decided to do so anyway. She strolled across the floor and quickly passed on the central theme – no, no-one had anything, except the right wing were getting very excited and maybe there was more behind their rejuvenation than simply that. As she said it, it didn't sound very convincing, and Emma didn't comment. Emma said that there would be a Gold Room update briefing for everyone at twelve. They'd meet up after, and April would probably find herself sent out to use her community contacts to see if she could pick up anything useful on the ground.

At twelve, the commander ordered all who could to stop work and pay attention. He summarised what April had guessed and what ninety percent of them already knew. Then he added a bombshell.

In the past few minutes, additional CCTV from the top floor car park entrance of a retail store, seized by police yesterday in Plymouth, had picked up the same man in grey located in the suspect's sniper position at the Drakes Mall Shopping Centre at the critical time. On this occasion he was carrying what analysts are saying was his sniper rifle case. The man was white, a sole operative, the same key suspect for the Guildhall attack. There was a good enough image of his face, this time a front view, to begin facial recognition software searches. These were now being done. A decision as to when to release the man's picture and to warn the public would be made shortly. There was an annoying problem with CCTV vehicle imaging from the car park and as yet they hadn't been able to identify his car, but hopefully before long they'd have that information too.

'Colleagues, we are finally on to something. The solid police work done by our recently transferred colleague from the Met, April Cooper has set us on his trail.' Everyone's head turned toward Emma and there was muted applause.

'We need to find this man. He's very dangerous and still out there. Get to it.'

50

Harry decided, against all recent practice, to spend his Sunday morning going to his local St Martin's Parish Church. Seeing the Archdeacon at the hustings the previous evening had reminded him that he had promised himself to see if he could forge a tie between his party and the church. He believed there must be votes in it if he could get it right. His family had, after all, given their support to the parish over three generations, and given the fears in the community engendered by the weekend's incidents, a bigger congregation than usual would probably turn out.

The more people in church and the more of an occasion, the greater the gain for his public profile. The local news had been reporting the churches' help in the crisis and the prayers being offered today. With luck he might be able to sign a book of condolence.

He also thought it would go down well if he got his parents to attend with him. It was only after some animated discussion over breakfast that they eventually agreed to come – family had to support each other sometimes, he'd argued. Finally, they'd caved in. They discussed how long it had been since they last attended and concluded that beside Michael's funeral it was, in reality, probably several years.

They decided to walk, the distance only a matter of a couple of streets. As they left the house, in a line across the pavement, Harry made use of the time to make calls to Phil, Cherry and Stu to alert them to his plans. He didn't think he wanted Stu there at church – he looked too much like a football fan, even in his suit, but he wanted him around afterwards.

In front of them, someone had left a bunch of flowers on the pavement, and Harry silently recalled this was the spot where Cathy had died. He again visualised the red blood running from her ear, and quickly carried on walking without altering his stride.

Cathy's death had left gaps and he needed to think about additional help. His mind began turning over how he'd manage. Phil knew he had to get Andy over to handle photographs and the social media; Twitter feed he'd do himself. Cherry, well, she'd sent him the piece about his grandfather, but it looked long and he hadn't yet had a chance to read it – they'd need to talk after the service too. Stu would need to go through the programme for the final days up to Thursday, and to tidy up the loose ends.

Then they were there. Churches always had that musty almost damp smell thought Harry as he sniffed the air on entry. A look of panic and concern showed in the face of the lady pacing just inside the porch, whose job it was to welcome the McNamaras into church. Harry wasn't sure she wanted to say 'Good Morning' to them, but in a noticeable tone of embarrassment she said it anyway. Harry didn't recognise her, nor did he think she was important and without slowing he walked on inside. There seemed to be plenty of empty seats from which to choose.

An elderly man with a stick showed them to some seats near the front – a more prominent position than his parents had wanted, but a position in front of the pulpit that suited Harry perfectly. Hushed murmurings indicated people had clued in to who they were – the words "the McNamaras are here!" were going round like Chinese whispers.

Harry gazed around him in the few minutes he had before the robed choir processed in and the service began. Then he felt unsettled, for he wasn't the one in charge – and he was being more closely scrutinised than he cared to admit to himself. He reminisced about past periods of boredom he'd endured attending family services as a child, and as he let his mind wander, he gazed around him.

He spotted memorials to unknown past worthies, then he saw a shiny more modern brass plaque on the wall with Michael McNamara's name engraved on it. The small lettering beneath was unreadable from where he was sitting and he resolved to look at it more closely later.

As he looked, he became aware of people talking to each other in the rows behind. He turned, and it struck him that the sea of faces looking his way were a complete cross-section of ethnicities and ages – something he hadn't anticipated, and he wondered what had become of the Church of England since he had last visited. Maybe coming here wasn't such a wise choice.

The rumblings continued until finally, with a clatter, several people appeared to leave their seats and exit the church just as the service was starting. People near the door had a hurried conversation to try and prevent them, but they were clearly adamant and disappeared.

Harry wondered what their problem was, and for some unknown reason his instinct for reading these things was not working so well today. Some kind of uneasy order then reestablished itself as the liturgical procession entered and the organ played. They all stood as the service began.

Harry went along with the monotony of it, rising from and resuming his seat as instructed by the Vicar. He realised how tired or bored he was, and when after a long series of Bible readings the Vicar ascended the pulpit to preach, he wondered if he'd be able to keep his eyes open. His mind totally elsewhere, his thoughts began to go through his diary, taking stock of the three crucial campaigning days left to him in the week ahead.

In an inadvertent moment of giving attention to what the Vicar was saying, he heard something about the meaning of friendship, and he heard a cynical voice inside him saying, the only true friend he'd ever had was his grandfather, everyone else had let him down.

Then the Vicar went on about the friendships that the weekend had created in the community, people coming together in the face of adversity to support and help one another. It was what the Christian faith was about – love in action.

Harry shuffled uncomfortably in his seat, before thinking better of himself for his own role in the previous day's community awards he'd presented, and he congratulated himself for thinking of it. He began to think about how friendships worked – people had to like the same things to be friends, share the same interests and want the same goals. Otherwise they didn't work. Why didn't the Vicar talk about enemies and dealing with them? From that point on Harry only listened to see if the Vicar would address how to deal with enemies, but he didn't and it made Harry boil inside. He was frustrated he hadn't been able to add some words of his own. Sermons, he decided were so one sided.

By the end of the service, when a 'warm invitation' to stay for tea or coffee afterwards was given, Harry was absolutely seething. It was as if the service had released some dark force within him he could no longer control. As soon as the organist had finished his rendering of a Bach fugue, he resolutely marched up to the Vicar; leaving his parents chatting politely to someone they obviously knew.

'Vicar, I hope you don't mind me saying so, but I was listening to what you said about friendship and was left wondering whether you have anything to say at all about how we deal with our enemies?' asked Harry, the words coming out more directly than he'd envisaged.

'Lovely to see you all here, been some time, and I know you've been so very busy,' the Vicar said graciously. 'Enemies – I'm not so good on. That's for another day – the Christian church teaches forgiveness, but not without holding alongside claims for justice and peace.'

'The Old Testament speaks of punishing the evildoer, the wrong doer, even killing those in the way of the people of God – we shouldn't forget that too,' said Harry, only slightly cooling.

At that point they were interrupted. A crowd had gathered around Harry and were wanting to ask him questions of their own. A coffee cup was thrust into his hand. He looked round for Phil and Cherry. They were too busy drinking coffee and not looking his way. A media opportunity was going begging and they weren't doing their job. Again, his anger started to rise, and he called out to them causing heads to turn.

'Oi, you two, over here,' he instructed.

They looked round, but so did everyone else, a sea of faces turning his way. Again, he'd been louder than he'd intended, it sounded rather all too like how he gathered his mates together at Home Park, having to shout above the noise of the fans. He noticed again how mixed the congregation was, and how unsettling he found it. This is not church, he said to himself, as he wondered what kind of place he'd stepped into, this is a waiting room for lost people.

'Mr McNamara, how do you square your politics with coming to church? I'm sure some of us would like to hear it,' said a woman waving her empty mug in his direction.

'My family have supported this church for generations. We are loyal to our community and yesterday I was invited to recognise what the good people do by presenting awards at Home Park. Some of you may have seen me. The awards came from my family,' Harry said, waving his arm in the direction of his parents a little way off.

'But you hold racist views,' said another woman.

'That would be an unfair caricature of our party's policies. We want to bring about a peaceful transition to a more just and fair society where the perpetrators of hate are given no platform. Surely that's what you all want too?' asked Harry trying to convince this congregation.

'Do you have any Muslim friends?' asked a man beside him.

The question caught Harry unawares and he didn't know what to say. Nothing came, and he realised he had none, not just no Muslim friends, but no real friends at all.

In panic he called over to Phil and Cherry once again, who were nearer to him now, to ask if the good people would mind if Phil took a picture of them standing 'with him'. But the remark seemed to have been misheard as he found himself isolated, only his Mum and Dad standing either side. Phil took the pictures anyway and then the five of them promptly left as a group, isolated, detached, marginalised.

'That wasn't one of your best outings Harry,' offered Phil as they moved quickly out of the door. 'I've never seen you stuck for words like that before.' Harry, silently remembered another occasion – the Businessmen's Breakfast.

Once outside, Harry realised, in all his distraction, he'd never got to read the words on the shiny plaque dedicated to his grandfather. Never mind, he thought, they weren't that important.

51

Job done, Carl shook his wet jacket and hung it on the back of his door. He'd left his kit safely hidden by dark windows in the back of the Range Rover parked well out of sight. Then he ordered a pizza to be left outside his room door as before and, after eating, he was soon soundly asleep.

When he woke at eight on Sunday morning he was anxious to be leaving the South West, a journey he'd intended to make later in the day. Mission complete, for the next few hours he had nothing to do. He shuffled uneasily, desperately wanting to head off east, reasoning that the sooner he could put any distance between himself and the pursuers he knew would be on his tail, the safer he would feel. He needed to ease the nervous stress of feeling so exposed whilst still lying low in the mission zone.

His plan was to check out of the hotel at the end of the morning and slip into the usual busy throng of Sunday traffic heading for the A38 and M5 and back to the metropolis after a weekend in the country. He showered, dressed, made himself a coffee, decided to forgo breakfast, and switched on the TV news channel to pass the time.

He knew that although the authorities on his tail never released all the cards they held in their hand, he was nonetheless pleased to see they really hadn't got any. That suited him just fine, but at any point they could get a break and be on to him. The thought made him feel unusually on edge.

After a quarter of an hour the cycle of news bored him with its routine of switching between bleeding heart stories, the evacuation of the areas surrounding the docks, and police statements as to the progress of the investigation. He flipped to an old Agatha Christie film and lay back on the bed.

Whilst lost in the intricacies of a crime thriller whose plot was set in a stately home, a thought suddenly occurred to him and he felt a shudder of fear. He pictured the man he'd taken down the previous night as someone just like himself. It took one military man to know another.

That guy had done his job down at the docks, and then the order had come to Carl – take him down. Maybe it was the Agatha Christie film, the hiding of evidence – the silencing of witnesses that had triggered the thought– but his blood went cold. He found himself asking a new question – how secure was Carl Reynolds himself?

End of mission satisfaction at the thought of a job well done was rapidly giving way to something akin to paranoia – what if The Circle wanted to tidy up by getting rid of him too?

He sat up and began to think hard. To live meant taking precautions, it also meant having something to bargain with. It struck him that the information he held was a strong bargaining counter that might just save him. He knew from past experience The Circle were ruthless, but they were also pragmatic. The last thing they wanted was a whistleblower and he realised he knew enough to blow a very loud whistle. His mood lifted a little as he realised the information he held could save his skin.

He was about to turn off the TV when Harry McNamara popped up on camera, the scene, a local hospital. Curiosity held his attention. On listening to Harry, he quickly learned, to his professional displeasure, that his target last night had survived his shot. The Circle wouldn't be best pleased, nor was he, berating himself for poor performance. He now had another problem, how was he to handle this unwelcome development?

He didn't see it as his role to let The Circle know, they'd pick up on it soon enough. As he reflected on his poor shot, he once more saw his personal future with a building sense of foreboding. Carl knew there would be no second chance to get his injured target – he'd be protected within the safety of the hospital like the crown jewels. Well, good luck to him – like himself he'd be wondering what lay round every corner for evermore. They were both two hunted ex-military men with poor prospects.

Then he came up with an idea – to write an e-mail report of all that he knew, but keep it by him as a draft document only to be sent if it became absolutely necessary. This would be his safety net. But who to address it to... who indeed? He realised with a shock how marginal he was – he had no family, no friends, certainly no-one he could trust. There just had to be someone – but there he was stumped.

Taking out his phone it took him nearly two hours to put together the kind of cover blowing story he required. It was complete with all the information he had been privileged to access through his own long service of The Circle. The names and contact details took a while to assemble, but were all included. A list of crimes the police no doubt had categorised as "unsolved", were set alongside enough evidential information as to what had truly happened that his e-mail was sure to gain someone a promotion. The final page of his e-mail detailed everything relating to the events of the past weekend, until only the recipient address remained empty. It stared back at him.

Carl read the whole thing through again. It made him feel sad, it read too much like an obituary, but at least he had been a somebody, a noble man who had served the true national cause.

Two things remained to be done, one immediate, the second more ongoing. Firstly, having finally made up his mind, he identified someone to send the e-mail to and entered the address before locating everything in the draft folder where it would sit until the time came, if ever, to send it into the ether. Secondly, he resolved from this point on, to view the day and the coming days, should he be so lucky as to live that long, as but a continuation of the weekend's mission, the final chapter being simply to keep himself alive!

To stay alive he would have to be vigilant, exercise cunning, and bring to bear all the skills of a lifetime in the military. Carl thought about disappearing for a while. It could be done, but being endlessly on the run felt to him like living as a dead man walking. No, he'd rather take his chances with The Circle, but with his safety net in place, through vigilance and his personal insurance, he might just stay alive.

Instead of checking out of the hotel at twelve as originally intended, he held on until room service staff were pressing him to go. He kept them at bay telling them he had to see the end of the movie. In the end he left at one-o-clock, settling his bill in cash. He observed the hotel car park from a lobby window for several minutes and then scanned the vista to the front of the hotel. There were lots of people about which made things feel safer and he couldn't see anything untoward to worry him. It was time to move.

He made his way quickly to his vehicle, and immediately started up and drove steadily away. Damn, he thought, he never looked underneath for any explosives that might have been attached. Such absentminded carelessness was foolish.

Once certain he wasn't being followed he pulled up, making the chassis check look as casual as he could make it. Finding nothing and once back behind the wheel he felt safer, for the present.

No cars had followed him, none pulled up when he did. No explosive device found, he judged that if a tracker had been attached to his car he'd almost have to strip it down to have any chance of locating it. If it was placed professionally, searching for it would be a waste of time. He took a chance there was none and pressed on, feeling a much troubled and hunted man, a contrast to the man he was only a few hours ago when he thought he had done so well and only rewards would come his way.

On the road, he soon joined the A38 and in the anticipated heavy traffic nonetheless moved swiftly away from Plymouth. After putting some Chopin on, the music began to help him relax, and he began to think more positively – maybe, just maybe, he had a chance of having his life back again. Maybe the Master would still trust him, find a new use for him in the cause. On balance they ought to have been well pleased with the weekend storm he had created.

So far as he could judge, the electoral tide had turned and he couldn't see any way that Harry McNamara could lose on Thursday. Surely that was more than they could want from him? That had to be enough to guarantee him a lifeline.

52

Though Harry saw his visit to St Martin's Church as one of the least comfortable, less successful parts of his campaign, he was absolutely delighted to see what Phil and Cherry had come up with between them to publicise it.

As he looked on his phone at various media platforms, he discovered that his attendance at church had been wonderfully framed in the most helpful light, and his mood switched from despondency to pleasure. He thought it all read rather like the Queen attending Morning Prayer at Balmoral – the account had all the right messages of Harry doing the right thing on a weekend of pain for so many. Harry could see how it would turn wavering voters, and above all the visuals give the subconscious mind a message – that the church was unwaveringly on board too. Couldn't be better, he told himself.

Just to complete the media picture, he couldn't resist posting a line on his Twitter feed to the effect that all good causes had to be built on the right spiritual foundations – it seemed suitable for the sombre public mood this Sunday. A glance at the number of his Twitter followers – up significantly again – further lifted his mood.

A Sunday lunch roast was a bit of a ritual at the McNamara home and today was no exception. His Mum had left something in the oven on the timer. It was invariably roast beef. He was feeling hungry at the thought as he accompanied his parents on the short walk back from church. The family together, had also made a nice family picture. However, as they walked, he realised his parents were unusually pensive and quiet and Harry picked up on their mood.

'Penny for your thoughts Dad,' said Harry.

'Not sure you'll want to hear them, Son,' he said.

'Come on – just been to church. Time for confession,' he jested.

'It's no time for laughs, Harry,' he said.

'Business good?' inquired Harry, thinking that was his Dad's main worry these days.

'Couldn't be better,' he replied. 'No, Your Mum told me you'd had a visitor yesterday. We talked about it.' Harry wondered where this was going and felt guarded.

'I get visitors all the time,' he said defensively, 'goes with the territory.'

'Don't try and smart arse me! He left you a lot of money, ten grand. Doesn't that bother you, Son?'

'Gave it to Mum to take care of – no, not really, since you ask. Not given it a thought since yesterday,' he said in all honesty.

'Well it should. Your Mum may do everything for you, but she's not stupid. She told me she didn't like the man, and she's a good judge of character. So what's the deal with the ten grand?' His Dad sounded like he all too often did - irritable and testy.

'No deal. He's just a generous supporter, we did no deal. Supporters can be very generous. Don't worry yourselves,' said Harry.

By then they were home, the opening of the front door releasing the aromas of the roast. Attention switched to getting the table set – it was a familiar domestic routine. Harry mainly watched, explaining he had to put on the TV to keep up with things.

The newsreader told of a manhunt under way, and then Harry had a terrible shock. The police image of the man showing on the TV for all the world to see was clearly yesterday's visitor. His Mum, also saw him and let out a startled cry.

53

April felt pleased that Prevent had had a positive contribution to make to the manhunt. Colleagues had asked what had triggered the investigation into the sinister "Grey Man" as he was being nicknamed. April knew it was something of a coincidence she had spoken to someone who was prepared to say they had seen something different, but she was happy to take the personal plaudits. Prevent worked best, she said when asked, if it was listening to people at the grassroots. People liked that and it gave the Prevent counter-terrorism profile a positive gloss it hadn't always had hitherto.

There was much still to be done. No definite leads had come in during the two hours since the picture was released to the press. Early days, yes, but Gold Room were desperate for things to gather pace – all knew the early window of opportunity was key to progress. Nerves were raw, edgy even, and tiredness was beginning to wear people down one by one.

At two on Sunday afternoon, Gold Room went quiet as everyone turned to listen to the Commander. Perhaps he had some news to share. His face was a picture of grim and haggard determination.

'OK everyone, listen up. Update time. Taking events in order. Exeter Guildhall. We now have cleared the building and can confirm we have twenty nine fatalities, with two of those injured still critical at the Royal Devon and Exeter Hospital. Eight others are still in hospital but out of danger. The Fire Service say the building's secure – no remaining fires or hot spots and an early forensic heads up gives us a military grade explosive, fingerprint Eastern Europe. In itself we can't read anything into that. All the CCTV footage we've seen and the witness statements taken point to "Grey Man" as a sole operative near the scene. Questions so far?'

'Will the High Street be open to the traffic and the public for tomorrow? Bus companies and business people are wanting to know if they can get into their shops and businesses.'

'Thank you. Yes. A real pressure to get back to normality. The local authority are erecting new barricades even as I speak. All being well, yes, open tomorrow seven a.m.' No further questions followed.

'Moving on to Plymouth, the Drakes Mall Shopping Centre. Here, sadly the sniper killed all twenty one of his targets. There are no injured in Plymouth. That's already fifty dead in total. We've worked out where he fired from and the site is being swept as I speak. A CCTV shot puts our "Grey Man" in the vicinity but unfortunately we have not yet got anything to tie him to the precise spot. The shot we have shows him carrying a case, commensurate with a sniper rifle grab bag. As you will appreciate, unlike the Guildhall, we're dealing with a big open site and it has taken a lot longer to do the forensics and make the searches. Again, thanks to the help from neighbouring police forces, we are hoping to reopen the area tomorrow by seven.'

'Sir, are we not risking the public? Shouldn't everyone be encouraged to stay indoors until we've apprehended this killer?'

'Good question. No, though risky, the politicians dictate that we should, true to our character as a nation, carry on calmly as normal. Just to add to what I was saying. There is little doubt that "Grey Man" is the person responsible for both incidents. He may or may not have had accomplices.' He paused.

'Last night, we had a third major incident at the Devonport Docks, potentially the most serious, with viable timed explosive devices fastened to all eight nuclear submarines docked for decommissioning. I can now report that after extensive searches and admirable bravery by Bomb Disposal, a total of nine limpet mines have been recovered and disarmed. There are not thought to be any more to be found and our man in hospital, Mr Collins, has finally talked and confirmed this.'

'Can he be believed? A lot hangs on this. We don't want to see a dirty nuclear explosion because someone missed another mine?'

'The bullet Mr Collins took served to inform him his paymasters saw him as entirely expendable and he has since been fully cooperative with us. Reports are that the information he's been only too willing to provide is 100% reliable.'

'Does that mean people can return to the dockside too, Sir?'

'No. That is being done more slowly. The plan is to allow that to happen from tomorrow afternoon, providing nothing untoward occurs in the meantime. People are being told as I speak.' There were murmurs of relief. Public resentment at being kept from their homes by the police was starting to rise.

'Finally, let me tell you where our investigation is headed.' People felt encouraged and lifted by the progress the commander's summary had shown and listened attentively and politely.

'So, three major incidents on this force's watch within twenty four hours – how are they linked, who's behind them and where's the investigation going next? No question they're all part and parcel of the same big picture and despite what the conspiracy theorists might be saying, claims that IS are responsible are unsustainable.' He paused and could detect the surprise amongst some in the room.

'We're looking here at something else. Our friends are telling us,' he said with a knowing nod to the regional counter-intelligence officer to his left that this increasingly looks like a right wing extremism mission. What we know currently is we have had two caucasian military, or ex-military operatives, putting the fear of God into the South West at a time when we have a by-election with an outspoken extreme right wing candidate in Harry McNamara whose policy stance is taking maximum political advantage from each and every incident. What Harry says makes UKIP sound like a teddy bears' picnic!' There were shuffles around the room.

'Further, these two men are not operating without having sophisticated back up. Mr Collins hasn't been able to tell us much on that front, simply because he hasn't been told much and hasn't personally met with people. His phone and the detective work on the things in his car are giving us leads, but yielding information only slowly. It was a clever ruse on their part to deploy Egyptian limpets and Eastern European rather than home produced explosive material, we could so easily have linked them wrongly, as it happens, with IS. We believe Mr Collins was singled out as a vulnerable individual and then groomed for the mission at arm's length by a third party. GCHQ and counter-intelligence are not giving away much on that front for now.'

'Don't you think it's time we had Harry McNamara in for a conversation at least?' asked Emma Stirling.

'That's the Chief Constable's call. She's already had her fingers burned for interfering in a by-election, so she's got a tricky decision to make. That's why she's paid more than you lot,' he added.

There was little more to add and people went back to their tasks knowing that it was a matter of urgency the shadowy "Grey Man", a key to the investigation, was quickly found. What everyone was desperate to see in the coming hours was the so far elusive lucky break. They felt it was coming but still tantalisingly just out of reach.

April returned to her desk wondering whether the Chief Constable had been informed as to Cathy Nicholls' death and who had reported it to the police, or whether in all the focus going on the big terrorist incident picture, this minor incident had been rather lost sight of. She was the one person in the room who felt it was well nigh time to ask Harry McNamara a few direct questions.

54

Harry had to think hard and fast, with Carl's TV image seared in his memory. He felt he was back in the old days, with his mates at an away match and trying to keep one step ahead of the rozzers. He'd always escaped a scrape by being quick thinking, taking the necessary decisions, and yes, sometimes being ruthless when necessary, and he admitted to himself sometimes when it wasn't. No one stood in his way when the chips were down. But first he'd try to rally his troops.

'Let's talk about this over dinner, shame to let the roast get overdone,' offered Harry. Five minutes later they were all sat down, his Dad silently carving the beef and putting slices on everyone's plates. Harry could feel the tension in the air. He didn't like it. Home was never meant to be like this.

It was only when they were finishing the apple pie and custard, Harry chose to return to the conversation; to what was uppermost in everyone's mind.

'What do families do when they're under threat? They stick together. We need to do this now. We're all implicated, just days before the election. We were all in the house when he called. Mum, you were even in a meeting with him. Now look, this man isn't here, we're not hiding a wanted man. We wouldn't, we're decent people.' Harry opened his arms wide to express innocence.

'If we knew where he was, if we were sure who he was, of course we'd need to call the authorities straight away. If they call us, if they ask, "Was he here?" we can tell them, he was. We've nothing to hide. Don't you think so?' he asked, but got no reply.

'If they want the donation to party funds he left with us, it's still untouched in the envelope isn't it Mum? We can hand it over. But for now, it would be prudent for us to sit tight, stand together. It isn't as if the CCTV picture is a definite likeness, we can't be sure our caller was him, now can we?' Harry dropped that thought quickly in the face of the incredulous looks he got in return.

'After all it isn't going to make one jot of difference to the police whether we call or not.'

'Harry, this isn't some game, we need to call the police now,' interrupted his Dad.

'I'm not playing a game, Dad. Look at Mum. She isn't with you on this. She knows she'll get into trouble. Do you want to put her through that? We can't do this to her for the sake of a little delay, it makes not a monkey's toss of a difference. And do you want to be the ones to scupper my chance of election – my big chance? Come on Dad, you were good enough to fund my nomination; you're the last person not to want a return on an investment. You don't want to throw my future away, do you? Think it through – a little pause, nothing wrong in that, no harm done. Mum, you think so, don't you?' Harry pleaded.

Head bowed, his Mum nodded and the argument was over. His Dad simply turned and left the room with, 'I've got things to do.'

'I have to get on too, Mum. Stu will be here any minute and we've only got three days of campaigning left. Any chance of some tea when he arrives?' Harry asked as he stood up from the uncleared dinner table and set off upstairs to his room.

Harry sat himself down on his bed thinking hard. For the first time in this campaign he felt he was up against it. This man Carl, whoever he was – Supporter? Terrorist? Both? He'd turned out to be a bloody nuisance. It wouldn't look at all good if Harry was thought to have sheltered the country's number one most hated, most wanted man. How was he to manage this one?

He decided he'd take Stu into his confidence, there was no one else he could trust. Stu had an unusual ability – he was invariably able to read situations well. He spotted Cherry's draft article left for him to read on his desk, lying in the half of his room cluttered with the detritus of a campaign office – well he'd nowhere else to go. As he was about to reach for Cherry's piece on his grandfather, the door bell went, he put it down again – it would be Stu.

Stu walked into the front room carrying two mugs of tea, and passed one to Harry.

'Your Mum was on her way with these. Is she all right? Is she well?' he asked, as he pushed papers off one of the chairs to sit down.

'Yeah, fine. The campaign is taking its toll on us all,' said Harry. 'In fact, I'm glad to see you. Something awkward's come up and I need your judgement on it.' He could see Stu was now giving him his serious attention, looking his way, waiting for more.

'Yesterday morning, around eleven, I had a visitor here. He'd booked earlier to see me, claimed he was a supporter, I'd never seen or heard from him before – strange man, a mystery man if ever there was one – left a large cash donation toward funds.'

'Nice kind of mystery man, then,' said Stu.

'I thought so, but I had a funny feeling about him. People don't threaten me normally, yes, he was definitely putting the pressure on, like he thought he represented a Mr Big, or something. His donation, well it was ten thousand, and in cash.'

'Bloody hell! Dodgy money, dodgy man,' said Stu, voicing what Harry knew to be true.

'I could handle it, but for one thing – he's the same guy everyone's looking for, for last Friday's terrorist attacks.'

'Hell! Did you call the police?'

'No, not yet.'

'It's a problem. I can see it. Could compromise the campaign. Your Mum knows doesn't she?' said Stu.

'Yes, Dad too. We talked about it over dinner just now. We decided to hold fire on calling the police for now – nothing to be gained – damage limitation, just three days of campaigning left. How do you see it?'

'Does anyone else know he came here?'

Harry suddenly remembered things were even more complicated by Cathy's death, she'd known, she'd called Harry and died for doing so. He'd called the police to report the hit and run, but not the conversation they'd had or his suspicions. He wondered if the situation was too bad to be contained. He decided to tell Stu.

'Yes. Now this really is just between us. After I met with Phil and Cathy yesterday morning, they left before this man arrived. However, I had no idea, but Cathy must have wondered who he was and let her curiosity get the better of her. She waited around, don't know where, and then followed him from the house. She called me when she thought she knew where he lived. She said he'd gone into a house, found out where he lived and "wouldn't I like to know". Told her she'd overstepped the mark, but yes, I'd like to know.'

'And where did he live?'

'Didn't make sense, the address she gave, I know Mrs Harris lives there, old lady on her own, been there years. I wondered if she had any relatives, and then I heard the crash, the sound of a vehicle approaching, the thud of a vehicle hitting her. The phone was still on as the vehicle drove off, then there was just silence, she never spoke back to me. I went out, found her round the corner, called the police when I got there. But I kept her phone, that's it,' he nodded to it on his desk.

'That makes it more complicated. They'll say you withheld evidence if they get the opportunity. What's in your favour is that chances are, the police are so busy with the terrorism, a hit and run isn't going to feature on their priority list for ages. They'll get round to investigating it, ask more questions after a post-mortem, maybe come back to you, but my guess is you'll probably have a few days, more likely even longer until they start sniffing around again. You'll need to have your answers ready, but I can see how you could justify your actions without being charged with anything – don't worry about it. You did the right thing in ringing for an ambulance, in getting help – that was the most important thing, everyone will understand that.'

Harry wasn't convinced, but he had run out of options and was feeling desperate to capitalise on the majority both polls in today's Sunday papers were promising him. That was enough to settle it. He didn't want to do anything to undermine his chances.

'OK Stu. Thanks. We'll sit on our secrets for now, just like old times eh, and keep things under review. Cathy's absence means I have to rely on your help all the more for the coming days' programme. She'd mapped it all out, booked all the arrangements and lined them all up, but you and I will need to spend some of this afternoon just rehearsing them through – she really was good at making me do that.'

At that, the afternoon's conversation turned to the business of attending to the final days of the campaign.

'Tomorrow morning we go to the site the Pilgrim Fathers sailed from. We are being met by tourism staff and will be handshaking with visitors, holiday, business and retail staff' said Stu. 'More nice pictures in it! Good messages!'

Harry thought of the irony. Being there he would be celebrating the departure by boat of people not welcome to stay in this country. Hadn't the pilgrims chosen a different religion to the Church of England, and in doing so become religious extremists – people who just didn't fit in?

My, how history repeats itself, he thought to himself, and for the first time that afternoon he allowed himself a smile.

'Stu, thanks mate. You've been a great help. Line up Phil and Cherry for the visit tomorrow, will you. Get Andy in, he does the best pictures. Right now I need to do some speech writing ready for the morning. So thanks, time for you to bugger off!' he said with a smile.

Stu saw himself out, carrying a nagging doubt in the back of his mind as to whether this time he'd really given his friend best advice. Harry was so headstrong it wasn't always possible to say things as they were – Stu went out on the street thinking this time his friend's folly would soon catch up with him, not in days but in the blink of a policeman's eye.

55

Heading north in a line of traffic on the M5, just south of Bridgwater in Somerset, Carl Reynolds knew his luck had run out. He briefly sped up to ninety five miles an hour just to confirm his suspicions, then took a last minute decision to pull off into the Bridgwater Services, using the hard shoulder to exit and by pass the queuing traffic at the roundabout up ahead.

The blue grey BMW in his rear view mirror had only just started tailing him about three miles or so back and now there was a second identical car. Both followed him on the hard shoulder as he swerved left and right entering the darkness of the enclosed low level grey concrete structure of the car park. He knew there would be no escape.

Pulling his car neatly and purposefully into the far left hand corner, the only available space, he was tight against the concrete wall. He leant low and reached left into his glove compartment, took out his still unused brand new ready loaded black SIG hand gun and held it at his temple in his left hand. He remembered doing the same to Harry with the gun and wondered what he'd thought. As he waited for the end, he took out his phone in his right hand and flicked it on. He was ready.

In his mirrors he could see they were, as he'd guessed, an armed response unit. He recognised they were following a well rehearsed drill and he could see they were out of their cars and closing in. Little time remained. He took one final look at his mobile, pressed his finger to the top right hand screen button and then reached for his SIG and pulled the trigger. It was four fourteen, Sunday 4th June. Carl Reynolds was dead.

Hearing the gun, the two leading officers warily approached the Range Rover. They'd heard the shot, guessed a suicide, but darkened rear windows made it difficult to be certain that what they suspected had actually occurred. Uncertain as to whether he was alone or whether the vehicle might explode, the lead officer was running on adrenaline, pumping him up and driving him into action. All the while the other officers were backing him up whilst giving live radio reports back.

The officers in the second car began hastily ordering the crowds in the busy service station to move back away from the area, whilst watching their backs and those of their two colleagues. Unlike most motorway services, the Bridgwater site felt cramped and with nowhere to send people to safety. They were desperate for the much needed cavalry to come riding over the hill. There was only so much a total force of four police officers, with divided attention, albeit waving guns, could do.

The lead officer used the concrete pillars for protection as he darted forward to the dark Range Rover. He instantly recognised "Grey Man" sitting upright, leaning against the driver's side blood spattered window, and spotted the pistol on the floor by his feet. No-one else appeared to be in the vehicle. The suspect appeared to be dead. The man stepped back behind the safety of the grey concrete pillar once more and talked into his radio. Surges of relief and satisfaction at a job well done pulsed through his adrenaline high body.

'We have him. "Grey Man" appears to be dead inside his vehicle. He's taken his own life, a hand gun beside him, a bullet hole clean through his head. Awaiting instructions before proceeding further.' Glancing again at the black Range Rover, he wondered whether the vehicle might be booby trapped and quickly stepped away and into the relative safety afforded by a concrete pillar – the vehicle was now someone else's problem. Call over, he could imagine the cheers back reverberating around Middlemoor HQ.

56

Late Sunday afternoon, Harry was sitting at his desk when his phone pinged to announce a new e-mail delivery to his inbox. So much mail, so many things to read and respond to, he didn't give it another thought, and it remained unopened, along with around seventy others. He must check them later, he told himself, as he turned his attention once again to the speech he needed to deliver at eleven tomorrow morning.

The venue Cathy had arranged was spot on. For a second he thought he actually missed her, and could hardly believe she had gone. In the morning he'd be standing between the Doric columns of a small colonnaded stone portico located beside the Mayflower Steps that led down to the water. To get there he'd wander through Plymouth's picturesque Barbican site, mingling with the summer crowds. With luck there would be plenty of people to hear him, queuing boat trippers wanting to use the quayside for trips up and down Plymouth Sound. It was where the crowds gathered.

His Mum tapped on his door at five.

'Tea, dear?' she said, timidly, before leaving a mug and two Rich Tea biscuits on the corner of his desk. 'I don't know whether you've heard, but there's a to-do at one of the motorway service stations on the M5. I think you ought to check it out – I do hope it's not another attack.'

Harry barely noticed she'd popped in, but after she'd gone, something clicked in his head. He lifted his head, put his mobile to his ear and called Cherry.

'What's happening in your world, Cherry? What's the word on the M5 motorway?' he asked.

'Hi Harry. Twitter feed says there's chaos following a shooting at Bridgwater Services. A man in a Range Rover. No news as to any more casualties, just the one, but the police seem to be getting very excited. It's definitely something other than the usual Sunday afternoon motorway incident. Some say there was a short high speed police chase first, the northbound carriageway, then a shooting. Nothing more yet. Will keep you posted.'

'Let me know the news as soon as you have it,' ordered Harry, suddenly coming to life. Instinctively, he thought this had to be connected to what had been happening in the South West and he went over to his TV to flick it on to see the live images already coming in to BBC South West.

A picture began to emerge. Apparently the incident had happened just after four ten. The trouble was, everything Harry really wanted to see was hidden somewhere inside the dark interior of the car park and the cameras weren't being allowed anywhere near.

With a dismissive shrug of the shoulders, Harry turned back to his desk. The outline of his speech was now put together, so he picked up his phone to see if there was anything of interest. Glancing through his inbox just in case he had overlooked anything important, it was then he spotted it – 'CARL' in capitals in the subject box. His unopened email lying amongst the scores of others. Time sent four fourteen. A chill ran through his veins as he pondered its significance. He opened it.

Harry had to read the extensive text twice to understand what he'd received. It was a dead man's last message, he was sure of that. More than that it was very dangerous information and implicated him in all that had happened over the past few days. He'd been set up and he was now the next fall guy in the line. The more he thought about what he was reading, the more frightened he became. He had no idea where else it had been sent. Things began to make sense as he understood how Carl had been part of a bigger picture, serving a cause banking on the naivety of Harry to fall in line.

As he read about the shooting of Steve Collins on Plymouth Hoe beneath Smeaton's Tower, and Carl's assessment of his fears for his own future, Harry too began to think that maybe he was also expendable – perhaps they wouldn't stop, ensuring he was dead too. He suddenly realised the fear, the hopelessness that had led Carl to shoot himself. How was Harry to save his own skin?

Harry felt lost, a drowning man. He had no idea what to do and had no solid back up plan to protect him in a time like this. Terror began to flow through his veins, the like he'd never known in his life before. What he'd suspected, he now knew, because the e-mail told him; Cathy had been killed to send a warning message to him, telling Harry, to fall in line or else.

This shadowy extreme group called The Circle, whose front man was Carl Reynolds, had been using him for their own political ends. He felt caught like a fly in a web in a trap not of his own making. His phone rang. Hesitatingly, he answered it.

'Cherry, more news. It's one man, unofficially, police chatter is that they've got "Grey Man". He shot himself before they got to him. Said I'd keep you posted. No-one seems to know what to make of it yet, but they soon will. Bye.'

Then Harry had a thought. Carl must have sent the e-mail about the time he died. He thought he might be disposed of, and he needed to tell someone. He's chosen me. But, he's dropped me right in it. His phone would now be in the hands of the police and the first thing they'll be doing will be to see who he's been in touch with. Top of the list – my name! More dark clouds on the horizon. They'd be sure to see what he's sent me. What did he do next?

Then he had the glimmer of a bright idea. He needed to beat the police to it, to call them himself to tell them he'd received some information that might assist them. Play the public spirited bit, put himself alongside the law, but especially to try and see if they might give him some protection, now he was in danger. He could tell them he needed protection, his Mum too.

Also there was now nothing lost in telling them that he thought this was possibly the same man who'd called here at his home briefly yesterday. Maybe he wouldn't mention the ten thousand yet, unless the police asked for it, treat that at arm's length like it was simply an administrative, party treasurer's matter, but it would help his cause, the tricky situation he was in, if he was showing cooperation with police enquiries.

He resolved to call 999 right away and then, whilst he awaited their visit, he'd sit down to talk to his parents as to the consistent message they'd need to give the police. Harry thought things through for himself – well isn't this how politicians have to think and act all the time? It was all useful experience for the future, onward and upward he told himself trying to lift his spirits.

His call to the police took some time before he was finally given someone to speak to.

'Commander Jim Abbotts here. Is that Harry McNamara?'

'Yes. I've information that may be helpful to your enquiries into recent terrorist incidents.'

'Please tell me more, Harry,' he said politely.

'A number of things have happened to try and derail our party's efforts to do well in the coming by-election on Thursday. Yesterday, a visitor came to our family home. He'd earlier asked if he could see me and I fitted him in at eleven, between meetings. It was no ordinary meeting and I have to say I didn't like the man. In fact I asked someone to sit in with me when he came inside. My first suspicions have been subsequently justified as I have just seen his picture on your wanted posters and I thought I should report this,' said Harry, pausing to see what was being made of his story so far.

'That's very interesting. Why do you think he came to see you?'

'Ostensibly to offer support, but I didn't like him and did nothing to encourage him. It was a brief meeting. I don't think I told him what he came to hear.'

'Oh, and then what happened?' asked the Commander.

'He left and I never saw him again. He did tell me his first name was Carl, but he wouldn't give any more details about himself. I hope this is helpful to you, might help you track him down,' offered Harry.

'And then?'

"Well, unknown to me, my political advisor, Cathy Nicholls, who had been in a meeting with me earlier in the morning, took it upon herself to follow this man. She had her suspicions about him too I think. She was an excellent judge of character, one of her strengths,' said Harry, making up his script as he went along.

'The same Cathy Nicholls you reported found in the street,' said the Commander.

'Yes. But I remember now there is more to tell than I was able to say at the time, in my shock at the loss of my dear friend and colleague.'

'Yes...'

'She called me on her mobile just before she died to say what she was doing, that she was following my visitor to find out more about him. I told her I didn't think that was wise, the cloak and dagger stuff is best left to professionals. I have to say, I then heard a vehicle, a thud, and silence. She never said another word. I didn't know what to think. I feared then something terrible might have happened.'

'Then what?'

'That was what actually led me to find her in the street almost opposite where I live. When I got to her, I held her hand until the ambulance arrived, and inadvertently I came away with her phone. I think she wanted me to look after it perhaps. She was dying Commander, she didn't speak again. I was in shock. As I told your colleagues, I believe she had no idea what had happened to her. Talking one minute, whoop the next.'

'Thank you, Harry. We'll be in touch. We'll arrange to get a proper statement in due course. Oh and did Carl say where he might be staying?'

'No. He was very evasive, mysterious even. As I said, I didn't warm to the man, didn't like him, it was only a brief conversation, like I said, fitted in between meetings, I was glad when he'd gone.'

'Thank you. An officer will make contact later today.'

'Hold on. Are you still there? I haven't quite finished. There's something else. I'm ringing now because the strangest thing has just happened. This man Carl sent an e-mail to me not half an hour ago. It's full of information I think you should have. It's about an international organisation called The Circle. It sounds as though he wasn't on his own, others were behind him. It's full of names, details, terrorist plots and so forth. I thought you guys need to have it as soon as possible. It may just be the ramblings of a mentally ill man, not for me to judge. I can't think why it's come to me, perhaps by mistake. What shall I do with it, forward it?'

'Harry, I want you to e-mail it to me straight away; to my e-mail address which I am about to give you and if you don't mind I'll get you to hold the line just to be certain it's come through OK. And thank you for your invaluable assistance.' Harry felt the praise given to his publicly spirited cooperative approach to be heartfelt, genuine and knew he'd pulled it off.

He sent the e-mail off within a minute and the call was terminated, Commander Abbotts saying he'd be sending a colleague round for a statement later that evening.

Harry came out of it all feeling he'd managed the call really quite well, and that it might mark the end of his temporary problems. Once again back on track, it was time to get back to his campaign planning. The clock was ticking and there was an election to win.

57

Monday morning saw Harry and three of his party faithfuls in the Stonehouse area, knocking on doors in a densely occupied city housing estate. It was productive work, the homes being so close together, many more people could be doorstepped. They were there early at Harry's insistence asking if people would actually come out and vote for him on Thursday.

He had another four, loyal BFDP people, working away in a spare office at the McNamara Metals yard who were trying to drive forward the social media side of his campaign – all the signs coming back from them were positive. Knowing that this aspect of his campaign was key to making a breakthrough, something the other candidates just didn't see, he thought it time to give them some personal encouragement in return for their efforts and called in to see them briefly at the factory office.

Moving swiftly on, his schedule was unrelenting. Glancing at his watch, Harry knew it was time for him to leave his two teams of party faithfuls, his front line troops behind and head for the Barbican and the Mayflower Steps. Stu was his driver today and he was beckoning Harry over to the car, also anxious as to the time.

After the short drive, Harry decided to walk the last few streets and told Stu to drop him, park up and meet him down there. Passing waterside businesses he grabbed a take away coffee at a quayside cafeteria with its bright plastic chairs and matching sun awning.

Gratified to find people recognised him on the street, words were cheerfully exchanged, most wishing him well and assuring him he had their vote.

There were wastrels too – homeless, alcoholics and druggies, occupants of doorway pitches hoping for food from the bakery or coins from a cashpoint user, all people he had no time for. The area had always attracted its share of social misfits as he saw them, mindful that when he came to power, they'd be cleared away. Maybe he'd make them useful – put them in work gangs somewhere. He gave one man who touched his shoulder hoping for something, a quick 'bugger off' and 'get yourself a fucking job.'

Harry had timed his arrival at the waterside to perfection. The first of the day's boat trips to the estuary had yet to leave and a crowd of people had gathered adjacent to the Mayflower Steps – a ready audience. Phil and Cherry were already there and Stu would be with them shortly. He looked at the embossed slab beneath his feet, marking the spot where the Pilgrims embarked. It stated baldly, "Mayflower 1620".

A second more informative plaque which he couldn't be bothered to read gave the story of these early travellers and their hope to create a new life for themselves in America. He'd invited some of the city's tourism officers to join him. Flattered at the chance of publicity, four of them had come along. It helped swell the crowd – gave official respectability to proceedings.

Above him, the Union Jack and Stars and Stripes fluttered side by side, and he strategically positioned himself under the little Doric arch portico, built to mark the point of the Pilgrims' historic departure. The light Monday morning

411

breeze was coming in from the glistening blue sea behind him – Harry thought it would carry his voice perfectly. It was eleven-o-clock precisely. A few more people were wandering up the quay, his audience was building.

'Good morning everybody,' he began, realising he sounded rather too like a headmaster at a morning assembly.

'This week we hope to see Plymouth once again making an historic impression on the world. Just as the Pilgrim Fathers and Mothers made their historic fresh start four hundred years ago. This city is going to rejuvenate itself as it moves forward united as one, like never before.' More people were joining him. He took a sip of his still too hot coffee.

'This past weekend our city has been on the receiving end of despicable attacks, designed to de-stabilise everything we hold dear. We have seen some of our dearest people die on the streets, we have seen the whole city put at risk by explosive devices fastened to nuclear subs sitting at Devonport Docks.' He paused, and asked that as it was eleven-o-clock, a respectful minute of silence be observed. As people fell silent and heads bowed only noisy seagulls dared interrupt.

'Changes are needed to make our city safe. My party is committed to bringing about these changes. We will say the unsayable, we will name the evil in our midst, we will be ruthless in keeping our people safe.' There was some polite applause.

'Part of our problem is our news. We are told untruths. My party has been maligned and misrepresented and lies have been told. Contrary to what they say about us, about me – we are not racist, we are not extreme, we are not violent. We are people of peace, but we will be ruthless in driving out the evil hiding on our streets.'

'I am a caring person, Plymouth is a hospitable caring city. When the Pilgrim Fathers came here on their way to America, they'd left Southampton down the coast and only put in here because the weather in the English Channel was so bloody awful! We helped them out. We gave them shelter, we even fixed their boat and then saw them off on their way again. It's what we do here, isn't it?' More applause.

'Today, we need to do the same with all these migrants. When things are bad we help them, but now we need to help them on their way again! You see these steps here, the Pilgrim Fathers went down these steps to leave this city never to return. They made a go of it in the land where they felt they truly belonged. We need to send off overseas all those who have overstayed their welcome and abused our hospitality – send them somewhere else, back where they came from, so they can prosper and thrive where they truly belong.' He took another swig from his now drinkable coffee.

'But we need to do more. The Muslims among us have allowed nests of evil terrorists to find shelter. Their violent faith is not ours. Now, whether or not they were the ones who attacked our cities in the South West these past few days,' Harry said, changing his earlier stance.

'They need to go. It's time. Our streets are filled with fearful people, those who have lost jobs to migrants, those who see the precious resources of their health, schools and other public services handed over to the undeserving migrant – well, let me tell you, you vote for Harry McNamara and it will stop.' Louder cheers this time. Harry spotted Phil and, to his delight, Andy also busily taking pictures.

'Let me tell you, we have seen the numbers of police on our streets fall so dramatically in the past seven years, we can no longer protect ourselves when we're threatened. I will change that. I will see our local police are equipped to do the job of protecting us. How many armed response units were there in the South West on Friday when trouble broke out? – Let me tell you, not enough to stop a fight in the Queen and Anchor down the road there,' Harry said, the crowd laughing.

'I need you to turn out and vote for me on Thursday. The Tories don't know the people of Plymouth Moor View Constituency like I do. And Labour, they are hand in glove with those doing harm to us. A real change is needed and this is your chance to tell the government. Vote Harry McNamara! Vote for Plymouth! Vote for our nation! Britain First!'

Hand shaking ensued as the clapping subsided. Harry turned to Stu, 'How about strolling down to the Queen and Anchor for a pint of Tribute? It's my round and there's another good photo in it.'

'That's fine. We've another thirty minutes on the parking meter ticket. I'll bring the car down to pick you up from there after. There's always a good crowd in that pub. I'd get yourself a sandwich or pie to see you through while you're there,' offered Stu. 'Do you mind me asking Harry, you sounded like you weren't blaming Muslims for the attacks, do you know something?'

'Well, I'm glad someone was listening to my every word! Stu, when we get to the pub I'll try and update you on a few things. There've been further developments since yesterday.'

When they arrived and had their drinks in their hands, had spoken to the people lining the bar and crowding the seats outside in the warm midday sun, the two finally had the chance to talk.

'I made a statement to the police last night, told them about Cathy, told them I'd recognised their wanted man,' said Harry. 'They really think I was phoning to help them, and they still do, I hasten to add, but there's more to this. That guy who saw me at home Saturday, this Carl Reynolds guy, now dead at Bridgwater Services, he was the one involved in the attacks. I now don't think it was Muslims at all. So we need to be careful what we say over the next couple of days. Everything has changed – I can't be made to look a fool, someone else's fall guy.'

Lunch – a pie consumed and pint drunk, and it was one thirty. Stu who'd been back to feed the parking meter was set to drive Harry to a Sixth Form Academy for a forum with the upper school. Harry put some mint gum in his mouth; the smell of stale beer didn't go down well in a school.

'It'll be detention for you if you're late, like in the old days,' chided Stu. 'Car's round the corner. Oh, and I've just picked up today's paper. Two things you should see. That guy, Adam Taylor and his girl Rita whatsit, they're back in town. They've got a spread on page five about working with Muslims today to offer tea and chat to anyone who wants to call in at the Islamic Mosque Trust – all, it says here, 'in the cause of good community relations'. Starts at four, both here and in Exeter. Look, even your friend the Archdeacon is quoted as supporting what they're doing,' he said wagging his finger derisively at the newspaper.

415

'And what's the other thing I should see?' asked Harry snappily, his earlier optimistic mood rapidly changing.

'That article Cherry wrote about your grandfather, Michael – it's right here.' Flicking over the page Stu pointed at it with his index finger – a long article with two pictures, a full page. One picture showed Harry in his suit, whilst facing was Grandpa Michael in his Blackshirt uniform.

'Where did she get that picture? Bit controversial I'd say. I'm surprised at her really, at you as well to be honest – didn't think you'd have OK'd it,' said Stu, passing him the article to read as they walked the car.

'I didn't,' said Harry, remembering to his chagrin the untouched draft Cherry had left him to read, still sitting on the side in his bedroom. He'd damn well forgotten to read it! Now the papers were portraying him as a fascist. Would the people mind? Things once again felt as though they were beginning to slide. With two more days of campaigning left, he just couldn't tell – might he hang on in there or would everything fall apart like a house of cards.

58

The mood in Gold Room on Monday morning was totally different to that of the day before, and quite unlike any normal gloomy Monday routine. Progress on an investigation was a marvellous medicine, a miracle cure elixir for flagging spirits.

Feeling much revived herself, April caught the mood when she checked in at eight, her skipper Emma no longer having grey rings beneath her eyes. She was beginning to feel she belonged, one of the team, though every now and then she still heard people expressing their wariness of the Prevent programme, of which she was a part. Even Nick had picked up the oft quoted line about it going too far, spying on the community. People always remembered the early mistakes, but as to the true value of the programme, she herself had no doubt whatsoever.

As she made her way across to a vacant workstation, she noticed how, after only three days, the Room was already taking on the feel of a permanently on-going investigation and was no longer looking clinically empty. The clutter of personal effects lying on desks and chairs betrayed a more lived in feel to the space – it had come alive with spirit of comradely endeavour – after all it had been home for many officers for three long days.

The Gold Room Commander gave a briefing at eight thirty, the rapidly gathering pace of the enquiry surprising everyone. The focus of the investigation had dramatically changed and those lucky enough to have had a rest day were astonished. Early unease that GCHQ and counter-terrorism had had about purported IS claims were now declared as self-evident truths, for behind everything that had happened an international right wing extremist group called The Circle and its mission operatives, Carl Reynolds and Steve Collins, were known to have taken centre stage.

Still under armed guard and in hospital, Steve Collins, now out of danger, was in Commander Abbott's words, "singing like a canary" and telling all he knew, though it had soon become clear he didn't know very much. Collins was described as a vulnerable individual; an about to be pensioned off royal naval engineer who had been successfully groomed by The Circle. About the shadowy Circle itself, little was yet known for certain and a national and international manhunt had been triggered.

The Carl Reynolds e-mail suicide note to prospective MP Harry McNamara and forwarded almost immediately by him to the police had been the kind of intelligence material spooks had spent dreaming of getting hold of for decades.

Investigators were poring over it and its authenticity was, so far, beyond doubt. Actually getting hold of the e-mail's named individuals was, however, proving a much more difficult task, The Circle's members seemingly having well laid plans to hide themselves in the shadows, staying always one step out of reach.

The Gold Room Commander withheld from his colleagues the fact that earlier he had sent a secure memo for the Chief Constable's eyes only – a preliminary report examining Harry McNamara's part in what had happened.

In it he'd outlined how it was clear to the police that Harry had not looked for nor directly aligned himself with what The Circle had been trying to do. Rather, they had seen in him as a vehicle for their own purposes and they had clandestinely used terrorism and public fear to generate further support for this extreme right candidate. A brick thrown through Harry's window at his home early on in the campaign, purporting to be a Muslim attack, was now known to be nothing of the sort. Carl's e-mail made clear how a local individual, whom he had not named, was paid to deliver "the message".

Harry McNamara had swallowed the line he'd been sold and he was unknowingly on their hook. Only late in the programme, two days ago, Saturday morning, had Harry been directly contacted by The Circle, which was when Carl had called round to see him at eleven. Even then, if Harry himself was to be believed, Carl only presenting himself in the guise of an anonymous backer, someone Harry would hear more from in due course.

The Commander concluded his précis saying, 'Harry McNamara could or should have begun to have had suspicions from that point, but we've no way of knowing and Harry denies it. Whether that's true or false, I couldn't possibly comment.' He looked up to read people's faces before continuing.

'What he undoubtedly did learn soon after that meeting was that his political advisor Cathy Nicholls had followed Carl, because she was curious as to his identity, and although Harry says he didn't add two and two together immediately, it was Carl who ran down and killed her in order to send a message to Harry about the seriousness of expectation that he align himself with The Circle.'

The Commander's concluding assessment was that it wasn't possible to say at which point in time Harry McNamara was truly aware of what was going on behind his back. He was

419

satisfied, given the evidence he'd seen so far, that Harry McNamara had no prior knowledge of the Guildhall explosion, the Drakes Circus Shopping Mall attack or the attachment of limpet mines to the nuclear submarines at Devonport. His taking Cathy Nicholl's phone away from the scene was open to different interpretations but again there was no evidence to tie Harry to her death and it was a foregone certainty the CPS wouldn't think there was enough evidence to take him to court over the matter.

What helped Harry's position was that he had more or less immediately contacted the police when he received the Carl Reynold's e-mail. The impression given, whether entirely sincere or self-serving, was that he genuinely wanted to assist the police.

The Commander and the Chief Constable were all too aware that the by-election was only three days away and it was turning into a fiercely contested acrimonious campaign. To single out any one candidate for police attention at this point could be counterproductive in maintaining the peace and safeguarding the reputation of the police. He had asked the Chief for her urgent response to his report. After such a summary and due praise of the efforts of all in Gold Room, the meeting concluded with everyone in high spirits.

It wasn't until late afternoon, the Commander alone at his desk, the Chief's reply came back; to his surprise, not in writing, but as a direct phone call.

Devon and Cornwall Police Chief Constable, Wendy Armitsted, still relatively new to her post, had throughout the weekend been in close contact with the Home Office providing them information as to the progress of the investigation, but more importantly for herself, to seek

Home Office support. She had immediately called London at nine that morning on receiving Commander Abbotts' e-mail, this time asking for urgent confidential advice.

Five hours later and much to her surprise the Home Secretary had called back in person to outline what should be done. It was underlined that what was happening in Devon had national ramifications and that the matter had been a significant element in the COBRA meeting discussions in the Cabinet Office earlier in the day. Beyond the immediate terrorist threat, hopefully now contained, there was a crucial political dimension to be considered. The Home Secretary had come to a view on Harry McNamara's situation. It was this order she was now passing to Commander Abbotts.

She relayed the order to the Commander, discernibly reading from a prepared script. He understood how orders from above worked.

Nonetheless Commander Abbotts' jaw dropped when he heard what she had to say. 'You want to me to do what?' he said. 'Very well Ma'am.'

59

Monday morning was far busier than either Adam or Raqiyah had anticipated. They weren't used to organising social events and since Sunday evening they had been non-stop phoning, messaging, posting on social media and getting themselves ready for Monday afternoon's open mosques events in both Exeter and Plymouth. Archdeacon Peter had proved amazingly helpful, finding discretionary funds and volunteer helpers.

Bilal and Raqiyah had drawn lots to see who was going to Exeter and who Plymouth. As luck would have it, Adam and Raqiyah, not without a sense of some foreboding, ended up with a trip to Plymouth. Fortunately for them they were going to travel by minibus with a group of volunteers from Exeter mosque, and that gave him confidence. Even so, Adam made a double check this time to see he had his medication with him.

The minibus collected them from the house in Pinhoe Road at eleven thirty, the argument being they could hopefully get to Plymouth in time for mosque prayers around one. Adam was reassured by the fact that everyone was friendly towards them, indeed they were expressing gratitude for taking a good idea and putting it into practice.

Before they left, Adam thought he'd just send April Cooper a last minute message to let her know the event was going ahead as planned and they had no reason as yet to have any real concerns. Adam was all too conscious of recent earlier visits to Plymouth turning out badly.

Later, after a trouble free journey, they were arriving at the Islamic Mosque Trust in Plymouth. He could already see that colourful gazebos had been erected on the pavement and tables had been put in place. There was an almost carnival spirit as people set up bunting and banners proclaiming an open invitation to the community, 'Welcome 2-7pm Today'. To Adam's surprise he spotted The Archdeacon mixing with the Muslim volunteers, clearly feeling quite at home.

Adam tipped his head in his direction to alert Raqyiah to his presence before going straight over to speak to him.

'Just wanted to say thanks for your support. Everyone's so come on board with this idea. Neither Raqiyah nor myself felt comfortable with the polarising politics going on and the terrorist attacks since Friday, and we had to do something.'

'Glad you did. Some of the other faith leaders have promised to put in an appearance. I was particularly delighted the Jewish Synagogues in both Exeter and Plymouth wanted to show support. They said their own experience of anti-semitism gave them an insight into what it felt like for the Muslims today.'

'I can understand that.'

'So many good people I talk to are really concerned at the direction things are going and want to do something to help turn the tide. People are hurting and frightened. In such circumstances, drinking tea together has always been a good option,' the Archdeacon said smiling warmly. Adam was reminded of his aunt, Ruth Churchill and the efforts she made for her parish in north London. He really ought to get in touch with her again soon; the call long overdue.

'Have you any press contacts, some way we could give what is happening a wider audience. TV even?' asked Adam. He realised as he spoke how much he was driven by this and how much he was now seeing it as a personal way of getting back at Harry McNamara.

'That's a good thought. I'll talk to our Comms Officer at the Diocese, she's always trying to be helpful. Give me a minute,' and he strode off to one side to make his call.

Adam, lost for a minute as to what to do with himself, got talking to a young Muslim guy standing idly by, much the same age as himself.

'Hi, I'm Adam. Salaam Alekum,' he said offering his hand in friendly greeting. There was a warm response.

'How do you know how to greet Muslims then?' he said, surprised.

'Got a good teacher,' Adam replied, glancing knowingly at Raqiyah.

'It's Ali,' he said.

'Oh,' said Adam, 'I knew an Ali once, but that's all in the past.'

'I'm here to defend our community,' Ali said.

'So am I,' said Adam, though wondering if they both understood the same thing by it. Adam let it pass.

'You a student or working?' asked Adam.

'Neither, my Dad's an Imam. I'm kind of helping out here with the educational programme. I hear you're a student at Exeter Uni. What you do there?'

'Islamic Studies,' said Adam.

'You a revert, a convert or something?' asked Ali puzzled.

'No, guess if anything, I've got Christian roots, well my family have. I needed to know Islam better, understand it for myself.'

'Wish more people would,' said Ali.

'So what happens in your educational classes? What do people learn?'

'Well, they don't learn to be terrorists, that's for sure!' he said laughing, before adding, 'it's more about how to be a good Muslim – it's not so straight forward living in a non-Muslim land.'

Archdeacon Peter broke into their conversation at that point.

'I got through, Adam, and got a positive reply. A reporter and photographer are on their way down, might even get a TV news crew around four,' his chubby face beaming with satisfaction.

To Adam's relief, there were samosas, chilli sauce and sweets to eat and he took the opportunity to tuck in. A steady stream of local people had started to mingle and gather in the shelter of the gazebos, and Adam was delighted that things looked to be so friendly. It all seemed genuine stuff, the atmosphere relaxed and something warmed inside him as he felt good community vibes spill over into him.

He looked over to Raqiyah who was laughing and smiling as she chatted with some of the other young women. As he watched her, he realised how deeply fond of her he was, how dependent they had become on each other in the eighteen months since they'd become friends and lovers. How these past weeks they'd carried each other through difficult times. For a moment he couldn't imagine not being with her.

Glancing at his mobile to see what was happening in the world he spotted a Twitter post from Exeter Mosque. The Mayor had dropped in, so had the Chief Constable, and the whole thing had snowballed into a crowd event as lots of people had started getting behind a positive alternative to what they had been living with for the past three days.

Adam also noticed the whole news coverage of the terrorist incidents had shifted away from an IS focus to an extreme right wing take in the coverage. Just how this would play out in the public arena was too soon to say. He wandered over to Raqiyah.

'Hey, look at this. It's the Exeter Mosque Open Day,' he said pointing to the post. Raqiyah read it and her face broke into a broad smile.

As word spread and it became late afternoon, more and more people started turning up. Everyone helping was finding themselves fully occupied and just after five, yet more people seemed to be arriving on to the streets as rush hour got under way and warm late afternoon early June sun invited them to stay outdoors after days of scurrying for cover from drizzle or rain.

Adam didn't notice the photographer at first, working his way round, accompanied by a reporter firing questions with a recorder in her hand. As they were approaching his table he saw Raqiyah's face freeze. She glanced over at him, a look of deep apprehension in her gaze and Adam immediately moved across to her side.

'Adam, these two, they were at the meeting Clive and I had with Harry. They're his friends. What are they doing here? What shall we do?' He put his hand on her back reassuringly.

'The Archdeacon said he was arranging for some media coverage, guess he got them to come. Look, it's a public event, they're not after you, not even noticed you in all likelihood. Keep a low profile. After they've got their pictures and story they'll be off. You wait,' said Adam encouragingly.

But, as Adam watched, he saw they were in no hurry. So after leaving Raqiyah with a group of women from the mosque, he decided to act. He walked over to Ali.

'Ali, can I just give you a heads up on those two,' he said, pointing to the two press people, now set a little apart from everyone and conferring with one another. 'They're from the press, just that they're Harry McNamara's supporting press, and could mean trouble. Just thought you ought to know, just in case.

'Thanks Adam, we'll keep half an eye on them,' and he returned to stock the table with more soft drink bottles to replenish dwindling supplies on the tables.

Adam was thinking that with only an hour or two at most left, they'd soon be back on the minibus heading back to Exeter and home. He tried to tell himself there really was nothing to worry about. Strange though, those two were still waiting, hanging around, the woman now chatting into her mobile. He watched them warily.

A minute or so later a car pulled up, and out from the front passenger door stepped Harry McNamara. The two started fêting him like a pop star – photos, microphone under his chin. He was striding their way.

'Ali,' Adam called sharply. 'Told you. Look who's turned up.' Ali just nodded as Adam moved himself ever backwards, further out of sight.

Harry followed, dogging Adam's retreating footsteps, a broad grin on his face, both moving toward the entrance of the mosque. A crowd had now assembled around him. There was tension building in the air.

Harry paused, looked up at the mosque building and looked intent on going inside. Adam noticed the policeman and his PCSO colleague were glancing at each other, looking every bit as if they hadn't expected this turn of events. The PC turned to one side and could be seen speaking into his radio.

But instead of going inside, Harry turned, his back to the mosque entrance looking for all the world as if he was about to address everyone, maybe make one of his poisonous speeches. Adam could almost feel the electricity in the air crackling around him as faces turned this way and that.

To his alarm he realised he'd lost sight of Raqiyah. His anxiety levels were rising fast.

60

'Friends, People of Plymouth, lend me your ears. I come from an afternoon with school pupils at a nearby Academy and they asked if I had ever been to Plymouth Islamic Trust. I told them I'd done one better – been in the magnificent Suleman Mosque in Istanbul. The Head teacher told me you were open to all visitors this afternoon. Not one to shy away from stepping into the lion's den, I thought I'd come along, join the party.'

People were looking at one another, not knowing what to make of this intervention. The relaxed mood of earlier had become uncertain, even threatening. Harry's skinhead driver, after parking up Harry's transport, had come and stood next to Harry as if he were his loyal foot soldier and bodyguard.

The two police personnel were still standing by the entrance looking unsure as to what to do next; clearly ill at ease that Harry was standing just in front of them. Inadvertently they looked as if, one either side of Harry, they provided his guard of honour.

'I have to say you have made a valiant effort this afternoon,' said Harry, sweeping his arm to point to the tables set out on the street, 'but it isn't enough. You know it, I know it. Muslims here are like leopards that never change their spots. I've seen what can happen when people take their Muslim faith to heart – it leads to terrorism, a cancer within wider society, trying to subvert it and weaken it. The purity of a people, a nation then comes under threat.' Harry glanced this way and that. There was a movement in the crowd as someone stepped forward.

'That's enough Mr McNamara. We've had enough of your poison here,' said Ali.

'We don't need any troublemakers,' replied Harry nodding first to the policeman at his shoulder and then to Andy, his photographer.

'Just back off and keep the peace, Sir,' said Harry almost spitting out his words, but Ali kept coming.

'I'm here to defend this mosque and these people. We're not prepared to listen to any more from you. Go home Harry McNamara. Crawl back under the stone you came out from. Go Home! Go Home!'

Then the crowd started joining in chanting, 'Go Home! Go Home! Go Home!' and as their chants rose, Harry couldn't be heard any longer. He had no PA system, no way to compete, drowned out. He was lost, it was like being caught in the visitor's end at Home Park when your mates were somewhere else.

Ali suddenly had half a dozen strong looking young men round him moving in on Harry and Harry knew a fight coming when he saw one. Worse still he knew when the odds were stacked badly. He nudged Stu, futilely pushing his friend forward, but Stu was hopelessly outnumbered. He was grabbed by the arms before he could throw a punch and frog-marched to his car and told to get inside as his head was pushed downward. Somehow a punch connected with the side of Stu's face when he hesitated. He needed no further persuasion.

Harry turned to the police officer at his side, 'I'd be grateful officer if you could escort me away to safety,' he said as he vainly tried to salvage some personal dignity. He reflected he had recently developed the habit of straightening his tie whenever things became stressful.

The officer told his PCSO to stay by the door, as he then stepped forward to lead Harry back towards the car. They had not walked five paces when someone kicked Harry hard in his knee, causing him to call out and stumble. He looked around him, but couldn't work out where it had come from. As he tried to stand, a fist flew from his right, hitting the side of his head, and another, and another. The powerless policeman was bundled to one side buried somewhere in the growing melée. Harry thought all was lost. Then there was a shout.

'Stop! Stop! My brothers. In the name of Allah, stop!'

It was the Imam emerging from the mosque, flanked either side by the mosque trustees and some older men. There was a pause, and as quickly as it had begun, the crowd became quiet and orderly.

'This is not how true Muslims behave. We are a people of peace, a people of the book, and the day we have been celebrating must not be marred by violence when we have so many welcome visitors. Shame on Mr McNamara and his kind for inciting trouble at a holy site, shame on you. Leave now I ask of you. Leave in peace.'

Harry needed no second bidding; he knew when he was beaten. Nursing his bruises and pride, he clambered into the car next to Stu and ordered him to drive him home. As the car pulled away, Harry had the sinking feeling that all he believed in and had worked for was slipping away like sand through his fingers. He'd watched as Phil and Cherry had caught the whole thing, photographed and recorded it all. Even they would find it hard this time to make good use of what they had.

Those two were maybe slipping from his control – who knows what they would do with the scoop that had just been handed them? New news was the only capital they understood.

Stu drove away in silence, occasionally rubbing his cheek. Harry knew from the look on his rueful face that his closest friend, who read things better than anyone, didn't need to speak; he could also see the writing was on the wall.

61

April Cooper was surprised to be told by her Skipper that the Chief Constable wanted to speak to her immediately and in her office.

'No, I don't think it's because you've done something wrong,' said Emma. 'But why she wants you in hasn't been shared with me,' she said with an edge, clearly resenting being cut out of the loop. In her eyes April looked every bit the rising star, and she herself felt passed over.

April tidied her appearance as best she could as she strolled quickly along the corridor and announced her presence to the duty desk PA outside the Chief's office.

A green light, April stepped inside and was told to sit down. Chief Constable Wendy Armitsted remained seated the other side of her desk scrutinising the new arrival before speaking.

'Well done April for the excellent work you did in putting us on to Carl Reynolds. That was a classic demonstration of grassroots police skills and due recognition will find its way into the paperwork in due course.'

'Thank you Ma'am,' said a genuinely grateful April.

'I've called you in for another reason too. I've been asked to organise something rather unusual. Orders from on high. You were sent here from the Met just a few weeks ago because someone thought the Plymouth Moor View by-election campaign might trigger something. Whoever thought that certainly got it more than right. We have had both the most vitriolic and divisive political campaign I think any of us have ever witnessed, and unquestionably the most serious round of terror incidents this country has yet seen. I hate to think what would have occurred if the Plymouth nuclear sub mines had exploded.'

'Indeed.'

'Let's get to the point, shall we. A Chief Constable's lot is not always a happy one. One moment having to back away from aspiring politicians so as to clearly not intervene in the political process, and the next, well, to do precisely the opposite.'

'I don't follow Ma'am,' said April puzzled.

'Two things have led to your being summoned here this afternoon. First, your being part in the Prevent programme. Under Prevent, you're supposed to spot and stop people getting radicalised and you're supposed to make places that are vulnerable to radicalisation safer, more resilient. True?'

'Absolutely right, Ma'am.'

'Strange as it might sound you've got a job to do. Mr McNamara, the parliamentary candidate for the British First Democratic Party, is being formally referred to Prevent.'

April's jaw must have dropped. She didn't know how to respond. 'If you don't mind me saying so, that's slightly irregular, Ma'am.'

'You heard me right. Harry McNamara is considered by officials at the Home Office to be at risk of Radicalisation. I won't go into the detail now, but you will find that within the next twenty four hours you will be getting a call from him asking if he can submit himself voluntarily to a programme of de-radicalisation training under your care. Why you? Well, it's to be low profile. The matter is still politically sensitive. I've spoken to the Local Authority Chair of the Prevent Steering Group and he has agreed it can be handled as a matter of confidentiality under his personal say so.'

April was trying to take in what was expected. Repugnance, challenge, surprise, apprehension – in that moment her feelings threatened to overturn her professionalism. How could she manage him, such a powerful personality, and holding such forceful views? This was beyond daunting – no it was impossible!

'I want you to go, plainclothes, to his home after he calls, and arrange for him to meet with people you think will help him move from his presently toxic and frankly fascist views. I've been reading reports of what he's been writing and saying. There's no doubt of the efficacy of the Home Office decision as you read the material. For some reason, he has been radicalised and needs help.'

'But it's voluntary. He surely won't comply?' asked April.

'I think he will. Counter Intelligence will be paying him a visit. Mr McNamara's Mother, Jessica McNamara, has handed us ten thousand pounds Harry received in an envelope from Carl Reynolds which Harry had immediately passed to her for safekeeping. Harry doesn't know this yet, but his Mother has, she tells us acted for the first time in defiance of her son. She says he needs help. He has, as she put it, "lost his way".'

'Is that enough to gain his compliance?'

'There's more. He is so closely aligned with Carl Reynolds it is difficult to fully believe he truly had no idea what was being done to support his election at arm's length. Aiding and abetting terrorism is not so difficult to prove with the new laws open to us. He will be advised that we could, if we were so minded, take him through some lengthy court proceedings, and he could end up in prison. Furthermore, some of the things he has said amount to incitement to racial or religious hatred, and that path looks far more certain for a successful prosecution, should we choose to take it.'

'So you want me to run a de-radicalisation programme for Mr McNamara, starting asap?' still not quite believing her ears.

'Yes, that's the sum of it. Not my decision. Comes from on high, from as high as it gets. You'd better start thinking how you're going to do it and I want daily report updates direct to me, for my eyes only. I will see your Skipper knows just enough and will ensure you are resourced for the task. Let me know as soon as you get that call from Mr McNamara. Counter Intelligence in Gold Room have also been told to give you all the help you need. They know on a need to know basis, but no-one else. Understood?'

'Yes, Ma'am.'

'Dismissed.'

April rose, walked back to her desk in a daze, needing to collect her thoughts. This was a poisoned chalice if ever there was one. Hardly run of the mill Prevent work, highly irregular. If she failed, she knew she'd be sent back to London, ostracised by everyone and hung out to dry; it would be the end of her police career.

Her mood darkened further when she realised she hadn't asked the Chief the important question as to how all this fitted into the climax of an election campaign. It was late Monday, the next couple of days could see her at the centre of a firestorm.

Then she recalled her former colleague Bob Steer, and drew inspiration from having served alongside someone who did what it takes, even if it cost him dear. Somehow, she thought, I'll find a way to get through this. "Good coppers have solid gold inside" he once told her and that thought was enough for her to believe in herself.

62

As Harry made his hurried, unplanned and humiliating exit away from Plymouth Islamic Trust, Adam and Raqiyah found their spirits lifting once again. Ali came over to them with a broad grin as they watched Harry disappear and he offered Adam a hand.

'Thanks for warning us. Guess my Dad was right to call a halt before we all laid into him. Unfortunately I think he'd have got more public sympathy if we'd kicked the living daylights out of him, as I wanted to.

'It's been a day we've been waiting for,' said Adam. 'We had no idea that our hopes for getting back at him would ever be fulfilled. But this afternoon, well he got sent packing, given his comeuppance.'

'I realised after we spoke that you're Adam Taylor. You were caught up with…'

'Yeah, another guy by the name of Ali,' and in their shared feelings of relief, the two fell about laughing.

'We need to start clearing up soon. This afternoon couldn't have gone better. Why don't you come over and meet my Dad. I know he'd like to say "Hello". He was asking earlier whose bright idea today had been. He must meet you. Come on.'

Ali led Adam and Raqiyah off into the Mosque. Introductions were made and Adam was made to shake hands with two of the Mosque trustees. He felt like a minor celebrity and somewhat embarrassed by the fuss they made of them both. There was genuine warmth and appreciation expressed, genuine interest in his pursuit of Islamic studies and after exchanging pleasantries they made their excuses to go and help with the dismantling of marquees and clearing away of a busy afternoon's detritus.

It was just after seven and the Exeter bound group was back in their minibus waiting to set off back North. As they were about to depart Ali rushed over, leant his face into the bus to show his mobile to Adam.

'Is this your e-mail address?' he asked.

Adam confirmed it, and they were waved off, with many 'thank you's' echoing as they pulled away.

'That feels so much better,' said Raqiyah to Adam, leaning against him. 'But Harry could still win on Thursday, couldn't he? One not so successful event for him probably won't make any difference to his lead, will it?'

'I'm not sure about that,' said Adam, 'I get the sense the tide has turned.'

When the minibus was well on to the A38 trunk road, moving quickly on a quiet dual carriageway, Adam received an e-mail.

'Look at this Raqiyah,' said Adam. He passed his mobile over to her to read it for herself. It was a jointly written e-mail signed by both Exeter and Plymouth Imams and by the Archdeacon of Plymouth. It was addressed to the Vice Chancellor of Exeter University, copying in Adam and Raqiyah.

'Well that won't do either of us any harm will it?' said Raqiyah, her face beaming with satisfaction and contentment. The e-mail was a glowing tribute to the efforts both had made toward building the "common good" and was described as an "outstanding piece of voluntary work by these two students at a time when some were trying to destroy the integration and harmony long enjoyed in our multi-cultural, multi-religious and multi-ethnic South West of England."

'So that was why Ali wanted to check my e-mail!' said Adam.

Before putting his mobile away he looked once again at social media sites, to discover that the afternoon's events outside the Plymouth Mosque had indeed been photographed and reported on. Adam's heart sank and his mood changed as he realised things hadn't been all the success they'd hoped for.

'Raqiyah, look at this, it's not so good,' he said. 'Harry's friendly photographer and reporter are saying he was set upon by a riotous crowd outside the Mosque and was lucky to escape with his life!

'That's not how it was at all, Adam, you know that. We all know that. Isn't there anything we can do about the lies in the news?'

'I'm going to ring April Cooper, she'll know,' said Adam.

Adam was rather surprised to have got hold of April at the first attempt. He thought maybe she'd be off duty by seven thirty, but she answered him cheerfully and asked how the day had gone, apologising for not having got along to the open event herself. Adam explained all that had happened at

Plymouth, thankful to hear that in Exeter the event had had just the opposite kind of coverage, everyone giving it plaudits. When Adam said there was a policeman and PCSO on duty when everything kicked off in Plymouth, April said she'd speak to them and see what they said before coming back to him.

It was as the minibus was leaving the M5 at the Exeter junction, April rang back.

'I had a really useful conversation with both PC Fraser and PCSO Williams, who saw it all happen before their eyes. There is no doubt in their minds that the whole incident was sparked by Harry McNamara provoking the crowd by what he said.'

'You can't believe how good that is to hear,' said Adam.

'It was inevitable something would happen and there only being two police present meant they were powerless to do much to stop it. Their greatest fear was that innocent people would get drawn in to defend the mosque and end up with a serious criminal record by acting against the law. Thankfully, nothing like that happened, the worst of it being some scuffling and an ignominious departure by Mr McNamara to escape the scene. I'm going to ask that the two of you trust me to deal with Mr McNamara. I can't tell you how, but watch this space.'

When Adam and Raqiyah were finally dropped off in the High Street back in Exeter soon after eight thirty, Raqiyah had an idea.

'It's about time we called Clive, he'd be pleased to know what happened today. Let's see if we can meet up.'

442

63

When Harry got home on Monday night he was feeling sore. Not only the bruises that were coming up – they were minor, but also more significantly the damage to his pride and reputation. By laying it on the line to Phil and Cherry, he thought he'd done a reasonable job of turning the story they'd been going to print into one putting him in a more favourable light. As he stepped in through his front door, his Dad was there in the hallway. He looked at Harry's face before commenting.

'I see you've been back to your old ways, Harry. I'd get some ice on that if I were you,' he said coldly, his face red in repressed rage; he turned and disappeared into the living room.

Normally Harry's Mum would bring him tea when he came back in, but this evening she wasn't there, which felt strange.

'Mum, cup of tea would be nice,' he yelled in the direction of the kitchen.

'Get your own, Son,' called back his Dad from the lounge, 'She won't hear you.'

'Why the hell not?'

'She isn't here. Gone to Birmingham to stay with her sister for a few days. She's left a note for you on the kitchen table. You'll need to make yourself a cup of tea, and while you're at it, make me one too, please,' said his Dad.

Harry felt ill at ease, and strolled into the kitchen to read his Mum's note. This wasn't at all like her, it felt strange, he was lost. He couldn't recall her ever going off unannounced like this before. The unmissable letter was there as his Dad had said. A white envelope, leaning up against a vase of red tulips on the kitchen table. Uncertain, he began reading.

'Son,

You'll have to fend for yourself for a few days. I've finally decided that I need a break. These past few weeks have been an unbearable strain. When you came back from Istanbul last summer, a national hero, I was so proud of you. We all were.

Then you decided to go into politics. Of course me and your Dad supported you again – we always have. But it hasn't worked out, for me any roads. I've always done for you, but lately I've ended up being your skivvy, running around for you without so much as a thank you. Probably my fault for always spoiling you, you being an only child, but I now see it's got out of hand. At first I was glad to support you, but it's got me down, especially as you started losing your way.

I mean, you got really nasty Harry. I've stopped being proud of you and I've decided to stop supporting your campaign. I'll come back home after a few long overdue days with my sister, that'll be after the election is all over.

You once said, the one person who really understood you was Grandpa Michael. Well, you need to read that piece Cherry wrote, remind yourself of what he did and take a long hard look at yourself. Otherwise Harry, I just don't know what will become of you, and I can't bear to think about that.

Love,

Mum.'

'Bloody hell!' said Harry out loud. 'Have you read this Dad?' shouted Harry.

'Yep, and for what it's worth, I agree with every word of it,' came back the stark reply.

'Then go to hell!' said Harry, pouring hot water into his own mug, adding milk, then stomping off upstairs to his room.

He was shaking with rage as he slammed the door shut to his room. The tea was too hot to drink. As he put it down his eyes were immediately drawn to Cherry's draft article about his grandfather, still un-read on the side and he decided it was high time he read it – more miserable reading he guessed. He'd best get it over with all in one go.

Lying on his bed, his feet resting on his grandfather's metal trunk, Sir Oswald Mosley gazing down on him from above, he began reading. Why, he wondered, had it caused such a stir?

After five minutes of studying her article, he suddenly understood what Arnold, the man at the breakfast had known, and now Cherry and the world knew. Michael McNamara had, in the end, become disillusioned with the Blackshirts, and he'd locked away all his right wing politics in his trunk where they had lain hidden until Harry claimed them on his death as they were about to be thrown out.

The article told how the change in Michael had begun. After Cable Street had so shaken his faith in Mosley, he'd met a Jewish woman, a reporter, who had escaped from Hitler's Germany and had told him what the pure Aryan state was like for people like her living within it. Michael had at first not believed her, but their relationship had blossomed and

445

before their ways parted, he had formed a deep attachment to her and had decided to turn entirely away from his right wing leaning, promising her his future support to help her community.

When Hitler bombed London, the young woman was killed in the Blitz. Harry looked up and down the page, but her name was not given. Michael himself never spoke of her again, nor would he talk of politics. As he read, Harry recognised what Arnold had claimed was right. Michael had indeed turned traitor to the cause.

The realisation slowly dawned, he'd got the Grandfather he idolised all wrong. He was a traitor to his right wing brothers. Harry struggled with the idea.

There was one other thing he spotted in the article before putting it back on the side. There was reference to a memorial plaque in the local parish church, the one he'd noticed that morning and hadn't had time to read. It had been erected, "in eternal gratitude by Michael's friends in Plymouth for his support of the Jewish Community and its ancient Synagogue."

Harry threw it back on the side. Bloody hell! What was he to make of this? Disappointed in his Grandfather for being so easily misled, he discounted the value of Cherry's article as something that wouldn't be read by the readers, and if they did they wouldn't make any connection between it and their candidate today – Harry McNamara. He kicked himself and then punched the wall in frustration at his own carelessness in not reading the draft before it was published – all his own fault.

It was whilst sipping his tea, his mobile rang. The man at the other end was, or claimed to be, a senior officer in counter-intelligence. Harry couldn't risk cutting him short, and as he listened to what he was told, he knew the man was every bit the person he said he was.

'I have an offer to make to you which you need to consider most carefully,' he said, as he went on to tell Harry exactly what was expected of him. 'Should you choose not to take the voluntary option open to you, then the full force of the law will be applied. Remember that it is entirely your choice. If you choose badly, you will be promptly arrested. You will be prosecuted and believe me, you will go away for a very long time.'

Finally, after Harry's political and personal future had seemingly diminished to nothing before his eyes, he was asked to take down a precise form of words he was to use when speaking to PC April Cooper at precisely nine a.m. the following morning Tuesday. The phone number to ring was provided before the anonymous caller hung up.

Harry knew he could do nothing else but as instructed, even so with the clock ticking, he held on to the faint vestiges of hope, that a slim chance remained he might win an election.

A couple of days, that's all, everything now hanging in the balance, he told himself. Harry McNamara wasn't beaten into submission that easily.

64

Harry got up early on Tuesday morning. He'd had a restless night. Unlike most nights, he'd tossed and turned, his mind at the boundary of wakefulness and sleep as confusing ideas kept passing through his mind.

Who really was his Grandfather? Did he really know him? Should he like him or hate him? Who had called him from counter-intelligence and what would this call to April Cooper mean for his campaign? And how would he keep things on track when the terrorism attacks were now known to be perpetrated by the extreme right wing, exposing him as an easy target for his political opponents? Would he win? Could he win? Questions, questions, questions.

At six thirty he got up and turned to some physical exercise for help. After twenty minutes spinning hard on his exercise cycle, he followed that with a work out session with his weights, pushing himself hard. Dripping with sweat, his straight hair stuck to his dripping brow, he had a shower. Then came the first set back.

His Mum hadn't left his clothes ready for the day. Swearing, he threw his towel and sports kit on the floor in the corner of the room and yanked open a wardrobe door. For the first time since he didn't know when, he'd have to find himself things to wear. Next thing he knew, he'd end up having to learn how to wash and iron, he thought.

As he rummaged through his clothes, he considered whether he needed a woman in his life but couldn't resolve the conflict in his mind between having a glamorous blonde model of a wife to escort him or someone who could do all the back-up stuff at home. Rarely did they come with both qualities in a single package.

He thought of Cathy, even she had gone and left him and he cursed again. He doubted his on-off ongoing search to find someone who held all the qualities he wanted in a woman would come good any time soon and resigned himself to a life of single-hood.

A further setback followed when he saw that he'd have to get some breakfast for himself. He quickly abandoned the idea, left the kitchen and called Stu. 'Breakfast meeting at Coffee Bright,' he declared, trying to sound cheerful, giving Stu no room for dissent. 'Pick me up in ten minutes.'

Before leaving, Harry called out upstairs for his Dad, but heard no reply, and concluded he must have gone off to work early as usual. He scooped up the message and telephone number for his not to be missed nine-o-clock call and in the few minutes he still had left, looked at social media and news feeds to see what was happening in the world.

His eye caught a local newspaper sponsored poll that had been conducted by telephone only yesterday, Monday. It seemed to show that far from losing out as the terrorism investigation proceeded, Harry's support was remaining solid and his two political rivals were still trailing. Harry not believing his good fortune, feeling very much encouraged by this, made a mental note of the figures. Then the sound of Stu's car pulling up outside told him it was time to move.

Stu was apparently none-the-worse for the mosque visit. At Coffee Bright Harry thought Stu was showing good foresight these days, as he laid out a sheet for the day's programme, fighting for space on the bacon butty and coffee mug strewn table. He might even take Cathy's place one day. Harry cast his eye down the itinerary.

'Looks good to me, but you'd better call Stonehouse Community Tenants' Association to say something urgent's come up and I'll be a little delayed, perhaps by fifteen minutes.'

'What's that then, Harry? Something missing here?' asked a curious Stu.

'Urgent phone call to make at nine. Police matter. Actually, it's nearly nine, I need to make the call now. I'll use your car as an office. You can stay here, settle up.'

With that Harry picked up Stu's keys off the table and walked outside to the parked car.

At precisely nine, he called the number he'd been given.

'April Cooper, Police Prevent, here. How can I help?'

'Harry McNamara. You'll be expecting my call. I've been given a few lines of shit to read, but let's take it as read and cut to the chase. What do you want me to do?'

'That's fine, Sir. I have indeed been told to await your call. Your name's been passed to me as someone who is said to be at risk of radicalisation and I have been asked to facilitate an appropriate mentoring programme for you. Prevent is of course a voluntary programme, people submit themselves to a learning experience that we organise for them, always tailored to suit the individual, so a good place to start would be if we were to meet up. I guess you would prefer to be discrete about this, and given the busyness of your political campaign, you probably won't want too much in the diary before Thursday. Who knows which way things will go after that?'

'Nicely put officer. I've just been looking at my diary commitments. Any chance we could do this in two weeks' time?'

'Yes, providing we first meet to deal with preliminaries today or tomorrow, that would do nicely, Sir. Do you have any friends from other ethnicities, races, religions?'

Harry thought this a strange and unexpected question. He'd been asked it before recently, but couldn't place where, it was one that he had no reply to, other than to acknowledge their absence in his life.

'Can't say that I have,' he simply said.

'Well, shall we say, our first session in committee room D at the Police HQ in Exeter at 5pm today will give you the chance to meet one or two? You know where police HQ is don't you, Sir? A trifle inconvenient I know, but the advantage is it's well away from your home.'

'Fine, fine,' said Harry, thinking he would cut short his afternoon pressing of palms at the shopping Mall. 'What time will I be able to get away? I've a local radio station slot from seven until eight back in Plymouth.'

'No problem, Sir. I'm sure you'll be back well in time. Would a police escort suit?'

'And that's it? And forget the police escort, I know the bloody way.'

'Well, this will be the first session we'll have together, but others will have to take place after Thursday.'

'No problem,' said Harry, making the effort to sound politely compliant.

The call over, Harry wondered what he'd let himself in for. He'd need to tell Stu something as Stu would be driving him. Stu was waiting out on the pavement discreetly placed a few paces away from the car. Harry leant across and pushed open the driver's door.

'Hop in mate,' he shouted. 'We need to get going to Stonehouse.'

Five minutes into their journey, Harry had an announcement.

'We've got an addition to the programme for later this afternoon. The police have asked for my advice on a sensitive community matter, I'll need you to drive me to Exeter for five.'

'No problems. You're the governor,' said Stu only to happy to serve.

65

In April Cooper's experience, the bringing together of people of different backgrounds was one of the best things the Prevent programme did. Like Harry, she knew that those who were sliding down the slippery slope into extremism, or indeed were well on their way there already, had had little opportunity to have a healthy conversation with a person from a different cultural background holding opposite views to themselves.

This time she thought she'd start Harry off by sitting him down with a Muslim retired businessman from Exeter mosque. Mr Hussain had a good reputation for the work he had done with radical youngsters in nearby prisons, successfully offering several young men ongoing mentoring support. She needed to ring him to discuss what she had in mind for later that day.

At five, Harry presented himself at the reception desk at Middlemoor. There were a few curious glances in his direction, but if anyone thought any more of it, they concluded he was there to give the police his support in matters under investigation.

April went to receive him and took him to a small private committee room, Room D, where Mr Hussain was already helping himself to a cup of tea. Pleasantries were awkwardly exchanged, Harry taking tea too whilst looking quizzically at this unexpected third party. After introducing each to the other, April began by explaining the house rules, before, rather to Harry's surprise, leaving him alone in the room with Mr Hussain.

The conversation began with Mr Hussain asking about Harry's family. He said family was very important in Islam. He was fortunate in having a wife, two sons and a daughter, all of whom were now married.

'When did you all get here?' asked Harry.

'My wife and I came here first in 1972. If you know your history, that was when Uganda's Asians were expelled from the country by a man called Idi Amin. I lost my home, my business, everything. I left the country with only a Qur'an in my hand, and my life.'

Harry began to wonder what to say. He himself was wanting to see Muslims thrown out of Britain.

'That's because you were trouble – terrorists,' said Harry unsympathetically.

'Not at all. We were a very integrated part of society. My business was very successful, we built electrical switchgear and serviced the country's electricity industry.'

'Then what did you do to get yourself chucked out? Must have done or said something?'

'No – we were the scapegoats for Idi Amin. We were accused of disloyalty to the state. I was told I was corrupt and my business practice exploited the indigenous population. Idi Amin claimed he wanted to give his country back to the indigenous population. The trouble was, those like me in commerce, business and retail, we were the ones making the country prosper. In the year before my family were expelled, Amin had passed a law to cancel our citizenship.'

'But you, Muslims, they wouldn't have wanted to rely on you, they'd have rightly feared future terrorism.'

'Only a small proportion were Muslim, most were Hindu or other faiths. All were from the Asian subcontinent. But I never heard any talk of terrorism. There was never any terrorism. We all got on, where I lived near Kampala, we had Christmas together, that kind of thing. At the time we were all kicked out there was an economic crisis in Uganda, that's what turned things.'

'Things change,' said Harry. 'So have you and yours been living off benefits since you got here?'

'No. I began working in a foundry factory on night shifts near Birmingham. Saved hard. Began buying and selling engineering services. Then in 1985 I started my own welding workshop in West Bromwich. It expanded, I bought up two other small engineering premises. The recession nearly took us in the late 1980s, but the business survived and continued to grow and then I moved my business down here when my wife's job changed. The factory's on the Sowton Estate, here in Exeter.'

'And your wife, you said she worked?'

'Yes. In local government, an accountant and finance officer.'

'What about your three grown up kids?' asked Harry.

'Doctor, policeman and teacher,' said Said Hussain proudly.

'Which one's the terrorist?' said Harry, poking fun, but without a smile on his face, only then realising it was a poorly judged remark.

'Oh, no, we are all very much against that kind of thing. It isn't Islam. We follow a religion of peace.'

'That's not how I see it,' responded Harry. 'I was out in Istanbul last summer and saw first hand what Islamist terrorists want to do to us. They claim to follow Islam too. Now you tell me, which one is the true Islam?'

'Personally, I always worry when people start using religion for political purposes –then it gets subverted by power.'

Harry let the comment pass. 'I was reading earlier that they think we've got almost a thousand returning IS terrorists coming back to this country. We've got numerous extremist preachers stirring up support for them. What's even more alarming is that we are seeing an ever escalating level of threat to ordinary people from Islamic extremism – that's so, isn't it?'

'I saw that too. We were talking about it over breakfast. At the mosque we want to find ways of addressing this. It's a terrible threat to us all. Did you know more Muslims are killed by acts of extremism than any other group? All this linking of terrorism with Islam is felt very painfully at the Exeter mosque. There is something we say, 'Not in our Name'. We're keen to talk to government about finding ways to address these issues. To be frank, Muslims themselves are probably best placed to find good solutions to the problem of terrorism that we all face.'

'I've got my own answers. We need to follow Amin, expel all Muslims. Cleanse the population. You might be an exception, but I don't trust Muslims, they need to go.'

'What about the extremes of other kinds, like the people behind the attacks this weekend. They're doing great harm to the community and are a threat to us all.'

'I don't know about them,' said Harry cagily.

'The papers say it's extreme right wingers who killed so many and threaten us all. They're also wondering if you're in sympathy with such people – are you?'

'I'm a man of peace,' said Harry, shuffling uncomfortably as he said so, thinking of all the scrapes and fights he'd had in football matches over the years and how often he'd landed a punch or kick himself.

'So am I, Harry, a man of peace. Let's shake on that and see where things go from here.'

Where did that come from? How did we get to this? In spite of himself, Harry shook the warm firm hand of Said Hussain. The grip held him for longer than he expected and Harry felt embarrassed at actually beginning to respect, if not like the gentle man opposite him. This wasn't what he'd expected.

'Our hour is almost up, Harry. I look forward to continuing our conversation after the election. But before you go, what I'd like to ask you about, Harry, discuss with you next time, is what you think is acceptable speech, and whether you think free speech should have limits? If you don't mind me saying so, you say things very directly to people, so much so some people might say you actually incite trouble, and there are laws to protect society against that kind of thing. I was wondering whether you agree with the need to protect society from extreme views as well as extreme acts? I know you've come here in a voluntary capacity today to meet me and for us to talk about Islam and extremism and so on, but some people are now saying we need to put extremists, whether from IS or the extreme right, through compulsory de-radicalisation programmes. I'd be interested to know what you think about that too. We might also chat a bit more about Islam. I get the impression you've only heard one side of a story. OK with this?'

What could Harry say? He was spared having to give a reply for at that point, as if on cue, April Cooper walked back into the room. 'Mustn't keep you Mr McNamara, your driver is waiting for you in reception.' And at that, Harry, rather lost for words after his encounter, was walked back to his car and seen on his way.

Once in the car, Harry was quiet. He was thinking how much he hated Idi Amin for what he did to the Ugandan Asians, and then realised his own policies and pronouncements had been along exactly the same lines. At that point Stu interrupted him.

'Useful time?' he inquired, curious to know more about the urgent visit Harry had had to make to the police station when the diary was so full of pressing campaign engagements.

'Oh, shut your face, Stu,' retorted Harry. 'Watch what you say. Didn't you know idle talk can be dangerous to your health?' Harry regretted his words as he said them.

Stu, his loyal sidekick through thick and thin deserved better. Even so Harry couldn't bring himself to say sorry. He simply stared ahead, trying to get his mind round his next political appointment. The only one to get him out of the hole he was in was himself. Friends, family – they didn't cut the mustard. In the end everyone let you down – someone had to pay.

66

At ten on Wednesday evening campaigning ceased. Polling day followed. Harry had been tireless, using his fitness and energy to get on the streets, in the shopping areas, in the pubs and clubs, and above all knocking on doors.

On Thursday evening after a quiet day, Stu drove him back home at quarter past ten, leaving him there, and promising to be back after midnight to pick him up to take him to Plymouth's Guildhall where the count was taking place. Both were feeling uncertain as to which way it might go. There had been a very raw, edgy, bitter feel to the last twenty four hours of campaigning.

When Harry opened his front door to leave the house he was surprised to see his Mum standing there. She was looking troubled, a far away look in her eyes, as if something was wrong. Harry felt awkward, didn't know what to say.

'What's up? Didn't expect to see you back?' he said.

'It's your Dad. He hadn't called me, so I came home,' she said, her words coming slowly.

'Think he's been very busy. Haven't seen him myself, come to think, he's always out the house before me. Sorry about the mess in the kitchen. Won't take you long,' he said about to step past her.

'He's in hospital, Harry. Had a stroke in his head. Unconscious, he is. I've just come home from being with him.'

'What! No-one told me. When did this happen? Are they keeping him there? How long's he likely to be in?'

'Harry, he's seriously ill. They say he may not recover, and even if he does, his brain has been so badly damaged he may not be able to do anything very much for a very long time. They say it's still really too early to tell, to be certain of things,' she said.

'Now, now, Mum. Dad's always taken care of himself and the business. He's tough, he'll pull through, you'll see.'

'Not this time, Harry. You'll need to take charge for a bit.'

'I've never done any work at McNamara Metals, wouldn't know what to do. Anyway, I'm hoping to go off to parliament, make a few changes in the world. Look, make yourself a cup of tea and calm down. Mark my words, it'll be all right. He'll be home before you know it.'

As his Mum wandered in to make her way slowly into the kitchen Harry felt his words might have sounded unsympathetic, hollow, even unkind. Maybe he should have given his Mum a hug and a kiss, but then he didn't usually, so that would have been unnatural. He didn't know how he could help. He wasn't good with sick people, and his Dad had become unwell at a most inconvenient time. He had an idea. The least he could do would be to ring the hospital, to express best wishes.

'Ward Sister Sarah Tomkins here, how can I help.'

'Harry McNamara. Believe my Father's on your ward. How is he?'

461

'Mr McNamara, a question. When did you actually last see your father?'

'Err. Err. Sunday afternoon. We had Sunday lunch at home.'

'That was the last meal he ate. We think he'd been lying on the floor in his room since Monday morning.'

'My Mother's been away at her sister's,' he added plaintively. 'I've hardly been in, what with the election campaign. How is he now?'

'Unconscious. He may not recover. I really think you ought to come in.'

'It'll have to wait. Oh, and thank you. I think our NHS staff do a wonderful job,' said Harry, wishing he'd not made the call. He turned to chase after his Mum. Stu was waving to him from the car, trying to get him to leave the house.

'Mum. I've just phoned the ward. Dad really isn't very well is he? Maybe you should get a taxi up there and be at his side. I'll call one for you,' he said, before she could say anything to the contrary.

Stu left with Harry before the taxi he called had collected his Mum. Harry, his mind on his speech, had jotted a few things down on a piece of card. On one side, his loser's speech, the other one for a victory. It was tucked away in his suit inside pocket. He reached his hand inside to check it was there.

On arrival at the Guildhall he was pleased to see Stu had rounded up his party faithfuls, some thirty or forty familiar faces smiled to welcome him. Also there were the dozen or so party workers who'd kept his campaign going. It pleased him to see how much younger and fresher they looked compared with those of the two other political parties who seemed to represent the third age.

Inside the hall, an official led him to his holding area and he was advised the last few votes were still being counted and checked, the result a matter of less than an hour away. Pundits were already saying the turnout had been high and the result too close to call.

It wasn't until two in the morning when there was talk of suspending the count, that all three candidates were finally told to follow the Returning Officer and make their way to the platform.

Harry spotted the UKIP candidate in the hall. The man who had thrown in his hand, late in the campaign, urging his supporters to vote Tory had then, last weekend, finally seen sense and urged everyone to vote for Harry. Harry was glad his Dad had been able to offer his son a job at MacNamara Metals. Maybe that was one of the last things he did before he fell ill, wondered Harry.

The Conservative and Labour candidates, whose names were alphabetically prior to his, were nearer centre stage. He followed on at the end of the line.

The Returning Officer stepped to the podium, she was ready.

'I, Yvonne Tracey Walker, Returning Officer for the constituency of Plymouth Moor View duly declare the results of yesterday's by-election to be as follows. Trevor Bayford-Jones, Conservative, fourteen thousand four hundred and twelve votes.' There were loud cheers of expectation.

'Pamela Cheryl Dane, Labour, fifteen thousand, eight hundred and sixty eight votes,' and even louder cheers followed.

'And Harold Michael McNamara, British First Democratic Party, fifteen thousand nine hundred and seventy two votes. I hereby declare the said Harold Michael McNamara to be duly elected to serve this constituency as Member of Parliament.'

There was a stunned silence, and then as Harry's supporters realised his position, they began to cheer and shriek as pandemonium broke out. The policemen and stewards on duty looked anxiously at each other.

Harry couldn't believe it. He turned the small card with preplanned speech notes over in his hand and stepped forward. Before giving his thank you victory address, he looked down at his phone impatiently buzzing in his hand to show him a new message –

'Congratulations, we'll be in touch – The Circle.'

67

Adam and Raqiyah's pleasure at what had been achieved on Monday afternoon with the mosque open days was short lived when they saw the election result on Friday morning. Disbelief and disappointment were mixed equally together.

They'd called Clive on Tuesday to tell him what they'd been doing with the mosques and arranged to see him for a final meet up before they all went their separate ways, finding a Friday morning rendezvous in Giraffe, Exeter to everyone's liking.

Over the past couple of days Adam and Raqiyah had been busily packing as they were vacating their digs, the university term finishing that coming weekend. The estate agent handling their current let in Pinhoe Road had just confirmed another place would be available for them in the coming September when they returned to commence their final year. All was settled and the paperwork signed off.

The election result had crystallised in Adam's mind his plans for the summer and he would share them with the others over coffee.

As they walked to Giraffe, Adam found his mind wandering and conjuring up the unlikely image of Ali Muhammed, the now dead IS extremist and Harry McNamara, the newly elected extremist MP walking side by side with the same skyward gaze as they looked toward the Houses of Parliament. What it all meant he wasn't sure, but he was convinced they had more in common with each other than either realised.

Soon they were at the boxy Giraffe cafe. On arrival they deposited themselves in the bright orange, bucket shaped plastic chairs. As they did so they were thrilled to see Clive had Kaylah, Winston and Jacob there with him. They'd all driven down to collect Clive, to take him back to London now that he'd successfully completed his access to nursing course.

There was much to catch up on, so much so that coffee ran into lunch and food was ordered. Kaylah described how her start up online jewellery business was flourishing and that Winston and she had finally moved out of the flat the Israelis had provided. They were very happy to be renting a small apartment near Enfield Town.

Winston was doing some mini cab driving, which fitted round looking after young Jacob when Kaylah was growing her jewellery business. Proud grandparents Sam and Shazee took their share of child minding very seriously, reported Kaylah. Adam, feeling on good form himself, was delighted things were going so well for them.

'Oh, there's another thing,' Kaylah added, 'Winston's going to be a Dad.' The smile on Winston's face couldn't be any broader.

'And who's the Mum?' asked Adam, cheekily, upon which Winston simply put his arm across Kaylah's shoulder.

'I've an announcement too,' said Adam more seriously, as all eyes turned in his direction.

'In the light of a disastrous by-election result in Plymouth, things in this country have taken such a downward spiral,

466

I'm going to spend my summer vacation away from it all –
in, Oman!'

It was the decision Raqiyah had been hoping for and she
could not contain her delight as her scream of pleasure
disrupted the scene, turning everyone's heads in her
direction.

Afterword

My original vision was to write a contemporary trilogy with the themes of cultural diversity and political extremism to the fore. In giving a serious treatment of these together with several other societal themes set in the genre of thriller I believe these novels to be unique. As sometimes happens with authors, once embarked on a course, it becomes hard to stop and ideas for three further books based around characters familiar to the reader are now in hand.

Beginning with the central stories of Adam, Ali and Kaylah the reader is introduced in **Flashbacks** to what has sadly become a reality – terror on city streets. Some of the storyline has been disturbingly prophetic.

Flashbacks was followed by **IStanbul**. It was a privilege for me to spend time in the beautiful historic city of Istanbul in the spring of 2016. Turkey is a country to watch. It lies in the borderland between east and west and has seen recent political upheaval and religious revival replacing Ataturk's secular republic. **IStanbul** imagines a possible future scenario in the course of which a visiting England football supporter Harry McNamara makes an appearance.

Harry is central to **Harry's England**, a novel which considers the possibility of an extreme right wing candidate being elected to parliament from the South West of England. I found local historian Todd Gray's well researched book 'Blackshirts in Devon' looking at local right wing extremism in the 1930s fascinating and it inspired me to ask the question, could it happen today?

In the course of writing I have been fortunate to have bent the ear of so many people and to have gained from their support and encouragement. Writers in Ottery St Mary and in the Exeter Authors Association have energised and advised. Editors like Jeni Braund, Steve Chapman, Ruth Ward and Margaret Whitlock all kindly advised on the text – the remaining errors are all mine! Many other people have answered my obscure questions, friends and former colleagues in the inter-faith and policing and Prevent worlds – you know who you are!

To those good people of Plymouth and Exeter who must have wondered why I was looking for CCTV cameras in public places or pacing out routes and locations whilst talking to myself and/or taking numerous photographs. One telling moment was to stand by Plymouth's landmark Smeaton's Tower lighthouse on the Hoe when I discovered I'd have to re-write part of the story because no-one could be shot from the war memorial as I'd envisaged. The curvature of the lawn on the Hoe, which I hadn't noticed before, opened a big plot hole that needed correction!

One thing I must underline is that the novels and their characters are fiction. There is no attempt to demonise anyone or besmirch reputations of fine cities and their people. Sadly though, the reality of extremism means the themes dealt with are deeply felt and all too many people's lives have been irreparably damaged by such events.

In writing my hope is that these books serve to prompt helpful discussion and I am always willing to hear from readers and reply to questions. Please contact me through my website:

http://jehallauthor.com

Suggested
Book Group Questions

1.   Harry McNamara is the central character. What kind of personality is he? How did you find his family?

2.   The plot depends on groups of people being susceptible to manipulation. Are people easily led?

3.   The Circle is a shadowy sinister group. They are interested in political power. How does that relate to the world we live in?

4.   April Cooper is the central police character. What do you make of her, the police and the Prevent programme? How does one tackle extremism?

5.   Adam Taylor and Raqiyah Nahawi's relationship is complex. What are the key elements you can identify? Has it a future?

6.   The South West of England provides the setting for this novel. Could events like those described ever happen here? Was the novel believable?

7.   How did you feel the story line developed and did the ending satisfy?

8.   Key themes in the author's writing are 'us' and 'them' – and how community works. Why did you think the author wrote these stories?

9.   What does the reader take away from this book?

Flashbacks

J E Hall

This, the author's first novel, introduces the characters featured in subsequent books.

In Flashbacks, Adam Taylor from Muswell Hill, north London, goes on an adventurous solo cycle ride across Europe to the Middle East before going to University. It ends unexpectedly. Is his life over?

Ali Muhammed is haunted by flashbacks since seeing his father shot before his eyes. He is subsequently trained by IS and is sent to London as a jihadist.

Kaylah Kone has Afro-Caribbean cultural roots. A business studies student in London, she finds her life becomes tangled up with Ali.

All three characters and those around them are drawn into a terrorist plot to attack an Armistice Day parade outside Parliament. Can Ali be stopped and tragedy averted?

'Controversially current, intense and compelling debut thriller, grappling with themes and issues pertinent for contemporary societies'

Dr Irene Pérez-Fernández
University of Oviedo
Spain

IStanbul

J E Hall

This novel is a sequel to Flashbacks.

Ali Muhammed's lone-wolf attack in London on Armistice Day is followed by plans for a new and ambitious terrorist initiative in Turkey. Forces are mobilised. Ali travels from Mosul to Istanbul, and with local help, he hopes IS can destabilise the country.

Adam Taylor, traumatised by the events of the previous year, begins a new life as a student. He is determined to understand Islam better. At the end of his first year he goes to Istanbul with three other students to explore and learn from this great city.

Kaylah Kone, in new circumstances agrees to help the security services.

Unimaginable tension and life-changing events in Istanbul take the reader on a compelling adventure.

'In the context of our multi-faith world and with a mix of the familiar and unfamiliar this drama succeeds in both entertaining and challenging the reader.'

Rt Rev Dame Sarah Mullally
Bishop of Crediton
Devon

475

What's Next?

J E Hall is currently working on his next novel.

It takes forward the story and transports the reader to the Arabian Gulf.

See the author's website for further details, for reviews and anticipated date of publication:

http://jehallauthor.com